AUTHOR'S NOTE

Thank you for reading *Courtship's Conquest*! Should you wish to see them, content warnings can be found in the back matter of this book or at abigailkkelly.com/content-warnings. For your convenience, a small glossary and pronunciation guide has also been included, but there is no studying required to enjoy this book.

Happy reading!

XOXO
Abigail

COURTSHIP'S CONQUEST

THE NEW PROTECTORATE

BOOK TWO

ABIGAIL KELLY

For those who are angry

may your rage carry you somewhere softer
where your tenderness will be safeguarded

may your rage keep you strong
until the day strength need not be a blade

but a bridge

CHAPTER ONE

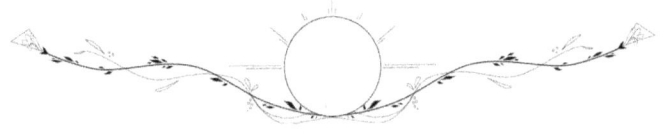

FEBRUARY 2045 - SAN FRANCISCO, THE ELVISH
PROTECTORATE

CAMILLE SOLBOURNE, FIRST COUSIN TO THE SOVEREIGN
ruler of the Elvish Protectorate and one of the last three living
descendants of the Dia family, turned a corner so sharply, she
nearly lost a heel.

Somewhere else in the cavernous warren of the Summit Hall,
a crowd's roar went up, shaking the walls and bouncing off of fine
marble floors. She didn't hear it. All she was aware of, all she could
feel and hear and taste, was *him*.

And that meant she had to run.

The Hall wasn't particularly familiar to her. She rarely left her
mother's Napa estate, and even when she spent time with her
cousins in San Francisco, they didn't care to pass the time in the
awe inspiring labyrinth where the elvish government made their
laws.

It didn't matter, though. She didn't need to know where she
was going. She just needed to get *out*.

Camille's skin burned as pheromones washed through her
veins. Her heart stuttered a wild, uneven beat. Sweat beaded along

her spine beneath the silk of her ice blue dress. Her bones felt ill-suited to their muscled confines. The beds of her claws ached. Even her vision was sharper.

All it took was one deep breath of his scent, one touch of his fingers to the soft, vulnerable underside of her chin, and she was changed.

Fuck!

Camille made another wild turn into an unfamiliar corridor, her heels clattering against the black marble floor, and spotted a door to a small, unused meeting room. Her preference was to get outside and as far away from Solbourne Tower as she possibly could, but what if *he* was out there? What if he waited for her by the steps or lingered in the shadows of the parking garage? She thought he darted after her when she fled the green room behind the sovereign's podium, but if he pursued her, wouldn't he have already caught her?

A more insidious inner voice than that of her anxiety whispered, *What if he isn't waiting? What if he's already forgotten you, like he did before?*

She shook the crushing doubt loose and kept going. She would not turn around. She would not look to see if he followed. She would not take *any* unnecessary risk.

It was much smarter to lie low until she was absolutely certain he was no longer on the small spit of land that was the elvish stronghold. Even if he wasn't looking for her, she couldn't risk it.

Intuition pulled her in another direction, away from any exits. *Don't expose yourself outside. Hiding is smarter.*

Camille darted down the hall, her breaths rasping in a throat that felt like sandpaper, and attempted to pry open the door. Her first try didn't do anything productive. Her hand shook too badly. Her glove, white silk with diamond-tipped claw-caps, slid against the bronze handle. Growling, she just managed it on her second try.

The room was small and dark, with a single, shuttered window in the far right corner. A wooden table sat in the center, framed by four chairs and overlooked by a large feed screen on one wall. It was a room that would have looked at home in any corporate office or government building, but to her it was a refuge. She would hide away until the day's meetings were over and her brother sought her out to give her the all-clear.

Camille dove in, her mind in a wild tangle of fear and desire, fury and desperation, yearning and revulsion.

How had she survived this once, only to succumb again? Why *now?* If her mother found out that she'd been in the same room with him, it would kill her — or, knowing Marian Dia Solbourne, she would try to kill *him* first.

Everything in Camille balked at the thought. Not that her mother stood a chance in her deteriorated state, but the idea of Viktor being injured made her stomach *roil—*

The door was on its return swing, sailing toward the jamb with all the force of a desperate woman's shove, when a tanned hand slid into the gap. Camille made a sharp sound of alarm and jumped back. She stumbled into a chair, knocking it onto the floor with a clatter.

She *knew* that hand. She knew that skin. She knew that tantalizing scent of salt and musk and clean, sweet sweat like she knew her own soul.

Gods, she thought, furious at the wash of relief and pleasure that swept through her, *he followed me.*

With a small push, the door swung open.

Viktor Hamilton, alpha of the Merced pack and figure of her sweetest nightmares, stood in the doorway. His beautiful face was cast half in shadow by the light from the hall, obscuring the fine lines of his features, the luminous quality of his cornflower blue eyes.

But she didn't need the light to see him, to *know* him. Camille's soul had been branded by the shifter nearly twenty years prior. She could never forget him, no matter how hard she tried.

"Cam..." Viktor's voice was a deep, jagged rumble. It lacked his usual lackadaisical cheer and was softer, gentler than it had any right to be. "I didn't mean to scare you off. I'm sorry about what happened in there."

He was apologizing for manhandling her, pulling her away from interceding in what could have been a politically catastrophic fight between her cousins, but all she heard was the bass rumble of his voice, that sensual shifter purr that made even the most sensible people beg for more.

Everything in her, instinct *and* soul, snapped to attention. Without intending to, she sucked in a deep breath, bringing more of him into her lungs until it felt like there were millions of tiny bubbles popping in her veins.

No! Run!

Her logical mind, the part of her that was all raw, wounded fury, had no plans to give into the pull that had rearranged her hormones and stolen her good sense. She'd done it once and suffered the consequences.

Camille gripped the edge of the table to steady herself — and keep herself *away* from Viktor — straightened her shoulders, and hoarsely demanded, "What part of me trying to get away from you as fast as possible told you to *follow* me? Get out!"

"I wouldn't have if you didn't look like you were ready to shatter into a thousand pieces," he shot back. "Did you really think I was going to let you run off after all that without even checking to make sure you were okay?"

Camille let out a distinctly elvish hiss. "I'm fine. Now get *out.*"

Viktor's eyes went from human to coyote. In the dark, his pupils suddenly expanded and glowed with the vivid green of a predator's vision.

With a flick of his wrist, the door shut with a resounding *bang.*

"*Cam,*" he tried again, moving a step closer.

She took a hasty step to the left. Viktor stilled and raised his hands in a placating gesture, but his eyes were still coyote bright and fixed on her with a hungry look she knew too well.

"You didn't have to run. I just want to talk to you. I'm not going to attack you or something." He sucked in a small, shuddering breath. "You know that. You know me. You can sheath your claws for a second."

A base, animalistic part of her almost wished he would lunge for her. Then she would really have a reason to flex her claws a little. "I don't know you, *Alpha Hamilton.* That sort of thing tends to happen when you haven't spoken to someone in twenty years. What could you *possibly* have to say to me now?"

Why would he bother seeking her out now, after so long? He had been very clear about what he wanted from her twenty years ago, after all. Humiliatingly, *heartbreakingly* clear.

Was it *pity* that drove him?

Gods, she wanted it to be anything but that. Even morbid curiosity would be better than pity.

Viktor took another step. The necessary gap between their bodies shrank. "I need to know that you're okay. You look exhausted, Cam, and it's not like you to lose your temper in front of everyone like that." His expression pinched with concern. "What's this about your mom being sick?"

She stiffened. "That's *private.*"

Viktor's eyes slid over her features, searching for something. "Cam, do you need help? I know you think your mother and your brother are your responsibility, but you don't have to deal with everything alone. Tell me what you need and I'll give it to you." He swallowed. "I know it's been a long time and that we're not— I *know,* but I'm here for you, Cam."

Rage snapped a tight band around her chest and squeezed the air out of her.

He didn't know anything, didn't even really care about her, and yet he thought he could corner her? *Gentle* her? He wasn't her confidant. He wasn't anything to her.

She owed him no explanation. He didn't get to see her grief, nor her pain. He didn't get to know that she felt like she was half a step away from crumbling under the weight of her grief, that she knew she was losing her mother more and more each day, and that as soon as Marian passed, her brother would jump at the chance to live his life.

He would go, her mother would join their father in Grim's domain, and she would be left alone to ache for a man who hadn't bothered to speak to her in *twenty fucking years.*

She let him see her softness once, when she was young and stupid. He would not get the chance again.

Camille lifted her lip in a snarl and darted away from the table. She dove around him as he stepped instinctively out of her swiping range, heading for the door he guarded. She might have made it, too, if he didn't have shifter reflexes.

"Oh, no you don't!"

Viktor's arm slid around her waist and hauled her clear off her feet. She kicked, but only managed to send her heels flying in two different directions.

Under her gloves, Camille felt her claws sink back into her fingertips, each one bursting with a flare of pleasure-pain. *Useless* against him.

Luckily she still had her claw-caps on — and *they* were diamond-tipped.

She yowled a protest as he wrestled her away from the door. He was saying something, his voice pitched to soothe, but she did everything in her power to block him out as she clawed at the arm around her waist. The fabric of his sleeve shredded immediately, but the moment her keen nose picked up the burst of coppery blood in the air, she froze.

Bile climbed up her throat as every muscle locked. *Can't hurt him. Can never hurt him. Gods, I've hurt him!*

The beast that lived in the heart of every elf wanted to bite and challenge its mate, but it never, ever injured. Fighting was a courtship game they played; a test to see who could come out on top and if they knew how to temper their strength. To know that she'd truly hurt him, even when he deserved it, made her stomach curdle.

"Shh, shh," he purred against the shell of her ear. "You're okay, Cam. Everything's okay. I'm here. Everything's going to be okay. You've just gotta tell me how to help you, sweetheart." One big hand stroked her short black hair back from her sweaty forehead. Only then did she realize that she had been letting out a high, keening note of apology.

Camille cut off the sound with ruthless will. Leaning forward as much as his grip allowed, she pushed at his injured arm but could not bring herself to look at it. If she stared at what she'd done to him, there was a large part of her that worried she would start stroking him, too.

Her voice was ragged and breathless when she bit out, "If you don't let me go now, I swear to every god, I'll tear your fucking head off!"

"Cam, I'm not letting you go until you calm down and stop *running* from me. Let me help."

Viktor's arm tightened around her middle. It was a band of hard shifter muscle. She *could* force the issue, but when she contemplated simply breaking it, she once more ran up against the solid wall in her psyche that was causing him pain.

Furious, Camille thrashed in his hold, hoping that if she wiggled and kicked and bucked hard enough, eventually he would be forced to drop her. "I would be calm if you *left me alone,*" she bit out. "I don't want anything from you! What about me not sticking around did you take as an invitation?"

"You want me to leave you alone when something's obviously wrong? Not gonna happen." It was a purely alpha bark, and so very *shifter* it made her want to roll her eyes. His arm tightened around her middle when he continued, "I'm not your family, Cam. I won't back off when you hiss and claw at me, and I'm for damn sure going to chase you when you run. I'm not leaving until you tell me how I can help you."

And then Viktor did something unspeakable: he *bit* her.

One sharp bite to the pointed tip of her ear, an unmistakable rebuke, made every nerve in her body short circuit. A flush of heat roared through her to settle, with profound viciousness, between her legs. Heat throbbed a low beat there.

Camille clenched her thighs reflexively and bit back a groan.

Every second in his arms, every breath laden with his scent, made the pull worse. She had to escape before she crossed that invisible line, that point of no return that would spell her grisly descent into madness — or, perhaps worse, before her rage melted into something hotter.

She needed to *go.*

Too bad she couldn't. Her limbs wouldn't cooperate, and the longer she stood there, the more muddled her thoughts became. Instinct battered at common sense with soft whispers. It told her to relax, to purr, to play rather than rage. It eased the grip of her claws on his arm and softened the muscles bracketing her spine.

It heated her blood, turned it molten, and demanded she turn, that she press her lips against the strong column of his throat in the most intimate of caresses.

Gods, she wanted the comfort of his touch so badly it *hurt.*

She felt Viktor's chest expand with a huge inhale and knew the moment he caught the warm thread of her desire in the air. That should have woken her up, pushed her to break the spell. It should have compelled her to break his arm and *run.*

His free hand closed over her throat, sealing her fate.

CHAPTER TWO

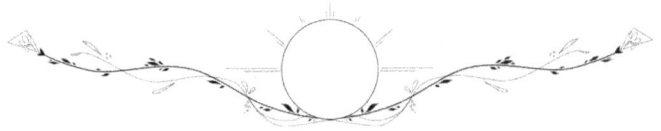

CAMILLE SUCKED IN A BREATH AND MELTED INTO HIM. It was raw instinct. Elves, unless locked in a life or death struggle, instinctively capitulated when their throat was clasped — by claw or fang. Handled by a consort, an elvish mate, it was a sign of trust and deepest eroticism.

"Cam..." She felt his warm breath stir the short strands of her hair when he let out a hard exhale. His voice dropped an octave when he murmured, "Is this why you ran from me, sweetheart?" There was a jagged, desperate edge to his normally smooth cadence. "Do you feel it, too?"

She swallowed hard as the arm holding her to his chest sagged, allowing him to skim the tips of his fingers along the thigh-high slit in her skirt. It was a small touch, but it sent another wave of molten heat to her core, making her ache like she never had before.

He breathed again, deeper this time, and exhaled a long, sensual purr that rattled against her back. His fingers slid against the exposed skin of her thigh, tracing the seam of her skirt.

"Did you think I wouldn't help you ease the ache?" he rasped. "Did you think I wouldn't chase you down and stroke you like you need me to? Is that why you want to claw my eyes out? You're all soft for me and that pisses you off, doesn't it?"

Viktor dipped his head to press a searing kiss to the corner of her jaw. She gasped, astonished by the potency of such simple, chaste contact.

They were roughly the same height, so he didn't have to contort himself to hold her, to smooth his lips over the curve of her cheek and swirl of her ear. Every brush of his skin against hers was torture — gorgeous, pleasurable torture.

"The best damn thing I ever smelled," he murmured, giving her throat a tiny, proprietary squeeze. "Like wildflowers and honey. I want to lick every fucking inch of you, sweetheart, and after that, I want to soothe every worry, everything that hurts you. And then do it all again. I'm *starved* for you."

Camille looked down to watch the progress of his fingers as they slid under her skirt, her breaths rapidly turning to pants. She knew that she should stop this. She knew that she still could. Viktor, for all that she had against him, was not a man who would force his attention on an unwilling partner.

But she was so, so hungry for him.

Not even twenty years of separation could stop that, no matter how much she denied it and fought it and buried it. Elves were possessive, touch-hungry beings. They dug their claws in and didn't let go — and to her body, to her instinct, Viktor was *hers*.

Anger and grief sweetened, transforming into the rich syrup of arousal in her veins. Two years of constant stress and worry momentarily lifted from her chest, allowing her one desperate, selfish breath, and by all the gods, it tasted like *him*.

Camille shuddered under the onslaught of yearning that rushed in through the gaps of her defenses. "Vik, I..."

"It's okay, sweetheart, I know." His touches were unbearably gentle, full of reverence, when he whispered, "I know. Let me make it better, then we'll talk."

What will it hurt? she thought, turning her head just enough to coax him closer, to ask for what she couldn't articulate with her lips and teeth and tongue. Pride would not allow her to beg.

I'm screwed anyway. The symptoms will be torture no matter what I do. Might as well make it worth the pain.

And after the last few years she had, Camille thought she deserved one awful, reckless decision. She couldn't have a lifetime of Viktor, but she could pretend for a moment, right?

Camille bit back all the things she wanted to say to him. She hemmed in her hurt and her anger, sweetened though both feelings were. She boxed them up and put them aside for later. *Now,* she wanted to feel something other than the raw, brittle heartbreak she'd carried for so long.

It wasn't giving in, she decided. It was taking what she was owed.

Her hands fell down to her sides and sought out the sturdy muscle of his thighs. Flexing her claws, she squeezed hard muscle and canted her hips back, pressing herself against him.

Viktor hissed against her cheek. She felt the tantalizing drag of his teeth as he scraped them against her jaw. His tongue followed, tasting the stinging flesh. "So sweet," he breathed against her damp skin. "I swear to the gods, you taste like my fucking dreams."

She closed her eyes, blocking out the sight of the darkened feed screen and the shadowy room.

In her mind, they were in a softly lit bedroom, one that smelled like him and her, and he was not wearing a suit but the battered jeans she knew he preferred. When she slid her palms up and over the rigid muscles of his thighs, tracing a sensual path toward his belt, she imagined that this was something special, something good, and not a strike that came with crippling pain.

Viktor let out a huff of air against her jaw when she gave his belt a sharp jerk, pulling his hips into the soft curve of her backside with unmistakable intention. He nipped her again, grumbling, "Bossy, bossy."

Without warning, he slid his hand into the opening of her

skirt and cupped her. Camille rocked up onto the tips of her toes, her eyes snapping open as the heat of his palm blazed through the thin, soaked material of her panties.

"Fuck," he rasped, slowly sliding two fingers up and down, tracing her aching center like he wanted to savor the task. She could feel his fingers through the whisper-thin material of her panties just as she knew he could feel every bit of her. His breathing stuttered. "Is this all for me, sweetheart?"

Camille made an inarticulate sound in the back of her throat. She wasn't capable of more than that when he began to slowly rub her, moving the wet silk over her skin with firm pressure and ruthless slowness.

His voice was tight, his desire a ragged note that struck her like a lightning bolt when he said, "You have no idea how many times I've imagined touching you. Tasting you." He dragged his tongue down the curve of her jaw again, seeking the thin strip of her throat not covered by the high collar of her ice blue dress. A deep, bone-rattling coyote growl filled the air when his lips hit the silk there.

"Fucking elvish clothes," he muttered, pushing down the edge of the collar with his thumb. She shivered, pleasure coursing through her blood like molten honey, as he gently nipped at the sensitive skin he uncovered.

Elves guarded their throats because the quickest way to kill an opponent was to go for the jugular. That awareness meant that *baring* one's throat to someone was a deeply intimate act of trust, one usually reserved for consorts and young.

But shifters were different. They didn't have any problem baring themselves to others. In fact, she knew that they enjoyed nudity and display — particularly when it came to *the bite*.

An elvish lover's embrace involved locking the jaws around a lover's throat, but they didn't actually bite. Not like she knew shifters did. When they mated, they sank their sharp teeth into the throat and held on, searing their wild magic into the m-paths of their partner, forever locking them together.

Camille knew that Viktor would never give her his bite. She also knew that she would never give him leave to embrace her like her basest instincts craved. He would never get that kind of trust from her again.

But she could let him kiss that small patch of skin he uncovered. She could let him scrape his teeth against it and taste her as he stroked her. She could pretend.

Camille rocked her hips forward and back, seeking out more from his fingers and the rigid bar of the erection she could feel through his slacks. Her fingers danced away from his belt to find it straining against his thigh.

Viktor sucked in a shuddering breath.

She suddenly wished that she was not wearing gloves. Of course she couldn't take them *off*, not when he might know what the sight of her retracted claws meant, but she wanted to feel his skin against her fingertips, to trace the length of him and soak in the heat he radiated like a furnace.

Hunger rode her hard. Letting out a small growl of frustration, she cupped him and squeezed firmly enough to make his hips jerk. "Viktor, I want you to *touch* me, not play with me."

"*Fuck*," he gasped, fingers losing their rhythm. The musky smell of him increased, thickening like a masculine perfume in the air — wild and aroused and *hers*. Making an innately coyote sound, he clawed through the material of her panties, sending the shredded remains to the floor. The action was raw, wild, absolutely lacking in civility; a far cry from the handful of sexual experiences she had previous to this.

When his fingers slid through her slick folds, Camille saw *stars*.

Viktor panted against her throat as he drew circles around her clitoris and then moved down, down, until he speared her with two fingers. No preamble, no warning. There was nothing but possessiveness in every line of his body, every sound he made, every wet push and pull of his fingers.

She cried out, her muscles rippling around the sudden intrusion, but he didn't give her time to adjust. His wildness was a buzz against her skin, threatening to drown her as she took what he chose to give her.

It was *glorious*. This was no gentle petting. There was no fear of rejection, of incompatibility. It was all raw carnality and it made her body *sing*.

A constant rumble, almost a purr but not quite, filled the air as he bit her jaw, her throat, the curve of her ear. With each nip and thrust of his fingers, he got wilder, more desperate. His movements were jerky and rough as he repositioned her against his front, bowing her back. Viktor rocked into the softness of her backside with abandon. It was as if he'd waited all his life to do this and now, presented with the opportunity, could not hold back.

Camille welcomed the burn of her muscles, the sting of his bite. She relished the way he thrust against her, seeking friction where their bodies met even as he drove her closer and closer to a perilous orgasm.

"Gods, you make me crazy," he gasped. "I want to look at you. I want to pet you. I want to taste you. I want to bend you over this table and fuck you until you can't stand anymore. But I *can't stop touching you*—" He broke off with a choked sound as she fumbled blindly with his belt and zipper. When they both gave way, she arched her back and plunged her hand inside to find him hard and aching for her. He damn near burned her through the silk of her glove.

His voice was taut as a bowstring, almost unrecognizable, when he continued, "*Yes, yes.* Touch me however you want, sweetheart. I want your hands everywhere."

Pressure built and built, the pleasure of his touch and his scent burning a path in her lungs like nothing ever had or would. Every nerve was a livewire. Camille chased her climax ruthlessly as she stroked him, as he plunged his fingers in and out of her, the heel of his hand grinding against her clitoris with almost punishing force. It was exquisite. It was the greatest sexual experience of her life.

It was also agony.

Fear battered at the edges of all that liquid desire drowning her good sense. With her rising orgasm and his hitched breath, she knew that this moment was coming to an end. Reality pressed close. It threatened to steal all that golden pleasure from her.

It would steal him, too.

Desperation to hang onto the moment, to the brief, shining lie, made tears prick behind her eyes. *Gods, this is going to hurt.*

But it was worth it. So worth it.

One moment was all she asked for. Only once would she be this selfish. Only once would she indulge. When it was done, she would cling to the memory for a lifetime.

Viktor's breath ghosted over her ear when he roughly commanded, "Come for me, sweetheart. Give me everything you have. Show me that I own this cunt."

Fingers curled inside her, he dropped his head to close his teeth over her silk covered throat and *bit*.

Camille bucked. Light burst across her eyelids as pleasure, hot and dark and rich as molasses, spread through her. Distantly, she heard Viktor curse. Through a haze of pleasure, she felt him cup her hand and squeeze hard as his hips jerked behind her.

His scent bloomed in the air — salty and fresh and distinctly him. She shuddered as another wave of pleasure rolled through her, tightening her muscles around his fingers in a pulsing wave.

For just a moment, she hung in that golden twilight where her release left her sated and the beast inside her basked in the scent, the touch of its mate. Viktor panted against her throat and kissed her there once, twice, a third time, as if compulsion demanded he do it again and again.

Home, she thought, drowsy and calm. *This is home.*

Except it wasn't.

Eventually, Viktor slowly removed his fingers, leaving her empty and cold as he skimmed her thigh, her hip, and her side. Gently, he began to turn her around. She was pliant in his hands, but as the seconds dragged on, cold reality replaced the sweetness with fear.

Chin down, Camille dared to stare up at him through the fringe of her lashes.

He was beautiful. She knew it, of course, but there was no escaping that fact when she turned around to find him flushed and disheveled, his cornflower blue eyes half-lidded and his suit ruined. Blond curls fell against a deeply tanned forehead and a small white scar marked his upper lip — a result of hitting a rock while surfing, she recalled. It was a testament to the wild young man he once was; the devastatingly handsome alpha he had become.

"Cam... Gods, I fucking missed you." He cupped her cheeks, his eyes seeking hers in the semi-darkness. A smile played at his lips. Every line of his lupine features was beautiful and made moreso by the joy shining there. "Ah, sweetheart. You're so damn pretty. I've imagined this moment for years." His thumb smoothed over the swell of her cheekbone. Humor danced in his gaze. "Though, I'll be honest, I didn't picture our reunion *here.*"

He leaned forward, eyes closing. Camille held her breath. He was going to kiss her, just like he kissed her that awful night—

Good sense chose that moment of shallow tenderness to reassert itself.

Gods, what have I done?

Camille lurched backward, stumbling out of his hold just as his lips brushed hers. The silk of her glove, wet with his release, felt like a brand.

She was halfway across the room before he even opened his eyes.

"Do *not,*" she gasped, pressing her back up against the wall. Her hands fluttered as she righted her skirt over her shaking thighs. Anger at herself, anger at *him,* made her voice thick when she said, "This is never happening again, do you understand me? I don't want you anywhere near me."

It was a scary thing, watching a powerful man go from relaxed to hunting-sharp in an instant.

Viktor's shoulders dropped and his knees bent slightly as his eyes flicked back to wild gold. If he cared about his undone slacks or the mess they'd made of him, he didn't show it. He remained perfectly still when he calmly demanded, "Explain why. Explain why you let me touch you but you won't let me see you again."

No, she thought, inching along the wall toward the door. *He can't know.*

Viktor grew up around elves, but she knew that even he didn't know everything. While she figured he knew that elves had their own matehood, she doubted Theodore would have told him about the pull. That was their most shameful secret — and their greatest weakness.

Besides the security risk it posed, she wasn't inclined to think that teenage boys throwing each other around on the sparring mats stopped to talk about mating habits, of all things.

If he knew, Camille was certain he would never let her go. He would hunt her down to the ends of Burden's Earth. Not because he wanted to be with her, but because Viktor was a man of honor and compassion. He would only want her because without him, she would lose herself to madness and eventually death.

Once, her mother had promised to put her down if the pull dragged her under. But her mother was dying, too ill to remember her vow, so the responsibility came down to Camille's twin brother.

If she couldn't escape the pull to be with Viktor, she would be dooming her brother to the greatest act of compassion their kind could conceive of — as well as a lifetime of grief.

For Cameron, for Viktor, for *herself,* she could not let the pull win.

Ignoring her fallen stilettos, she padded slowly toward the door, her eyes locked on the man who looked a half step away from shifting right there in the Summit Hall.

"I don't owe you any explanation," she answered, haughty

enough to cover up the tremor in her voice. "You were right earlier. We aren't family. We aren't even friends. What I do or don't do is none of your business, *Alpha Hamilton.*"

"Bullshit." Viktor's eyes blazed with the coyote's hunger, the wildness that spoke to something deep and dark in her. "You think I'm going to walk out of this room and forget this, Cam?"

Her gloved palm found the knob. "Yes." She twisted and pulled. A cooler rush of fresh air swept up her sweaty spine, fluttering the skirt of her dress around her legs. A chill settled over the raw wound inside her, numbing her to the pain, the brutal craving that was even now beginning to set in.

Camille lifted her chin as she swept one bare foot out into the hall. "You had no trouble when we were sixteen, right? Shouldn't be hard for you."

A muscle in Viktor's jaw jumped. His expression, normally relaxed and quick to smile, was stiff with tension. "Don't do this, Cammie. Don't walk away from me and think I won't chase you."

If she didn't feel like she was going to throw up, Camille would have snorted. Chase her? Viktor hadn't so much as glanced in her direction in twenty years. Just because he'd followed her this time didn't mean he would make any effort again.

Certainly, when she needed him most, he hadn't thought to follow her. Nothing had changed.

"You're a busy man now, Alpha Hamilton," she replied, easing backward into the hallway. "I'm sure you'll find better things to do than think of me." Another roar of noise went up, shattering what little remained of their intimate bubble. Eyes flicking down the hall, she added, "You should be at the Summit, watching my cousin make history. If you don't hurry, you'll miss it."

Dismissing him with a cool look, she turned on her heel and, even though it felt impossible, walked away.

CHAPTER THREE

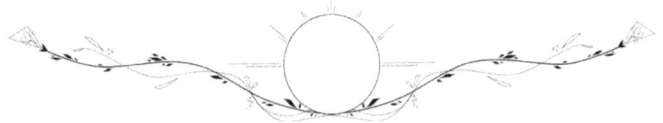

JULY 2045 - SAN FRANCISCO, THE ELVISH
PROTECTORATE

THE WATER OF CAMILLE'S BATH WAS COLD ENOUGH TO
kill. It stung every inch of her skin and threaded cold fingers
through her short black hair as she stared up at the ceiling of her
apartment's lavish bathroom.

Light poured in through a high window and struck a crystal
light fixture, a relic from another time, to burst against the walls
in a riot of colors. She could just make out each one through the
distortion of the water and the lazily drifting ice cubes passing
overhead.

She braced her hands against the sides of the tub, forcing her
body to stay still, to submit to the bite of cold, and tried to think
past the scream of age-old instinct.

...six one thousand, seven one thousand, eight one thousand, she
counted, lungs beginning to burn. She needed to get to twenty
before she would allow herself up for air. After a deep breath in,
she would dunk herself again.

Sometimes it only took one or two rounds to beat back the
craving. Sometimes, if the day was particularly bad, it took ten to

twenty. It was a miserable ritual, and one of the many things about San Francisco she would be happy to leave behind.

She knew from experience that things would get easier with distance. It *did,* but of course, she was forced to come back to the city after only a few months back in Napa. Regaining that distance was vital.

The ache in her bones would lessen. The unbearable itch under her skin would disappear. The hollow keening in her soul would peter out into cold, wounded silence.

The symptoms were worse than when she was sixteen, but Camille was optimistic that she would conquer the craving tearing its way through her soul with fang and claw once again. Viktor Hamilton could not be allowed to win. He would not break her. *Twice.*

Lungs aching, Camille surged upward. The muffled roar of water in her ears gave way to the soft strains of classical music in the next room and, very distantly, the hum of the m-lev train gliding through the streets below the Solbourne-owned apartment building.

Water dripped from her lashes as she sucked in a huge lungful of warm air. Her fingers curled over the edges of the porcelain tub. Her claws were sharp and diligently maintained — ten pretty, almond-shaped blades that could rend a man's head from his shoulders with a single swipe. Her skin, a shade of amethyst that reflected the light in pinks, lime green, and deep blues, stood out starkly against the bathtub.

Across the cavernous bathroom, her tablet buzzed on the cream colored marble countertop. Camille stiffened. She was damn tired of getting notifications. For someone who had been in what amounted to self-imposed isolation for the past month, she received a truly appalling amount of emails every day. That was just about the only aspect of her mother's death she *didn't* anticipate.

But these were important. Life-changing. If she was very, very lucky, they might even be life-saving.

Grimacing, she forced herself back under the water. The ice was melting fast, and she had no desire to fetch another bucket from her freezer. The notifications could wait a few minutes longer. Freeing herself of her involuntary bond to a shifter that didn't want her would always come first.

Three dips later, she finally allowed herself to unplug the drain and stand. The shivers didn't hit her until, with a raw, scouring pain, the lukewarm water of the shower sprayed down her back. Like always, she took it with gritted teeth and pure, spiteful will.

Her mother wouldn't have approved of her staying in the city. She would never have allowed her contact with Viktor in the first place. But she was dead. Two long years of suffering were finally at an end. Marian never even knew that her daughter had come into contact with her wayward consort at the Summit. She wasn't lucid enough to understand it even if Camille bothered to tell her.

She felt foolish for her misstep, but how could Camille have known her cousin would personally invite the shifter to the Summit? It was supposed to be safe. No one but elves attended the yearly gathering. Never in her wildest dreams did she imagine Theodore might break all the rules the moment he became Sovereign and actually *invite* him.

She tried to swallow down a familiar swell of bitterness at the thought of her cousin and his newfound happiness. A king in his own right, Theodore worked himself to the bone to be in a position where he could not be challenged — and where he could finally claim his consort.

Camille was happy for him, truly, and she might have liked Margot Goode well enough, if only their bliss didn't put her in danger of losing her mind.

Now that elves were free to mingle with the general population, every step outside was a risk. No Solbourne function was safe. Viktor was Theodore's childhood friend and newly minted political ally. If she agreed to show up for a family dinner, would she find him waiting at the table? If she stepped out for a trip downtown, would she stumble upon him at a table in her favorite cafe?

Gods help me, I need to get the fuck out of this town.

She couldn't blame everything on Theodore, though. Yes, he'd made a mess of her life, but she made things so much worse by allowing Viktor to corner her, to touch her. Perhaps her symptoms would have already begun to fade if she hadn't allowed him so much skin contact.

A moment of weakness cost her months of agony.

And yet... And yet she still did not regret it. Not completely. The fleeting moment of peace she'd taken with him lingered with her. When the grief of her mother's death became too much, rolling as it did in dark, brackish waves, she sank into the bliss of the memory. It wasn't healthy, not when she needed to *forget,* but she couldn't be forced to stop, either.

Camille shook out her long limbs, stubbornly willing away the last of her shivers, before she scrubbed her skin and hair with whatever products her staff stocked the shower with. She didn't care what they were or how much they cost, so long as they helped get Viktor's pheromones out of her pores and washed the memory of his touch away.

That done, she rinsed with quick efficiency and exited the shower. She never felt *better,* per se, after her ritual, but a little more in control. The beast inside of her quieted, and the craving became a smoldering ember rather than an inferno.

Drying off with a plush white towel, she padded over to where her tablet lay on the counter. A quick touch brought it to life. Camille's grip on the towel tightened as she read the notifications scrolling across the top of the clear screen.

A message from her brother, who had finally joined his own consort in Paris and looked to be living it up on a tour of France's finest vineyards, lit up the screen. He attached a photo of them both looking blissfully happy as they sat in little wicker chairs beneath a green canopy, wine glasses in hand.

A tight ball of anxiety momentarily loosened. *Good,* she thought, ghosting her fingertips over the image of Cameron's dear, usually somber face. *You deserve your happiness.*

Their mother was dead, after all. Though they both loved her, Camille didn't begrudge Cameron for ignoring the official mourning period to run off with his consort. Her brother finally felt free to *live.* She wanted that for him more than anything else in the world.

Reluctantly swiping his message away, the other notifications followed in a cascade: official documents about potentially selling her shares in their family vineyard to Cameron, client inquiries about shipments of wine, and, most importantly, responses from the families she and her mother had sent proposals to. Negotiations halted when her mother became too ill to function, but now, a month after her death, Camille decided it was time to pick things up again.

Apparently, the families agreed.

Wrapping her towel around her torso, she picked up the tablet and walked out of the bathroom. Marble floors gave way to soft carpet as she made her way to her bed. She perched on the edge and, ignoring the water droplets that slid down her neck, opened the first of several replies she'd received.

Miss Solbourne,

I am delighted to hear from you again. We would love to continue our discussion about a possible union between yourself and my son Cyrus. For your convenience, I have attached my schedule. Please let me know what day would be best for a meeting.

Regards,

Arabella Noor

Head of the Noor Family and Noor Foods Inc.

Camille's throat constricted as she scanned the rest of the messages. All but one response to her query was positive. Despite the fact that elves were now free to pursue romantic relationships with Others, the prominent families she reached out to hadn't changed their minds about negotiating a union with her.

Theodore threw open the door to the world, but people didn't change overnight. Not everyone was willing to leave things up to fate, after all. Contracted unions were mostly safe and politically expedient. In her case, they were even life-saving.

She let out a shaky breath and set her tablet aside. Relief mingled with queasiness. It appeared that her bid to find a spouse was still viable. That was a good thing, even if every instinct said otherwise.

Her mother's plan to get her safely ensconced in another powerful family's embrace would be a success. It had to be. Camille wasn't sure she could survive much more torture.

The only problem was that she didn't think Theodore would agree.

∼

Camille hated asking anyone for permission. It wasn't that she was unused to it, but rather she was *too* used to it.

After thirty-five years under her grief-stricken mother's thumb, Camille learned to despise her lack of agency. Her mother's rapid decline and death had propelled her into being the head of their small family unit, finally allowing her the space to take charge of her own life, but until the day she pledged her allegiance to another name, the ultimate authority would always lie with Theodore.

She hated it on principle even as the beast in her understood it was necessary. Her elvish nature craved the steadfast understanding of hierarchy. It *needed* to know its position in the world like her body needed meat and water and air. Theodore was her alpha, though elves didn't typically use the word. He made the laws by right of his strength and his sacrifice for the people under his care. Instinct recognized the safety to be found in his shadow.

That didn't mean she liked it, though — particularly when that position meant she was required to inform him of her upcoming nuptials.

Stepping out of her apartment for the first time since the internment of her mother's ashes in the Solbourne temple, Camille eyed her stoop warily. There was nothing there. It wasn't unusual, since her family owned the entire floor and she was the only resident at that moment, but in the last few weeks, she'd been dismayed to discover several packages on her doorstep.

Mostly, they held big containers of elvish food — raw meats marinated in rich sauces, as well as juicier, more snackable bits like rich heart and fatty liver — but sometimes it was dark chocolate, or a sumptuously soft blanket, or even a handwritten letter. She didn't dare take any of the gifts, nor check to see if they came with a name tag. Camille knew who they were from.

Her nose told her everything she needed to know.

At least today there were no gifts to pawn off on her staff, nor notes to keep carefully sealed in a plastic bag in her office, unread. There was no risk, as far as she could tell, of accidentally encountering Viktor Hamilton.

Hustling out of the door, she hit the biometric lock and waited for the perimeter wards to snap into place before she walked to the bank of elevators at the end of the hall. The *tap-tap-tap* of her stilettos was muffled by the sound-absorbing runner that spanned the length of the hardwood floor.

The apartment building was old compared to much of the city. The Solbournes built it only a few years after they took over the territory, and it had somehow survived both the calamity of 1906 and the Great War.

For what it lacked in modern conveniences, it made up for in beauty. Camille had a keen eye for design, and she loved the intricate molding and rich wood accents of the building. It had other benefits, too. Mainly, it wasn't locked on Treasure Island like the rest of the elvish population preferred, but situated in the heart of the Financial District. It didn't provide her complete independence, but it was near enough to make her feel slightly better.

The elevator was small and creaky, but it was meticulously maintained. She eyed it uneasily. Camille wasn't concerned about its ability to take her down to the ground floor of the building so much as *who* might already be in it.

Security claimed no one besides her staff had access to her floor, but she knew that couldn't be true. Viktor had somehow managed to get in and out without being seen at least five times. Coyote shifters were sneaky like that.

If I was smart, I would have already moved. Or at least pressed the issue with security, she thought, cautiously stepping into the narrow elevator. She didn't care to examine exactly why she hadn't done the latter.

The elevator was blessedly empty. Her shoulders rounded with relief as the gold-plated doors slowly drew to a close.

It was too bad that she was a Solbourne. Fleeing with her tail between her legs was never an option. Pride and spite were baked into her DNA. While moving her temporary residence to somewhere more secure would have been smarter, it also would have been a blow to that pride. She would not abandon her territory just because a clever coyote shifter thought he could enter and exit her life whenever it suited him.

She would be gone soon enough, anyway. If the negotiations stalled, then she would just have to make a break for her mother's Napa estate, where she'd spent most of her life in seclusion. She could continue to manage the vineyard while Cameron was on his *tour* and try to think of what in the world to do next.

Either way, Viktor would not be able to reach her.

Camille shoved her gloved hands into the pockets of her expensive black pea coat, her Solbourne crest pinned to her left lapel, and firmed her mouth at the thought of running away.

It's not running, she silently argued. *It's a tactical retreat.*

Never again would she *run* from Viktor Hamilton. She was not sixteen any longer, and she wasn't that frazzled creature from the Summit. If she played it smart, he would never take her power from her again.

When she exited the building, an m-enhanced town car was waiting for her by the curb. One of the many self-driving cars in the Solbourne fleet, it needed no driver to find its way through the gnarled thicket of San Francisco's streets or across the stately bridge. Camille needed only to briefly roll down her window to pass through the security checkpoint at the entrance of Treasure Island.

Solbourne Tower loomed overhead as the car drove itself down a single tree-lined street. Its gold accents glinted in the sunshine as the hard, monolithic face cut a stern shape against the powder blue sky. At its feet, smaller buildings housing secure elvish homes, nurseries, the Summit Hall, and Patrol barracks sprawled over the artificial island.

Elves weren't restricted to living on the island, of course. Many lived in the city and beyond, but there was a sense of security in closeness. With a population as small and insulated as theirs, it was nice to be near one another.

At least, Camille assumed that was the case. Her mother never let her and her twin brother stay more than a few days at a time with the rest of the Solbournes — and even that was under duress.

Marian Dia Solbourne went to Grim's arms hating the main branch of the Solbourne family with everything she had.

A swell of grief expanded in Camille's chest as the car passed under the gated entrance to the Tower's garage. As much as it confused and hurt her growing up, there was a comforting familiarity in her mother's vitriol and constant, useless plotting. She didn't miss either, but she did miss her mother.

Only the gods know why. I certainly don't.

Climbing out of the car, Camille reminded herself that she was fulfilling her mother's dying wish. She would not make the mistakes Marian had. She would not end up a bitter husk, wreaking misery wherever possible. She would live on her own terms or she would die trying.

Make a union. Get out of the family. Be free.

She just needed to secure Theodore's permission first. He wouldn't like it, but she doubted he would outright refuse her. How could he? Her union with a powerful elvish family would only strengthen his position. It wasn't like any of his brothers were in a rush to make alliances, so she would do what was in everyone's best interest.

CHAPTER FOUR

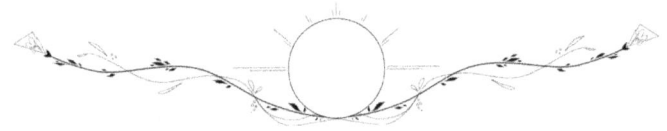

CAMILLE KEPT HER EYES AHEAD AND HER STEPS QUICK as she passed through the lobby, every one of her senses stretched to catch even the slightest hint of danger. The scent of shifter — coyote, specifically — was entirely absent from the people mingling in the luxurious, well lit lobby, but she didn't breathe a sigh of relief until she was in the elevator and riding up to the private floors.

The Sovereign's Guard, faceless and silent, nodded to her as they let her through the blast door and into the long, terrible hallway that guarded the Solbourne penthouse floor. Malevolent, watchful magic was thick in the air. Sigils painted in blood coated every inch of the ceiling, making it nearly impossible for intruders to pass through without being maimed, or scalded to death by their own boiling innards, or something equally horrifying. It made the Solbourne family apartments perhaps the safest place in the entire UTA.

Despite her semi-regular, enforced visits and the awful hallway, Camille never got tired of the Solbourne's penthouse floor. It was a massive estate suspended in the sky, over which a dome of stained glass threw candy-colored light. The metal door opened into an octagonal space lined with pillars and doors. Each door led to another wing, though most of them were empty.

Someday, they might be filled with Theodore and Margot's children and *their* families, but that was far enough in the future to be unimaginable to Camille. Her only concern at that moment was finding her way to Theodore's office and securing his seal of approval.

Camille didn't want to think about the promise of her cousin's future when hers hung on the edge of a knife.

She knew his guards would have already alerted him to her entry into the penthouse, but she knocked on the heavy wood door anyway. One didn't simply barge into the sovereign's office — not even when they were once nothing more than naked babies cavorting together in the private gardens behind the Tower.

"Come in, Cammie."

Breathe in. Breathe out. She steeled her spine. There was no backing out after this. Once she told Theodore, the whole family would know, and she was certain they would all have opinions on the subject.

But no matter how much she loathed asking for permission and wished she could continue to work in secret, Camille was no coward. She would be forthright with her plans. If Theodore disagreed with them, then she would just figure something else out.

Anything was better than living in perpetual fear of losing her mind, anyway.

She curled her gloved fingers over the door knob and gave it a sharp twist. It swung open on well-oiled hinges to reveal a room with a tall ceiling, glass-encased bookshelves, and plush leather furniture. A massive live edge desk stood in front of a wall of windows that show-cased the San Francisco skyline beyond the thin strip of deadly water.

Strangely, it looked as though the familiar desk had been... expanded. A new, curved piece of live edge mahogany had been artfully attached to the right side, and a smaller chair stood behind it. On the far corner, a small pile of ancient pulp sci-fi novels stood beside a framed newspaper clipping — specifically a paparazzi shot of Theodore and his consort climbing into a car after their secret wedding.

Oh, Camille thought with a small start. *That must be Margot's desk now, too.*

Theodore sat in a chair behind the desk, his usual suit jacket discarded and his elbows braced on the arms. One ungloved hand curled over his chin as he regarded her. "Hey Cammie," he greeted, baritone smooth and comforting. There was a cautious warmth in his voice. "It's been a while."

She stepped inside and closed the door behind her. Her eyes lingered on the empty half of the desk and then the bookshelves as she avoided looking at her cousin. He was dear to her in his own heavy handed way, but she found it difficult to look at him for too long without staring at the dark blue, healed marriage sigil between his brows.

It wasn't that it looked foreign or grotesque — though a subset of hardline elvish isolationists would argue the point — but rather that when she looked at the symbol of his happy marriage, she was filled with envy.

She wanted that. She wanted a consort and a happy partnership and love and babies and warmth. She wanted that more than she could properly articulate even to herself.

But fate saddled her with a consort who didn't really want her and never would, so she could only take what few scraps were available to her.

Reeling in her familiar anger, she politely asked, "How was your honeymoon?"

Instead of looking him in the eye, she watched his mouth curve in a wide, satisfied smile. "My time with Margot was wonderful. We swam in the lake and she took me *blackberry* picking, though I still don't see the appeal of the nasty little things." His smile dimmed as a chill entered his voice. "Being with her is everything I could have wanted, but I could have done without spending so much time with her family."

Camille's hackles raised. The low, almost inaudible rumble coming from Theodore's chest sent her instincts on edge. He wouldn't hurt her, but instinct was instinct.

Not that she blamed him for being upset. She didn't even know Margot and *she* was upset on her behalf.

Word traveled fast in their family, even when some of the members were intentionally distant. Camille heard from her brother, who heard from Theodore's older brother Sam, what exactly the Goodes had done to their halfling kin. It turned her stomach.

What kind of monsters mutilated their own young?

Babies were precious. *Rare.* Camille wanted her own, though she was practical enough to get herself an IUD so she could choose when she wished to have a child — certainly that would come up after her union was solidified, but hopefully not too soon.

To hear that Margot's mother had been blessed with a child, only to abandon her to people who did not know the proper way to care for an elvish child made everything in her bristle with rage.

They didn't feed her properly. They maimed her to hide her elvish traits. They didn't explain the *change* — that most vulnerable and traumatizing time in an elf's life, when they went temporarily mad while their bodies went through a rapid, extreme form of puberty. The memory of Camille's own change and the events that followed it haunted her, just as it haunted every elf. The acute hunger, the echo of bones snapping and muscles stretching, the hallucinations...

It was terrible enough when one knew what lay ahead of them. She couldn't imagine what it must have been like to be Margot, fragile and ignorant, locked away in the dark for a week as she endured the agony of sudden growth and the madness that accompanied it.

I'd have killed the whole lot of them, she thought, once more marveling at her cousin's restraint.

"I'm surprised you allowed it," she said, briskly unbuttoning her coat as she moved to take a seat in one of the chairs facing his desk. "And without bloodshed, too. You must have nearly ground your fangs to stumps."

She certainly wouldn't have done such a thing. If it was *her* consort that had been smothered and mutilated and starved — no matter how good the intentions were in doing so — Camille would have chewed metal filings before she let her partner play nice with those responsible.

Then again, she was a touch less gregarious than her esteemed cousin.

Theodore dropped his hand and sighed. "It was a compromise. It was my wife's dream to be married in her family's territory. I agreed only when *she* promised we would never step foot there again."

Camille blinked, more wrongfooted by his use of the word *wife* than anything else. It was such a... human word. "I see," she murmured, eyes skating away from the sigil between his brows. "Well, that is for the best. She has a new family now."

Her cousin smiled. Dimples creased his cheeks and made him look boyish again, just as she remembered. "Yes, she does, though she's still getting used to us." He paused, one clawed thumb tracing his lower lip thoughtfully. "You know, she could use a friend, Cammie. Someone I could trust to always have her best interests in mind. An elvish woman who can share things with her that I can't."

She stiffened. Even if she wasn't planning on leaving the city as fast as possible, Camille wasn't entirely sure she could stomach being in Margot Goode's presence long enough to *be* friends.

Oh, she seemed nice enough — really, who *didn't* like healers? — and Camille rather liked that she had a strong enough spine to stand up to a room of growling elves the day they met, but being pals with someone who had *everything* Camille would never have? No, she didn't think she could do that.

Folding her hands neatly in her lap, she answered, "I'm not sure I'm the best fit for the job, Teddy. I plan to leave the city soon." *Very soon. As soon as the ink is dry on the contract.*

Theodore cocked his head to one side. A black curl fell against his blue-skinned forehead, once again drawing her eye to that blasted sigil. "Why's that? Are you headed back to Napa? Alone?"

Camille did her best to contain her annoyance. It was his job to look after her and everyone else in the Solbourne family. He was just doing his duty. But that didn't mean the word *alone* hurt any less.

She breathed in and squared her shoulders. Keeping her eyes on his, she answered, "No, not yet. I am... I would like to negotiate a union." *No, that wasn't right. Not strong enough.* Camille cleared her throat and said more firmly, "I *am* negotiating a union."

Theodore's eyebrows nearly hit his hairline. For several torturous seconds, he simply sat there, his arm suspended in a strange, aborted gesture and his dark eyes fixed on her face. She did her best not to quail. She wasn't the sort, anyway, but it was vitally important that she not do so now. Any hint of uncertainty might tip the scales in the wrong direction.

"Cammie..." Theodore dropped his arm and leaned forward to brace his elbows on the polished surface of his desk. "Who are you looking to join with?"

She could feel his eyes scouring her features, searching for something, but she didn't care to figure out what it was. Instead, she dropped her eyes to her supple suede gloves and adjusted their fit. "Mother and I made a list of twenty candidates last year and then narrowed it down to ten men of similar rank."

Camille had then gone through and eliminated those who were outright enemies of the Solbournes, despite her mother's firm wish to make life as hard as possible for the main family. She had no desire to procreate with someone who wanted her cousins dead.

Clearing her throat, she continued, "When Mother got too sick, I froze the negotiations. Now that the mourning period is over, I've picked things up again." She raised her eyes to his. Theodore watched her closely, his brow furrowed. Her stomach sank. "I am happy to do this on my own, but as the head of the family, I need your blessing. So... here I am."

Theodore blinked twice before something dark passed over his expression. "What brought this on, Cammie? Why now? You're so young. You don't need to be thinking about any of this for decades — or ever. I would never ask you to join with someone you didn't care for."

His last sentence was laden with meaning.

Neither of them had their family's fabled talent for Foresight, so she knew he was not drawing on some sixth sense to uncover her secrets, but they had always been close. Theodore could read her easily. He also knew what happened between her and Viktor twenty years prior.

He knew that Viktor was her consort. The only question was whether he would accept her choice or make her life that much harder.

Camille's silver claw-caps dug into the thin material of her skirt. Little pricks of pain bloomed in the skin of her thighs. "You are bonded," she countered, striving to keep her tone civil. "We're only months apart, Teddy. Are *you* too young?"

He gave her an arch look. "That's different and you know it."

That was true. Camille *did* know the difference. She knew it better than anyone, which was why she was so desperate to escape.

Standing up abruptly from her seat, she announced, "I want this, Teddy. I want it more than you can possibly imagine. And I'll find a way to do it, with or without your blessing."

"*Why*, Cammie? Because you saw him at the Summit?" Theodore paused before he continued, hushed, "I didn't know you'd be in that room. I would have taken precautions to make sure you had no contact if I'd known. I wouldn't— I never wanted you to feel like you didn't have a choice."

"I don't blame you for that. Or *him*." Though Viktor was a lightning rod for her anger over the entire terrible situation, even she knew that it wasn't his fault her body betrayed her.

She stared down at her cousin's knowing face and gritted her teeth. Her fangs, four self-sharpening blades on her upper and lower jaws, squeaked against one another. "It's not *about* him." A partial truth, and one she knew he saw through with ease. Theodore *always* knew when she lied.

"I'm doing this because I want to start a family, Teddy," she bit out. "Are you the only one allowed to do that? Or do the rest of us have to follow your example to the letter?"

"No." He leaned back in his chair and scowled. "No, I'm not and I don't expect you to do things exactly as I do them. But I am allowed to ask questions when you decide to do something you'll regret for the rest of your life. Family asks because family *cares*, Cammie."

Anger burst in hot, acrid bubbles in her blood. If he wasn't her sovereign, if he wasn't the head of her family, she would have lunged across the desk and gone for his throat.

Who was *he* to think he knew what she would regret? Who was *he* to judge her for taking the only option that kept her sane? Who was *he* to look at her reproachfully, as if she was taking the coward's way out?

Camille wanted to scream at him, at Viktor, at herself.

I tried, she inwardly railed. *I tried! You know I tried! He wouldn't have me! He said he didn't want me, and then it was nothing but silence for twenty years. He could have found ways to contact me. He could have seen me. He never tried.*

While she suffocated under her mother's declining state and her brother's abject misery, doing nothing with her life, Viktor became an alpha and lived happily with his pack. He moved *on*, while she was stuck.

And it made her so damn angry to think that *now*, as she was finally trying to make something of her life, he thought to pick up right where they left off.

Instead of forcing those acidic words out, she snapped, "Family trusts, too. You don't think I know what I need? What's good for me?"

"I think you're fighting something that can make even the sanest elves lose their heads," he answered, measured and infuriating.

She took two steps away from his desk, afraid that if she did not put some distance between them, she would actually try to take a bite out of him. Theodore was kind, but he was also sovereign for a reason. One swipe of his claws, one heavy press of his palm or his boot, and she would crumble.

It was not just his physical strength that would subdue her, but the dominance he wore like a cloak. The beast that lived in her recognized him as a protector *and* a predator. It had no desire to rankle either side of him. If it came down to a fight, instinct would compel her to submit, even when her heart raged.

It took a moment, but Camille managed to find her voice. It wasn't polite, necessarily, but it was miraculously free of outright fury when she said, "That is not up to you to reckon with. My future is *my* responsibility, Teddy."

His expression was intense, dark with foreboding, but even then, she saw concern in his gaze. "Damn it, Cammie. I just want you to be happy. I'm afraid that doing this will destroy any chance of that."

Camille stared at him. Her anger ebbed, flowing back into the place it churned endlessly, and left her feeling cold. Tired. Gods, she felt like she had been running a marathon for two years. Couldn't he allow her a little bit of rest?

"Cameron is happy," she replied plainly. "Winnie and Delilah are happy. You are happy. *I* am just trying to take whatever I can."

Theodore swallowed. He swiped his palm over his mouth and pushed back from his desk, giving himself room to stand. She watched him circle the desk and chair she had just been sitting in, but didn't move away when his big hands curled over her shoulders. He tugged her against his chest with a low, soothing purr.

She held out for only a handful of seconds before she melted.

Elves needed touch. With her brother away celebrating his binding with Rufus, she'd gone without for too long. Theodore's warmth bled into her parched soul, momentarily soothing the ache that never, ever went away.

When she curled her arms around his middle and buried her face in his chest, he sighed and cupped the back of her head with one heavy hand. "Cammie," he murmured, "you aren't alone. I'm sorry you felt like you couldn't come to us when your mother was sick. I know you've been traumatized by the last few years, but this... You don't have to do this. You don't have to run away from us to find peace."

She dug her claws into his back, but Theodore didn't so much as flinch. He held firm against her, as steady and strong as the pylons that held up the bridge just beyond his window. "Yes I *do,*" she argued, choked. "You know I do. If I don't, I'll go insane like my mother, Teddy. I will. I can't do this again, and I can't *become* her."

"Have you spoken to him since the Summit?"

"No, and I don't plan to. This isn't about being a stupid teenager anymore, Teddy. He broke my heart— it sucks, but I'm a big girl and I've tried to move on. He's a stranger to me now." And even though the words tasted sour on her tongue, she added, "Maybe it's not fair to him, but I don't care. I'm not going to let him waltz back into my life and risk— risk becoming my mother. I can't do it."

"You're afraid," he murmured.

Camille's breath hitched. "Teddy, I'm fucking *terrified.*"

"Maybe if you actually sat down and talked to him—"

"What? So he can look at me like a charity case?" She swallowed a painful lump in her throat. "Never. I'll never do that. I'd rather live in a loveless union than know he only mated me because he *had* to. He can't know."

She released her hold on him and stepped back, out of the warmth and protection he offered. As much as she wanted to cling, the promise in Theodore's care was a lie. He couldn't really protect her. Only *she* could do that.

"Cammie..."

"You swore, Teddy," she pressed, staring into his worried face. Concern made him look older, wiser, so very different from the boy she once idolized. "You swore you wouldn't tell him. Remember?"

He shook his head. "That was twenty years ago. You really want me to keep that promise, knowing that he's unintentionally torturing you *now?*"

"Yes, I do. Teddy, I am *doing* this," she insisted.

He shook his head again, slower this time. She couldn't tell if it was sorrow, disappointment, or frustration that twisted his handsome face. Perhaps it was a mix of all three.

Bracing his hands on his hips, he sighed. "Fine. If it's what you really want, I'll look at the list you put together, and I won't tell him, even though I think it's a terrible fucking idea. We'll help you find someone who will..." His lips pressed into a hard, brief scowl before he finished, "...who will treat you right."

She mirrored his stance as well as his scowl. "I don't need you to do that. I need you to give me your blessing. I can handle the rest."

Theodore leveled her with a hard look that was all *sovereign*. "Not a chance. You want to do this? Then you do it with the family. That's my condition." He waved a dismissive hand, showing off long blue fingers tipped with razor sharp claws. Ever since his binding and shocking marriage, Theodore had eschewed the elvish practice of wearing gloves altogether. Unlike her, he no longer had anything to hide.

"I'm not sending you off with some stranger who will mistreat you," he continued, utterly immovable. "You've lost your mind if you think any of us will let you join a family that won't care for you, Cammie."

Camille closed her eyes. Massaging her forehead, she replied, "Fine. Whatever. As long as it gets done, I don't care."

Hearing Theodore's phone buzzing on the desk and content that she got what she came for, Camille took that as her cue to leave. Another tactical retreat.

She turned on her heel and strode back to the door, saying, "I have a virtual meeting with the Luz family tonight and one with Arabella Noor tomorrow. I'll send you the details."

"The list, Cammie. Send me the *whole* list."

She shot him an exasperated look over her shoulder. Theodore was back behind his strange, expanded desk already, his phone in his hand. He arched his brows expectantly.

"I'll send you the damn list," she muttered, pulling open the door.

"And Cammie..."

She was already stepping into the hall, but she sighed and turned back around to demand, *"What,* Teddy?"

"I expect you to have lunch with my wife tomorrow. Noon, at The Rotunda. Understood?"

Anxiety churned in her stomach, but she forced herself to nod. She would do whatever it took to see this done. "Fine," she answered, turning back around, "it's a date."

CHAPTER FIVE

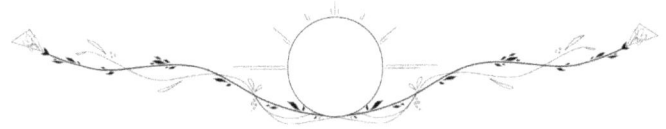

VIKTOR SHIFTED IN HIS LEATHER-PADDED CHAIR AND tried to ignore the ever-present discomfort that was his inner animal clawing at his insides. The damn thing wanted out, and it didn't give a damn that he was in the middle of the most important negotiation of his life.

Tension bunched the muscles of his neck and shoulders. His mind felt raw, bruised from the constant beating of his coyote battering his will. Only sheer stubbornness kept him in his chair, in his human skin, and away from the woman who consumed his every waking thought.

He wouldn't disrespect the Alliance by not paying attention, though. He was perfectly capable of listening to Alpha Andreas's concerns and worrying about his mate at the same time.

"I just don't see what you would bring to the alliance, Alpha Hamilton, that we could not get elsewhere and at a cheaper cost."

Viktor dropped his hand from where it had been idly tracing the corner of his jaw. It was an unconscious gesture he found himself doing more often in the days since the Summit.

Cammie used to touch me there, his animal reminded him, imaginary claws curling with unbridled rage. *Cammie liked to trace her fingers over my jaw when she felt bold, when she let me coax her. Why isn't she here? Why can't I touch her? What is she doing? Does she need me? Why does she not want to see me?*

Viktor's mind wasn't the only thing that felt bruised. The heart of the animal was aching — from separation, from her rejection. It didn't understand why she would continue to keep him out, just as it didn't understand the man's tactic of painfully slow courtship. It *hurt*.

Forcefully pushing old, painful memories aside, he calmly replied, "And what cost would that be, Alpha Andreas? Certainly not the territory on offer, seeing as it is currently being criminally underutilized."

He nodded toward the razor thin feed screen embedded in the center of the wide table. It showed a satellite image of the territory in question: a verdant landscape of lakes and greenery about an hour outside of Minneapolis. "Prairie hasn't had a pack since before the war. The town is dying. My pack would immediately infuse money into the area, as well as make much-needed infrastructure improvements."

The older alpha, a lean but powerful cougar shifter, looked down his long nose at Viktor. "I should think the issue is obvious."

"Oh?"

Andreas's eyes gleamed with a familiar malice. "Yes, *oh.*"

They were seated at a round table in the Alliance Landing, a building perched atop a deep red canyon that acted as neutral ground for all the shifter packs in the territory. Technically, the three capitals of the Shifter Alliance were neutral too, but in practice, each city belonged to one pack or another. Only in the glass-walled compound of Alliance Landing was the threat of violence truly at its lowest.

All but three of the ten shifters sitting around the table were predators, but every last one of them was an alpha — all of them dominant and proud, their rank unmatched within their own packs.

A lesser being might have lost his cool under the laser focus of so many powerful shifters, all of them older and more battle scarred than himself. Most sentient creatures would have wilted under the pressure of so much accumulated dominance in one room.

Viktor Hamilton, alpha of the Merced coyote pack, did not lose his cool and he did not wilt. Ever.

He met the eyes of Ruben Andreas, the alpha of the Aucilla cougar pack and nearly a hundred years his senior, squarely. The cougar's age didn't matter, and neither did the faint sneer that curled his lips when he went on to say, "Your friendship with the elves is unacceptable. We let you into the Alliance, we are effectively giving the elves and their stooge a foothold in our territory. Did you really think we wouldn't care that you're basically on Valen Yadav's payroll — and have been since you were a weepy cub?"

Viktor felt every eye on him, watching for his response to the insult. This, like every moment since he initiated contact with the Alliance, was a test. Would he lash out with the famous shifter temper and demand recompense for the insult, or would he lay down and take it, hoping to get in their good graces?

He let his usual good natured smile curl his lips. *Neither.*

Casting an unbothered look around the table, he scanned the faces of the most powerful shifters in the UTA with pure, stubborn confidence. "I understand that many of you come from an era when the lines between our people were rigid — with good reason. Elves were the enemy." He paused, thinking of soft lavender skin and a smile he hadn't seen in twenty years.

Everything in him said that she wasn't his enemy, that they could be so much more if only she'd let him near enough to coax. But longing for his elf took a backseat to *now*, when he needed to be at his sharpest. For her, for his pack.

"But so were the orcs, and the dragons, and the fey, and everyone else." He rapped two knuckles against the polished surface of the table. "That time is *done*. Gone. The Great War

shattered that world. This new age is going to be about cooperation and alliances, not suspicion and prejudice."

Viktor held Alpha Andreas's condescending stare when he
continued, "If you can't see why my formal, *politically expedient*
relationship with the wealthiest, most stable territory in the UTA
would only bring benefits to the Alliance, then you are a fool.
And if you recognize that fact but still refuse my pack's suit on the
grounds of prejudice, you are not *just* a fool. You are a bad alpha."

The cougar shifter's eyes flickered between vivid, catlike green
and dark brown. A subvocal growl vibrated the air around him as
the muscles of his lean body tightened with aggression. The
alphas nearest him, a bear shifter named Taisia and a wolf shifter
named Asbury, turned their bodies slightly, preparing to restrain
Alpha Andreas should he lunge across the table.

It was for his own good. Attacking another alpha in Alliance
Landing — even one that was just visiting — outside of the
bounds of a formal challenge would result in his pack's immediate
expulsion from the territory.

Killing another alpha would end with him losing his head.

Nobody wanted that, but Viktor didn't shrink under the
reproachful glances thrown his way.

It was one thing to call someone a bad person. It was quite
another to call them a bad alpha. One was a shallow swipe at character, while the other was an attack on the foundation of what
made an alpha who he was. They were born with the need to
protect and guide their packs, their loved ones, and questioning
their ability or their willingness to do that was tantamount to spit-
ting in their face.

A bad alpha wasn't just an asshole. They betrayed a sacred
trust. They got cubs and elders killed. They lost territory and they
broke vows.

A bad alpha was worth less than dirt.

And yet Viktor did not take it back. He did not try to smooth
ruffled feathers. He was right, and by the looks of some of the
alphas assembled around the table, they knew it, too.

A baritone voice cut through the aggression thickening the air. "Enough noise, Ruben. We're moving on."

Lee Seymour, alpha of a mixed pack but himself a take-no-shit elk shifter, gave both Viktor and Alpha Andreas a hard look. He was a broad man with silver hair and dark skin, and although the Alliance recognized no official leader, he was as close to one as any of them could tolerate. "Your concerns have been noted, Ruben. For the Council's awareness, Alpha Hamilton turned over all his correspondence with the Sovereign's office yesterday. We will discuss the Merced pack's connections with the Solbourne family in detail during deliberations, I'm sure."

Lee's eyes were a pale blue; a striking contrast to his dark skin and long, curling lashes. He was old enough to be Viktor's father, though he doubted the two had ever met — unlike Andreas, who was an old, cruel drinking buddy of his father.

If ever there was a definition of a bad alpha, Dominic Hamilton was it. Never in a million years would he have thought to petition the Alliance for a slice of their vast territory. To him, it would have seemed like groveling, and he would have rather watched his pack shrivel away into nothing than debase himself like that.

Alpha Seymour, on the other hand, was keen and practical. He had a level head and despite being just as dominant and aggressive as the predatory shifters in the room, rarely let his temper get the better of him. He was not the official leader, no, but he was a key founder of the Alliance, and when it came to tie-breakers, his opinion was the one that weighed the most. Viktor was confident that if he could win over Lee, most of the alphas would follow.

Unfortunately, he really didn't know if he *had* won him over.

Glancing around the table, Lee's lips pressed into a firm line. "If there are no other questions for Alpha Hamilton, I am going to say this meeting is adjourned." He leveled Viktor with a cool, impenetrable look. "We'll deliberate and then call you to let you know what we decide."

"And when will that be?" Viktor curled his fingers against his thigh, letting his tension out beneath the table, where no keen shifter eyes could see it.

Lee stood up from his seat. Broad shoulders straightened over a barrel chest. Sunlight streamed in from the glass walls, passing through the silvery strands of his tight curls to give him an even more intimidating look than normal. In his usual calm baritone, he answered, "When we're ready."

Nodding to the table, he didn't glance back to see if anyone disagreed with him before he strode out of the meeting room. Utter self-assurance and all alpha. Following his lead, several other alphas rose and drifted away from the table. Viktor held in the urge to growl.

He wasn't used to waiting on others for permission. Even though he was the one who initiated this infuriating process, he couldn't say he enjoyed it. A year into negotiating the Merced pack's move to the Alliance and he had begun to scrape the bottom of the barrel once full of patience.

An alpha was by nature decisive. They had to trust their gut and know when to act. Viktor made his choice, with the input of his pack, and he'd see it done. The only issue was that this *wasn't* the pre-war days, when anyone with enough might could take a territory whenever they decided it was theirs. The very institutions that made their world safer also chafed at his instincts.

Other things did, too, but at least in this he finally felt like he was making *some* headway.

Standing up from the table, Viktor met Alpha Andreas's eye and inclined his head. A small gesture of respect the man didn't deserve. In response, the other alpha scowled and leaned an elbow on the table, saying, "Your father is turning in his grave, welp."

"Considering I'm the one who put him there, I don't really give a damn," he answered.

Andreas clenched his jaw. Speaking through his teeth, he said, "He should have put you down when you were a weakling cub. Would have saved me the headache of dealing with you myself."

Viktor raised his eyebrows. "Are you threatening me, *Ruben?*"

"You're lucky I'm not challenging you to meet me in the fucking circle. You really think a coyote could beat a *cougar?*" Andreas planted his palms on the table and stood, his eyes locked on Viktor's. "I don't need to threaten you, welp. There is no way you're getting any Alliance territory. I may not have been able to take your head for Dominic, but I can neuter you." An ugly smile, so very much like his father's, creased Andreas's cheeks. "Politically speaking, of course."

A lifetime of dealing with his father's rage provided Viktor with the experience to know that the conversation should end there. If he continued to tolerate Andreas's vitriol, they would end up spilling blood right there in the meeting room where the Alliance was founded. *Not a good look.*

"We'll see, I suppose." Viktor smiled a bland, cordial smile. "Lovely talking to you, as always. Enjoy the vote."

Even if the vote came out in his favor, Viktor was certain that Alpha Andreas would be an issue in the future. Even without the ugly history between them, the man had a notorious temper and a vocal dislike for anything that smelled even remotely like inter-territory cooperation. He ruled his pack with an iron fist and was rumored to have cast out his own daughter, Lana Andreas, for insubordination.

He was hungry for a fight, and the kind of man who put his own desires before his pack's needs would not put aside his aggression just because the majority approved of Viktor.

It was just as well that Viktor didn't mind a good fight.

Saying his goodbyes to the alphas, who looked on with keen eyes and grim expressions, he buttoned his suit jacket and finally left the stifling air of the meeting room behind.

Alliance Landing was blessedly equipped with special air filters that worked to scrub most scent from the air, but even that could not entirely eliminate the aggression and dominance that hung around every single one of them. It was an energy, not a smell, and it was the exact reason Alliance Landing and the pageantry of this whole process was necessary.

If they went back to the old ways, he would have already been forced to tear out Alpha Andreas's throat. Viktor would have won his pack's place with might and fang, not with his nice, uncomfortable suit and his sprawling investments and his alliances. A simpler time, to be sure, but not one he wanted to raise cubs in.

And he wanted to raise cubs. He wanted a family with a keen yearning that cut deeper every day. The only problem was that the only woman he wanted to sink his fangs into, finalizing that beautiful, agonizing process of courtship, was the same one who wanted to disembowel him.

He would be lying if he said that wasn't a turn-on.

CHAPTER SIX

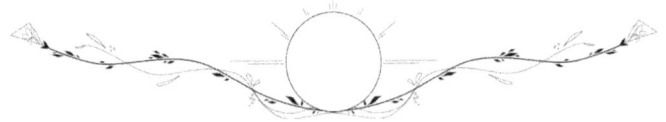

RUNNING A FINGER UNDER THE CONSTRICTING COLLAR of his crisp white shirt, Viktor headed toward the main floor and the security desk, where he could reclaim his phone from its assigned blackout box, as well as his second in command, who waited with the other alphas' seconds.

Benny was sitting on a white lounge chair, his brawny arms braced on his knees and his face turned toward the incredible view of Alliance canyon. As soon as Viktor stepped out of the elevator, his head turned. If Viktor thought *he* looked silly in a suit, it was nothing compared to Benny. The man was as big as an orc. In a suit, he looked like a trussed up turkey on steroids.

He was on his feet instantly, though Viktor waved a hand to let him know he didn't need to rush over. Walking to the reception desk, Viktor asked the neatly dressed, lushly figured fox shifter for his belongings. He felt more than heard his second come up behind him.

"You good, Vik?" His gravelly voice was pitched low, though there was no chance of really escaping shifter ears.

Always, Benny read Viktor's emotions like an open book. It was part of the reason they worked so well together. An alpha had to know that his command structure understood him implicitly. If they didn't, trust eroded.

And where there wasn't trust, there was no pack.

"Yeah, Benny," he answered, giving the receptionist a quick smile as she handed him the small blackout box. She flushed, her pretty green eyes sparkling, but he didn't feel anything more than mild gratitude for her quick professionalism when their fingers brushed.

Using his ID chip and a quick scan of his thumbprint to unlock the box and retrieve his phone, he winked at her and said, "Thanks for taking care of it for me, fox."

She blushed a darker, pretty pink. She smelled nice, like soft soaps and something earthy, but she wasn't for him. He wanted wildflowers and honey, razor sharp fangs and a pretty, pretty pout.

"Of course, Alpha Hamilton." The fox looked at him shyly, perhaps wondering if he would ask her for her number or, in the shifter way, simply invite her for a tumble somewhere private.

Viktor could only offer her a smile and a friendly wave. Everything else he kept for Camille.

Turning around, he found Benny rolling his eyes. "What?" he asked, walking them both toward the exit. Outside, a highly secure tram waited to take them back to St. George. From there, they would take an m-jet to San Francisco and be back in their postage stamp-sized territory before dinnertime.

Benny held the glass door to the tram platform open for him. Hot, dry air hit them like the heat from an oven, but they both breathed a sigh of relief to be out of the carefully maintained atmosphere of the hyper-secure building.

"I don't know how you charm them so fast," his second said, scowling. "If I tried winking at a woman like that, I'd get my eyes clawed out."

Viktor stopped by the open door of the tram for just a moment. Scanning the horizon, he let his animal closer to the surface of his mind as he savored the view.

It was wild, stark country. Craggy cliffs of burnt umber and deep, rusty red sloped down in a thin blue river. Patches of scrubby green clung to the places where moisture managed, against all odds, to accumulate.

The *sky*, though.

The sky was vast and almost unnaturally blue. Mountains faded into lavender ridges against its awe inspiring expanse, and huge, rolling clouds drifted overhead, dwarfing the canyon and every being below.

A coyote could have a good life in a place like Alliance Landing. But then again, they could have a good life just about anywhere. His people were adaptable in the extreme. All they needed was space to stretch their legs and they would flourish.

"It's not about charm," he finally replied, tearing his eyes away from the scenery. They settled on a faintly etched circle carved into the white, solar-conductive material of the platform. A cold chill briefly settled into his bones.

How many challenges had been met there? How many good shifters died in the center of that circle? Viktor had only ever fought in one circle, and he never wanted to enter another one if he could help it.

Shaking off the bloody memory, he stepped into the sleek tram and took a seat by an oval window. Closing the door behind them, Benny strode down the empty aisle to take the seat across from him. His big body, padded with generous muscle in a way that made him seem like more of a human boxer than a lean, long-legged coyote, folded into the seat.

"Is it your boy-next-door good looks that does it, then?" his second teased, legs spreading and big body relaxing. No longer on high alert around the other alphas and their seconds, his hard-edged face lost some of its tension.

The intercom system dinged, letting them know that the door had been locked, before the tram hummed and lifted seamlessly off the platform to drift down the canyon. It picked up speed almost immediately. Infused with m-tech, it went well beyond the speed of sound but muffled its sonic boom so effectively that even acute shifter hearing only picked up the faintest *pop*.

Viktor played with the sleek edges of his deactivated phone, familiar urgency making it difficult to follow the rules and wait until he left Alliance Landing completely to turn it on.

What is she doing? Has she eaten today? When was the last time she stretched her legs? Got some fresh air? Is she grieving all by herself now that her brother is gone? Has anyone checked on her today?

"No," he answered, almost absently, "it's my lack of intent."

"Lack of intent? Like, they don't get the feeling that you're going to tie them up in a basement or something?" He made a face. "Do *I* give off that impression?"

Benny's brow wrinkled, his lips turning down with alarm as he considered the possibility. With his glossy chestnut hair, golden brown skin, and watchful, hooded eyes, Viktor wouldn't say he was unattractive. Perhaps he wasn't conventionally pretty — he was a scrapper and it showed in his crooked nose and scarred knuckles — but he wasn't ugly. With the gossip mill of the pack churning constantly, Viktor knew for a fact that he managed to get enough lovers to never be *too* lonely.

Though, perhaps he was feeling his single status more keenly than usual, since his fledgling pursuit of Healer Goode had crashed and burned before it could even get off the ground. Viktor wasn't even sure that Margot knew his second was interested before her life went up in flames — literally.

Poor bastard had the bad luck to moon after Teddy's mate, he thought, wincing on his second's behalf. *That is a fight even I couldn't win.*

"No, I mean that I'm harmless," he explained, waving away Benny's doubtful look. "I *am*. Women can feel it when someone is really trying to get something from them — sex, companionship, whatever." He shrugged. "I'm safe because I don't actually want anything they could give me. Even when I *do* want sex, they know I'm not going to ask them for more."

And shifter women were notoriously reticent about that sort of thing. There was a reason they took courtship so seriously. Coaxing a woman into a permanent monogamous relationship could be a Herculean trial. It was worth it, though.

When the mating fever hit and two people decided to take the bite, nothing could tear them apart. There was no higher loyalty than what existed between mates.

"Not even that pretty fox?" Benny shook his head. His dark eyes took on a dreamy cast. Seeing that look on his bruiser's face might have been comical if Viktor wasn't feeling his own terrible longing at that moment. "Can't imagine. I'm tired of dancing with women who only want me for a night. I want to sink my claws into a soft, pretty woman and never let her go." He paused, considering, before he added, "I'd like her to sink her claws into me too, honestly."

Viktor eyed his friend critically. "You feeling the fever already?"

Benny rubbed absently at his chest, as if he could soothe an ache that was not physical, but deep in the heart of his inner animal. "Yeah, I'm starting to feel it." His hard mouth twisted into a self-deprecating smile. "Damn, man, I even found myself in a homegoods store the other day, thinking about getting all new furniture. Just got up one day and thought my den needed to be completely overhauled. Shit's crazy."

Viktor laughed, shaking his head, but he didn't feel any mirth. He knew what the fever did to a person. It was a clawing need that tore at every inch of one's life and drove all peace out the window. The desire to *decorate* was the least of what it could do to Benny's mental health.

Trying for cautiously concerned nonchalance, he asked, "You don't even have a mate yet and you're already going den-crazy?"

"Shut up." Benny flashed his fangs, but there was no real heat in it. "You watch out. Someday you're gonna find a mate, and then you're gonna wish you'd made a den as nice as mine *before* you met her."

Viktor's smile thinned.

He shared almost everything with his inner circle, but not Camille. He hoarded her close to his heart. Possessiveness and the fear of how the pack would react to an elvish alpha he couldn't even coax to his side meant he didn't tell even his closest friends that he had been working on his den for years, always with her in mind.

Not wanting to get into it *now*, of all times, Viktor swallowed his animal's rage and loneliness. He sent his second an arch look. "I've got other things to think about, you know. Like uprooting our entire pack, building us a better future. Little things like that."

Or big things like mile long legs of the softest lavender and wavy black hair that shone like oil in the light.

Like a soft, almost husky voice and a razor-sharp mind. Like the pleasure of watching her unravel under his hands as an orgasm nearly buckled his knees. Like a girl who'd given him her heart when she was at her most vulnerable and who would rather skin him alive than see him today.

"Uh-huh." Benny cushioned his cheek on one of his meaty fists, his expression more knowing than Viktor would have liked. "You keep telling yourself that, Vik."

"Hm. We'll see."

Reading him easily, Benny changed the subject. "How did the meeting go?"

"Great, until Ruben spoke up." Viktor blew out a breath. "Fuckin' hate that guy. Reminds me way too much of my dad."

"They *were* two shitty peas in a pod," his second astutely pointed out. "Remember when he and your dad used to fuck off to go gambling in the New Zone? Neither of them cared that they were taking money the pack needed to survive."

Old, dark rage made Viktor flex his fingers into the arm of his seat. "Yeah, I remember."

"We knew he'd be a problem, Vik."

Viktor nodded and breathed out slowly, releasing the old

poison that was his father's memory. "Yeah, we did. I'm just hoping he won't find a way to tank our bid."

"He won't," Benny replied, utterly immovable. "You are going to land this, Vik. I know you will. The only way that old bastard could take it from you is if he killed you."

"I almost wish that was still how we did things." Viktor smiled ruefully. "I mean, not really, but it would be way simpler than trying to work *with* shitheads."

Benny snorted. "Agreed."

Viktor thumbed his useless phone and stared out the window. He counted down the minutes until he could turn it on. He'd called in several favors to have Camille's building watched. Worry for her ate at him constantly, and he relied on the updates he received to calm a small but necessary fraction of his instincts. If he at least knew she was safely in her apartment — even though he was *also* worried about her self-imposed isolation after her mother's death — he could get through another hour, another day.

And that was all he could count on now. The promise of seconds progressing into minutes, to hours, to days.

He wasn't always so high strung. Twenty years was a long time to miss the other half of your soul, after all. He'd learned to cope, to find happiness in the day-to-day, to move on as best he could. With her almost never in the city, he'd managed to live a mostly normal life for an alpha in his prime.

He'd built strong bonds with his pack. He enjoyed his life. He took brief, nearly anonymous lovers when he needed to. He *managed.*

All that was shot to the underworld now, though.

If he thought the mating instinct, the fever, was rough when he was sixteen, it was nothing compared to the torture he experienced at thirty-six. Now that he'd seen her, held her in his arms, breathed in her wild, floral scent, watched her come and tasted her skin, it was like she'd torn him open and pulled a monster out of him.

That monster only wanted her. It wanted to be near her, to

rub its fur against her skin, to know she was in his den and safe, happy, sated, at all times. It *hungered* for her.

And she wouldn't fucking see him.

As soon as the tram landed on the platform in the private St. George airport, Viktor hauled himself out, his phone already flickering to life in his hand.

Truly, he didn't expect any new updates. Camille hadn't left her apartment since her mother's private funeral the month prior. It was unlikely that today of all days would be different.

Still, he gritted his teeth as he climbed the fold-out steps of the waiting m-jet. He ducked his head, stooping to avoid being clipped by the low ceiling, and fell into yet another luxurious seat as his phone began to buzz.

Notifications piled in, as usual. Packmates sent him updates, asked questions, and added themselves to his calendar. Pictures of frolicking cubs came through, as well as a report from his financial advisers on several new, risky investments they wanted him to consider.

Finally, amongst the cascade, a message from the demon he'd paid to watch Camille's building made it through. Viktor sucked in a ragged breath, his heart seizing.

Livia Hunt 11:02 AM: Left the apartment at eleven. Took a Solbourne town car.

Livia Hunt 1:15 PM: Came back at one. No guests.

Attached to the message were two photos. The first was of Camille, dressed in a black coat and dark turtleneck and small leather skirt that showed off her long legs, stepping out of her building's glittering entrance toward a waiting car. Her heartbreakingly beautiful face was set in a determined, almost mulish expression as her gloved hand held the door open.

The second photo was much like the first, except it was from the back. The light was different, and he could just make out her expression as she climbed out of her car. What struck him was not how much the sight of her made everything in him ache, but the way she seemed to have lost something in the time between the photographs.

Gone was the resolute expression. Even her color seemed to have dimmed slightly. Her eyes — gorgeous, violet eyes he saw everywhere, in everything — were glassy, as if she'd been crying.

Viktor swore.

Her distress was like a punch to the gut, a direct hit to the coyote that knew how to soothe only in the most primal ways. His helplessness was even worse. He didn't know what was wrong with his *mate*. And even if he did know, he couldn't fix it because she wouldn't even answer his calls or his messages. He didn't even know if she was even accepting the gifts he'd left her.

Gods, he just wanted to know she was well. Even if she never let him into the same room as her again, he could at least sleep at night if he knew she was happy and cared for.

He stared at the pictures, bile churning in an acid wave, as the coyote howled a furious, mournful song.

This was not happy. *This* was not cared for. It absolutely gutted him.

His mind raced, a whirlwind of worry and rage and unfulfilled longing making rational thought difficult, when his phone pinged again. The last of his missed messages came in, and Viktor's world tilted sideways.

Teddy 11:52 AM: Cammie's looking to contract a union. Now's the time to put up or shut up, Vik.

∼

Viktor didn't sprint off of the m-jet, but he walked damn fast. Benny hustled after him, all traces of teasing gone. While he didn't know what caused the shift in his alpha's mood, he reacted to his stress, the aggression that pulled his muscles taut. He was Viktor's shadow as they crossed the tarmac and climbed into their car.

As soon as Benny was behind the wheel, he asked, "What do you need?"

"Drop me off at The Palace," he answered, his voice barely audible beneath the coyote's growl.

It was well out of the way, considering their territory was only ten minutes from the airport and The Palace hotel was in the heart of the Financial District — completely across town — but Benny didn't complain. He didn't ask any questions, either. Putting the car in drive and syncing with the m-grid, he did exactly as Viktor told him to.

It wasn't blind loyalty. It was trust.

At that moment, trust was the only thing holding Viktor's frayed composure together. Trust that his second wouldn't ask questions he couldn't answer. Trust that Teddy had his back. Trust that Camille, at least for another moment, still belonged to him.

Gods. What the fuck am I going to do?

His animal pushed against the forefront of his mind, pacing in tight, furious circles. Viktor felt the confinement of the car, of his damn suit, like the bars of a cage pressing closer around him.

Sweat broke out across his skin as he tore off his suit jacket. Wadding it up, he chucked it into the back. The smart thing would have been to stop the car, strip, and shift. If he ran around Lake Merced enough times, eventually the rage would fall under the weight of exhaustion. Eventually he would feel like he could breathe again.

But what then? When the emotion died away, reality would still be there. He could wake up tomorrow morning and discover Camille had signed her life away to a mate who would never love her like he did. Nine months from now he could open up his phone to see the news that she'd given birth to some other lucky bastard's cub. Two hundred years from now he could lay on his deathbed, mateless, wishing he'd done it all differently.

Viktor couldn't survive that. He couldn't suffer seconds

turning into hours and hours turning into minutes knowing his mate belonged to someone else. Not after he had a taste of her.

He wouldn't do it. He *couldn't* do it; not until he'd done everything in his power to win her.

Viktor didn't say a word to Benny before he jumped out of the car in front of the gleaming arches of The Palace Hotel. After a moment's hesitation, Benny drove off, back the way they'd come. His second knew he would call if he needed him. One word and the entire pack would be by his side, ready to do whatever he asked of them.

But in this, they couldn't help him. Courtship was a private dance. And while Viktor knew he had to think about his pack, about how they would react to Camille if he was lucky enough to win her, he also knew that there was no stopping him this time.

He'd fought the fever once, and it cost him a chunk of his soul. He wouldn't survive a second attempt. This time, he would court his elf. He would coax her and pet her and earn back her trust.

He had to. He couldn't survive letting her go twice.

CHAPTER SEVEN

CAMILLE WASN'T STAYING IN THE PALACE HOTEL. SHE was staying in the old, elaborately styled apartment building just across the street, but Benny didn't need to know exactly where his alpha was headed, so Viktor didn't tell him.

Built by the Solbournes before the disaster of 1906, it stood out amongst the skyscrapers clustered around it. Viktor was familiar with it in ways that Camille probably didn't even realize.

Being an angry, inquisitive kid got him into a lot of trouble, but never moreso than the day he decided to break into that very building.

All of ten years old, totally unsupervised and eager to get away from a home that reeked of unhappiness, he'd taken a shine to hating the Solbournes. It was easier to blame them for the misery at home than it was to acknowledge it was his father, his *alpha's* doing. Perhaps it was his father's rants about the elves that pointed him in their direction, or perhaps it was simply the directionless anger of a neglected child that did it.

He picked a day to break into their special apartment building. He did his recon, knew that they mostly spent their time on the top two floors. With a lot of fury, a coyote's cunning, and very little good sense, he slipped in through an old, defunct service shaft once connected to the bank next door and made his way up the emergency stairs to the penthouse floor.

His plan, so far as he could recall, was to use his claws on everything they owned. He wanted to smash every mirror and rend every curtain. He wanted to tear down the massive oil paintings and shatter every vase. He wanted to act on the vitriol his father had filled his head with. He wanted to let the coyote out and howl in what should have been their territory if only to feel like he was *doing* something.

What he got was *caught.*

It was bad luck and pure foolishness that landed him squarely in Valen Yadav's sights at the end of the hall, his hand on the doorknob he now knew he never could have opened without his biometric scan anyway.

Viktor remembered that moment with the perfect clarity of an animal's perception: Valen, huge and intimidating, looked nothing like the men he was used to. Dressed head to toe in black, his neck covered by the signature elvish collar and his claws capped in gleaming silver, he looked like a specter out of Viktor's childhood nightmares. His jewel-toned skin shone in the light from a small window.

So did the flash of his fangs when he opened his mouth to ask what *exactly* a coyote cub was doing in a high security penthouse.

Of course Viktor made a break for it, but there was no chance of success. Valen was an elf in his prime — and General of Patrol to boot. He was a living weapon honed in fire. Viktor, by comparison, didn't even have all his adult teeth in yet.

When Valen grasped him by the scruff of his neck and hauled him into one of the apartments, Viktor was certain that the elf would rip his throat out.

That's what elves did, right? They killed — violently, without hesitation or remorse. That's what his father told him. One of the many lies he spewed when he wanted to blame his failures on their elvish overlords.

The predator in Viktor respected the ruthlessness, but the boy was just terrified. Not enough to stop fighting for even a second, though. Even at home, where he knew he could never hope to win, he kept fighting. He would always fight.

Even when he cried, he fought.

In hindsight, that was probably why Valen took such a shine to him, and why he didn't just dump him on his ass in front of his father, demanding *he* mete out bloody retribution for the trespass. Valen saw something familiar in the stupid, angry kid, and, astonishingly, took mercy on him.

He couldn't have predicted that he would go on to spend some of his hardest *and* happiest moments in those fancy apartments, nor that he would, twenty-six years later, find himself breaking into them once more.

Viktor didn't care that the old service shaft was a tight fit for his adult body. He didn't care that he had to disable the alarms and, the first time he tried it, use a small laser torch to cut through a new steel access panel. There were no barriers tough enough to keep him from Camille.

The only person who could really accomplish that was the elf herself.

Racing up the emergency stairs two steps at a time and deftly avoiding the security sensors he knew only scanned in regular, exploitable intervals, Viktor felt his senses sharpening, his claws prickling at the tips of his fingers as his animal fought to burst free. It was damn sick of waiting for him to act, and it blamed *him* for what might be the permanent loss of their mate.

By the time he slid out of the fire door — alarm disabled, of course — his heart was racing and his eyes were no longer blue, but a wild coyote gold. He sank into a very canine half-crouch. The need to hunt, to track, was a wild call in his blood.

Immediately, he picked up the scent of her in the air. It was faint, but he would be able to follow that scent through driving snow or sleet, in his sleep or drugged, through complete darkness or across a scorched desert.

Wildflowers and amber. Rich like honey, but with a floral

edge that reminded him of a childhood spent tumbling in the grass.

It lived in his pores as surely as Camille lived in his soul.

Biting back a snarl, Viktor was down the hallway and in front of her door in a flash. This time, he had no gifts to leave her, no way to show her that he cared, that he would *always* care, even when she didn't want him to. He had only himself and his need for her.

That need demanded he kick down the door to her apartment and force her to look at him, to see reason before she committed herself to someone who didn't love her, but the part of him that was still a man knew that was a bad idea.

For one thing, she wouldn't take that sort of invasion of her space well at all. For another, he knew for a fact that the doors were reinforced with sigil-lined steel. The Solbournes might have kept the antique look of the building, but that didn't mean they neglected security.

Mostly, he thought, a tiny bubble of amusement making its way through his panic as he recalled the service shaft. He'd have to tell them about the security breach at some point. Just not yet.

Viktor braced his palms on either side of the door and tried to get his ragged breathing under control. He squeezed his eyes shut.

I shouldn't have come here like this.

He knew it in the car, but now that he was actually standing there, grappling with the compulsion to howl until his mate was forced out of her den, he felt like he was being torn to shreds. It was stupid to think he could do this rationally when he rode a wave of pure possessive fury.

He should have waited. He should have let himself cool down. He shouldn't have allowed the thought of her with someone else to drive him half insane. She deserved better than that.

Camille had every right to live her life without him. He forfeited any claim on her the day he rejected her. Viktor *knew* that.

He just couldn't stomach it anymore.

Claws, coyote sharp, dug into the wallpaper on either side of the door jamb. Every sense was strung tight as a bowstring as he wrestled with himself. He could smell her, clear as day, but he could also make out every chemical cleaner the staff used, the smell of someone's perfume, even the faint hint of earl grey tea. He could hear people moving around the floors below them, and if he strained, he thought he could make out the slightest sound of a woman's voice in a room far beyond the door.

His spine went rigid as he strained to listen to the faint, husky notes. The animal in him knew, without a shadow of a doubt, that the voice belonged to his mate.

In that instant, any chance that he might have gathered his senses and left without making a scene, fled.

His mate was in there. She needed him. He needed *her*. The time for going back had passed.

Viktor curled the fingers of his right hand into a fist and knocked on the door.

～

Camille was in the middle of a video call when a knock echoed through her cavernous apartment. A chime sounded from the speakers discretely embedded in the ceiling, unnecessarily alerting her to the presence of someone at her door.

She was too well trained to express her unease, but she felt her perfectly poised spine tense. *He's here.*

"...and a furnished home in Henderson, on the edge of the Sloan Nature Preserve. You would retain it as a private residence, but would of course be expected to appear regularly with Epifanio at *The Luz* for social functions."

Cammie swallowed, her focus torn between the keen, catlike features of Elio Luz and the furious presence she could feel buzzing just outside her door. She didn't possess any powerful psychic abilities like her cousins, but she *knew* who stood out in the hallway. Her intuition was damn close to Foresight and had yet to steer her wrong.

Energy, violent and searching, buzzed against her skin.

I guess he doesn't care to hide this time, she thought, stomach dropping. There was only one reason she could think of for the sudden change in his behavior, though she didn't want to believe it.

Theodore had betrayed her.

Gods-fucking-damn you, Teddy. You meddling snitch!

"...appearances at the openings of any new ventures. We would be more than happy to discuss a collaboration with your vineyard as well." Elio's eyes gleamed. "I'm sure we could work out a lucrative joint venture."

"That is reasonable," she found herself replying, her voice cool and detached, as if she wasn't on the brink of hyperventilating or, just as likely, smashing her mug of tea against the wall in frustration. Elio was not an elf she wanted to show weakness to. He was just as much a predator as the man knocking at her door.

He might even be worse. At least Viktor wouldn't slit her throat for a perceived insult.

Ignoring her visitor, she folded her hands in her lap and continued, "And of course, should we move ahead with the negotiations, we can discuss a permanent living and custody arrangement. I will require at least a few months each year in Napa with any offspring Epifanio and I produce."

Her stomach curdled at the thought, but Camille pushed past the feeling. The business deal style negotiation, the detached references to intimate relations, and the cool discussion of *children* with Elio's son, an elf she'd never met, were all de rigueur.

Unions weren't passionate things. They were necessary and lucrative business arrangements.

Elio was a shrewd man with a reputation for cold cruelty. His skin was a remarkably luminous teal, and though he was beginning to show signs of his advanced age, he was still a handsome man. She might have admired the clean cut of his features and silvery hair if he didn't look like he wanted to squash her like a bug.

He was an elf of her grandfather's generation — haughty, bloodthirsty, and cold. In any other situation, she would have happily gone the rest of her life avoiding him, but she was smart enough to know that a union with his son would benefit the Solbournes immensely. The two families were not exactly enemies, but they weren't allies, either. If she could bring another powerful voting block into the fold, it was a chance she would have to take.

Elio sat in a glass-walled office. The sun had not even begun to set, so she could make out the glittering skyline of Las Vegas over his shoulders. No doubt he was on the top floor of *The Luz,* his family's casino and the center of their empire. It was one of the finest luxury resorts in the world.

The Luz family was not old or particularly powerful. They had only earned their seat amongst the Families a generation ago. That meant they were hungry for clout, for legitimacy. Seeing the cold, greedy look in Elio's eyes, Cammie had the uncomfortable realization that she wasn't entirely sure just how far the Luz's were willing to go to get it.

"That will be discussed and put into the contract," Elio replied, no hint of uncertainty in his lined face. As if she'd already made the choice, despite the fact that this was just a preliminary meeting. Nothing would be decided until she met Epifanio face to face. And nothing would be *official* without Theodore's blessing.

Elio raised a hand and flicked his claws, covered in matte black caps, in a dismissive gesture. "My son will require you to be flexible with your schedule. He is an exacting man, but you are used to the Solbournes, so perhaps you will find his structure a nice change of pace from the chaos of your household." A small, chilly smile curled the corners of his lips. "When can we expect you?"

Another knock, more insistent this time. Not knuckles tapping, but the meat of a fist hitting the door in a blatant demand. Her proximity alarm chimed again.

Something about Elio's presumption, the way he looked at her through the camera, raised her hackles. This time, Camille didn't just feel her heart jump in her chest. She felt the prickle of dread under every inch of her skin. It wasn't the same as seeing the future, but her intuition was very rarely wrong.

The beast that lived in her recognized a threat from the one in him. In that moment, she decided that the coyote at her door was the lesser of two evils.

"I apologize, Mr. Luz, but it seems I have an unexpected visitor. I'm going to have to cut this meeting short." She smiled, but it was a reserved, tight-lipped thing that gave nothing away. "I will get back to you with my schedule. Please give Epifanio my regards. Have a lovely evening."

She saw him open his mouth, his silver brows turning down in a flash of raw elvish annoyance, but her finger was already on the controller sitting beside her on the couch. Elio Luz and his avaricious gaze disappeared from the feed screen in an instant.

Camille stood up from the couch in one fluid movement and raked her ungloved claws through her hair. Without intending to, she oriented her body toward the entryway, where she knew — she *knew* — Viktor stood.

Her heart beat fast and unevenly in her chest. Her skin felt hot, prickly. Even though she knew it was impossible, she thought she could smell him: salt and soap and the wild, musky scent of animal fur.

Of course, she knew that he had been close enough to leave things at her door, but she didn't actually consider what she would do if he demanded to speak with her.

There was nothing she *could* do. It wasn't like opening the door was an option. Neither was ignoring him. He had to know she was in the apartment or he would have given up already.

Not that coyotes — or shifters in general — were known for their lack of tenacity. They were famously stubborn. When they wanted something, they were dogged in their pursuit of that thing. They were cunning, too.

Shifters were coaxers, ambush predators. They used any means necessary to get what they wanted.

They were quite unlike elves, who simply *took*. No games. No obfuscation. When an elf felt the pull to a consort, they didn't suffer long courtships or dance around their intended. They *acted*.

As Camille had acted all those years ago, when he told her he didn't want her.

A bolt of anger shook her out of her panic. It streaked through her, hot and bright and biting. The beast in her snarled, claws flexing. It wanted to sink its fangs into him and *shake*. It wanted to make him hurt as he made her hurt, even now.

Who was *he* to demand her attention? Who was he to invade her space? Viktor Hamilton did not belong anywhere near her, let alone on her stoop.

Throwing open the door to the hallway, Cammie charged toward the entryway on bare feet.

The knocking stopped as soon as she stepped into the entryway. He must have heard her with those sharp shifter ears. *Good,* she thought, storming up to the door. *That means he'll have no trouble hearing me through the door.*

There was no way in Glory's radiant name she was going to open up that door and expose herself to the pheromones or the beautiful face that would doom her, but that didn't mean she had to keep quiet.

Standing a foot from the door, fingers curled into fists, she glared at the reinforced wood with every ounce of venom she possessed. "Go *away!*"

There was a scraping noise — the unmistakable sound of claws dragging down the door.

"*Cam.*"

CHAPTER EIGHT

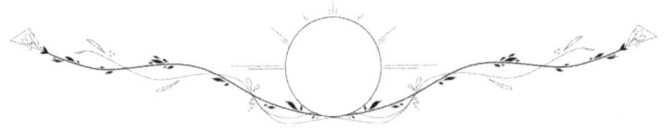

HER HEART STOPPED, STARTED AGAIN, AND THEN firmly lodged itself in her throat.

Gods, who gave the man the right to say her name like that? What divine entity had she pissed off enough to give him a voice that made her knees weak? It was smooth and low, but not *too* low. It was the kind of voice that sounded best in a close whisper, spoken just for her ears alone, and it called to the snarling thing in her like nothing else had.

Camille's arms shot out to brace herself against the door jamb. Her claws dug into the elaborate molding, anchoring her to the present, to *her* side of the door. A pounding beat thrummed through her veins and traveled, with alarming swiftness, to settle between her thighs.

One word. That was all it took for her instincts to spin completely out of her control. One word, and she'd gone soft and wet for him.

"Cam, open the door. Please."

There was no way she could do that. Even if there was no risk of exposure to his pheromones, she knew that she couldn't resist him if they met face to face. Their last encounter had cost her greatly, and she wasn't certain she would have that kind of strength of will again.

Her fingers flexed, sending a flurry of splinters and chipped paint to the floor. Her arms shook with the effort it took to hold still. "No. Why are you here? You have no reason to bother me."

That was a lie. Camille knew why he was there. She just wanted him to say it. She wanted him to admit that he cared, just so she could throw it back in his pretty face.

She knew that she would never, ever matter to Viktor like he mattered to her. He was her consort, but she would never be his mate. Still, he seemed to have some sort of fixation on her — just as he had when they were teenagers, sneaking around her mother to spend stolen hours together at the beach, in the garden, behind the waterfall in Yerba Buena Plaza.

Whatever drove him to seek her out, it wasn't enough to make her open the door. It was just enough to torture him a little, though.

She heard the rough sound of claws again, and then a hard exhale. His voice was muffled by the thick door, but close enough for her to hear the telltale shifter purr when he said, "Teddy told me about the union, Cam."

The metallic taste of betrayal lingered on the back of her tongue. At least it appeared that he hadn't told Viktor *everything*. She wasn't sure she would have been able to stomach seeing Theodore again if he broke that one, sacred promise.

"He shouldn't have told you anything," she snapped. "That's none of your business. And you know what? It's none of his business either!"

She'd done the proper thing by telling him her plans and getting his blessing, but if this was how he treated family, then she didn't give a flying fuck what he thought going forward. Clearly, he was not on her side. He was on *Viktor's*.

Hurt swelled beneath the heat of her fury. It was immense, brutally hot, and heavy in her soul.

All she wanted was an escape; her own little slice of happiness.

Instead of letting her have that, he turned around and spilled her secrets to the very man she was trying to run from. Was that what family did?

Camille knew what her mother would have said: *The Solbournes can't be trusted. The only people you can rely on are me, your brother, and yourself.*

Marian was cruel and narcissistic, blinded by the grief of her lost consort, but at least she always kept her confidence. Camille never worried that her mother would betray her. She wasn't a kind woman, and she wasn't a very good mother, but she was loyal to her core. That was more than she could say for Theodore.

"Don't take your anger out on Teddy," Viktor warned, as if he could read her mind. "He just wants to protect you, Cam. He wants you to be happy. Just like I do."

"You and I haven't had a relationship in twenty years. What I do is not your problem. You can take your concern and shove it up your ass, *Alpha Hamilton.*"

A low, coyote growl rumbled through the door. "Damn it, Cam, just open the door so we can talk properly. I'm not doing this in the hallway."

"I'd rather bite my own claws off," she snarled back.

"Fine!" The word was barely discernible beneath the animal growl. "Then tell me why you're doing this. Tell me what could have possibly brought this on. For godsakes, Cam, a *union?* You deserve better than that!"

Oh, she wanted to bite him!

Camille heard the crack of wood splitting under the force of her grip. Everything in her demanded she open up the door and lunge at him, claws and teeth bared.

The pull made her more aggressive — no moreso than to her consort himself. It was instinct to swipe, to bite, to test. If he cared for her, he would fight back and subdue her without doing harm. He would *play.*

But she couldn't do that. If she opened the door, she would expose herself to him and undo all the hard work she'd done to combat the bone-deep craving that was the pull. And when he rejected her again, she knew she wouldn't escape unscathed a third time.

No matter what instinct demanded, she would not give Viktor Hamilton another chance to break her.

Hissing through clenched teeth, she asked, "You want to know why I'm doing this?"

"*Yes.* What's wrong, Cam? Is this because of your mom? What—"

"Because I want a *mate,*" she bit out, using words she knew he would understand. "I want a *den.* I want *babies.* I want my own life away from politics and the city. How I go about getting those things is none of your fucking business."

If she had to sign a piece of paper, if she had to barter her time and her womb like assets in a business deal to get the life she wanted, Camille was fine with that. At least it was something. Anything was better than knowing her consort was out there and that he didn't want her, while she remained alone, forgotten by her twin and no longer needed by her mother, left to be used as a political pawn by people who once shunned her side of the family.

Besides, at least now she didn't have to worry about one day stumbling across her consort after she was contracted to another. She knew exactly who he was. The trick would be avoiding him — something that would be much, much easier when she tied herself to a family far beyond his territory.

Viktor was silent for several moments. She could just make out the sound of his harsh breathing. With her claws still gouging holes in the wall, she allowed herself to lean closer to the door. Her feverish cheek rested against the cool surface as she counted every exhale.

Something deep and wounded keened inside her, *Open the door. Let him in. It will finally stop hurting if you give in.*

But that way lay madness, so Camille did not give in. She did not yield. Not even when he breathed, "Cam... Please open the door." His voice broke. "I just need to see you. I need to see that you're okay. If this is what you really want—"

"You don't need to see me to know that." Pain reverberated through the fine lattice of every bone, every muscle, every fiber of her body and soul. The sound of him hurting didn't give her the satisfaction she craved. It just made the ache worse.

Still, she had to be strong. Always, always, she was the strong one.

For Cameron, she was the buffer between them and her mother's random, often inexplicable outbursts of rage and malice. For her mother, she was a constant source of support and the caretaker who was there all the way to the undignified end. Now, she would be strong for herself, even when she didn't want to be.

Sucking in a deep breath, she pried her claws out of the door jamb and rested her forehead against the door, her eyes closing. "I've already started the process," she told him, firm, but softer than before, a small concession to the aching beast who wanted to claw and to soothe. "Negotiations have begun. This is done, Viktor, and it has nothing to do with you."

A thread of challenge entered his voice. "What if I wanted it to?"

Her heart lurched. "Then you should talk to *Teddy,*" she answered, summoning some of that protective anger to shield herself from poisonous hope. Taunting him was easier than being gentle. He hadn't *earned* gentle. "He's the one who gets final approval of the list of candidates. Maybe if you ask nicely, he'll consider you."

She snorted at the idea. Unions were for elves. A shifter would never in a million years consider an arrangement built around business, politics, and loveless procreation. They believed in matehood before all things. To them, a union would seem blasphemous. Unnatural.

"You think I won't do it?" Viktor seemed somehow closer, as if his voice managed to reach through the barrier between them to wrap around her with a possessive caress. The desperation and the frustration vanished. It was replaced by the smooth timbre that made the skin on the back of her neck prickle. "You want me to do it your way, Cam? I will. Believe me, I will."

She might have balked if she truly believed he'd do it. As it stood, she'd been seduced by him once before and knew how this would end. Viktor took her on as a challenge. His damn coyote inquisitiveness had drawn him to her when they were sixteen, and she had no doubt that it was what drew him to her now.

He saw her as a conquest, not a mate. In the same way that he liked picking locks, he enjoyed getting under her skin, breaking down her walls, only to disregard what it was that he discovered inside. It wasn't the treasure the lock protected that he cared about. It was the challenge the lock *represented.*

She didn't see it when she was sixteen, but Camille saw it clearly as a grown woman.

Her lip lifting in a silent snarl, she braced her hands on the door and taunted, "You do that, Alpha Hamilton. If you can even make it on the list, I'll have to see how you stand up to the elvish men I have in mind. No promises, of course. I'm afraid I already have my favorite picked out."

There was a beat of taut silence. *"Who?"*

She smiled. He didn't sound so confident anymore. *Good.*

"That's none of your business," she replied, silky smooth. "But good luck with Teddy. Seeing as you're so close, I'm sure he'll love hearing from you."

This time, he really did growl her name. *"Camille—"*

"You have ten seconds to step away from my door and crawl back into whatever tunnel you used to get in here," she warned, tapping her claws against the smooth plastic of the control panel by the door. She knew he would be able to hear it.

When they upgraded the building, they didn't bother putting in feed screens by the doors, but they did link every apartment to the security floor. One tap of her claw and she could have the squadron of Patrol soldiers stationed there on their way.

Viktor could probably put up a good fight, but it would look awful for the alpha of the Merced pack if he was caught brawling with Patrol. His pack depended on him having a level head and they both knew he couldn't afford that kind of bad publicity.

His growl rattled the door, but she got the sense that he'd moved away. "You want to challenge me, sweetheart? Fine. You're not the only one with claws. Remember that."

"Then swipe at me, mutt," she challenged, blood hot to the point of boiling. "See what happens."

His voice, dark and full of promise, slid against her senses. "I intend to, sweetheart."

And then, prowling on silent shifter feet, he was gone.

CHAPTER NINE

"THAT IS *NOT* WHAT I MEANT!"

"Well, what did you expect me to do? Nothing?" Viktor rubbed the back of his neck, hoping to ease the painful tension there.

Theodore stood by an elaborate drink cart in the corner of the Solbourne's private sitting room. He was dressed in dark gray athletic gear, his hair was mussed, while his skin was flushed and sheened with sweat. Viktor caught him just as he was heading back from the training floor, where he kept sharp and socialized with those under his command. Viktor was more familiar with that floor of the Tower than almost any other.

It was where Valen took him that day he caught him breaking into the apartments. It was the place where he met the Solbourne boys for the first time. It was where he learned to defend himself and those who needed his protection. It was also where he'd gotten the shit kicked out of him by elves three times his size on a regular basis.

It was there that he learned what he needed to challenge his father when the time finally came, and what it meant to care for the people who trusted you.

"I expected you to talk her out of it entirely, idiot," Theodore growled, one clawed hand wrapped around the neck of a crystal decanter. He poured a splash of whiskey into an elaborately cut glass and then set the decanter aside. Bringing the glass to his lips, he muttered, "You were supposed to coax her, Vik, not make her dig her claws in *deeper.*"

Viktor squeezed the muscles bracketing his spine hard enough to bruise. "I *know.* I just... I freaked out, Teddy." He looked up through his blond fringe to glare at the man who was, even after twenty years of stony silence, a brother to him. They'd spilled blood together, fought side by side, became young men of worth as one seamless unit. That kind of bond never really died.

"What would you have done? If it was Margot who signed herself up to be sold to the highest bidder, how would *you* have handled it?"

Theodore lowered his glass just enough to flash his fangs. "I would have made the competition irrelevant, one way or another."

"And what competition would that have been?" Margot's voice, soft and full of fondness, drew his attention to the doorway that cut off their private penthouse from the rest of the family floor. Dressed in a soft blue skirt and white blouse covered with an unbuttoned Healer's Coat in charcoal gray, she leaned against the door jamb and smiled at her husband with unvarnished pleasure.

She was, at least to Viktor's eyes, a completely new person.

The healer he met almost a year prior had a desperate, wounded air to her that stirred every protective instinct. Her cheeks were thin, her smiles brittle. Even her scent had been... wrong. Washed away with astringent over the counter scent blockers, but still somehow carrying a note of sickness to it.

Healers were always soft, always in need of protection from the predators around them, but she was a special case. Not once did she ask for help, but he'd felt her desperation in his bones anyway. When she started healing members of his pack with extraordinary skill, asking for neither compensation nor explanation, it was only a matter of time until he began to think of her as one of theirs.

Her sharp wit and easy compassion didn't hurt — and neither did her pretty face. At one point, Viktor was pretty sure half the eligible single people in his pack were infatuated with her, most especially his second.

But the woman who screamed for coddling, for a soft den and a gentle hand, was not the woman who stood before him now.

She was comfortable, entirely at ease, and she wasn't just a witch. She was a proud halfling — witch and elvish. Her ears, revealed by her slowly unraveling updo, were very gently pointed. Now that she'd stopped using a dizzying amount of Noscent, she smelled crisp and clean and wild.

Elvish, but with a twining scent of ozone and magic that was distinctly *witchy.*

I knew there was something familiar, something that reminded me of Cam, about her, he thought, a tiny fraction of his tension easing at the sight of her. It was something about the air healers carried. Some tangible compassion that lingered just out of sight, easing stress and pain without even a touch. Healers just had that effect on people, though he wasn't sure they always realized it.

"All the suitors looking to steal you from me," Theodore answered. He set down his glass and walked across the room to cup his wife's cheeks, which were creased with a bemused smile. His blue hands dwarfed her delicate bone structure. "I would never let any of them near you, my brilliant, beautiful wife."

Margot's pert nose wrinkled. "I never even *had* suitors."

"Not true, sunshine," Viktor argued. He grinned, knowing he was probably about to start some trouble for his gruff second in command. "Benny was pretty damn hung up on you, remember? Still is. Can't say I blame him, of course."

Theodore's head snapped around to pin him with a hard look. "Your *second?*"

And because he was a coyote who loved to play, he answered,

"You know Benny. Big guy. Dark skin, good smile, looks like he could crush steel girders between his thighs?"

"Viktor, are you *trying* to get Benny killed?" Margot smoothed her hands down Theodore's chest, petting him, soothing him. Magic hummed between them. It was almost tangible enough to make the air shimmer, though he didn't know if that was a symptom of the witchbond he knew they shared or something deeper.

"He only came by when you all had teenagers that needed healing. Benny was sweet, but he barely spoke." She patted her husband's chest. "Besides, I knew right away that he wasn't who I was looking for. I knew I wanted Theodore from the moment I saw him, though I couldn't exactly admit it."

Viktor could make out the sound of Theodore snapping his teeth together from across the room. "See? It only took me a week to bind *and* marry my consort." Theodore slid his hand around the back of Margot's neck and pulled her close. She sighed and wrapped her arms around his waist, her eyes dropping to a relaxed half-mast as he stroked her nape. If she cared that he was fresh from a workout, she didn't show it. "It wouldn't have been an issue even if Margot was spoken for already. We were a done thing from the start."

"Yeah, and you didn't have a history like Cam and I do," he argued, suddenly annoyed by all the open affection oozing through the air. He didn't usually feel bitter, seeing as he lived in a very openly affectionate pack, but something about the relationship between Theodore and Margot made him sick with envy.

"No," Theodore dryly replied, "we just had a nascent psychic bond, a looming death sentence, and a life changing secret keeping us apart."

Margot poked his side. "Don't forget the bomb."

"*And* a bomb."

They did not, Viktor noticed, mention the fact that the bombing in question was orchestrated by Theodore's own sister, the terrifying Delilah. Last Viktor heard, Theodore had quietly banished her from their inner circle and confined Delilah to her post in the UTA Congress in the New Zone until tempers died down.

"Fine, but it's not the same." Viktor stood up from the couch to pace, his hands on his hips. His animal clawed at his insides, snarling to be let out, to hunt down their mate, but he restrained it with a ruthless mental grip. He couldn't mess up again. If Camille wanted him to chase her, to challenge her in her own territory, then by the gods he'd fucking *do* it.

"Are we talking about Cammie's betrothal or whatever it's called?"

Theodore answered her with words when all Viktor could do was snarl. "Yes. Vik wasn't able to talk her out of it *or* find out what prompted this."

"Don't give me that shit. She wouldn't even let me through the door!"

Theodore sent him an arch look. "Wouldn't have stopped me."

"Oh, shush." Margot rolled her eyes. "You're the man who sat out in the hallway like a pitiful little puppy until I let you in. You have no room to tease him."

"It worked, didn't it?"

"Only because I'm a pushover." Margot ignored Theodore's emphatic denial in favor of peering at Viktor, her expression thoughtful.

He expected her to ask why Camille hated him so much, but she simply asked, "What are you going to do?"

Viktor pinned Theodore with a hard look. Jabbing a finger in his direction, he announced, "I'm going to get on that fucking list."

"That's not how that works." Theodore shook his head. Sliding his hand down Margot's back, he gently guided her to sit on the couch in front of Viktor. When she was settled, he sprawled out beside her, his arm slung over her shoulders. Neither seemed to care that he was sweaty, nor that Margot had clearly just come in from a day of working in the Healer's Ward of Solbourne General, San Francisco's premier medical institution.

They were perfectly domestic. It made him want to gnash his teeth.

"Vik, this isn't something you would understand. She's making *business* deals, and it's not a process open to Others."

Gods, the idea of Camille turning her life into nothing more than a business arrangement, of her having cubs with someone because it was stipulated in the cold lines of a contract, made him feel ill.

Theodore was right. He *didn't* understand it, but if he had to play this sick game to get his mate back, he would do it.

He wasn't even sure how it would work if he succeeded. The Alliance was his pack's chance at a new, brighter future. They could expand, stretch their power, secure a place for their descendants that would forever remain under their own authority.

All of that was already jeopardized by his public connection to the Solbournes. If he took Camille as his mate, that connection would be utterly irrevocable.

The smart thing would have been to wait until *after* he secured their place in the Alliance. Once his pack was settled into their new territory, expelling them would be much, much harder than simply denying them entry. But he couldn't wait. Camille forced his hand, and finding a way to have her and provide for his pack wouldn't be simple or easy.

Doesn't matter.

The part of him that was more coyote than man knew with the certainty of instinct that he was doing what was right. He would just have to figure out how to make it work. There was no other choice.

"*Make* it open," he insisted, a deep growl rumbling through every syllable.

Theodore rubbed the heel of his hand into his eye and sighed. "Vik, I can put you on the list. I can even insist that she consider

you and follow the proper courtship protocol to secure my blessing, but I can't actually make her give you the time of day."

That he knew. No one could make Camille do anything she
didn't truly want to. As much as she bent to accommodate her
vicious mother, and as much as she liked to please, when Camille
got something into her head, she became a whirlwind of claws
and teeth and fury.

He *loved* that about her. Always had.

"You let me worry about that. I just need you to open the
door for me."

He'd won her twenty years ago, despite the divisions of class
and race and enmity. He could do it again. All he needed was an
opening, something to force her hand into spending the smallest
sliver of time with him.

"What will happen if it becomes public knowledge that
Viktor is being considered for a union with Cammie?"

Theodore ran his claws through the wispy strands of hair that
had escaped Margot's updo. "I'm not sure, to be honest. I hadn't
considered it. My hope was that unions would become defunct
when the moratorium on Other consorts was lifted, but we're a
stubborn bunch, so I guess I'm not surprised by its staying
power."

He looked at Viktor. The softness bled out of his voice. "If
word gets out, it could swing one of two ways: Either elves could
see it as a remarkable opportunity for new and lucrative unions
across the UTA, or they'll lose their minds all over again."

And, Viktor thought, pacing again, *it will tank our chances
with the Alliance.*

He didn't say that, though. Theodore didn't know about his
negotiations with the Alliance, and Viktor was keen on keeping
him in the dark until things were settled. What his pack did or did
not do wasn't the sovereign's business unless their actions were in
violation of the law — though the elves rarely saw things
that way.

Which was why his people needed their own territory outside

of the smothering oversight of the EVP. They needed their autonomy. *True* autonomy.

And that was what they stood to lose if it leaked that he was in negotiations with the Solbournes. Not simply because it would look a lot like he was double dealing, but because shifters would find the idea of an arranged mating repugnant, unnatural. It would look like he was not only betraying an instinctive honor code, but an entire way of life.

It was a massive risk. On one side, his pack — the people who had supported him, who were his family, who believed in him even when he was a boy trying to learn how to be a leader.

On the other side, Camille — the woman who made him feel a wild, fierce sort of joy that he could compare to nothing else, and the woman who made the thought of the future bearable.

The loyalty to mate and pack were never supposed to come in conflict. One was the other. To feel like he couldn't have both made something deeply fundamental in him wither.

But if I do this right, if I win her before word gets out, then it won't matter. Certainly, the Alliance might still reject him, but they were still shifters. If they knew she was his mate, they would understand and respect the sacred bond between them.

If she wore his bite, there wasn't a damn thing they could say about it.

Viktor pulled himself upright, his shoulders moving back as the tension eased out of his muscles. *Yes,* he thought. *That's what I have to do.*

Everyone, including the Alliance, would be forced to accept her if he claimed her properly. If he had to play elvish games to make that happen, he would do it.

But he had to do it fast.

"Tell me about how this works," he demanded, rounding on Theodore.

"Well, typically a family makes a list of eligible partners and then they put out feelers to see if anyone is interested in discussing a possible union." Theodore frowned, his distaste for the practice clear. "Obviously, word usually gets out unless things are kept firmly behind closed doors, and offers can be submitted to the head of the family for consideration. For instance, if you were an elf, this wouldn't be that unusual. You heard Cammie is looking for a contract, so you petitioned the head of her family for a place on the list."

He shifted so that Margot could lean her back against his chest. She looked up at him with big eyes, her expression intent. Obviously, she was just as new to this as Viktor was, and appeared just as eager to learn.

"After the final list is approved, a contact is made with each family. First in writing, to confirm that both parties are willing, and then in a series of meetings to negotiate terms and assess compatibility." He paused, expression tightening. "It is considered deeply insulting to pull out of negotiations with any family before the final meeting. It is a sign of respect to give every family a fair shot. If everyone played favorites from the start, it would make the gene pool that much smaller — something we can't afford to do."

Viktor smiled thinly. "So if you approve my place on that list, she *has* to meet with me."

"Yes. Though, knowing Cammie, she will try to find a way out of it."

He waved that thought away. Of course she would try to outsmart him. That was another thing he loved about her. She made him *chase*. "And what do these meetings involve? Do you have to be there?"

"No." Theodore shuddered. "Gods help me, I don't even have time in my schedule for that sort of thing. Three meetings with every family? I'd rather jump off the bridge." He sniffed, clearly relieved that he didn't have to manage Camille's suddenly crowded social calendar, though Viktor might have felt better knowing she had her cousin there looking after her.

"No, Cammie is technically the head of her family unit. She took the dominant position when Marian passed. That means she is fully within her rights to negotiate her own union, so long as all assets brought to the table are in her name only."

That, at least, he understood. The elves were very similar to shifters in their hierarchy. It wasn't based on age or gender, but on the readiness and willingness to lead, to take care of those below you. Camille was strong enough to take over her small family, but nowhere close to dominant enough to rest control of the *entire* Solbourne family from Theodore, putting her neatly under his supervision.

In the same way, the families that made up his pack were tiny packs of their own, with their own internal hierarchies giving them structure and security. Those families ultimately looked to him for guidance, but they would always have a level of autonomy within themselves.

"The meetings are not terribly structured, but they tend to escalate in terms of contact and length as the negotiations progress," Theodore continued. He began to tick points off on his fingers. "First, a brief meeting with the head of each family to discuss basics — major points within the contract like living arrangements, social obligations, young, and so on. Nowadays, this is typically done virtually. Second, an in-person meeting with the head of the family and the interested parties. This assesses compatibility."

He briefly dipped his head to nuzzle Margot's hair. Viktor watched, envious, as Theodore's catlike pupils expanded in a rush, like even the scent of his consort was something intoxicating. "Finally," he continued, softer, "the last meeting is the longest and the most private. It can be anything from the pair having dinner to spending a week together in a villa, assessing everything from routine compatibility to sexual attraction."

Viktor tensed when Margot made a soft sound of surprise. "Wait," she said, sitting up a little, "you mean a *meeting* could be afternoon tea or a week-long sexathon? With *every candidate?*"

"The point, my love," Theodore replied, "is not just about business or politics, but procreation. What happens if you contract yourself to someone, only to discover you can't stand it when they touch you? Sure, you can attempt artificial insemination, but with odds already stacked against having children, it becomes nearly impossible to create a viable pregnancy that way."

Viktor tried to breathe past the roaring fury currently tearing its way through his chest, but it was no easy task. The thought of his mate trying out every man on her list made him want to go absolutely *feral*.

It wasn't going to happen that way, he decided. He wouldn't let it.

By the time it came to the third meeting, she was already going to be his. The time she spent with those other men would be perfunctory at best. In and out, with a cold rejection tacked on at the end.

He wanted the thought to cool his temper, that territorial rage that made him want to bite and claw until he was too exhausted to do anything but sink into blissful darkness, but the memory of Camille's voice coming through the door wouldn't allow it.

If you can even make it on the list, I'll have to see how you stand up to the elvish men I have in mind. No promises, of course. I'm afraid I already have my favorite picked out.

Who? Who was her favorite? Was it someone she was already attracted to? Someone she *wanted* to spend a week in a villa with, "assessing their compatibility"?

It was enough to make any fevered shifter want to rip his hair out. Mates didn't sleep around. Mates were sacred; the bedrock of the pack. They were loyal to one another above all things. To think that *his* mate might find comfort and pleasure in the arms of another was the keenest kind of agony Viktor could imagine.

He had to take several deep breaths before he was capable of speech again. "Put me on the fucking list, Teddy," he growled.

Theodore arched a brow. "Yeah? And how do I know you won't fuck it up again?"

"Because," he grated, "by the end of this week, we're all going to be one, big, happy family."

Chapter Ten

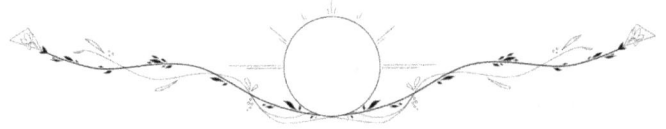

Viktor didn't bother calling Benny for a ride. He was too keyed up to sit with his second and pretend that nothing was wrong, so he hopped on the m-lev and rode until he hit the boundary of the Merced territory.

Theirs was a small but beautiful enclave of greenery in the otherwise technologically advanced city. At its center sat Lake Merced, a marshy body of water with low, scrubby vegetation around its edges. Sturdy coastal trees clumped together in dense thickets, obscuring the homes of his pack members and the thin, winding trails they created. A long stretch of cold, windswept beach was only a short run away and closed off for the Merced pack's use.

The territory itself was only a small corner of the city, but it had been theirs for nearly three hundred years — long before the elves swept in to take control. Back then, it was a mess of feuding factions and people looking for a new start in a freshly discovered territory. The shifters, easily adaptable and vicious, might have taken control of the area entirely if the elves hadn't marched in one day, claws at the ready, and swept nearly the entire West Coast into their pockets.

It wasn't that shifters weren't capable of taking them on.

Viktor could heal faster than any elf could, and though he lacked the diamond sharp claws and steel bones of the elves, shifters were elastic. They could take enormous amounts of damage and bounce back unscathed.

The issue was that elves, even when they hated one another, acted as a single unit for the best interest of the group. Shifters never could manage that.

Pack was the heart and soul of a shifter. It was what tied the animals in their hearts together, gave them a sense of purpose in a world that would otherwise not make a damn lick of sense to them. To live in a pack was to be important, no matter your position in the hierarchy. It was to know that you were loved, that someone would always be looking out for you, and that you had a place.

But between packs, the intensity of that loyalty could become a poison. The Alliance was as close as they came to truly putting their differences aside and pooling their political power.

Even that, as Viktor knew firsthand, was a shaky thing.

Still, it was better than living in the confined sliver of territory they were afforded by the EVP. He would take an uneasy truce over watching his own pack eventually wither away, families melting into other packs as they sought more space, more freedom to let their cubs roam.

He loved Lake Merced. As he shucked off his dress shoes and tied the laces together, he thought of what it would be like to say goodbye to the salty breeze blowing off of the ocean and the call of wrens in the hazy time between night and blushing dawn.

He imagined it would feel a bit like tearing out a chunk of his soul.

Viktor's throat constricted as he wadded up his socks and shoved them in his pocket. He slung his tied up shoes over his shoulder and crossed the border into the intensely monitored perimeter of his territory at a loping run into the darkness.

His eyes changed automatically, shifting to the superior vision of the coyote's. They glowed with reflective green as he wove through cypress and fir trees. Normally he would have already ditched his clothes and shifted, but he only had the one good suit left, so he was forced to satisfy the urge to run as a man.

The deeper he ran, the more he felt the ache of impending loss, as well as the bone-deep understanding that this was for the best.

The animal in him loved its pack, but it balked at the unnaturally cramped quarters they had been forced into. He should not have been able to see the homes of his packmates through the trees, though they were a familiar and comforting sight.

One's den should never be immediately visible to outsiders. It was where mates and cubs were kept safe, where each pair had their own tiny territory. Although they had gone to great lengths to disguise their homes so that they blended in with the scenery, they were still obvious to anyone with eyes. There just wasn't enough room to sprawl out as they should, to give each den and its family space.

Viktor knew that his pack felt a deep loyalty to the land on which so many of them had been born and raised their own cubs. He also knew that they felt hemmed in, exposed to the outside in ways that the animal could not accept.

The last straw had been the loss of three young families. All of them cited the same reasons for leaving the pack: they didn't feel right raising their cubs in a cage. If he weren't the alpha, bound in blood and magic to serve his pack, he might have made the same choice as them a long time ago.

As it stood, he *was* the alpha, and he couldn't just sit and watch his pack die a slow, suffocating death.

No one stopped Viktor as he ran, though he felt the presence of several packmates pass him in the dark. They were quiet and moved like quicksilver even in their bipedal forms, but he would always know when they were near. They lived in his blood and in the wild heart of the animal that connected them all.

He was grateful that they sensed his aggression, his need for space. He knew they all wanted updates on their progress with the Alliance, but he could not give them that time tonight.

Tonight, he ran until sweat slicked down his back, until his lungs burned with exertion, and then doubled back around to do the circuit again. By the time he felt like he'd finally let off some steam, dawn was already starting to creep into the velvet dark.

His den was situated in the heart of their territory, on a tiny jut of land that nearly cut between the two halves of the lake. Swathed in darkness cast by massive, old growth trees and under-brush, the clever use of mirrors and proprietary m-tech nearly hid it from view.

It was not the home he grew up in. *That* den was knocked down after his father's death. Viktor could no more stand to live there again than he could look at his father's picture. It didn't matter that it had been nearly twenty years since the old bastard met his gruesome and well deserved end. He would never stop hating him.

Slipping through the hidden door, he didn't bother turning on the lights as he padded into the main living area. Like many shifters, he had an aversion to most walls. The only kind he found permissible were those that protected cubs from the cold and wet. Inside, only small concessions for privacy were made for even crowded homes.

Seeing as he didn't live with anyone else and hadn't brought a lover into his space *ever,* he only bothered with blocking off his bedroom and the bathrooms — mostly so nosy packmates didn't accidentally catch him in a compromising position.

That didn't mean he didn't care about his living space, though. On the contrary, Viktor was obsessive about the state of his den. Not a single corner went uninspected or piece of furni-ture came into it without meeting every last one of his exacting standards.

Was it sturdy? Did it smell good? Could it hold up to claws? If a cub stood on it, would they risk a broken neck? Would his mate prefer a soft mattress or a firm one?

Camille had different dietary needs than he did, so he'd gone out of his way to secure a specially designed refrigerator meant to store large amounts of meat.

She liked light, so he had large, reflective windows installed.

He knew she liked clothes, so he'd even gone so far as to build her a walk-in closet. It, like everything else, sat empty, unused. Waiting for her.

Camille had no way of knowing that he had spent the last twenty years building his life around her. Even when he didn't think he would ever have her in his life again, she went into every decision he made.

He thought of her as he stripped and stepped into his shower, big enough for two. He thought of her as he scrubbed the sweat from his skin and stared at the small, violet tiles he embedded with his own hands into the wall. Each one was made of cut glass that caught the light with an iridescent shimmer.

He was glad, at least, that he would not have to give up his den when they moved. All their homes were modular and made to fit seamlessly in with the surroundings they found themselves in without damaging the environment.

When they left Merced, it would be as if no one had lived there at all.

Viktor turned his back on the hot spray and shuddered, tracing one of the tiles with the tip of his finger. His mind was a tangle of conflicting needs, but he knew that he could not back down from the chase again.

He needed his mate. He needed to touch her, to know she was well, to look into the violet eyes that sparkled with humor one moment and burned with ire the next. He needed to know that she was his, and he *needed* to put his mark on her, the consequences be damned.

Closing his eyes, he took himself back to the Summit.

He knew the moment he made the choice to pursue her down the winding hallway that he wouldn't let her go again. It was as if his coyote had simply sat inside him, waiting for the moment to slip his leash. When he saw her walk into the green room, all fury and long legs, the leash *snapped.*

Viktor couldn't have stopped himself from chasing after her if he tried. The need to be with her stole his breath, his common sense, and when he caught her and smelled the sweet, honeyed scent of her desire...

Viktor braced one arm above him and reached down with the other to squeeze his aching cock. The damn thing hadn't given it a rest since their interlude in the meeting room. He was perpetually half hard, and even the *memory* of how her skin tasted, the scent of her, drove him wild. She made him ache like he never had before.

The elders weren't fucking around when they called it *the fever.* It was like a sickness raging in his blood, this need for the woman who let him have only a taste of her sweetness.

The same as every day since he had the privilege of making her come, Viktor stroked himself to the memory. Hot water pounded against the tense muscles of his back as he remembered the feeling of her slick skin under his questing fingers.

Perhaps he should have been gentler with her, but instinct told him to be rough, that she wanted him to make her bend. And when he plunged his fingers into her silky soft cunt, so wet and ready for him, he knew he was right.

It was a frenzy, and the pace of his hand stroking and squeezing his flushed cock matched the memory. Desperation and the crazed desire to sink his fangs into her before someone else did only made the lust burn hotter, more furious. Pressure built as he recalled the prick of her claws in his thighs and the way she reached back to handle him.

He rutted against her ass like a damn teenager, but she didn't seem to mind. Her gasps were soft and needy, her inner walls a molten ripple around his thrusting fingers, and when she squeezed the head of his cock like she wanted to punish him—

Viktor came with a shudder, painting those lovingly placed tiles with his release.

Sagging against the wall, he braced his forehead against his arm and breathed deeply. The scent of water vapor replaced the wildflowers and honey of his memory. The heat of the water washed away the silk of her skin. A sense of keen loss quickly over-shadowed the temporary euphoria of his orgasm. His closed eyes stung.

Viktor curled his fingers into white-knuckled fists.

He'd let her go once, but that was a lifetime ago. Viktor was no longer a scared boy, wondering how he could keep an elvish mate safe in a world that would reject them both. He was a man. He was an alpha. He was *hers*.

All he needed to do was make her see those things, too.

Chapter Eleven

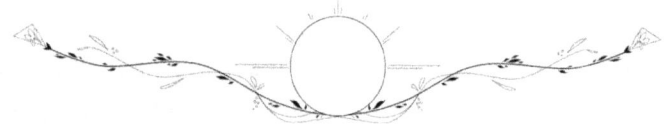

The Rotunda was a San Francisco landmark. It was also one of the handful of restaurants in the city that actually served elvish food, probably because the Solbournes owned it.

Situated at the top of a sprawling, high-end shopping center, it got its name from the fact that it was, in fact, a rotunda. The restaurant itself was a series of tables scattered along a circular balcony. If you looked over the elaborately molded railing, you would see shoppers milling about in the floors below you, crossing gold-veined marble floors as sweet instrumental music filtered through hidden speakers all around them.

The walls and decor were cream and gold leaf, modeled in a slightly toned down rococo style, and the tables were elegantly arrayed with silver cutlery on top of pristine white table cloths. Above it all, a massive oval-shaped dome of stained glass soared overhead.

Sun shone through caramel-colored glass painstakingly placed to look like swaying foliage and filigree. A blazing sun crowned one end of the dome, spreading its rays of light out over the scene set in the middle: an astonishingly large ship riding the green waves of a wind-tossed ocean. At first glance, the blue sky behind it seemed faintly patterned, but upon closer inspection, one found that it was actually emblazoned with hundreds of subtle Solbourne crests.

It was a glass monument created to celebrate the day the Solbournes took the city, but every time Camille saw it, she rolled her eyes.

It was gorgeous, of course. Like any elf, she was awestruck by anything that enhanced the radiance of Glory's light. She just didn't think her family was one particularly worth celebrating.

Sitting in the Solbourne's private booth, Camille looked away from the dome to glare at the appetizer that had been laid out on the table. She wasn't and hadn't been hungry in weeks. The pull stole appetite, but so did stress.

And she was, if nothing else, *stressed.*

"Gods, Cammie, I'm so sorry I'm late!"

Camille turned her head to see Theodore's consort hustling toward their table, her cheeks flushed and a frazzled looking maitre d' trailing after her. A few steps behind *him*, two glamoured guards stalked between the tables of gawking onlookers. There were other elves scattered around, too, but they at least were smart enough to avert their eyes from the black-clad figures. Unlike the average diner, *they* knew how deadly the guards could be.

Instead, their eyes found a safer target: the sovereign's consort.

Margot Solbourne née Goode was pretty in a delicate sort of way. The fact that no one clocked her as a halfling didn't surprise Camille at all. Petite and fine boned, with red hair that leaned toward gold and eyes of a striking copper, she hardly looked elvish. Her features were almost vulpine — the look in her eyes cunning, distinctly *witchy*, but softened by that vulnerability that all healers carried with them.

If it weren't for the small points of her ears and the distinctly elvish note in her scent, it never would have occurred to Camille that the healer sliding into the chair across the table was anything more than a witch.

Margot cast her an apologetic smile before she gave the

sweating maitre d' her order for a cup of tea. "Oh, and please bring some coffee as well. We have one more guest coming."

The wire-thin fey nodded twice, eager to please, before he hustled off. His wings, mostly vestigial, twitched with unease against his suit jacket. Camille had no doubt that Margot would have her order in moments. No one would dare keep the sovereign's consort waiting.

"Who are we expecting?" Camille asked, flexing her claws in her lap. Anger, fueled by betrayal, bubbled through her veins. "If it's Teddy, I'm not making any promises that I won't make a scene when he gets here."

Margot shook her head. "No, he's busy." Her lips twisted in an aggrieved grimace. "So busy, in fact, that he didn't bother telling me I had a lunch date with you until approximately half an hour ago. *After* I made plans with another friend of mine."

Relief mingled with a small splash of disappointment. It would have been nice to really lay into Theodore for betraying her to Viktor so quickly, but she knew that it would do her little good in the long-run. All the anger did was slap a bandage on the hurt. It didn't actually fix anything.

"Well," Camille began, happy for an excuse to escape, "I'd hate to ruin your plans with your friend. You can tell Teddy we had our lunch and go—"

"Oh, no, Cammie. I'm not canceling on you. I just invited Petra to join us."

Camille was already nearly out of her chair. She sank back down with a barely disguised scowl. "I see."

Margot gave her a sympathetic look. "I know you don't want to be here. Theodore thinks we need to be friends, but I'm not exactly the most social person myself." She shrugged, her dainty shoulders rolling under a soft white sweater. Just behind her, the two guards stood, their heads turning every few moments as they scanned the room. "I've never really had friends before, but I'm trying to get better at it."

Right, Camille thought, *because your family kept you in isolation your whole life.*

Empathy pinched her. Neither of them wanted to be there, so Camille didn't feel right taking her anger out on her new kinswoman. "I'm not great at making friends either," she replied, looking down at her cup of coffee to avoid staring at Margot's marriage sigil. She licked her lips. "My... mother didn't want us socializing with the family, so I grew up mostly on our estate in Napa."

Camille swallowed hard. Trying to cover up her awkwardness, she lifted her porcelain teacup to her lips and took a long, bracing sip of unsweetened coffee. She wasn't used to being *open* with people, but she was also a loyal sort of person. Margot was family. The least she could do was make some small effort to connect with her.

"Then you understand how overwhelming it can be to suddenly have people pushing you toward strangers. Feels a lot like punishment, doesn't it?" Margot replied, crisp and to the point. Camille glanced up in surprise and found the healer's coppery eyes glowing with an exasperated sort of humor.

"Yes." A smile quirked the corners of her lips. Setting her teacup down, she announced, "And I'm sorry for... for how we met. I wish I could have made a better impression on you."

Margot's expression softened. "Don't worry about it. I would have reacted the same way in your position."

That was probably true, but Camille still wished Margot hadn't seen her at her worst. She'd been thrown into a frenzy when Valen showed up at their estate, demanding to see her mother. When she refused him and his Patrol squadron entry without explanation, things only got worse. But what was she supposed to do?

They wouldn't tell her why they wanted her mother, so she wouldn't tell them why they couldn't see her. Simple as that.

Camille never promised her mother that she would hide her illness from the Solbournes, but she did it out of respect for Marian's fierce pride. If the main branch of the family knew she was ill, they would have tried to step in, to *help*, and the humiliation would have killed her that much sooner.

So Camille refused them entry, and for that she and her brother were dragged to the Summit. Valen figured that Theodore would be able to get to the bottom of what was going on and where Marian was hiding away. However, the truth was that if he'd simply *explained* that their mother was the only suspect in the bombing that had shaken the entire EVP, Camille would have caved.

Not that she *blamed* them for suspecting her mother. The main family was well aware of the fact that Marian tried to plot their demise on numerous occasions. It was part of the reason they were fine with her self-imposed exile in Napa. They thought it kept her docile.

Camille would never tell them just how many of her mother's plots she had foiled before they ever got off the ground. What they knew of was only a tiny fraction of Marian's machinations. Never once, not even in the throes of her rapidly deteriorating health, did Camille's mother let go of her hatred for the people she blamed for her consort's death.

The bombing, however, was *not* her mother's doing. By the time Margot's Healing House was destroyed in a brazen attempt on her life, Marian slept more often than she woke.

And when she *was* awake, she wasn't lucid.

Margot first encountered Camille when she was confronting Theodore for the accusation against her mother — and, unknowingly, when she was thrown headfirst into the pull once more.

Viktor was in that room. The scent of him, the feeling of his eyes on her, had nearly driven her insane.

It wasn't a good look for anyone, least of all for a woman who knew better than to lose her cool in a room full of predators.

Camille cleared her throat and watched, thankful for the distraction, as a server came with Margot's tea and coffee. When they'd bustled off again, she changed the subject. "I heard that you've been accepted as a junior healer at Solbourne General."

Margot's expression brightened. "Yes! I've been there about a month now."

"Couldn't you have gotten a higher position?" Camille had trouble imagining anyone giving the sovereign's consort a *junior* position in anything.

Margot grimaced. "Believe me, Theodore tried to coerce me into letting him *help* with that. I refused. I went through the entire interview process under a false name so I wouldn't get any special treatment."

She found it deeply charming that Margot had gone so out of her way to stick it to Theodore's heavy-handed interference. She only wished that she could do the same. "And when they found out who you were?"

"Oh, I got a call from the board, apologizing and offering me a better position." Margot waved a hand, her annoyance with the favoritism open. Disgust was clear in every line of her pretty face. "I told them that I didn't want it and was insulted that they'd offer it in the first place. Good gods, what if I'd been an unskilled healer? Don't they care about what kind of damage I could do if left unsupervised or properly vetted?" She shook her head. "It was appalling."

Camille leaned forward, enticed by the very elvish bite she picked up in Margot's tone. She had no fangs to flash, but there *was* elvishness in the lifted lip, the way she flicked her clawless fingers. "And what happened after that?"

"Well, *clearly* they couldn't be trusted to do their jobs well, so I asked Theodore to look into the board. So far, three of the seven members have been found violating the ethics code and one was fixing contracts for a ridiculous cut. We expect their resignations soon." Margot eyed a lemon popover on a silver dish for a moment before she chose a cranberry-speckled scone from the one beside it. While her focus was on the appetizers, her expression was still hardened with intense disapproval.

"Honestly, I couldn't believe it. Playing with lives and billions of dollars in research like that. Some of the violations we've found, Cammie, would turn your hair gray."

"I believe you." Camille watched, intrigued and a tiny bit revolted, as Margot spread some jam across a sliced half of her scone. She knew healers had trouble with meat, since it tended to *"jump"* in their mouths even when it was thoroughly dead, but she still struggled to wrap her head around the fact that Margot didn't even think to try the fine cuts of veal or tender, marinated beef that sat between them.

For godsakes, there's even fresh, lemon zested lobster tail by her elbow, she thought, scandalized, *and she goes for pasty breads? No wonder she's so small.*

Camille was tactful enough to keep that observation to herself, of course, but she made a mental note to inquire into what Andy, the Tower's Houserunner and unofficial Solbourne grandmother, was doing to help supplement Margot's foul diet.

"Anyway, we're working on getting things in order. My main concern right now is making sure the people making bad decisions are stopped from making any more. We can sift through the mess later. It'll take time, but we have lots of that. I've also reached out to my old mentor, Healer Mason, to see if we can poach her from the hospital I apprenticed at. She'd get the ship in working order again."

Margot nibbled at her scone and appeared, as far as Camille could see, entirely ignorant of the fact that she had effectively usurped authority of the EVP's premier hospital without even trying.

No wonder she and Teddy are such a good fit. They're natural-born leaders. In Teddy it at least fit with his air, his look, the way he carried himself. With Margot, it was markedly more surprising — and amusing.

"So, you enjoy being a junior healer?" Camille asked, trying to hide the unreasonable glee she felt knowing that this little slip of a halfling was effortlessly dominating an entire institution. She wondered what it would be like to be a fly on the wall in that boardroom as a bunch of stuffy, overpaid louts took orders from a woman half a step up from a green intern.

Camille *had* always been a fan of scrappy underdogs.

"Oh, I love it," she gushed, "I liked running the Healing House, of course, but there was no challenge in it. Being a healer in an active ward means I get to push myself and actually make a difference in people's lives. All I ever wanted was to be useful — to help people with the abilities I've been given. If you have the ability to stop suffering but don't use it, the feeling of failure is like poison. It's a slow sort of death."

Margot paused for several seconds, her gaze lost somewhere in the middle distance. As the silence stretched, magic began to hum around her in a thick haze that smelled like bright ozone and metal. The hair on the back of Camille's neck rose.

Of course she knew Margot was a gloriana, the most powerful rank a witch could be, but it was one thing to *know* it and quite another to *feel* it.

In that instant, Camille could swear she felt the witch's power humming in her *teeth*.

The sensation only lasted a moment before Margot shook herself, her expression clearing. Whatever it was that held her magical focus seemed to vanish as soon as it appeared.

She took another bite of her scone before she finished, as if she never stopped talking, "It's good to finally be able to help people, at least." She smiled, soft and satisfied.

Camille suddenly understood why Theodore had nearly worked himself to death to have her. Margot's aura fairly pulsed with her compassion, with a healer's warmth and a gloriana's blazing power.

Even if Camille *wanted* to dislike her, she wasn't entirely sure she could.

"Anyway, since junior healers only work part time, I've been spending the rest of my days going through the archives." Margot paused to take another sip of her tea, her eyes glittering over the rim of her cup. "Theodore's wedding gift to me was my own clinic in the Tower. I'm trying to study up on all the secret elvish research I now have access to so I can hopefully use it for some good in the near future."

Camille's brow wrinkled. "What are you focusing on?"

"Well..." Margot set her cup back on its saucer with a small *clink.* Her eyes lingered on the platters of food between them as her fingers skated over the finely wrought handle. "Mainly I've been looking into the pheromone problem."

A chill slid down Camille's spine. "I see."

She knew all about *the pheromone problem.* It was a catch-all term elvish healers used to cover both the *pull* and the madness that had begun to take out her mother's generation of elves. It was rumored that they had been working for decades to find a cure for the problem — a way to eliminate the draw to consorts completely.

The concept made her stomach clench with instinctive disgust, but Camille couldn't deny how much of her yearned for a cure. The pull was all well and good when you were like Margot and Theodore — destined to be together, willing to take on any obstacle to make it happen, *soulmates* — but most people weren't.

Many elves were like her: shackled to someone they couldn't have, existing in a state of constant fear that they would lose their minds due to devastating hormone imbalance.

And then there were the consequences they were only now coming to understand. The moratorium on Other consorts had been in place for a thousand years. That spanned two generations of elves, many of whom went on to procreate with partners who were not bound to them in the way they were supposed to be. It had not only narrowed their gene pool significantly, but had a cascade effect on the children produced by those unions.

The healers who had diagnosed Camille's mother didn't have an explanation other than the circumstantial evidence that children born to two generations of unbound elves were dying fast.

Marian's parents and *their* parents had all been unbound, their offspring created through loveless unions. Camille had lost sleep wondering if that genetic legacy had played a role in her mother's lifelong misery, only to culminate in her pitiful death.

Swallowing around a jagged lump in her throat, Camille asked, "And what have you found so far?"

Margot leaned back in her seat, her fingers half curled around the delicate handle of her teacup. Her angular features took on a look of frustration when she answered, "A lot and also nothing."

"What do you mean?"

"I mean that in the effort to keep all of this a secret for so long, the actual pool of research is painfully shallow." She heaved out a large sigh. "It doesn't matter how much money you pour into something if you don't have the right people looking into it. If the issue had been put on the medical radar across the world a hundred years ago, we might actually have an idea of how to help people by now. Or at least we could have warned you that elves were steadily poisoning their own population with unions."

Camille held very still. She could feel her heart beating faster in her chest, the frenzied pulse echoing down to her fingertips. Guilt and anxiety twisted her stomach into knots.

Was she making the same mistake as her ancestors by pursuing a union with an elf who was unbound? Would her children suffer the same fate as her mother?

It didn't matter that all available information pointed toward Camille herself being safe. *Her* parents were consorts, which seemed to wipe the genetic slate clean. But what about her own children?

"If we eliminated the need for pheromone binding in the first place, none of this would be an issue," she breathed, thinking of her own torture, of the uncertainty of her future. Bitterness laced every word.

"I'm not sure that's true." Margot's voice was prim, lacking any false sympathy or pity. When Camille glanced at her expression, she found it thoughtful. "And what I do know is that the better part of all that money and research *has* gone into trying to find a *'cure'* for the pull — to absolutely zero success. The body needs hormones to function, Cammie, and you can't turn off one without causing a ripple effect across the entire, complex system."

Camille dug her capped claws into the edge of the table, the tips sinking through the white tablecloth all the way into the wood below. "How do you know for sure?"

Margot's expression darkened into a grim mask. "Because I have access to highly confidential records, Cammie, and I can tell you that more than one team *tried* it."

She sat back suddenly, cold astonishment stealing her breath. Camille wasn't even aware of the kernel of hope that had existed, buried in her breast, until the life was snuffed out of it. "I..." She closed her mouth, only to open it again a second later. "What happened?"

"They died."

CHAPTER TWELVE

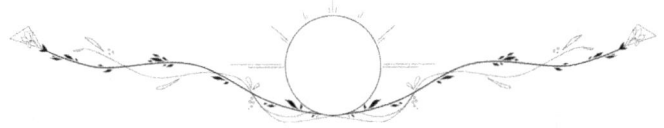

MARGOT LOOKED AWAY, HER LIPS PRESSED INTO A FIRM, bloodless line. There was a lengthy pause as they both digested the grim truth.

When she spoke again, a thread of anger wove itself into her soft voice, "The results didn't stop them the first, or second, or third, or even the *fifth* time. Six trials, all with desperate volunteers, ended with the death of the subjects due to rapid tumor growth, irregular hormone regulation, or heart attacks induced by shock."

It was stupid, Camille thought, that she felt like crying over something that had never been a possibility to begin with. But she did.

Camille blinked hard several times and turned her face away, ostensibly to examine the beautiful restaurant but really to hide the devastation she knew was written across her face.

Her voice cracked when she said, "So there really is no hope."

For her. For others like her.

The choice would always be impossible. Either you found a way to be with your consort or you suffered. If you dared to try and find some happiness on your own, you might very well doom those you loved to a miserable end at some indeterminate point in the future.

For her, there was no winning.

"I'm sorry, Cammie," Margot murmured, soft and full of feeling. "I wish I could give you a better answer. I really, really do."

She *knew* it hadn't always been like this. Not everyone found their consorts even before the moratorium, after all. Was it simply that they had tipped the scales too far in their pursuit of isolation? Perhaps the poison couldn't get a foothold when the majority of babies were born to bound couples, but when that number flipped...

We've cursed ourselves, she thought, assailed by grief and useless rage. *Gods, there is no saving people like me.*

A soft hand touched her arm, just above where her royal blue gloves ended. When Camille's eyes darted up in surprise, she found Margot reaching across the table, her expression creased with concern. "Cammie, if you ever want to talk about—"

"Madam Solbourne." One of her guards appeared by Margot's elbow, his large, black-clad form bent slightly at the waist to speak near her ear.

Margot slowly removed her hand, though Camille's skin tingled with warmth for several seconds afterward. Even when they weren't actively healing, a healer's touch was a balm.

She turned her head to look up at her guard. Her brows pinched with a look of obvious concern. "Yes, Aman? Did you or Erez want something to eat?"

Speaking through the distortion of the smoky glamour obscuring his face, the man Camille knew to be one of Theodore's most loyal soldiers and the newly promoted Captain of the Consort's Guard said, "No, madam. You have an unauthorized visitor requesting access to your table."

Camille tensed, her eyes swinging toward the entrance. She couldn't quite see anything except the shoulder of another Guard stationed by the maitre d's little stand.

"Who is it?"

The glamour hid things like inflection, but Camille could swear she heard a note of annoyance — and the faintest southern drawl — in Aman's voice when he answered, "Your brother, madam."

Camille felt her eyebrows nearly hit her hairline. *"Olivier du Soleil* is here?"

"Ugh." Margot looked vaguely dismayed. "Did he say why?"

"Only that he wishes to see you, madam. Would you like us to escort him away from the building?" Again, Camille thought she detected more than a hint of eagerness in that strange, inflectionless voice.

Margot made a soft sound of annoyance in the back of her throat. Shooting Camille an embarrassed look, she answered, "No, no, I should see what he wants."

Aman nodded sharply before he rose to his full height and lifted an arm to gesture at the guard across the restaurant.

Margot leaned over the table to whisper, "I'm sorry. I had no idea he'd show up or else I would have said no to going out completely. If you want to leave, you can. I won't blame you."

"What is Olivier even doing here? Doesn't he mainly stay in Malibu?" she asked.

A heavy sigh drifted over the table. "He bought a *house* here, Cammie."

"Is that so bad?" As a twin, she couldn't imagine being upset by her sibling's nearness.

"Yes," Margot answered, surprisingly mulish. "It means he's never going to leave me alone now."

Camille watched the guard by the entrance step aside. Immediately, the imposing figure of Olivier du Soleil strode past him.

As clean cut as an ice sculpture, Olivier was devastatingly pretty and equally untouchable. She'd never met a man as cold as Margot's half brother, and amongst elves, that was saying something.

All elves were born hungry — for power, for touch, for prestige, for the stability of hierarchy — but some wore that hunger closer to their skin than others. Olivier was one of those people. He walked like the universe had personally wronged him, and he intended to eat it all up, one bite at a time, as recompense.

Wearing a black on black suit with a distinctly elvish half cape slung over his shoulders, his pale gold skin and white blond hair stood out like a beacon across the room. Chair legs screeched as people hastily moved out of the way of his long-legged stride.

When he arrived at their table, Olivier took a moment to stare down his nose at Camille, the black lenses of his sunglasses hiding his expression, before he turned to address his sister. Every line of his body was sleek, powerful, and elegantly adorned. Even the air around him simmered with a biting sort of sophistication that set her fangs on edge.

When he spoke, his voice was as cold and sharp as a knife's blade. "I'm having lunch with you."

"Olivier, you can't just crash our lunch!" Margot's tone took on a tartness that Camille rather liked.

"I can when you stop answering my messages." Olivier pulled off his sunglasses and tucked them neatly into his breast pocket, revealing eyes of the same striking red-gold as his sister's. In the shade, they looked almost like copper. In the light, they glowed with Glory's topaz.

He dropped into the chair to Margot's left. Helping himself to the waiting cup of coffee there, he took a long sip before he leaned over to cup the back of his sister's head and plant a firm kiss to her hairline. It was a startlingly warm gesture for one so cold.

Pulling back, he commanded, "Stop avoiding me."

"I was *working* yesterday." Margot wrinkled her nose and sat back in her chair. Despite her retreat, Camille thought she spied a cautious softness in her eyes.

"And you could have answered me today, but you didn't. My point stands."

"Don't you have better things to do? Have a business empire to run? Dreams to crush?"

"Nothing is more important than family," he replied, quick and unbothered. "Besides, I am between meetings and currently out of innocent dreams to crush. I fly back to Malibu this afternoon. I wasn't about to miss a chance to spend a moment with you."

Though his tone didn't actually change, Camille got the impression of some great heaviness in his last sentence. That was reinforced when Margot's expression abruptly lost its annoyance. Tenderness took its place.

"Well, I guess that's fine," she murmured, reaching for her tea like she needed a distraction.

Olivier leaned back into his chair and turned his cold gaze on Camille, blatantly assessing her. That wasn't anything new. It was standard practice to take in an elf at a glance, picking out the clues of rank and ability, dominance and power, unabashedly.

She supposed there was also an element of sexual attraction in that assessment as well, but Camille saw nothing of the sort in Olivier's pretty topaz eyes. They were as cold and hard as the stones they resembled.

Thank the gods.

She had no desire to tangle with someone with so many sharp edges. Camille wanted passion, *fire,* not ice.

Unbidden, memories of Viktor's hands on her body, his rough voice in her ear, made her skin prickle with harsh, violent want. Beneath the table, she squeezed one hand into a fist and tried to breathe through the wave of frenzied longing that rushed her.

Oblivious, Olivier took another long drink from his pilfered coffee before he bluntly announced, "I've heard you're looking to contract a union."

"Olivier!"

He glanced at his sister, one white brow arched. "What?"

"You can't just roll into a personal subject like that when you haven't even said *hello* to Cammie yet." When he just stared at

Margot blankly, she explained, with palpable annoyance, "It's *rude.*"

"It's *business,* pearl." He turned his stare on Camille again, fixing her with a look of cool curiosity. For all the passion in Olivier's gaze, he might as well have been looking at a brick. "Who are your top contenders?"

Camille tilted her head, her eyes narrowing on the lean but powerful elf sitting by her elbow. It didn't surprise her that word had already gotten out. She doubted her own family had leaked the news — Theodore's transgression aside — but any family she sent feelers out to might have. "Why should I tell you? It's not like you're on it."

One corner of Olivier's mouth kicked up in a fleeting smile. "How disappointing. I would have liked to reject Theodore's overture to his face."

She might have told him that he *had* been on her mother's first few lists, just out of spite, but Camille didn't want to give the arrogant man more reasons to think he was better than everyone else.

"My apologies," she replied, perfectly flat, "I do hate to disappoint."

"Hm." Olivier glanced down at the spread on the table. Reaching out with one black gloved hand, he plucked a paper-thin slice of prosciutto off of a dish with the tips of his gold-plated claws. After popping it in his mouth, he used his knuckle to nudge the plate toward Margot. "Eat, pearl."

She looked as revolted by his offering as Camille was by her scone. "No, thanks."

Olivier rolled his eyes but let the subject drop without a fuss, as if they'd had the same conversation a thousand times. "If I'm not on your list, then at least tell me who the favorites are."

Camille snagged a piece of prosciutto for herself, if only to take some away from him. "Why?"

"Because I'm good at business," he bluntly replied. It was a vast understatement. Olivier had built a reputation as one of the most ruthless businessmen in the world. "And I don't care about you, so you can trust I won't sugarcoat my criticism."

"Olivier."

He let out an exasperated sigh. "It's not rude. Trust me, it's the polite thing to do. I'm an objective observer. Her family is not."

That was true. Better than that was the fact that Olivier might have had much more personal interactions with some of the men on her list than she did.

Taking a chance, she straightened her spine and bluntly told him, "Cyrus Noor and Epifanio Luz are the current favorites."

Olivier sat back in his chair, his gloved hands folded over his trim middle in a thoughtful pose. "Hm. Why Cyrus Noor? His family's rank is below yours. Their developed territory is laughably small. You stand to gain virtually nothing from the union, while they rake in credibility and your cut of the Dia holdings. It's an uneven bargain."

Camille shrugged. "They have a strong sense of loyalty to their family. That's its own benefit. Besides, the Noor family owns half the produce distributors in the EVP. If they decided to throw their power around, they could starve millions of people within a week. Even you can't deny that not all power lies in who owns the most skyscrapers, Mr. du Soleil."

All that was true, but neither point moved her. There was no way she'd explain to Olivier that she held a certain affection for the soft spoken elf who ran the Noor agricultural empire beside his mother.

Sure, the Noor family didn't have a grand city to their name like the other Families, but they were whip-smart and loyal to their bones. And she liked living in the country. Most elves weren't big on nature, but she'd spent her life in the verdant countryside of Napa. Their sprawling property in Sacramento Valley would suit her just fine.

That, and I already know I can tolerate Cyrus.

They had, after all, mutually agreed on an exchange of

virginity five years prior. It was customary to make such an arrangement around thirty, and although she felt no great passion for Cyrus, he was gentle and attentive. He would treat her and their offspring well. More than well. He might even love her, though she could never return the feeling in the way he deserved.

The thought sent a terrible, ripping pain through her chest, but Camille chose not to acknowledge it. What was a little more guilt on top of the rest, anyway?

"And why Epifanio?" Olivier pressed, pinning her with an inscrutable look. "He is much older than you."

"But he would bring a powerful new family into the Solbourne fold," she argued. "And his wealth outstrips mine."

Camille could feel Margot's stare on the side of her face but chose to ignore it. She had no doubt that to her, a woman raised amongst humans, their frank assessments of her possible spouse's relative worth was jarring. However, Olivier was right.

It was just business.

"True, but he and his father are..." Olivier tilted his head to one side, then the other, clearly looking for the right word. "*Intense.* There is no love between them, and the few times I've spent more than a minute in Epifanio's presence, I left with the impression that he is a man who does not do things by half measures — not in business and not in his personal life. To be frank, I'm not certain you could handle him."

Interesting. Camille made a thoughtful sound in the back of her throat and considered all that she'd heard about Epifanio over the years. Certainly, he was handsome, but she'd also heard that he was meticulous, short tempered, acquisitive, and dominant in the extreme. Perhaps he was too much like his father and *that* was why they didn't get along.

Feeling her phone buzz in her lap, she replied noncommittally, "I've heard something similar. His father is pushing hard for the union, though." *And my intuition says I shouldn't touch that snake with a ten foot pole.*

"I imagine he would, considering he's been clawing his way

upward since the day he disemboweled his own mother." Olivier took a slow drink from his coffee. His topaz eyes cut to his right to take in Margot's appalled expression. "Don't worry, pearl, she deserved it. Or at least, that's his version of the story."

Margot dropped her fork onto her plate, a half eaten cube of melon stuck on the tines. "Gods, that's awful."

"Oh, certainly, but that's the way things were before the war," he explained. A foreign note of warmth began to thaw some of the coldness in his voice. Olivier appeared to actually wish to be *gentle* with his sister. *How unsettling.*

Like he was giving her a bite-sized history lesson, he continued, "I believe she cheated the family somehow and poisoned her spouse with iron — this was, of course, before the metallurgic inoculation. Iron poisoning was... incomprehensibly cruel. It was a just execution, considering the crime."

"But his own *mother?*"

Olivier shrugged. "If I had my choice, I'd prefer to die by the hands of a kinsman than an enemy."

Margot stared at her brother for a moment, her lips parted in a look of frozen horror. "That's— That's *awful.*"

"It's *nature.*" He snagged another piece of prosciutto. "Ask any shifter, any dragon, most especially your *in-laws,* and they'll tell you the same thing."

While he and Margot debated that point, as well as the mode of murder, Camille pulled her phone out of her pocket and checked it under the hem of the tablecloth.

Two text messages waited for her. One was from Theodore and the other was from a number she didn't recognize. Still smarting from his betrayal, she chose to check the other message first.

Unknown number 12:46 PM: Looks like I made it onto your list, sweetheart. We've got a call at 4 PM. I'll be wearing something nice, so don't be late. xoxo

Camille felt the blood drain away from her face in one great rush. Heart hammering, she quickly checked Theodore's message and prayed it would not say what she *knew* it did.

Teddy 12:50 PM: I added someone to your list. Call @ 4. And yes, I'm making it mandatory. Try not to hate me. Love you. -T

She had to curl her claws into the armrests of her chair to stop herself from swaying. *Godsdamn it, the crazy coyote really did it.*

Dread was a lead weight in her stomach, but below that, an ember of something warm and soft glowed. Of course she was horrified that he'd somehow managed to convince Theodore to do what *should* have been out of the question, but she could not deny that a secret, shameful part of her was terribly, terribly pleased.

I am not done with my coyote yet.

It shouldn't have thrilled her, but it did.

"...Cammie? Are you all right?"

Margot's voice filtered in from far away. It broke through the fog of disbelief and exhilaration that had blocked out the chatter of the restaurant, the smell of food, even the sound of her own thundering heartbeat.

"I have to go." Ignoring Margot's concerned questions, she shot up from her chair, nearly knocking it over, and turned on her heel to rush out — only to nearly bowl over a golden-haired witch approaching their table.

Camille only got the impression of a heart-stoppingly lovely face and a glorious, burning energy before she breathed an apology and nearly sprinted out of The Rotunda.

Behind her, a woman's voice dryly noted, "Well, I must have missed something interesting."

CHAPTER THIRTEEN

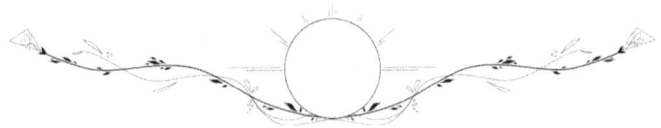

"YOU'RE AWFULLY TENSE."

Viktor didn't look up from his task to reply, "I don't know what you're talking about."

Mia Larkin, mother of two wild teenage coyote shifters and his childhood babysitter, leaned her hip against the picnic table he was helping clear. Around them, pack members of all ages milled around, swapping gossip and speculating about the future. Cubs ran between legs, yipping and laughing, their bellies full of pasta salad and chips and way more pudding than was healthy. It was a beautiful day.

When the summer heat came from the inland, it tended to hit a solid wall of coastal mist, creating a soupy fog that blocked out the sun. Occasionally, though, summer managed to break through.

Today was one of those rare days. The sky was a crystalline blue, cloudless and vast, and the sun made the air shimmer with heat. Everything felt charged; more full of life and color. Anticipation hummed in the air like the low buzz of insects hidden in the scrub around the clearing they gathered in.

Viktor used the occasion to personally speak with every pack member, giving the adults and elders an update on the Alliance.

He also checked in on all the teenagers, as well as the littlest ones, though they were not privy to the same information as their parents. The teens knew something was going on, but he didn't want them to worry about being uprooted for nothing. If the negotiations fell through, it was better to let them live in ignorance.

But it wasn't stress over the Alliance that made the muscles of his shoulders tense. It didn't matter that he'd gone out of his way to appear relaxed, to give no hint about what he was struggling with.

Pack always knew.

They were connected not just by blood and memory, but by a thin, remarkably sturdy latticework of magic. It bound them together — cubs to parents, mates to one another, pack to alpha. It was a tapestry of bonds, each one as important as the other, their threads woven tight enough to make something unbreakable.

Usually he found an untold amount of strength in those bonds. At that moment, however, he could have used a little *less* closeness.

"I'm fine, Mia," he replied, shooting her an easy smile as he stacked sealed food containers into a tower by the edge of the table. All the leftovers would go home with the elders, though they never went without ready made food to begin with. Pack looked out for everyone.

"Uh-huh." Mia crossed her arms and looked at him with the knowing, motherly gleam in her eyes she'd perfected when she was barely sixteen. She was something of a mother to him when his own couldn't be, though she was just a child herself. "Is that why half the pack is ready to run, fight, or fuck?"

Viktor rolled his shoulders, hoping it would loosen the painful knots that had taken root under each shoulder blade. "I don't know what you're talking about. It's summer. The pack always gets rowdier in the summer."

Even he knew that was a weak excuse, true though it was. He

and the rest of the dominant adults had been forced to break up no less than four scraps since the start of the picnic, and he didn't want to consider exactly what was going on with the teens that snuck away half an hour prior.

Everyone was restless, hungry for something they couldn't quite put their fingers on.

Of course *Viktor* knew what was going on. He was damn near coming out of his skin with the fever, fighting every single second against the compulsion to hunt down his mate and lick every inch of her until she clutched at him with those pretty claws.

Because he was the alpha, he sat in the center of the pack's tapestry. Everything flowed through him — everything flowed *out* of him and into the rest of the pack. It was no wonder that every young, single packmate looked like they were dangerously on edge.

That's how *he* felt.

"Vik, I know this isn't just about the Alliance bullshit," Mia pressed, sidling closer and lowering her voice. Her fingers skimmed his bare forearm. He felt her gaze searching his profile. "Are you courting someone?"

He clenched his jaw hard enough to make the hinges pop. *Yes,* he wanted to say. *I'm courting an infuriating, gorgeous elf who hates me. Everything is great.*

But he couldn't say that. Admitting that he was courting someone would open up a whole line of questions he wasn't yet ready to answer.

Except he couldn't rightly say no, could he? Viktor was honest to his core. Lying to his pack was anathema to who he was as a man, as a leader.

He was also violently stubborn.

He *would* win Camille to his side. There was no other option for him now. While he'd spent the better part of his life keeping her a painful, beloved secret, the time was rapidly approaching when he would have to share her with the rest of the pack.

If he wanted Camille to be his, she would have to be *theirs* too.

But that didn't mean *now* was the time to tell the whole pack who she was. Until he knew for sure that she wasn't going to slip through his fingers again, he would keep her identity to himself.

He'd try, at least.

Viktor opened his mouth to answer her with a vague affirmative, knowing Mia would spread the word to the rest of the pack as soon as she possibly could, but was cut off by the sight of Benny jogging into the clearing. His expression was bewildered, but there was an underlying tension in his muscular frame that Viktor knew well.

Standing up straight, Viktor moved around Mia with a small touch to her spine. Benny quick-stepped around a couple of brawling cubs, their silver fur streaked with dust and bits of grass, to meet his alpha at the table.

Viktor's eyes went coyote gold. "What's wrong?"

Jabbing a thumb over his shoulder, Benny told him, "There's someone at the border asking for you. They're waiting at the end of the corridor."

"Who?" Viktor felt the hair on the back of his neck rise. It wasn't unusual for uninvited guests to show up at the corridor, the narrow strip of unfenced land that connected their territory to San Francisco's premier university and the rest of the city, but his instincts told him this was more than just a friend popping by.

He could feel Mia's eyes on him when his second answered, "You'll never believe this, but it's an *elvish* woman. Pretty purple, with the meanest scowl I've ever seen in my damn life."

Well, fuck me. There goes that secret.

Not that he cared, really. The moment the words left Benny's mouth, Viktor snapped into the hunt, his coyote prowling just under his skin. He heard Mia make an astonished gasp, but he was already moving, his long legs taking him out of the clearing without conscious thought.

Wearing only an old t-shirt, faded jeans, and sneakers, his

speed wasn't restricted by a suit or stiff dress shoes. When he ran to meet his mate at the border of their territory, he *really* ran.

Only a handful of minutes later, he burst through the trees that closed in around the Merced pack's end of the corridor. A wide expanse of well tended park rolled out from the border to the street. On the other side sat the sprawling campus of San Francisco Protectorate University.

Technically the public had access to the park, but no one really used it. Neutral or not, the land belonged to the coyotes, and no one wanted to risk life and limb by overstepping their bounds so close to where the pack raised their cubs.

Viktor caught sight of the sleek silver vehicle immediately. Sunlight bounced off of it in a blinding display, spilling light across the woman who stood stiffly beside the rear wheel.

His heart jackhammered in his chest. It'd been *months* since he saw her last, since he tasted her skin and held all that fierce warmth in his arms. Seeing her there, in the flesh, staggered him. Gods, he was so damn hungry for her it *hurt*.

Her short black hair was tousled by the breeze that blew toward him, blowing the sweet, wild scent of her straight into his lungs. Camille was dressed in an elegant cotton dress with a high, buttoned collar, her long lavender legs exposed, and her dainty feet encased in strappy stilettos. The ever-present Solbourne pin, cast in gold and pinned above her heart, winked in the sun.

Fuck, he thought, going instantly, painfully hard at the sight of her in those dainty, sharp-looking heels. He wanted to know what it was like to feel them bite into his back.

Without realizing it, Viktor slowed to a stalking gait, his shoulders slightly rounded as he moved in the shadows between the trees. He would have to leave them sooner or later, since there was no cover close to the street, but until he got there, he wanted to bask in the sight of her.

She didn't look happy, but he knew she'd look even more upset when she caught sight of him. In the seconds he had left before that happened, he wanted to take in the way she looked in the sunlight, how her silver earrings dangled from her ears, how she adjusted the fit of her little blue gloves almost nervously.

They'd never met in secret here, back when everything was different. He couldn't risk his father finding out that he was willingly spending time with an elvish girl, and she couldn't risk getting caught fraternizing with a scrappy coyote shifter.

Usually they met on the beach, where the borders blurred, or behind the waterfall in Yerba Buena Plaza after he finished a training session with her cousins. His father had been informed that Viktor's punishment for trespassing was being meted out by Valen himself — a good excuse that kept his father from becoming too suspicious of the time his son spent with the elves. For a while, anyway.

But Viktor had always wanted to bring Camille to his land. He wanted to show her his den, to see her eyes light up when he explained why he'd chosen what he had, how he'd kept her in mind every step of the way. He wanted her in his *home*, no matter where that was.

To see her there, dressed like she was ready to join the picnic, made his chest tighten with an indescribable feeling. She was so godsdamned pretty and growly and *his*.

He didn't bother reining in the coyote when he stepped out of the shadows several feet away from where she stood. He wanted her to see it. Maybe if she actually saw how much every part of him craved her, she'd let him in.

"Finally," she tartly exclaimed, making his lips twitch with a wide smile. "I've been waiting for— no, you stand *right there.*"

Viktor halted his approach, his smile vanishing under a confused frown. "Cam, I'm not going to talk to you from halfway across the park." He shot her a hungry smile. "I swear, I only bite when you ask me to, sweetheart."

Her chin jutted out at a familiar, stubborn angle. "You stand right there or I'm leaving, Vik."

Exasperated, he held out his arms. "Why? Are you afraid the big bad coyote is gonna gobble you up?"

Not far off from what I want to do, he thought, tactfully refraining from saying it aloud.

He watched, pleased, as a violet flush darkened the skin of her cheekbones. They were about twenty feet away from one another, but he had no trouble making out the way her eyes narrowed and her fists clenched by her thighs.

"No," she ground out, "maybe I just don't want to smell musty fur. Ever consider that?"

Viktor's grin was sharp, full of the coyote's need. "You had no problem with my scent that day in the meeting room."

"A massive lapse in judgment."

"A massive something, maybe, but I wouldn't say *judgment.*" He dared to take a step forward and watched, eyes narrowed, as she took a matching step backward. She was nearly plastered to the car.

No part of him liked that.

Sure, the coyote and the man liked the chase, but the way the flush drained from her cheeks, the sight of the stark outlines of her neck muscles tensing under her collar... none of that was play. It wasn't a game.

Camille really didn't want to be anywhere near him.

He understood that he'd hurt her — and damn, if she'd just let him *talk to her* maybe they could start working through the thorny brambles of the past — but he didn't think it warranted twenty feet of empty space between them.

Voice dropping into a growl, he pressed, "Why are you doing that, Cam? You came to talk to *me,* remember?"

"I did." Camille braced one hand on the roof of the car, as if she needed the support, and announced, "You are going to withdraw your name from consideration."

Viktor didn't move. Didn't blink. He didn't even twitch. He simply stared at her, letting the silence stretch until she began to shift uneasily, before he answered, *"No."*

Camille's lip lifted in a snarl. "No? Why on Burden's Earth *not?*"

"Because I don't want to."

"This isn't a *game*, Viktor!" The hand clutching the car turned into a fist. Her voice rose, pitched high with fury and some other, desperate emotion that set his teeth on edge. "You can't play with my life like this! Not again! Go satisfy whatever it is that makes you think torturing me is fun *somewhere else!*"

"*Torturing you?*" Gods, was that what she thought he was doing? When all he wanted to do was to talk to her? To kiss her? To tell her that a day hadn't gone by in twenty fucking years when he did not think of her?

What did she know of *torture*, anyway? Torture was giving up the thing shifters held most sacred for her own good. Torture was watching his mother slowly waste away and die under his father's neglect, knowing that he had turned his back on his own mate. Torture was wondering every day if he'd made the right choice, if the pain of being without her was worth it, if she cried over the awful things he said.

She didn't know torture. Elves took mates, but he knew nothing about the process. He doubted it came with even a little bit of the raw, agonizing want that wracked *him*.

There was no way she could comprehend what it was like to be *him*.

That didn't mean he would take the comment laying down.

His shifter pride, the heart of him that loved her beyond anything the human mind could articulate, howled in outrage at the insult.

Viktor's temper, already a problem in the grip of the fever, began to lick at his insides. A growl rumbled out of his chest. It was deep and furious, a sound that anyone in his pack would have known as a signal to stand down, to submit.

He watched as Camille's eyes widened, her plush mouth parting in an astonished little *o* before she scrambled to circle the car. Only then did Viktor realize he'd begun to prowl toward her.

"Let me make one thing very clear, sweetheart," he rasped, halting at the line where the sidewalk and the grass met, "I am not *torturing you.* I'm *courting* you. There is no one else. There will never be anyone else. This isn't a game and I'm not fucking playing. Got it?"

From across the car, Camille sent him a wild-eyed look of disbelief. "You can't be serious. You— you— *Now?* Why? Do you think that you can just decide that after—"

"Cam, we were *sixteen,*" he snapped, lifting a hand to rake his partially shifted claws through his hair.

"Exactly! You've had plenty of chances since then to make your move. So why now?"

Viktor tried to gather the frayed edges of his temper, but it was a losing battle. He hated fighting with her when all he wanted to do was soothe, but damn, she was the most stubborn woman he'd ever met. He wasn't trying to cage her or swipe at her, but with the way she acted, one would think he'd been nipping at her damn heels.

Half snarling, he snapped back, "Why are *you* so insistent on a union now, huh?"

"That's none of your damn business!"

"Yeah, well, maybe my reasons are none of yours either!"

He didn't see it, but he *knew* she stomped her foot. "They are when they involve trying to sabotage my entire future!"

"Well, *your* reasons are my damn business when they involve you selling yourself to some fucking elf who doesn't even care about you!" Viktor fought the compulsion to charge across the sidewalk, prowl around the car, and kiss the fury right out of her. He didn't think it would work, but he didn't really want it to. He hated fighting with her, but he loved her fire, the way she was totally unafraid to snarl at him.

Camille looked like she wanted to lunge across the car, her claws curled and ready to tear into him when she hissed, *"Remove. Yourself. From. The. List."*

He propped his hands on his hips. *"Fuck. No."*

She made the sweetest, scariest little growl, and bared her four fangs in a purely elvish display of ire. Camille wrenched open the passenger side door, clearly intending to leave him in the dust.

She was already halfway in when he barked, "Four o'clock, Cam! *Four o'clock!*"

"Gods, I hope a bear shifter comes along and *eats* you, you insufferable mutt!" Gesturing over his shoulder to where he could feel a packmate watching, she added, "You *and* your audience!"

She sent him one last seething glare before she disappeared from view. The windows of the car were tinted, so he couldn't make out what she looked like in the back seat, but he could hear the slam of the door perfectly well.

Knowing she was watching him, he raised his eyebrows expectantly and tapped his wrist. "Four o'clock, Cam!"

The car rumbled to life and, as it was pulling away from the curb, the back window rolled down *just* enough to see Camille flipping him off.

CHAPTER FOURTEEN

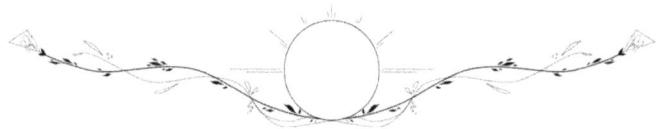

IT WAS STUPID TO GO TO VIKTOR. SHE KNEW THAT EVEN when she was doing it.

But not confronting him wasn't an option. While her instincts howled for the joy of challenging him, the rest of her was galled beyond belief by his sheer audacity.

Deeper than that, buried beneath the indignation and the fear, the flame of hope grew a little larger, a little more dangerous.

As Camille prepared for her second virtual meeting, she tried to smother that hope down into cold, smoking embers. She could not hope. Hope led to trust, and trusting Viktor had once led her to make one of the stupidest proposals of her life.

Run away with me, she'd begged him, breathless with the first wave of the pull. *Run away with me. I'll be your mate. We can be happy anywhere, can't we? Away from your dad, away from the elves. Just you and me.*

She was certain he'd say yes. Everything Viktor had ever done, every touch, every look, every word, assured her that he wanted her as much as she wanted him. There was no doubt. There was no second guessing herself. Viktor loved her.

Until he didn't.

It was the memory of those frigid moments after her

proposal, when warmth hemorrhaged out of her, as his silence stretched and stretched, that made Camille wish she could tear her feelings for him out by the root.

He looked her in the eye and told her, with a wild, caged expression, that he didn't want a mate. He didn't want her.

And *now* he did? Because he didn't like that she was forging a union with another man, or perhaps because of what happened in the meeting room?

Certainly it wasn't because he loved her. It was some twisted sense of honor, or even an unintentionally cruel coyote game that she didn't understand that motivated him. Camille wished that thought didn't slice her to ribbons, but it did. Better he not care at all than get her hopes up.

She could survive his indifference. She couldn't live through another heartbreak.

So Camille firmed her chin, forced her roiling feelings aside, and got ready for her afternoon meeting with the Noors.

Donning a simple, professional dress of black silk and white piping, she carefully combed her hair back behind her ears and secured the cropped curls with a silver clip. Checking to make sure her high collar was securely buttoned under her chin, she smoothed out any wrinkles and forced herself to breathe deep.

Do not think of Viktor. Think of Cyrus.

She *liked* Cyrus. He'd spent time with her at the Dia vineyard, helping them find new and more environmentally friendly ways to cultivate their grapes. He was a good man and a gentle soul. Though she knew that she had to go through with the other meetings for the sake of propriety, she'd always known that if the Noors were interested, she would choose Cyrus in the end.

Until Viktor ruined everything.

No, she had to stop thinking of him. It didn't matter that her meeting with him was less than thirty minutes after the scheduled end of her meeting with the Noors. Viktor could not factor into any decision she made. His suit wasn't real. His motivations were suspect.

She didn't need to consider him at all.

And yet she thought of him as she settled onto the couch facing the feed screen. She thought of the way his skin gleamed like polished bronze in the sunlight; how it stood out against the soft white of his t-shirt. She thought of how he looked at her, eyes coyote gold, like both halves of his soul wanted to eat her up.

She thought of the way his expression changed when she told him to stop torturing her — how it went from stricken to darkly furious in a blink.

Camille carefully posed herself on the edge of her seat, her legs crossed at the ankle and tucked demurely to one side, her spine straight, her gloved hands folded in her lap, and squeezed her eyes shut with enough force to make her see stars.

Stop. Stop it, Cammie. He'll destroy you. Cyrus won't.

Cyrus would love her. Maybe not passionately, maybe not romantically, but he would. Was that not good enough? *More* than good enough, under the circumstances?

Viktor was passionate and he lit her blood on fire, but he was also danger and old, bitter heartbreak. Better that she be safe than risk the dire consequences of losing whatever game the shifter was playing with her.

Her feed screen chimed with a call alert.

Camille's eyes snapped open. Sucking in a deep breath, she reached for the small remote by her thigh and accepted the call.

The feed screen in her sitting room was large enough to give the impression that the people displayed on it were life size. With the crystal clear picture, it was as if Camille was sitting in the Noor family estate, surrounded by rich color and gleaming copper furnishings.

Warmth bloomed in her chest. "Arabella," she greeted, pleasantly surprised. "Cyrus, good afternoon. I didn't realize you'd be sitting in on the meeting."

Arabella Noor sat on a low, richly embroidered sofa, her deep sapphire skin and inky black hair mirrored in her son, who appeared beside her. Where she was slim and delicate, her son was thickly built, with strong, roughly-hewn features and eyes of the softest feeling. She felt the warmth in his gaze even through the screen.

"Seeing as you are already familiar with my son, we didn't think the formality was necessary." Arabella was direct, as always, with a crisp, professional demeanor that barely hid the deep well of warmth Camille knew she possessed. She was ruthless and dominant as any head of a large elvish family had to be, of course, but Arabella was also kind.

Only a loving mother, a kind one, would cultivate the gentleness of Cyrus's spirit. Camille's own mother would never have done so.

"I'm glad," she replied, unafraid to be honest. "It is so good to see you both. It's been too long."

Cyrus leaned forward and clasped his hands between his knees, his heavy brow furrowed in an expression of open concern. "How have you been, Camille?"

Her throat tightened. "As well as can be expected." She tried for a smile, but it came out shakier than she wanted it to.

Cyrus's lips, lush and soft, turned down at the corners. "I'm sorry about your mother. I know how dedicated you were to her."

"She was lucky to have you as a daughter," Arabella chimed in, firm even in her kindness. "Your loyalty to your mother and her care is something to be proud of, Camille, even as you grieve her death."

Loyalty? Camille considered the word as she swallowed the hard lump in her throat.

Had she always been loyal? No.

No, there was a shining moment where she hadn't been loyal to her mother at all. She'd been beautifully selfish for once in her life. Camille had been willing to throw her mother's opinion away, to abandon her twin, for a shot at a future with her coyote.

And that moment taught her the most valuable lesson of her life: the only people she could trust were her kin.

It was her mother who whisked her away from San Francisco

as soon as Camille confessed about the pull. It was her mother who held her as she cried, her viciousness subdued in the face of her daughter's acute agony. It was her mother who helped her find ways to purge herself of him, to free herself of the painful grip on her instincts, to move on when it felt impossible.

Guilt was a sour taste in her mouth as she remembered Viktor's hands on her skin, his husky words in her ear. She'd promised her mother that she would get away from the Solbournes, not fall prey to the pull the moment it reared its head again.

I am trying my best. It's not my fault Viktor decided it was his business.

Clearing her throat, she said, "Thank you, Arabella. I appreciate it." Summoning a smile, she waved a gloved hand in the universal gesture of *moving on.* "But that's not what we're here to talk about, is it?"

"No, it's not." Arabella laid a hand on her son's arm. Glancing at him, she said, "We were pleased to receive word that you had begun negotiations again. We were concerned that your cousin's recent marriage would have changed your mind."

"The sovereign hasn't banned unions." Camille watched their faces closely, looking for any signs of true discontent. While she liked the Noors, she *was* a Solbourne. Her awareness that someone might try to feel her out for information, or even as a potential ally against her family, was always high. "He merely decided it was time we stopped pretending that our strategy is working. That doesn't mean all of us will be as lucky as he is in love, however."

Arabella nodded, her expression inscrutable. "True. There were unions before the moratorium."

"They have a valuable place."

"Certainly."

Cyrus's voice, soft and smooth, drifted from the speakers. "I know that if we joined our families there would be great financial and social benefits, but... I hope that our union would not be only about that." He swallowed. "I enjoy your company, Camille. It would be an honor to be your spouse."

Camille's heart ached as she watched Cyrus' blue skin flush a darker navy. His expression was wary but hopeful, making the ache in her chest worse.

Gods, Cyrus was a good man. Thoughtful, kind, decisive when he needed to be. He wanted to love someone as much as she wanted to be loved.

So how come, when she looked at his dear, handsome face, she only felt a twisting sense of unease in her gut?

There were no butterflies. There was only the steady feeling of friendly warmth and *guilt*.

"Thank you, Cyrus. I want that as well," she managed to reply, though the words tasted like ash in her mouth.

She *did* want that. Just... not with him.

Cyrus's smile was wide and shyly pleased. He shared a look with his mother, who simply nodded and gave his bulging bicep a small, affectionate pat.

"If there cannot be fate, then there *must* be affection," Arabella proclaimed. "Otherwise I would not have agreed to negotiating a union at all. We have not had much need of them in the past."

"Yes, I know that your family has been very lucky." Almost absurdly lucky, in fact. Of the last four generations, only a handful of the Noors had produced offspring through a union. Glory had blessed them again and again with elvish consorts, making the necessity of a loveless agreement moot.

Arabella nodded. "We have, and I was prepared to let my son find his way naturally, but..."

"I insisted." Cyrus reached up to touch his ear — a nervous habit she noticed all the way back when they first met in the vineyard years ago. He looked at the camera through his long, curly lashes, a smile playing at the edges of his lips. "I know we're not consorts, but I like spending time with you."

"I enjoy spending time with you, too, Cyrus. You *and* your

family." She forced a smile and, out of sight of the camera, fisted her hands so tightly the seams of her gloves creaked. "Now, let's talk about what you might want out of a union. I want to be sure our needs are compatible as well as our personalities."

Cyrus rubbed his ear again. "Well, I'd like for us to live together, if it wouldn't bother you too much. I'm not a city person, though, and I worry that will upset you."

Gods, he's such a sweet, honest soul.

"It wouldn't upset me," she firmly replied. "I don't particularly like the city. I prefer to live in the countryside if I can."

"Would you keep the vineyard?" Arabella asked.

"Only if I were contracted with someone who didn't wish to live together." Someone like Epifanio, though she wouldn't know that for certain until they met. "Otherwise, I would most likely leave it to my brother and his consort to run. It wouldn't do well without someone consistently on site."

"You would give up the vineyard to live with me?" Cyrus peered at her, his eyes wide.

"I would, yes. It's better for children to live in one place consistently, anyway." Besides, she wasn't as attached to the wine making business as she seemed. Camille enjoyed it, certainly, but it had also been her mother's choice of pastime — one that she'd forced on her daughter. It wouldn't be too great a hardship to leave it behind.

Cyrus and his mother shared a look. Turning back to the camera, Arabella said, "Well, perhaps you would be interested in taking over some of our wine operations. We would not want to uproot you from everything and give nothing in return."

Camille was touched by the gesture. Her voice was husky when she said, "That is... very kind of you. Thank you."

"Of course," Cyrus insisted in his soft, serious way. "I only want to make you happy."

Again, guilt twisted her up. Guilt over her slip-up with Viktor. Guilt over her potentially dangerous choice to pursue a union at the cost of her offspring. Guilt that she could not think of a future with Cyrus without imagining Viktor in his place.

The guilt hadn't been so bad when she spoke to Elio, but that was a purely business arrangement. Speaking to Cyrus, Camille was aware that it was *personal.* He liked her. He might even have feelings for her.

It should have made things easier, perhaps bring her a measure of relief, but it didn't. Instead, it just felt much, much worse.

CHAPTER FIFTEEN

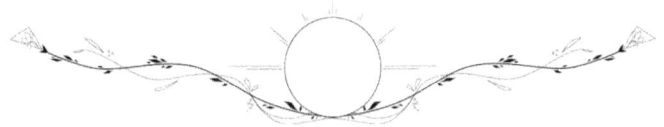

"I *KNEW* YOU WERE SEEING SOMEONE!"

Viktor stabbed his fingers through his hair, pushing the wet, freshly washed strands back from his forehead like it might give him some illusion of style. "Benny, I swear to every god listening, I will throw you out of this den if you say *one* more word."

His call with Camille was in fifteen minutes and he was trying, unsuccessfully, to get his second to leave him to stew in anxiety in *peace.*

Benny leaned against the door jamb of the bathroom, a beer in hand, and grinned like the damn Cheshire Cat. A disgraceful look for a canine shifter, honestly.

"An elf, too," he said, shaking his head. "Didn't know you had a death wish."

Viktor braced his hands on the edge of the sink and met his second's eyes in the mirror. "It's new."

"Is it?"

"What do you mean by that?"

Benny shrugged. Swirling his beer, he answered, "Just think it's awfully coincidental that you'd suddenly get the fever for an elf that just *happens* to be cousins with your former best friend. That's all."

"I haven't spoken to her in twenty years," Viktor flatly replied.

He wasn't lying, but it wasn't exactly the truth, either. This thing *was* new. Whatever they'd had as teens couldn't come close to what roared between them now — whether Camille acknowledged it or not.

He felt Benny's stare as he turned to exit the bathroom, but Viktor was too wound up to play along with the ribbing his second wanted to give him. Maneuvering around him, he padded into the kitchen on bare feet.

"So, when are you gonna tell the pack?"

Viktor tensed. Forcing himself to rein in a snarl, he rummaged around for a glass and filled it with cold water from the tap. "When she says yes."

"Don't you think you should give them a heads up beforehand?"

Swallowing a cool sip, he rasped, "I know, Benny. I know. I'm just— We've got baggage with the elves, and with the Alliance shit hanging over our heads, I..."

"What baggage?" His second snorted with dark amusement. "You mean the kind where her family killed half our pack and made your shithead grandfather alpha when they moved in next door? *That* baggage?"

Viktor set his half empty glass down on the countertop with too much force. The cup, made of sturdy, biodegradable plastic, cracked down one side. "Yes, *that.*"

Benny threw a heavy arm around Viktor's shoulders. Suddenly serious, he said, "I get it, man. I do. But you've got to trust pack. If you want her, then they'll trust you made the right choice. You gotta give us the chance, though." He reached up to tap the rim of his beer bottle against Viktor's temple. "Don't make assumptions. I know you think everyone hates the elves as much as your dad and grandpa did, but it's a new generation, Vik. We're moving on."

It was annoyingly ironic of Benny to call him out using an

almost identical admonishment to the one he'd leveled on Alpha Andreas.

Was he shortchanging his pack by keeping his suit secret? Guilt was a heavy stone in his belly.

He'd kept his feelings for Camille to himself for so long, it was hard to let go, to share her.

It was a selfish impulse, and fundamentally against everything that made alphas what they were, but damn, he hadn't even gotten her back yet. Asking him to share her, even in thought, with the whole pack made his instincts bristle. The coyote wanted her to *himself.* Was that too much to ask after so many years of loneliness?

That didn't mean Benny was wrong, though. In fact, Viktor *knew* he was right. Knowing it just didn't make it any easier.

"I'll tell the pack," he grunted, stepping out of Benny's one-armed embrace. His skin felt sensitive, his senses raw — the fever made everything seem more intense, even glancing contact with packmates he'd known his whole life. It made the magic in his veins boil — preparing itself to erupt the moment he sank his canines into the soft skin of her shoulder.

Running his fingers through his hair one last time, Viktor used his other hand to give Benny's meaty shoulder a shove toward the door. "I'll tell the seniors tomorrow. Until then, you have to get the fuck outta my den. I've got a date."

Benny held up his hands — and beer — in surrender as he trotted toward the door. "Fine, fine! Gods help me, I'd rather gnaw my tail off than get between an alpha and his pretty elvish mate."

"Damn right." Viktor opened the door and gave his second one last shove out into the evening sunlight. Benny's laughter trailed after him even after the door was firmly shut.

He checked the time. Only a handful of minutes had passed. Was time moving slower or faster than it should? He couldn't rightly tell anymore.

Flustered, Viktor strode into the open living area in the center of his den and hastily rearranged the pillows on his couch, the press of instinct demanding he make his den absolutely perfect before his mate saw it.

Camille loved beautiful things. He remembered watching her flip through feeds on her tablet as they hid away together in the small, usually deserted park by the train yard south of Market street, and the way she would gush over the color of a wall or the arch of a window.

Even if he wasn't a shifter and therefore hardwired to care about his den, he would have been nervous. No, she wasn't stepping *inside* the space he had so lovingly designed for her over the years, but she would *see* it — or, whatever the camera bothered to show her, at least.

Heart jackknifing in his chest, Viktor checked the time again and sat down in the center of his soft gray couch. He swallowed hard. It didn't matter that he just drank water; his throat felt like sunbaked asphalt.

Before he could reach for the controller and begin to agonize over hitting the call button, the cellphone in his pocket buzzed.

Scowling, he contorted himself to yank it out of his back pocket. The only thing that stopped him from sending the call to voicemail and silencing the damn thing was the name on the screen: *Ruben Andreas.*

Staring at the dark feed screen on the far wall, Viktor held the phone up to his ear. "What do you want?"

"Did you really think we wouldn't find out that you went to Solbourne Tower the moment you got off the jet? Are you fucking *stupid?*" Andreas's tone was outright gleeful.

"Did you really think I was *hiding* it?" Viktor didn't bother to smooth out the annoyance in his voice. "Obviously you weren't listening at the meeting yesterday, *Ruben,* or you would have heard me disclose my personal relationship with the Solbournes — the *benefit* I bring to the Alliance."

"You were running back to your masters like a fucking

lapdog," Andreas sneered. "Which is exactly what I told them you would do, and what I said *again* when I showed the council the video of you leaving the Tower."

Viktor checked the time and inwardly cursed. "I don't have time for this. If you think I didn't know you had someone watching the Tower, then *I'm* not the stupid one. Furthermore, I don't give a shit if the council knows I visited the Solbournes. I've been clear about my relationship with them from the start."

Did he think it might tip the scales if they knew he was pursuing a very elvish *union* with Camille? Yes. But seeing as Theodore, Margot, and Camille herself were the only people who knew that, he didn't back down or waste energy worrying about the council knowing of his visit.

One of the very first things he did when applying for the Alliance was disclose his relationship with the Solbournes — as well as his pack's history of autonomy despite living in the very heart of the elvish territory. They were no elvish lackeys, no matter what Andreas thought.

"Do you really think they'll let you into the Alliance now that they've seen proof of you running back to—"

"I *think* the alphas on the council will make up their own fucking minds on the subject given all the facts available to them," he snapped. "I *think* that if you really had the case you wish you did, then you wouldn't be calling me to shake me up right now. And I *think* that you can shove this weak intimidation tactic right up your ass, *Alpha Andreas.*"

"You want intimidation?" Andreas snarled. "If you think I'm going to let you bring elvish poison into the Alliance, you're dead fucking wrong. Your father didn't think you were worth the effort of getting rid of, but I'm not him."

"You're right," Viktor coolly replied, "because he's dead."

Andreas's voice dropped into an icy growl. "I'm going to fucking—"

Viktor pulled the phone back from his ear and ended the call.

Whatever threat Andreas wanted to deliver wasn't worth his time. Until he decided to actually work up the guts to challenge Viktor to a fight in the circle, it was all hot air and not worth his time.

Checking the time again, Viktor blanched. He didn't have time to calm down from the call, nor to overthink things. It was time. Biting his lip, he reached for the controller and, after a moment's hesitation, hit the *call* button.

It rang once. Twice. A third time.

Viktor felt the tips of his fingers shift into claws with a familiar burn. The razor sharp tips dug into the tops of his splayed thighs as he watched the screen, unblinking.

On the fifth ring, the feed screen lit up. *Call accepted.*

Camille appeared and his breath froze in his lungs. Every muscle in his body tightened as all of his focus narrowed into a pinprick — shifting to her.

She sat in an opulently furnished living room swathed in sophisticated shades of gray and deep blue. Perched on the very edge of a velvet couch, his mate sat with her back ramrod straight and her chin set in a stubborn angle.

Camille had changed her clothing since he saw her in the green corridor. Instead of her soft white sundress, she wore a sleek black number with white piping, emphasizing every delicious curve and giving her an austere, sophisticated look.

For a taut moment, they simply sat there, staring at one another on the other side of the feed screen. He wondered if she felt the same way he did — almost surprised that she showed up at all.

Well, if she expects me to back down from a challenge, she doesn't know shifters well, he thought, a slow grin spreading across his face. *We love to chase.*

Despite the fact that they were separated by miles, Viktor *felt* her suspicion, the wariness his grin inspired.

"Well?" Her voice was an icy whip through the speakers. Damn if the sound of it didn't make him hard even when she was pissed at him. "I'm here. Are you just going to keep looking at me like that, or are you actually going to participate in this farce you've strong-armed me into?"

"Can't I just admire you for a minute?"

"No, you may not."

Viktor sighed, but it wasn't an unhappy sound. He didn't bristle when she snapped at him. Certainly, he would have preferred it if she wasn't angry with him, but he also felt... comfortable. Nostalgic, even. This was, after all, the place from which they began their relationship.

Chest aching, he leaned back into the cushions. In a soft voice, he asked, "Do you remember when we met, Cam?"

Immediately, her annoyed expression shifted into outright wariness. "That is not what a union negotiation is about, *Alpha Hamilton.*" Her reply was stiff, uninviting. Nothing about it or her expression encouraged him to continue.

He did anyway.

"We were fourteen," he murmured, watching her closely, "and I swear, that moment I saw you out in the garden, I thought my heart stopped. You were the prettiest damn thing I'd ever seen." Viktor pressed his palm against his heart, as if it could help contain the warmth of the memory that glowed there. "And then you told me that if I kept staring at you, you'd be happy to give me a closer look at your claws."

Camille looked away, her cheeks turning a deep purple that made him want to stroke every inch of her skin. "What about it, Vik? None of that matters now."

His smile widened. "It matters, sweetheart."

"*Why?*"

"Because this thing between you and me — it didn't start gently. You never liked soft for too long. You always wanted a reason to use your claws, even when you were pleased with me." Viktor breathed deeply, his chest expanding as if he could take in the scent of her from all the way across the city if only he tried hard enough. "You like a challenge as much as I do, sweetheart."

He knew that like he knew his own soul, his own strength.

Camille hissed and clawed only because she enjoyed the tangle as deeply as he did. She could be soft — oh so, so soft — but only when he *worked* for it. That dance of chase and play and submission was a siren's song for a shifter like him, an alpha in the prime of his life who knew, without a shadow of a doubt, what he wanted.

"You forfeited the right to any *challenge* twenty years ago," she flatly replied, like she didn't feel the heat, the tension that drew him to her every second of every day.

"You want to talk about that? Fine. Let's get it out of the way." Viktor sat up straight, his hands loosely curled on his thighs. In a hard, matter-of-fact voice, he said, "Cam, we were sixteen. Fuck, you have to know it would have been a shit-show if we ran off together. My dad would have hunted us down and killed you in front of me — and *your* family would have flayed me alive for even thinking of taking you from them."

And *gods,* it still fucking hurt to talk about it. How many times had he relived that night, playing it out over and over again, wondering if he made the right choice?

Shaking his head, Viktor continued, "It wouldn't have worked. How was I supposed to protect you from my shitty alpha *and* your family? And even if we could hide out somewhere, what kind of life would it have been for you? For our cubs? I couldn't do that to you, Cam."

Camille's features, beautifully sculpted and so very dear to him, tightened. "You didn't even think to try," she accused, voice trembling with decades of hurt, of rage. "You didn't ask what we could have done. If I recall correctly, you said *I don't want a mate,* not, *I want to protect you.*"

Viktor winced. "I was a stupid kid, Cam. I meant *right now,* not—"

"You didn't even consider what it might be like if my family actually *approved* of you, did you?"

Viktor went very still. "What are you talking about, Cam? Elves weren't even allowed—"

"Do you know what the *pull* is, Viktor?"

CHAPTER SIXTEEN

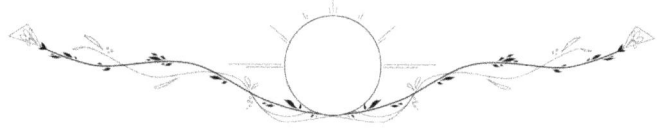

OH GODS, IT'S NEVER GOOD WHEN SHE USES MY NAME like that. Icy fear trickled through his veins. "No," he rasped. "No, I don't know."

Camille leaned forward slightly. Her expression was hunting sharp, like everything in her was poised to go for his throat, when she continued, "Of course you don't. You didn't even think to *ask* why I would be so keen on running away with you. Why it mattered *that night* of *all nights.*"

"Cam, I don't—"

"For the record," she continued, steamrolling over his objection, "us running away together was for *your* sake, not mine. Knowing what your home life was like, I knew what your father would do if he found out about us. I wanted to get you out of there as fast as possible. But *my* family? My mother? She might have been *delighted* to hear we were together, if only to make the Solbournes look bad. Yes, I would have given up a lot to be with you, but not what you assumed. And nothing I wasn't prepared to live without."

Viktor wracked his memory, trying to recall every specific detail of that awful night, when he'd rejected the only mate he'd ever have.

Camille had been gone for months, but that wasn't unusual. Her mother hated the Solbournes and only brought the twins into the city when absolutely necessary. He and Camille had worked out how to privately message one another and fell asleep to the sound of the other through an audio feed every night. It wasn't the same as being together, but it was close enough.

The week prior to her ultimatum, she had been strangely silent. His messages went unanswered. His calls went to voicemail. Viktor had about gone out of his mind with worry, but when she finally called to tell him that she was going to be in the city, he only felt relief.

When he saw her next, she looked... different. Not in a huge way, but subtly. Her body looked softer, her cheekbones more pronounced. There had been other signs that something changed, but he was too distracted by her offer to properly investigate them — or get answers about her disappearance.

He didn't know what triggered her sudden desperation to run away with him that night. Viktor simply assumed that something had happened with her mother during that mysterious week — perhaps she discovered their messages, or otherwise found out about their budding relationship. It made sense to him at the time.

Elves, after all, did *not* take outsiders as mates. Everyone knew that.

Viktor shook his head hard, a growl building in his throat. "Don't act like your mother would have been jumping for joy if you and I ran off together," he bit out, a brewing storm of disbelief and guilt churning in his stomach. "Until a few months ago, elves weren't even allowed to mate with shifters — or anyone else. I don't care how much the Solbournes liked me. They never would have let me take you as my mate."

"You underestimate how much my mother hated the Solbournes." Camille looked away from the camera, her expression shifting into something distant and terribly sad. "You never asked, Viktor, why I wanted to be with you. Why it mattered so much. You never asked."

A tremor ran through his body as his coyote pressed up against the surface of his mind, demanding to be let out. It howled in response to the sound of the sorrow in his mate's voice.

"Tell me now," he demanded, ragged. "You shut me out after I said no. You didn't give me a chance to ask again. So tell me now."

If he'd known that night would be the last chance to speak to her, to hold her, Viktor wasn't sure he would have had the strength to reject her offer.

He didn't know that, come morning, she would block him on every messaging service. He didn't know that when he showed up to train with Theodore in the afternoon, he would convey the message that he was never again allowed contact with Camille. He didn't know that he and Theodore would come perilously close to killing one another that day.

In a moment, he lost his mate and a brother. It sat beside the death of his mother as the single worst moment of his life — but at least he understood what had happened, what went wrong, and how it had all been for her own good.

And when the years dragged by without contact, he accepted her decision to end things, though it tore the heart out of him to do it. He respected it right up until that day of the Summit, when he just... couldn't anymore.

To feel the dawning horror that accompanied the realization that he might have been *wrong* to assume he knew what was best, that he didn't actually understand what had happened...

Viktor's stomach rolled. Bile crept up the back of his throat as Camille stared at him through the camera, her expression shuttered.

In a flat voice, she explained, "It is a chemical reaction that happens after an elf has reached maturity through the change, a week-long stretch of hormone induced madness and body growth where we are isolated for our own safety. Our mating imperative, the *pull*, is a hormonal shift that takes place when an elf meets their consort and takes in their pheromones for the first time. After that, they experience increasingly intense compulsions to be near their consort and share skin contact, increasing their intake of pheromones until a chemical bond is in place. It's meant to help procreation, and often results in pregnancies with multiples."

She said it with no inflection, as if she was reading from a medical textbook rather than telling him something that made cold sweat break out across his chest.

"When the bond is not put in place, the consequences of pheromone withdrawal range from severe discomfort, paranoia, and aggression, to loss of motor function, uncontrollable rage, and finally, madness." Camille looked down at her lap. It took him a moment to figure out that she was methodically peeling off one of her skin-tight leather gloves.

Lifting her bare hand, she showed him her pale purple claws and her lovely, finely wrought fingers, and continued, "The only outward sign of the pull is the retraction of claws. We are biologically incapable of harming our *mates,* as you would put it."

Her eyes, a beautiful, luminous violet, gleamed with a hurt so deep, it shook him to the core. "I went through the change when I was sixteen. It was six days of torture and madness in the padded cellar below our house. Days of pain and fear — then relief and exhaustion when it was over. A week later, I asked my mother to take me to the city to celebrate. I wanted to see you. I wanted to know if I was right. That night when we met in the plaza, my claws retracted, just like I knew they would."

Viktor's mind spun. He couldn't breathe. He couldn't even see. The feed screen mounted on the far wall blurred, becoming little more than a smudge of blues and grays and lavender. His voice was all rough syllables and ragged edges when he said, "You... have mates. *I* am your mate."

Of course he knew that elves had a form of matehood. He'd even known, to a small degree, about the *change.* He'd seen the mate bond in Valen and Andy, as well as in Theodore's terrifying older sister and her partner, but he never thought they felt a draw to a mate like shifters did, like orcs did.

He never dared to hope that Camille would feel the bite of instinct like he did; that she would feel devoted to him down to the cellular level as he did. But *now...*

Viktor sucked in a deep breath and felt his heart hammering against the cage of his ribs, threatening to break through muscle and bone to reach her. "Cam, I didn't know—"

"No, you didn't." Camille looked down as she primly pulled her glove back on, as if she still needed to hide from him, from the world. Her tone had lost its flatness, but was made altogether worse by the brisk, professional note it had taken on instead. "And it doesn't matter now, regardless. I purged you from my pores once, Viktor, and I have no intention of putting myself at risk of madness and death for you again."

Settling her hands in her lap, she lifted her chin and said, with great dignity, "And that is why I am telling you to back off from this ridiculous suit of yours. Whatever care you have for me, whatever responsibility you feel like you have for my wellbeing — *disregard it.* Nothing is more dangerous to me than you are. So unless you plan on taking me as your mate in front of the gods and all the world, then *leave. Me. Alone.*"

Viktor realized two things simultaneously: first, that his mate thought, with every ounce of conviction she possessed, that he wished to hurt her.

Second, that he *did* hurt her.

Agony rippled through him. It permeated every corner of his mind, tainted every sweet memory he held close to his heart. It stripped him of his certainty in his actions with acidic ferocity, peeling away two decades of denial to reveal the horrifying truth.

Camille needed him, even when she had been set on saving him from his own father. On a chemical level, she *needed* him.

And instead of asking her why she chose that moment to ask him to run away with her, instead of fighting against the wall her family had put between them after his rejection, he sat in his absolute certainty that, whatever else happened, it was the right choice for *her*.

Gods, I'm going to be sick.

Viktor leaned his elbows on his knees and covered his face with clammy hands. Inside him, his coyote paced, whimpering and sick with grief, in the darkness of his mind.

"Did it hurt you?" The question burst out of him like a spray of poison, toxifying the air he drew into his lungs.

There was a beat of silence, then, quietly, "Yes. The first time. And the second."

Everything went quiet inside of him for the span of several heartbeats before, with a tearing, furious cry, Viktor's hands shifted to claws and swiped at the coffee table. It skidded across the floor, its surface gouged with ten jagged lines, as he fought to keep the horror, the rage, directed at himself.

A small part of him was furious with her for withholding the information from him when he could have *done* something, but he knew that wasn't fair. In her place, he would have done the same.

Fuck me, I did do the same, didn't I?

He hadn't exactly told her about the fever, about the choice his coyote made that day in the garden. A part of him had always just assumed she knew — how shifters mated was common knowledge, after all — but he never actually *said* it. Was that why she hadn't been open with him? Did she think that he had just been playing with her, coaxing her for a lark, all the way back then?

"Vikt—"

"Give me a minute," he grated, head hung low and claws fisted on his knees. The muscles of his back and shoulders trembled as he fought the urge to shift, to get out and hunt her down so he could—

What? Apologize? Expose her to my pheromones? Force her to bond with me so she can't *choose anyone else?*

A different kind of horror snapped across the surface of his mind. It was cold and hard; a blade that slid neatly through the blinding fury that threatened to consume him.

She didn't trust him because he'd been actively, if unknowingly, attempting to steal her choice without so much as telling her that she had always been *his* choice. In a moment of perfect, brutal clarity, he realized that she must have seen nothing but history repeating itself.

But that wasn't going to happen.

Raising his head, Viktor stared at the stark, pale face of his mate and announced, "Cam, you're my mate. Always have been. Always will be."

He watched, heart twisting with fresh pain, as her eyes widened. "I... what?"

"I'm yours, sweetheart," he rasped. "I'm so sorry. I didn't know. I thought— I thought you knew, and when you cut me off, I just assumed you..."

Camille made a sound that struck him like a blow: half gasp, half growl. Gone was the fierce, hissing elf. In her place was a woman who looked like she was ready to run as far and as fast as her feet could take her. "No, Viktor, you don't get to do this to me. You don't. I won't let you play your games with me anymore. I'm going to contract a union and I'm *going* to be free of the pull. You don't get to just— just *do* this now!"

In that moment, he felt the gulf of time between them yawning open, dark and cold. His mind raced. How could he get her to see him *now*, not the boy she knew?

Gods, I'm an idiot.

She didn't know him. He didn't know her. Twenty years had gone by as he kept the idea of her, the memory of their brief time together, locked safely in his heart. That girl was gone — replaced by a woman honed to a razor's edge, determined to keep her pride and live her life as she chose.

It was with agony and wonder that he realized he did not know *this* Camille's dreams, her habits, her dislikes. He didn't know what she wanted or who she dreamed of being. The things that drew him to her in the first place remained, but there was so much more to her than the feisty little elf he'd toppled head over heels for.

Viktor stared at Camille with wide eyes, comprehending, for the first time, that she was not the girl he'd loved, but something more, something precious and irreplaceable.

Pride in her swelled into a tidal wave inside of him, washing some small measure of his grief away. Urgency coalesced into ruthless decisiveness. *Think, Vik. Think. If this was a woman you'd just met, how would you fix this?*

"I've fucked this up," he said, blinking hard. The image on the feed screen blurred, for just a moment, as he tried to get a hold of the coyote yowling with pain in his mind. "I'm sorry, Cam."

Camille didn't reply. Her expression loosened with surprise. "I... well, yes, you have." He watched the little pearl buttons holding her collar together wink in the light when she swallowed. "Will you withdraw your name from the list now?"

Viktor smoothed his palms over his thighs, wiping away the clammy sweat. "No."

It was her turn to blink. "For godssakes, Viktor, *why?*"

"I said I was sorry, not that I was giving up." Consciously unbunching the tense muscles of his shoulders, he did his best to seem nonthreatening, to reel in the hunting instinct. Gentling his voice, he asked, "Cam, if I said that I wanted you to be mine, that I wanted to court you and know you for real, what would you say? No pretenses, no games. Just you and me."

She was very still. For a moment, he worried that the feed link had glitched, freezing her image on the screen.

And then her expression, shell-shocked and unreadable, cracked.

Even though her voice wobbled, there was an unmistakable fierceness in it when she whispered, "Don't be cruel, Vik. I can't take it."

Fuck. The itch to run to her, to wipe away the tears he saw glittering in those arresting violet eyes, was a real, physical ache in his chest. "I swear I'm not," he assured her, rough and painfully sincere. "I mean it, Cam. Let me prove it to you."

"How?"

The idea came to him in an instant, half-baked but good enough. "Meet me at our beach tomorrow night — midnight. Let's just talk, get to know each other like we used to. If you still don't want me to... if you want me to take myself off of the list after tomorrow night, I will. I swear."

For her, he'd do anything — even break his own heart all over again.

Viktor watched her look away, one gloved hand lifting to toy with the buttons at her throat. She gnawed on her lower lip with a pearly fang. *Don't say no,* he silently begged her. *Don't shut me out. Give me a chance.*

Her brow puckered and her shoulders firmed. Dread crept in, but Viktor didn't let it get far. Before she could deny him, he rushed out, "It'll be outside and I'll stay downwind. I won't try to touch you or anything. We'll just sit and talk." His voice cracked. "I'm not trying to take your choice from you, Cam. I would rather die than do that."

As he said it, he recalled their meeting in the corridor: how she danced away from him, always managing to keep the wind at her back. Viktor wanted to give himself a good, hard punch to the head for missing something so obvious.

Clearly he didn't need his brain in working order since he wasn't *using it.*

For a second, he thought she still intended to refuse him. In that moment, her lack of trust in him scored his soul like nothing ever had.

What was an alpha without trust? *Just a bossy asshole.*

What was mate without trust? *Just a stranger.*

When he felt his hope tumbling like a house of cards, the gloved fingers at her throat curled into a tight fist. Camille sucked in a deep breath and, with all the wariness of fox in a snare, answered, "Okay."

Chapter Seventeen

CAMILLE STARED AT THE CEILING OF HER BEDROOM AND the blue-black shapes of each dangling crystal of the chandelier that swayed, ever-so-slightly above her bed. Light from the busy street below her window spilled through the crack between heavy silk curtains — tangerine orange and sickly magenta and the sweet-toothed teal of neon. The colors sparked on the sharp edges of the crystal droplets, limning them with a vibrant glow for just a moment before the crystal swayed again, catching a new light, a different color.

Despite the perfectly calibrated air flowing through the apartment, the atmosphere in her bedroom was warm and heavily scented with the perfume of her shampoo. Camille breathed slow, measured breaths and felt the slide of her sheets over her bare skin. She listened to the sound of cars moving through the throbbing veins of the Financial District outside her apartment's walls.

Sleep, like peace, eluded her.

What am I doing?

Why had she indulged him with that call, with her agreement to meet him? It was foolish, dangerous, bound to hurt her in the end. She wanted to blame it all on Theodore, but she was nothing if not honest with herself.

She didn't speak to him because she truly worried her cousin would pull the plug on her union. She did it because she *wanted* to talk to Viktor.

But why in the gods' names did she tell him *everything?*

Somehow despite her regret, she couldn't stop the bubbly, fizzy feeling of excitement in her chest. Every nerve in her body hummed with it. Her muscles flexed and relaxed again, as if the beast that lived in her wished to jump out of her skin and run to him, heedless of the tremendous risk it took in doing so.

She'd felt both too exposed and utterly over-sensitized after their call, so she showered and climbed into bed nude, hoping to sleep the tension away. Perhaps if she finally got a good night's rest, she would wake up in the morning with a clearer head and a stronger will.

But she couldn't sleep. She could barely even close her eyes.

Whenever she tried it, all she saw was him: high cheekbones, deeply tanned skin, wind-tossed curls of sandy blond hair, eyes of beautiful, clear blue that flickered to wild amber and back again. Even now, his voice rumbled in her ears with a low, hoarse purr. She saw the vulnerability in his eyes when he said, *I'm yours.*

Gods, if that's true...

Camille shifted under the blankets, her breath quickening with excitement and dread, desire and trepidation. Longing made her ache as surely as arousal did.

In a perfect world, he would be here with me now, she thought, remembering the way his calloused hands felt on her bare skin.

In a perfect world, she would not have cried on their call, nor would she have had any reason to in the first place. *He would make you happy,* instinct pressed. *He would take the ache and the pain and the loneliness away.*

It was not simply because he was her consort. She knew deep down that it was a deeper connection that drew her to him again and again, despite the danger. Viktor held a solid core of fierce goodness that called to her. It always had.

I watched that core shake today.

Camille turned on her side, one hand tucked under her pillow, and stared at her night stand. *When I told him the truth, it was like I nearly broke something in him.*

She thought it would make her feel good to watch him hurt, to hear the horror in his voice when he realized what she'd been through, but it didn't. All she felt was hollowed out and lonely, aching for that connection hanging just out of her reach.

It was with an awful, sickening jolt that she realized *his* hurt was hers, too.

Peering through the soft shadows, her wandering gaze landed on her phone. It sat innocently on its charging pad beside her stained glass Tiffany lamp.

Her fingers twitched under the cool pillowcase.

No, Cam, you can't. She gritted her fangs together and tried to force herself to flip onto her other side, but it was like her body refused to follow the order. Instead, she lay there, staring at her phone, gutted by how easy it would be to soothe the ache.

Just the press of a button, her traitorous inner voice whispered. *It was so easy before, and the risk so minimal. What is a call, anyway? One click and you could hear his voice again.*

The temptation of a promised reward was almost too much to bear.

The uncomfortable prickling of her skin would fade. Her heartbeat would slow. Peace could be hers for another stolen, selfish moment.

A blink and her phone was in her hand. Camille squinted at the bright screen, her slit pupils contracting into razor-thin lines as her vision adjusted. "Don't call him," she sternly ordered herself, an edge of pure desperation in her voice. The phone shook in her trembling hand. "Don't do it, Camille."

If she needed to talk to someone so bad, Camille decided, she could just call her brother. He was worried about her, and she knew he'd be up. Even if he wasn't, he would take her call.

But calling Cameron would open up more wounds than it would close. Their bond was such that he would know immediately that something was terribly wrong with her. She had no doubt that he'd cut short his vacation with his consort and rush home as soon as the call ended.

Camille couldn't bear that. Her twin had only just come up for air after spending so long suffering under their mother's withering disapproval. He deserved his happiness, his peace.

And I know who I really want to talk to.

She chewed her lip, her eyes fixed on that innocuous string of numbers that had sent her the text during her lunch with Margot.

Would he perceive her reaching out to him as weakness? Would it matter if he did? Camille vacillated with not caring either way — he had seen her at her most vulnerable that evening, after all — and shuddering at the idea of him knowing their call had shattered so many of her defenses.

She began to lower the phone, her gut soured by the idea of giving in, but couldn't quite bring herself to let it drop onto the blankets.

What's the harm? He already knows everything. Maybe if you're lucky, he won't answer.

Now that the idea of hearing his voice again was in her mind, she couldn't shake it loose. Even as she tried to reason her way out of doing it, Camille lifted the phone again and, with one trembling thumb, dared to hit the *call* button.

Checking to make sure it was on audio only, she lay back in her pillows and squeezed her eyes shut. It rang and rang, each discordant note striking a blow in the warm darkness. Dread settled over her. *He's not going to answer.*

That was good. It was foolish and sentimental to call him in the dead of night, anyway. They had their meeting planned. Surely she didn't need to add one more bad decision to her roster for the evening.

Mind made up and stomach roiling with self-recriminating

disappointment, Camille moved her thumb across the screen to end the call.

"*Cam?*"

Viktor's voice came through the line crystal clear. It brushed across her senses in a silken caress, both soothing and anxiety-inducing. He didn't sound sleepy, but he still had that peculiar note to his voice that people got when they were laying down.

Her breath hitched. Words fled. Now that she had him on the line, what was she supposed to say? Panic and embarrassment overwhelmed her.

"Sweetheart, I can hear you breathing. Are you okay?" She heard a faint rustle before his voice changed. Camille imagined him sitting up in bed, his hair tousled and his skin bare, and gripped her phone tight enough to make it creak. "Cam, sweetheart, say something so I know you aren't bleeding out on the bathroom floor or something. *Please.*"

She forced herself to swallow, despite the fact that her throat was dry enough to light a match. "I'm fine. I just wanted— I'm sorry, I shouldn't have called. It's late. I'm sorry, I'll just—"

"Sweetheart." Viktor's low purr stopped the progress of her finger, which had been inching toward the *end call* button. There was a lilting note of surprise in his tone when he asked, "Did you call just to talk to me?"

She briefly considered lying, but the idea didn't get far. What would she say? No, *I called the wrong number?*

Biting back a low, pained groan, Camille leaned her head back into her pillow and tartly replied, "This was a mistake. If you'd rather be sleeping, I can let you go."

"Camille, the day I'd rather be sleeping than talking to you is the day you should put me in the ground."

"Yes, well..." She paused, flustered, and cleared her throat. "Now that I'm talking to you, I don't know what to say."

"Why'd you call, sweetheart? What made you want to talk to me? Is everything okay? Don't get me wrong— I'm fucking ecstatic you called, but I thought after tonight you'd want some space."

Her eyes roved over the ceiling, tracing the intricate molding designed to look like bunches of leaves and flowers and fruit. *Gods, I should not admit this to him.*

But she was already in deep, wasn't she? He knew about the pull and she was the one who made the choice to call *him*. If he really wanted to know why, then she supposed it wasn't unreasonable of him to ask. Letting out a slow breath, she braced herself for what she was about to say.

"The pull is... difficult."

His voice lost its playfulness when he asked, "How so?"

"It makes you feel like something is undone — like that crawling feeling you get when you realize you've left the bath running or a candle lit." Focusing on one particularly robust bunch of plaster grapes, she continued, "It's a compulsion to be near you, and when I don't follow through with it, my body fights me. It's uncomfortable." She paused, knowing it was a mistake to continue but unable to stop herself. "It's... it's painful, in a sense."

He was quiet for a moment, but she could hear his steady breathing, count each deep inhale and exhale like the ticking of a clock. "Sounds an awful lot like our fever, if you ask me."

"Does it?"

"Yeah." The sound of fabric shifting came again. Was he laying on his side? On his back? She pictured him lounging against his pillows, one arm bent behind his head, showing off every beautiful inch of his chest and stomach.

Camille squeezed her eyes shut and clenched her thighs, trying to will the image away.

"Once we pick a mate, it's like... Well, it's like you said. A compulsion. The animal can't stand to be away from its mate. The body starts to— ah, it's hard to describe. It's like everything gets ramped up. Our magic goes haywire. Adrenaline goes overboard. Even our body temperatures rise. We're aroused *constantly*.

We get territorial, short-tempered, and go den-crazy. Especially when mates aren't marked yet."

"Den-crazy?" She blinked. "Is that like... nesting?"

"A bit. But it's not like how a newly mated dragon will buy out an entire store's worth of blankets as soon as they Choose. It's more like the *whole* den. Everything has to be perfect. Usually a shifter will start working on their den years before they even find a mate."

"Oh. Elves don't do that." Camille caught herself before she dared ask what *his* den looked like. She gnawed on her lower lip, trying to remind herself that she was a big girl, that she shouldn't get comfortable with him just because he opened up to her a few hours ago.

Still, curiosity nipped at her heels.

If she gave in to the pull, if she trusted him, would he go den-crazy? She wasn't sure why the thought made her chest tight, but it did.

Viktor felt none of her hesitation, apparently. His eagerness came through loud and clear when he asked, "What do elves do, then?"

Eyes popping open, she sputtered, "What do you mean?"

"I mean what do elves do when they find their mates, sweetheart?" There was an unmistakable note of rich laughter in his voice. It damn near melted her. "If you don't make a den and you don't buy a bunch of blankets, what do you do?" He paused. Voice deepening into a hoarse whisper, he asked, "If I was there with you right now, what would it be like?"

Her breath stuttered. A rush of hot arousal flowed through her veins to settle between her thighs, making her ache more fiercely than she ever had before. Control — *reason* — slipped from her grasp like so much smoke.

"We don't bother with a nest or a den," she answered, knowing he could hear how quickly her breaths came, how raw her voice had become. "We want — need — skin contact above all things. It's like we're starved for touch, for the smell and taste of our consorts, and when we get it, we indulge until we're drunk on it. If... if you were here, we would be in bed, skin to skin, until my scent lived in your pores and vice versa."

There was a beat of complete silence. Camille had the startling realization that he must have been holding his breath.

Finally, he asked, "Is that all we'd do?"

CHAPTER EIGHTEEN

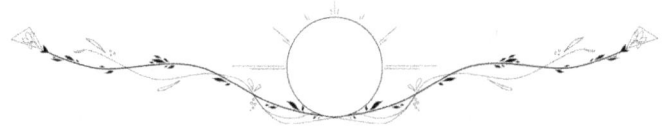

"No," she answered. Her free hand dug into her duvet, each claw piercing a perfect little hole in the butter soft cotton. "No, that's not all."

"Tell me, sweetheart."

"I... shouldn't. It's a bad idea."

"But you want to, don't you?" Viktor's voice was a stroke to her senses. She swore she could feel it against her skin, caressing her in that rough, proprietary way she associated with him and him alone.

She sucked in a shuddering breath. "I..."

"It's okay, sweetheart. Your *pull* sounds a lot like our fever, right? I *know* that ache. If this is what you need, then I'm here to help you. Tell me what we'd be doing right now if I was there."

A streak of pleasure arrowed down her spine in response to that crisp, masculine demand. A completely involuntary whimper escaped. Camille couldn't tell if her instincts wanted her to claw at him for the audacity or clutch him closer for it.

"Ah, that's my girl," he breathed, making the ache worse. "Go on. Tell me what I want to know, and then maybe I can help you take care of that needy cunt."

Camille flushed, at once shocked and aroused by his crass

language, the scorching lust she heard in every word. She *wanted* to hate it. It would be better to find it repulsive. That way she could feel something when a man like Cyrus, gentle to his core, touched her or whispered sweet things in her ear.

Instead, she only felt hotter and slick between her thighs. Worse than that was the unwavering compulsion she felt to *obey*.

Drawing in ragged breaths through her nose, she answered, "I'd want to taste you, to bite you and claw at you until you pinned me down and *took*." Her hips rose unconsciously as her thighs fell apart beneath the sheets. "If you could hold me, you would bite my throat and slide between my thighs."

A low sound came across the line: part growl, part groan, all pleasure. "You want my bite, sweetheart?"

Gods, did she want his bite. Camille had never known the pleasure, but she'd heard of it. The most intimate of embraces could bring pleasure like no other. It released a rush of endorphins, melding sex with pure instinct until they were indistinguishable.

During their brief liaison, Cyrus hadn't asked and she hadn't offered. Though she trusted him to never hurt her, Camille shied away from anyone coming that close to ending her life — or seeing her that unguarded.

Anyone except Viktor.

"Yes," she whispered into the dark, guilt and old hurts be damned.

"Fuck." The sound of fabric rustling came again, making her ears twitch. What was he doing? The possibilities were endless and each more tantalizing than the last. "I don't think you know what a shifter's bite entails, sweetheart. It's not meant to hold you."

When had her hand snuck under the sheets? She couldn't remember. All she knew was the grating edge of his voice and the pounding heat in her core — that twisting, empty ache that begged for relief. Her voice shook when she asked, "What does it entail, then?"

Viktor hissed out a breath. It crackled through the speaker pressed against her ear, sending goosebumps over her sensitive skin. "It's meant to *claim.*"

Exhilaration and lust burst like bubbles in her mind, drowning everything else out even as her focus on him became the only thing that mattered, her only tether to reality. He was the only one who could soothe the needy, grasping thing inside her.

"Sweetheart, when I bite you, it's not going to be some elvish dominance play," he continued, ragged. "I'm going to sink my fangs into that pretty shoulder and make you mine. You can snarl at me all you want, but when the time comes, you'll submit — and purr while you do it."

The beast in her balked, lip lifting with the snarl he spoke of, but the woman who craved passion, possession, the heat of raw challenge, was blindsided with desire. Secretly, both the elf and the woman *wanted* what he offered, but were wary of letting him that close without first proving himself.

The beast wanted a test of claw and fang. The elvish courting dance was an intricate one of violence and restraint, lust and aggression. A partner had to be tested in order to sort out their own personal hierarchy, after all. Could the weaker of the pair trust that, even when they bite or swiped, that the stronger would always protect, never harm? If not, then the dance of dominance continued until the matter was settled.

The woman, of course, wanted a test of a different kind.

While she yearned to throw off the yoke of past hurt, she grappled with guilt and fear of the future. What if he left her? What if she became her mother? What if her choice to form a union was a terrible idea? What if she was already in too deep to end it?

To silence those doubts, she would need *trust.* Unfortunately, she had no idea how to test for that sort of thing.

But in that moment, Camille was not thinking of the past, nor of the future. She was thinking only of Viktor, his voice in her ear, and her body, strung so tight with arousal it *hurt.*

"Vik," she murmured, a plea and a prayer rolled into one syllable.

"Fuck, that is the sweetest fucking sound." And there it was: the unmistakable sound of skin on skin.

She gasped, picturing his fingers wrapped around his cock, stroking rough and fast. The idea that he was unabashedly taking his pleasure while he spoke to her in that low purr was almost too much to handle.

Camille's fingers slid between her legs. A low, keening sound escaped her throat as she felt how wet and hot she was, waiting for the touch of a consort who was not there.

Although it was unspeakably erotic to hear him stroke himself, Camille wanted to be the one to do it. She wanted to be the one who wrapped her fingers around his cock, that watched his face when he came. She wanted to claim that heady sense of power over a being so strong and beautiful — that taste of exquisite connection that terrified and tempted her.

"Shh," Viktor soothed, breathing hard, "I've got you, sweetheart. Focus on my voice. I'm there with you right now."

Frustrated tears pricked at the backs of her eyes. There was pleasure to be had in her own touch, but it wasn't enough. It wasn't *him.*

"You're not. You're *not* here." Camille was horrified by the whine in her voice, the accusation. It sounded like she was pleading with him to come to her — because she *was.*

I've finally lost it. Her control had snapped and the beast roared to the forefront of her mind to take over her mouth.

"I know, sweetheart. I know you're hurting." Viktor sounded as pained as she felt, which went a small way to soothing her frustration. "As much as I want to jump in my car and hunt you down right now, I know I can't. So let me take care of you in the only way that's safe for you, sweetheart. Let me talk you through it."

Despite the frustration and the ceaseless desire, Camille felt her chest tighten with an uncomfortable tenderness. She breathed out a shaky exhale. "Okay."

"That's my girl." A little electric *zing* went down her spine. "Where is your hand right now?"

"Between my legs."

A low, very *coyote* growl rumbled through the speaker. "How long has it been there, touching that pretty, pretty cunt?"

Camille swallowed thickly. "A... while."

"A while, huh? You must be wet right now, sweetheart. Slick and warm and mine. Do you feel it? How much your body wants me?"

She bit her lip as she stroked down, fingers sliding through slick, swollen skin. "Yes," she whispered.

"Tell me how much it wants me. Tell me how wet your panties are, sweetheart."

"I'm not wearing any."

Viktor let out a huff of air against the mic. "I... What are you wearing right now, Cam?"

Camille lifted one leg, slowly dragging it against the sheets as she propped her foot on the mattress. There was no way he wouldn't hear the sound of fabric rustling against skin. "Nothing."

He swore.

"Gods save me, Cam, as soon as you say yes, I'm going to make myself a new home between your thighs." The sound of skin on skin picked up tempo, tantalizing her. "You have no idea how much I want to touch every inch of you. I want to *see* you. I've been dreaming of it for twenty godsdamned years. I know you're going to have the most perfect skin, the softest curves. I want to explore every inch of you."

Fingertips sliding carefully upward to avoid pricking herself with her claws, Camille began to circle her clitoris, seeking that delicious friction that would send her over the edge. She strained to listen to every word and every illicit sound.

"I'm not going to ask if you remember that day in the meeting room," he continued, panting slightly. "I *know* you do. Tell me, sweetheart, are you imagining it's my hand between gorgeous legs? Are you remembering when it was me rubbing that little clit? My fingers inside of you, making you come so hard your knees shook?"

Camille pressed harder, used more force than she normally would have, chasing the memory of his callused fingers and rocking hips. *"Yes,"* she answered, desperately.

"Do you remember how hard I was for you? What I felt like in your hand as you came around my fingers?"

Gods, I'll never forget it.

Silky smooth and hot as a brand, he was everything she could have wanted — and she never even got to look at him.

Moving her hand faster, both legs drawn up now, she answered, "I remember. I— I think about it *constantly.*"

"I was a fucking idiot that day, but I don't have one damn regret. I've never felt anything like you before, sweetheart. You're *perfect.* I want to spend every night of the rest of my life with my hands on all that pretty skin and wake you up every morning with my mouth between your thighs."

"Gods!" Camille rolled her hips into her hand, chasing the edge of an orgasm that hovered just out of reach. She needed *his* hand, his scent, his lips and teeth and tongue. Without him, it felt as though pleasure would remain just on the periphery, driving her slowly insane.

As if sensing her urgency and her growing frustration, he said, "That's it, sweetheart. I know we can get you there. Focus on my voice."

"Vik, I—"

"It's *my* hand on you," he growled, something dark and possessive entering his voice — as if he took her struggle as a personal affront to his claim. "Those are *my* fingers on your clit right now, sweetheart. I'm the one who feels how wet you are for me, how your cunt holds me so fucking tight. I'm the one who gets to kiss you until you can't breathe, and when I let you up for air, *I* am the one who gets to *bite you.*"

The image of Viktor leaning down to clamp his fangs over her throat short-circuited her mind. Camille's fingers stuttered, their rhythm failing as her orgasm rippled through in short, hard bursts. She cried out. Distantly, she heard him hiss a curse, the sound of skin on skin picking up into a frenzied beat until it stopped abruptly with a long, masculine moan.

Together, they panted in the darkness, their ragged breaths *whuffing* across the line.

Camille felt the sweat begin to cool and waited, breath held, for the regret to come. She expected it to sour her stomach as it had the day of the Summit, but it didn't.

Instead, she felt languid, her muscles relaxed and her mind pleasantly fuzzy. The urgency hadn't gone away, but it was briefly dulled. Enough to let her close her eyes and not feel as thought she had made another horrible mistake.

Setting the phone down next to her head on her pillow, Camille slowly turned on her side. In a small, hushed voice, she whispered, "Viktor?"

She heard his breath hitch. "Yeah, Cam?"

"Thank you."

"Ah, sweetheart," he grated, "please believe me when I say it was my pleasure."

Her lips twitched with a small smile. "Still."

"Yeah, I get it." Viktor's voice changed again as he — presumably — laid back down. "I'd do anything for you, Cam. I know that's hard to believe right now, but it's the truth."

It *was* hard to believe, but she wasn't in the mood to pick a fight. Instead, Camille chose to let it go. Softly, she asked, "Can you tell me about your den?"

Viktor sucked in a breath. "Well... Damn, you have no idea how much that hits me right in the instinct, sweetheart." He chuckled. "Makes me want to preen like a fucking peacock or something. My mate, asking about our den? Don't think there's anything as hot as that, weird as that sounds."

My mate, asking about our *den?*

Camille's heart lurched. Hope, traitorous and hungry, spread like ink in her mind, staining everything it touched. "So... are you going to tell me about it?"

"Nah."

"No?"

"Nope." She could hear the smile in his voice when he explained, "I want you to see it. The first time you step into our den, I want you to be surprised."

"What if I don't like it?"

"Well, then I'll change it." He was utterly matter-of-fact. There wasn't even a hint of worry or annoyance at the prospect of years of work and thought being erased on a whim. "It's *our* den. If you don't like something, then that's that. I couldn't fight the urge to make you comfortable even if I wanted to."

"Oh."

They were quiet for a while, simply listening to each other breathe as pleasure melted into soft drowsiness. Eyelids heavy and heart aching, she finally murmured, "I should probably let you go. You've got a pack to look after tomorrow morning."

While she had... nothing, really. Paperwork from the vineyard and union negotiations didn't hold a candle to the important choices Viktor made every day. He *lived* for his pack. She used to feel bitter about that, but now she only felt sad.

It must be nice, she thought, biting her lip, *to know you're doing good every day. To know that so many people trust you. To have a place in their hearts.*

"Cam..." Viktor's voice softened and became strangely uncertain. "Would you mind if we just... kept the call going?"

Surprised but tentatively pleased, she dared to ask, "Why?"

"So I can hear you breathing for a while longer. It feels a bit like you're here with me, sleeping in my bed."

Camille dragged her blankets up over her shoulders. Fingers

peeking out from under the fabric, she rested the tips of her claws on the screen of her phone. "Yeah," she whispered, "it does feel like that."

Equally hushed, he replied, "Then we'll keep the call going, and you'll be the first voice I hear tomorrow morning."

She drew her legs up, hugging them close to her chest — which felt too full, too fragile, like the protective cage of her rips might shatter at any moment. "I'd like that."

His sigh was long and relieved. "Good."

"Goodnight, Vik." She let her mind drift, imagining he was beside her, falling asleep slowly. Every breath, every rustle of cloth, was a comfort.

"Goodnight, Cam. Sweet dreams."

Chapter Nineteen

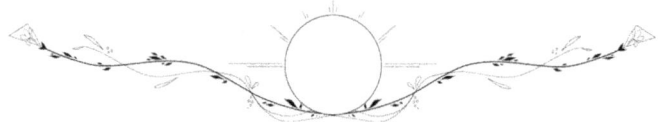

For the first time in years, and certainly since the day of the Summit, she slept well.

Not once did she wake up in a cold sweat, wondering why her alarm had not woken her to check on her mother in the middle of the night. When she cracked her eyes open the morning after their call, the first thing she noticed was the soft, even sound of someone else's breathing.

She held her breath, straining to listen. The events of the previous evening rushed back with a heady flush of embarrassment and desire as she counted Viktor's even breaths puffing through her phone's speaker. She'd left it resting on the pillow next to her.

The sound of his breathing, the position of the phone beside her ear, and the rush of contentment that filled her stomach with butterflies — all of it brought on a wave of nostalgia that made her eyes sting.

How many times had she woken up like this as a teenager? For nearly a year, they'd spoken in secret every night. Most often, they fell asleep together, drifting off mid-conversation as the late hour took its toll. They rarely *chose* to stop talking.

The sound of Viktor's breathing had been one of the most

disorienting losses after that disastrous night. At some point, Camille had forgotten how to sleep without it. Learning how to rest without the comfort of his presence was a brutal addition to the torture that was pull withdrawal.

"Good morning, sweetheart." Viktor's voice was gravelly with sleep. It startled her out of her painful reverie.

Self-consciousness reared its ugly head when she cleared her throat to reply, "How did you know I was awake?"

"Your breathing changed. The coyote always notices that sort of thing."

A deep pang of longing struck her. Without thinking, she replied, "It's been a long time since I..."

"Yeah," he gruffly replied, effortlessly deciphering what she could not say. "Yeah, it has been awhile."

Camille grasped the rumpled edge of her sheet and pulled it up under her chin. In her mind, she saw Viktor as his other form: a sleek gray coyote, about double the size of the non-shifter sort, with long, black legs and luminous gold eyes. He was lean and cunning-looking. Even when he was lupine, she saw the familiar lines of his human face, the intelligent gleam in his eyes, the good humor that glowed with warmth.

For the first time, Camille acknowledged that she did not simply miss Viktor the man, but the wildness of his coyote, too. They were one and yet not. Fate said they were *both* hers, though a large part of her still resisted its call.

The silence that had settled over them was broken by the rustle of cloth. When Viktor spoke next, his voice was closer to the mic and had lost the rough edge. "I've got to get ready for work, Cam. Will you be all right today?"

Her heart squeezed. She wanted to curse him for the note of real regret in his tone, but held her tongue. They'd crossed about a dozen lines last night. Her usual acerbic responses, programmed to keep people at a safe distance, no longer felt right.

Instead of telling him where he could shove his concern, she took a deep breath and slowly answered, "Yes. I... think I'll go to the nursery today."

Viktor paused. Was he as surprised by her genuine, if hesitant, response as she was? "That sounds like a good plan, sweetheart." It was a warm, smooth croon full of approval and it made everything in her *melt*.

Desperate to chase that feeling and knowing she couldn't keep him on the line much longer, she hastily asked, "What work are you doing?"

"Ah, you know, alpha stuff." The sound of movement came across the line. She imagined he had shifted the phone to his other ear as he levered himself out of bed.

Camille turned onto her back and stared up at the chandelier. "What kind of *alpha stuff*? A lot of growling and chest beating?"

She could hear the smile in his voice when he answered, "Cute, but I think between the two of us, *you* do more growling than I do." She thought she heard the faint sound of a drawer sliding open. "Mostly it's high level life management stuff. The pack invests in a lot of m-tech and entertainment ventures. I oversee all of that while Benny focuses on security."

She had to work hard to dredge up exactly who *Benny* was. Camille sought out information on the state of the Merced pack when she was feeling particularly weak over the years, so she could only vaguely recall hearing that a man named Benjamin Reeve had been promoted to his second after a more senior pack member stepped aside.

"This morning I have a meeting with a new start-up working in audiopathy, and then after that I have to swing by a few elders' homes to check in on everyone. In between, the *work-work* stuff and the pack stuff, I also have to deal with disciplining teens and talking to the seniors about their duties — security of the territory, community events, stuff like that."

Camille blinked, surprised by how busy his life was. She knew that the Merced pack was wealthy — due in large part to Viktor's keen business acumen — but she didn't quite expect to hear that so much of his day was taken up by interpersonal business.

She used to think that elves and shifters weren't terribly different in their need for hierarchy, but it sounded like there were several key facts she had missed. Elves never got quite so *involved* in each other's lives as shifters did.

"You sound busy," she said, feeling suddenly awkward. He had so many people depending on him, so much to do, that she felt her lack of purpose keenly. "I shouldn't be taking up your morning—"

"Sweetheart." Viktor's voice took on a firm edge. "I will *always* have time for you. I'm not gonna fuck up again by not telling you exactly how important you are to me. A happy alpha makes a happy pack, and I'm happiest when I'm with you, okay?"

Camille's heart skipped a beat. *Goddess.* "...Okay."

"Good. Now I've gotta go shower. As much as I'd love to take you with me, I don't think it would be very satisfying for either of us," he teased. "Are we still on for tonight?"

His tone was light, like it was any other casual date, but even after all the years between them, she knew him well enough to pick up the subtle tension there.

He was giving her an out.

If she felt like she wasn't ready to meet him, she knew he wouldn't press. Uncertainty made her curl her toes into the blankets, as if she needed to brace herself for the fallout of her decision. Still, she answered, "Yes."

A quiet sigh came across the line. "Good. Good. Okay." He cleared his throat. "Have fun at the nursery today. If— I mean, you don't have to, but if you could maybe let me know when you get home, I'd— Fuck me. It would just make me feel better, is what I'm trying to say."

Camille's brow furrowed. "Are you worried I won't make it home?"

The idea of being *unsafe* in Theodore's city was so beyond her comprehension it sounded like he'd spoken another language. She was a Solbourne in *Solbourne territory*. There hadn't been a credible threat to her safety since the day Thaddeus II lost his fool head.

Besides, she was an *elf*.

Viktor huffed a laugh. "Cam, I've worried about you every single day for twenty years. And before you bring it up, yeah, I know you've been trained in defense. Doesn't mean I can't worry about my girl."

It was like he'd knocked the wind out of her. Camille could barely catch her breath when she whispered, "I... Okay. I'll text you when I get back to the apartment."

"Thank you, sweetheart." He paused before adding, "I'll miss you today."

"You're seeing me tonight, remember?"

"Seeing you tonight means I'm not seeing you *now.*"

The pull was half challenge and half driving need to please. In that moment, Camille wrestled with the overwhelming urge to tell him she was on her way. If he wanted to see her, the beast that lived in her soul was more than happy to oblige him. Gods, did it want to oblige him.

Digging her claws into the mattress, she forced herself to say, "You should go shower, Vik."

"Yeah, s'pose I should."

"Bye."

There was an unmistakable thread of longing in his voice when he replied, "See you soon, sweetheart."

The sun was out, but thick gray clouds lingered on the horizon as Camille stepped out onto the sheltered patio of the Treasure Island Nursery. A stiff wind laden with brine blew the dense clouds closer and tossed her short hair around her cheeks.

The patio overlooked a large, heavily guarded play area scattered with tricycles, elf-proof jungle gyms, and a crowded sandbox. Everywhere, elves ranging from one to twelve years old ran around, shrieking with delight over a caught ball or tumbling to the ground in a heap of jewel-colored limbs.

Scattered around at regular intervals were those elves trusted with the highest honor — looking after their young. Dressed in svelte uniforms of deep blue, they did everything from teaching arithmetic to changing diapers to breaking up a bloodthirsty feud over access to the monkey bars.

Everyone was encouraged to visit the nurseries, since it gave even solitary elves a sense of deep grounding to interact with their young, but only a select few were trusted with their day-to-day care and protection.

One of those people was her friend Linnea Stafford.

Camille shaded her eyes with her hand and scanned the yard, looking for a pale pink face and a head of corkscrew curls. It only took a moment to find her with a cluster of toddlers playing with large foam shapes in the grass. Dodging squealing, carefree children, Camille only stopped to help up a fallen little boy with chubby cheeks and dark green skin before she came to stand next to her friend.

Like always, Linnea did not appear to care that her uniform was covered in grass stains from sitting with the babies, nor that the little one currently in her lap was happily drooling on her shoulder. She was perfectly at ease amongst the chaos, and when she spotted Camille, her grin was immediate.

"Cammie! It's so good to see you!" Linnea reached out to tug on Camille's hand, urging her to sit down in the grass.

Wearing charcoal gray jeans for this very reason, Camille gracefully sat down beside her friend and opened her arms to the toddler who, without so much as a wary look, crawled into her lap. All the children felt perfectly secure with adults of their kind. It was a deep, hardwired instinct all elves carried.

Violence amongst adults was common and even encouraged in the right spaces, but *children* were another matter entirely. Young were universally off-limits. As a result, it was rare to meet an elvish child who felt skittish around strangers. Adults could come and go in the nursery without fearing they would upset the children, allowing both to take comfort in a sense of community.

Camille let out a long, relieved sigh and rested her cheek on the silky hair that crowned the toddler's head. For her, there was little in the world more restorative than time spent in the nursery.

"Hey Linnea," she breathed, stroking the little one's back as he began to fiddle with her gloves and babble semi-coherently. "It's good to see you, too."

Gently untangling a sticky, clawed fist from her curls — so pale pink they were almost blonde — Linnea gently asked, "How are you doing?"

"Better." She could hardly believe it, but it was the truth. Despite everything, Camille was leagues better than she had been when Linnea saw her at her mother's funeral.

"I'm glad to hear it," she replied, her voice as sweet and high as a songbird's. Addressing the wide-eyed toddler in her own lap, she asked, "Isn't it good to see Miss Solbourne again? We missed her, didn't we?"

There was a chorus of agreement from the toddlers, though Camille didn't think they had any idea what they were agreeing with. She knew from experience that few people had a way with children like Linnea did. When she spoke, they very rarely fussed, and generally did whatever it took to earn a kiss on the head or a treat in their fists.

Camille *loved* children, but even she didn't have a way with them like Linnea did.

"I've missed you, too," Camille replied, reaching out to adjust a sun hat over the eyes of a little girl attempting to stack a foam cylinder on top of a rectangle with the utmost concentration. "How have you been, Linnea?"

"Oh, busy, as usual." Linnea's lap companion began to squirm, so she helped him stand on chubby legs before she let him wander off toward the elf standing by the refreshment cart. They both watched him babble before the elf nodded sagely and handed him a sugar-free juice pouch.

"I'm thinking of taking a sabbatical."

Camille turned her surprised gaze on her friend, who was still watching the little boy messily suck on the thin straw of his juice pouch. "What? Why? Is everything all right?"

"Everything's fine," Linnea was quick to reassure her. "I'm just feeling a bit... I don't know, restless, maybe?" She let out a wistful sigh. "With all the change happening, it makes me realize how much of my life I've spent caged in here."

Camille nodded. "I get that."

She knew that Linnea experienced a similar level of isolation as she had, though for markedly different reasons. While *she* was sequestered because her mother was a pariah and refused to play nice with the main family, Linnea was not only a halfling, but a magically gifted one. Her specialty was warding, or protective barrier magic, and she was in charge of teaching young elves the basics of the craft.

In fact, she was *so* rare amongst their kind that she was exempt from all but the most basic martial training for fear of harming her. Linnea had been swaddled and smothered from the moment she threw up her first effortless ward.

The only reason Camille got the chance to know her at all was because her father ran the Dia-Solbourne household. They'd known each other their entire lives and despite their initial disparity in rank, were good friends.

"What are you thinking of doing?" She asked, worry for her friend's wellbeing and sympathy for her situation tightening her voice.

"Traveling. Meeting new people. Getting into trouble." Linnea's eyes, a deep, dark pink that bordered on red, glowed with enthusiasm. "I want to see the UTA and know what life is like outside of *this*. Doesn't that sound like fun, Cammie?" She gasped, momentarily drawing the attention of the assembled toddlers. "You could come with me!"

"That *does* sound fun," she hedged, struggling to imagine the sheltered, happy-go-lucky Linnea running wild in, say, the New Zone, "but I don't think I'm going to be able to join you."

"Why not?" Linnea leaned over to gently but firmly discourage one of the toddlers from testing her fangs on another's arm.

"Well, I'm..." Camille trailed off.

Gods, she really didn't have a succinct way of describing the mess that was her life lately, did she?

Linnea sat back on her hands to stare wide-eyed at her friend. "Wait... the rumor isn't true, right? You're not contracted to *Epifanio Luz* are you? You are legally obligated to tell me if you are!"

Camille reared back with surprise. "*What?* No! Where did you even hear that?"

"It's all the buzz around the Tower," Linnea answered, unblinking, as if she feared she would miss some vital clue in Camille's expression if she dared close her eyes for even a moment. "I heard from Darren, one of the receptionists, who heard it from Julia, the fey who works on the Luz PR team, who heard it from — oh, nevermind, you get it. Anyway, I didn't believe it, of course. He's way too old for you. But if you're too busy to travel the UTA with me, then..."

Camille stroked the silky curls of the toddler in her lap in an effort to soothe her irritation. Clearly, Elio Luz had been running his mouth. Considering she had already decided against his son even *before* the complications with Viktor, she knew she'd have to deal with that sooner rather than later. No matter what happened with her consort, she wanted *nothing* to do with the Luz family.

"I am *not* going to be Epifanio Luz's spouse," she firmly announced.

"So you *can* travel the UTA with me."

"I didn't say that." Camille shook her head, wondering if Linnea really grasped how caged she was. Would her parents even let her go? Would the nursery? She doubted the social pressure to stay would be *light*.

"Then what? Are you taking a class or something?"

"No, I'm... I *am* negotiating a union." Her lapmate began to squirm, so Camille gently let him go. Chunky legs took him all of a few feet before he settled down amongst his fellows and began to chatter away to himself, claws reaching for the foam blocks with more determination than skill.

"Oh." Linnea gave her a studiously blank look. "What about Vikt—"

Camille felt her cheeks heat with a dark blush. "What *about* him?"

"I just mean that you had a thing with him when you were teenagers, right? I always got the feeling that you and him had more than you let on. I guess I just figured that with this whole thing with the Sovereign and his healer, you'd..." She made a vague gesture with her hand. "Live a little, maybe?"

Live a little, indeed. She'd done more than a *little* living last night, and the day of the Summit, too.

Before she could come up with some noncommittal response, Linnea drew a toddler that had begun to fuss into her lap to rain kisses down on her soft cheeks.

Baby fangs peeked out in a wide grin and a rattling, high-pitched purr bubbled out between squeals of laughter. Playfully popping her out of her lap and back onto the grass, Linnea wistfully continued, "I always thought shifters were dreamy. They do courtship so much better than we do. An elf is all grabby and *let's just do it before I flip out.* When shifters meet their mates, I hear they write *love letters.* Can you imagine?"

Camille stilled. "Yeah... I *can* imagine."

Chapter Twenty

She didn't text him as soon as she got home. Instead, Camille rushed into the office attached to her suite and frantically dug for the letter she'd angrily discarded amongst the paper copies of all the official, death-related paperwork she had to file in the family vault at some point in the future.

It took her several agonizing minutes to recall where she'd stuffed it. In a fit of ire, strung out on grief, she took the letter Viktor left her and shoved it into a plastic bag before, *apparently,* dropping it behind several boxes of replacement staples and ball-point pens in a drawer of the desk.

Sweating a little, Camille sank onto the Persian rug. Her legs splayed in front of her as she eyed the sealed letter in her hands.

Her name stared up at her in slanted, angular handwriting she would recognize anywhere.

She found it partially stuck under the front door the week after her mother died. At the time, she'd been nearly inconsolable and exhausted and furious at the world. The sight of Viktor's handwriting had nearly compelled her to shred the damn thing as soon as she saw it, but Camille couldn't quite bring herself to do it.

Instead, she stashed it away, unable to face the reasons why she couldn't bear to be rid of it.

I hear they write love letters.

But was it a love letter? How did she know it wasn't just another condolence card, or something equally disappointing? Why did it matter, anyway? What would she do if it was? What would she do if it wasn't?

Camille gnawed on her lip as she considered the ramifications of opening the bag. She didn't think his pheromones would stick around on the paper long enough to be a problem, and if they had, they would be in such negligible quantities as to not make much of a difference to her, all things considered.

Besides, an insidious, yearning voice whispered, *you aren't even really trying to avoid him anymore, are you? You didn't even take an ice bath this morning.*

Camille swallowed hard. This wasn't making a choice. This was just... knowing all the facts *before* she made a choice.

Sliding the tip of a claw into the seam of the plastic bag, she parted it with a quiet *suuuuuhp* sound. Immediately, the air in front of her was ever-so-faintly perfumed with his musky scent.

Heedless of the consequences, she sucked in a deep breath. Camille's slitted pupils expanded to swallow nearly her entire iris before they contracted again.

Gods, he smells so good.

Luckily for her self-control, the thrill was as short-lived as his scent.

Shaking off the brief wave of goosebumps that broke out across her skin, she delicately extracted the letter with the tips of her claws. It seemed very *Viktor* to use a regular paper envelope instead of, say, a text or an email, and even moreso that he wouldn't bother properly closing it. He simply tucked the flap inside the envelope rather than peel the paper off of the complimentary adhesive strips inside.

Suppressing a reluctant smile, she gently pulled out the slip of lined paper from inside. It looked like he'd torn it out of a notepad, though this time he took the care to tear off the jagged edge on the perforated line.

It was a single page, folded in half, and inscribed with blue ink in his usual slanted hand. Holding her breath, Camille scanned the writing quickly once, to determine whether it was what she dared hoped it was, before she blanched and read it a second time.

Cam—

I'm not very good with words, but I need to try harder because you deserve all of the best ones.

I know that right now you think the world is ugly and dark. I know that you're grieving, and that grief doesn't ever really end. I know that you are hurting by yourself.

I'm here, Cam. I'll always be here. I'll be here when you need me and when you don't. It was the biggest mistake of my life letting you face this world by yourself.

You're my heart. My very first pack. My first and only love.

I adore all that you are and all that you will be, with or without me.

You are not alone, Cam. I'll come when you call, and if by chance you never do, I'll love you every day anyway.

Yours,

Vik

Camille couldn't catch her breath. She couldn't see the page through her tears. When she set the letter oh-so-gently aside, she barely felt it leave her trembling fingertips.

She sat there with her back pressed up against the desk's drawers for nearly a half an hour before she sniffled, wiped her eyes, and sent Viktor a simple text.

I'm home.

He sent a cascade of hearts and, a minute later, a question: *Mind if a coyote begs at your door for a little while? I've got time between meetings and I miss you.*

No, she answered, chest aching. *I don't mind at all.*

When the knock came less than forty minutes later, she had secreted the letter away beneath her pillow and at least somewhat composed herself again. Her emotions were in upheaval, knocking loose all the convictions she'd relied on for so long, but she still didn't dare allow him into her space.

If not because of the pull, then because she simply couldn't imagine him seeing her in the state she was in after reading his letter.

So instead of letting him in, she disabled the proximity alarm and softly greeted him through the door. "Hey, Vik."

"Hey, sweetheart." She heard the faint scrape of skin against the wood of the door. She imagined he trailed his palm down the smooth surface like he might graze her cheek, her shoulder. Camille skimmed her fingers down the same path. "How are you feeling today? Was the nursery good? All the elflings doing all right?"

"I'm good," she answered, trying to keep the shakiness out of her voice. "The nursery was great. I— I played dodgeball with some of the kids and then helped with lunch."

She could hear the smile in his voice when he asked, "Were you wearing your heels?"

Camille glanced down and peered at her white suede stiletto booties, which were liberally sprinkled with bits of grass and smudges of dirt. "Yes."

"Perfect."

"How was your meeting?"

"It was good. I'm always looking to invest more money for the pack, so I'm happy to meet with people trying to do cool shit." There was rustling on the other side of the door before he spoke again. This time, his voice was lower to the ground. "Sit with me, sweetheart."

Camille turned and pressed her back against the door. Sliding down until she could tuck her legs under her, she asked, "How do you keep getting in without security noticing?"

"I'm a coyote. We're good at that sort of thing."

"By *that sort of thing,* do you mean picking locks and trespassing on private property?"

"Exactly."

A small laugh bubbled out of her throat, but it faded quickly into a heavy silence. Camille stared down the hallway, towards the sumptuously decorated sitting room, though she didn't see it.

Into the quiet, she whispered, "I'm sorry I never gave you a chance to ask."

She felt a faint *thump* against the door and guessed that he had tilted his head back. "You were scared and heartbroken, Cam. I don't hold it against you."

"I know you don't." Viktor didn't hold grudges. He wasn't like her family, who never forgave or forgot a slight. He wasn't like *her,* who took out her anger on those who loved her most. "But things could have been different."

"I don't know..." He sucked in a deep breath. "Would things have been *better?* I don't think so. I wouldn't be my pack's alpha and you wouldn't be who you are today — which is someone I happen to like very much, even if you keep clawing at me."

Camille let out a watery scoff. "It seemed like such a good plan in my head. I thought we'd run away together, maybe to the New Zone, until people forgot about us. Then we could come back and everything would be okay. No one would mind."

"Even if your mother approved of us, Cam, you have to know your family would have hunted us to the end of the Earth. Teddy was ready to take my head off for rejecting you. I can't imagine what he would have done if I *stole* you."

And despite what she had coolly asserted the previous night, there really was no telling what Marian would have done if Camille chose to leave her side for Viktor. A volatile woman even before her sharp decline, there was a fifty-fifty chance that she would think it was a grand way to get back at the Solbournes. If her mood swung the other way, she might have done something dangerous and explosive, like putting a bounty on their heads.

Camille was mature enough to look back and know it was a

bad idea, but there would always be a part of her that wondered what it would have been like to jump from one seedy motel to another with him; how it would have felt to have him be her first. More than that, she would always wish she could have succeeded in saving him from what the future held.

"I never wanted to come between you and Teddy," she admitted, eyes stinging. "He wouldn't tell me what happened, but I knew it was my fault."

"It wasn't your fault, sweetheart. It was just... the way it happened. I would have done the same thing if I was in his place."

Guilt crawled up her throat. Camille wasn't sure she really wanted to know, but she had to ask anyway. "What happened?"

"Cam..."

"I want to know." She curled her hands into fists and pressed them against her thighs. "I need to know."

Viktor was quiet for the span of several heartbeats before he quietly admitted, "We fought."

Her throat wanted to close around the words, but she forced them out anyway. "How bad?"

"Bad enough that Valen had to call in the Guard to separate us."

Camille closed her eyes. *Fuck.*

That meant they must have come very close to killing one another. The Guard wouldn't have stepped in otherwise. Generally speaking, elves were left to solve their own disputes.

You picked a fight, you were the one who suffered the consequences.

To know that members of the Sovereign's Guard — at the time under Delilah's command — had to step in to stop the fight was a horrifying testament to just how bad it must have been.

"And then you were left to face your father alone." Camille wrapped her arms around her middle and drew her legs up to her chest. Resting her forehead against her knees, she choked out, "You were alone because of me."

Viktor's voice was a raw croon when he said, "I wasn't really alone, Cam. I knew that if I really needed the Solbournes, I could always ask for help. But I was always going to have to face my dad by myself. I knew it from the moment I could walk. He was always going to be my responsibility. It's... just the shifter way."

The beast in her understood that. It was the same part that recognized that sometimes protecting the people you loved meant facing a horror that should never have existed in the first place. Her own father had done the same thing — and died for his trouble.

Like Theron Solbourne, Viktor was a good man willing to do the hardest thing to protect his family. Camille respected that as much as she feared it. If she made that final choice, would she just end up meeting her mother's fate anyway? Would she choose him, only to have Viktor ripped from her because he needed to stand up for what was right at some point in the future?

Viktor had faced his demons and survived. His violent, selfish father was dead and his pack was flourishing. But there would always be more demons. There would always be more threats.

That was part of the allure of a union, she realized. There was so much safety in knowing that you would be okay if something happened to your spouse. She would be devastated if Cyrus passed away, of course, but it would not kill her.

Camille could not say the same thing about Viktor.

Her voice was slightly muffled by her knees when she admitted, "I'm scared, Vik."

"I know, Cam."

"I've made a mess of everything." Camille shuddered. A heavy weight settled over her chest and shoulders, making it hard to breathe. "I don't know what I'm going to do."

Why had she rushed into a union so fast? If she had only waited—

"We'll figure it out," he firmly replied. The softness had vanished from his voice and was replaced by a hard authority that made her want to straighten her spine, to *please*. "You don't have to make any choices right now, Cam, but when you do, every-thing will be okay. *We'll* be okay."

Camille let out a huff. He didn't know about Epifanio, who apparently thought things were a done deal, nor about Cyrus, who might very well truly be in love with her. He didn't know how she wrestled with the potential consequences of her choices — for herself, for the Solbournes, for the promise to her mother, for her future offspring. He didn't know anything.

And yet she felt the muscles lining her spine begin to relax anyway. Because Viktor promised everything would be all right. Because when he spoke, something base and desperate in her listened. Because he was steady, and kind, and when he said that he would be there for her even if she didn't choose him, a mad part of her had actually begun to believe him.

Chapter Twenty-One

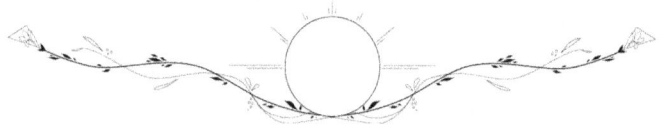

What in the gods' names am I doing here?

Camille felt the thought swirl around the contours of her mind for the tenth time as she climbed up a sandy bluff. The air had cooled significantly from the heat of the day and the wind whipping off the dark water threatened to cut through her light jacket. The sun had already set, though a glow still lingered in the velvety sky, glittering on the waves that frothed over the dark sand.

Picking her way around low, coastal plants, Camille once again considered turning around and walking right back to her car. Had she really gone through all the trouble of negotiating a union only to give it all up *now?* Her mother would turn in her grave — if only elves buried their dead.

Not that her mother's approval mattered anymore.

Camille frowned as her sleek black running shoes sank into the sand. Grief was a steady tide, rising and falling with each day. Mostly she felt relief knowing that her mother was released from a miserable existence, but she was angry, too, at the injustice of that life.

She was dead. Camille understood with a predator's frankness that death was not cruel, nor willful. Sometimes it was even a kindness, though it never quite felt that way to those left behind. Marian was finally at peace, her ashes mixed with Theron Solbourne's and lovingly interred in the Solbourne family temple. Despite her hatred for the family, she requested her final resting place be with her consort — together again at long last.

Will I end up just like her? Am I not already on that path?

Camille's throat tightened. Doubt and experience told her that sentimentality would only hurt her in the end. So why did she continue trudging through the sand, following a path seared into her memory, to meet the man who could steal her future with the smallest touch of his hand?

Because hope is tenacious.

It held her in its claws no matter how hard she tried to shake herself free. No matter how many times she tried to talk herself out of meeting him, all Camille could see and hear was Viktor's stricken expression, his ragged voice when he begged to meet her, and the hasty scrawl on that cheap piece of paper.

That was not the roguish, mischievous young man she'd known. That boy would have simply outmaneuvered her, found some way to trick her into seeing him again. He wouldn't have begged simply because he didn't feel like he had to, not when he intended to use that easy confidence to get what he wanted.

But *this* Viktor, a seasoned alpha with twenty years of growth between then and now, *asked.*

And that was why she couldn't refuse.

Camille cinched her coat more tightly around her waist as she crested a familiar rise. Twenty years had done very little to change the landscape of this secluded stretch of the Merced pack's private beach. Jagged sandstone cliffs loomed over the windswept coast, creating small alcoves insulated from the salty wind. Greenery, leathery and plump with stored water, was a thick carpet over the tops of the cliffs. Vibrant pink and purple blooms dotted the strange, stubborn plantlife clinging to inhospitable sand.

She was intimately familiar with all of it. Not even twenty

years could tarnish the clarity with which she recalled their time together in their own little alcove. The ghost of the thrill of getting caught whispered down her spine as she peered over the ledge, down to where she knew Viktor expected her.

And there he was.

He was shirtless, in only a pair of loose athletic pants, his feet bare and one knee drawn up to his chest. A fire crackled in front of him and, on the other side, a neatly laid out blanket awaited her.

Camille's breath caught in her throat. *Gods, he's so beautiful.*

As if he could hear that tiny sound, Viktor's head snapped up and swiveled in her direction. He didn't stand, but she could tell even at that distance that he'd tensed, the muscles and sinews of his finely honed body coiled and ready to spring.

She felt his eyes on her as she gathered her courage and slowly picked her way through the foliage to stand at the edge of the cliff. *It's now or never, Cammie.*

It was her last chance to decide to trust the man he'd become or listen to reason and run back to the safe misery she'd left.

The scent of decaying ocean life and brine filled her nose as the wind rippled around her. Somewhere in the distance, a ghostly, warbling call went up — a warning to any being foolish enough to step into the water. Full dark had settled in, and now the water folk were free to do as they pleased in their territory.

Her pulse thrummed in her ears. Instinct said one thing while her head said another. One side promised a chance at happiness; the other a lifetime of cold safety.

I'm a Solbourne, she thought, firming her jaw. *We don't back down from a challenge and we are no fucking cowards.*

Camille took a step back, bent her knees, and jumped off of the cliff.

She landed the nearly two hundred foot drop in a graceful crouch, her elvish bones and muscle taking the impact into the damp, packed sand with ease. Pebbles crunched under the soles of her shoes as she stood.

"For fuck's sake," she heard Viktor growl, nearly matching the timbre of the roaring waves, "are you trying to give me a heart attack?"

Camille felt a grin rising, but forced it down. Turning slowly, ever cautious of the direction of the wind, she found Viktor standing by the fire several feet away. His fists were clenched by his sides, knuckles white and his eyes blazing. "What? Have you never seen a woman land a two hundred foot jump before?"

"A little warning next time, that's all I ask." Viktor propped his hands on his lean hips, his expression forbidding. He looked damn good. All sharp lines and sloping muscle carved by a lifetime of vigorous activity, he couldn't have been more perfect even if she'd conjured him herself.

The fact that a faint sheen of sweat caught the firelight and illuminated every delicious, lickable inch of him didn't hurt, either. Desire threatened to seize her, but Camille forced it down.

"Did you run here?" she asked, walking the long way around to avoid even a hint of his scent on the wind.

Viktor watched her with an unblinking stare — all coyote gold. "Yeah. Needed to release some tension."

"But you aren't wearing shoes." She was only ten feet from the fire now, and her voice echoed strangely against the sandstone walls that closed in around her. Between them, the fire crackled merrily. Smoke curled up and away, toward Viktor, before it was swept out into the night.

She took a deep breath. There was no delicious musk or scent of clean, sweet skin. With the wind whipping toward him, carrying his scent away from her, there was only the salty ocean spray and that distinct note of ocean decay that clung to the sand.

He watched as she slowly lowered herself onto the blanket. Relief gleamed in his predator's eyes. "I shifted," he explained, easing himself back down onto the sand. She glanced down in time to see his fingers curl into the grains, as if clutching them might steady himself. "Carried everything with me in a pack. Figured the fire would help keep everything safe."

"Safe?" She blinked. "From what?"

Camille struggled to imagine any predator stupid enough to attack a fully grown elf *and* an alpha shifter. Unless they came with a unit bursting with weapons, it would be an extremely bad idea for their health and continued existence on Burden's Earth.

A corner of Viktor's mouth kicked up. "From me," he answered, jutting his chin toward the fire. "The smoke will move with the wind. That way we'll always know if you might be in danger of smelling me."

Her throat constricted. "Ah. Thank you."

Viktor's gaze was warm, utterly focused. "I meant it, Cam. This isn't a trap. I'm not trying to take your choice from you."

She had to look away from his earnest expression. Hope burned in her chest, unbearably hot, even when she reminded herself that there was still so much standing between them.

"I know you didn't mean to," she admitted, compelled by the memory of the guilt and horror she saw on his face during their call. "You didn't know."

"Why didn't you tell me before?"

She shrugged. Swirling the tip of one capped claw in the sand by the edge of the blanket, she answered, "We don't like to talk about it. The pull is— well, you can see how it can be a vulnerability."

"I know you told me some— Well, we talked about it a little last night, but I want to know more. Is it like taking the kohl?" he asked.

Camille tilted her head to one side and then the other, considering his question. He wasn't far off. What orcs called *taking the kohl* was their own mating imperative. "It's pretty similar, though there are some key differences." She licked her lips, amazed that she was telling him this at all. That they were even having a civil conversation while the urge to get closer to him ate up her insides in great, heaving gulps. Even without his scent in her lungs, she craved him.

"Explain, please. I want to understand."

"Well, for starters, we don't experience any skin pigment alteration." Camille lifted her hands and wiggled her fingers near the fire. Sealed in supple black leather and polished silver, her claws looked particularly wicked. "The only real outward sign of it is the retraction of our claws, like I told you... before. Hence the gloves. It's considered... indiscreet to go without them."

She glanced up, eager to see his reaction, and found Viktor raking a hand through his blond hair. The strands were bleached by the sun and saltwater — a result of all the time he spent outside with his packmates. A sharp spike of jealousy pierced her. What would it be like to be part of his pack? To tumble with him in the wild?

She imagined it would be like shedding a thousand-pound weight from her shoulders, or surgically removing the steel rod from her spine. To be free to play, to tumble and run, with no one waiting to see her slip up or looking for a weakness to exploit, was a luxury she could only imagine.

"Okay," Viktor breathed, brow furrowed over troubled eyes. "What else? What other symptoms are there?"

Camille shifted her gaze away and tried to banish the longings that threatened to steal her voice. "Mostly it's internal. Increased aggression, a compulsion to initiate skin contact. Things like that."

"Is it reversible?"

His heavy gaze was as tangible as hands on her skin. Goosebumps broke out across her body as she struggled to find an answer to his question. Habit and old wounds demanded she lie, to cover her weaknesses lest he exploit them, but...

But she was *there,* on the beach with him, in the place where they had first become friends, and she didn't want to lie. *I am no coward,* she thought again.

If she could jump off one cliff, surely she could leap off of another.

Taking a deep breath, she quietly explained, "Yes and no. Once contact is made, there really is no *reset button.* The craving will always be there. But if no other contact is made, the harm can be mitigated. There are steps you can take to purge yourself of their pheromones and get mostly back to normal."

Viktor's voice was terribly strained when he said, "It hurts you."

"It's not pleasant, no." She thought of her ice baths, of the withdrawal, of the itch under her skin and the keening pain in her soul. "But there's a reason it's worth it."

"Because you don't want to be mated to outsiders." His tone was flat, non-judgmental, and yet she felt a wealth of hurt radiating from his side of the fire.

"Partly," she admitted, looking up at him through the fringe of her lashes. The firelight made his bronze skin glow. Even with the hard look on his face, he was so, so beautiful. "Not for me personally, though. The main reason is that..."

She shook her head, struggling to find a way to explain such an intricate, private thing. Viktor waited patiently as she gathered her thoughts. "It's that there's this... invisible line. You can cut off contact and go back to being mostly normal until suddenly one day you can't. No one knows how much contact it takes, the amount of exposure necessary to flip the switch, but at some point it becomes irreversible. Once that happens, binding yourself to your consort isn't just a compulsion, it's lifesaving."

Viktor's eyes went hunting sharp. The skin covering his cheekbones went taut with tension when he asked, "What do you mean? Will it kill you?"

"The pull itself? No. Not physically." Camille rubbed her palms together, sending grains of sand back to the ground. Her voice was whisper-soft when she continued, "The hormone imbalance drives us insane. Aggression gets out of control. Paranoia sets in. Sleep stops. Appetite vanishes. Eventually you wither into nothing, but only if your loved ones don't take pity on you and execute you first."

She heard his sharp inhale, but felt too raw, too exposed to look at him. "It is what it is. The only cures are isolation or capitulation. You find a way to live with it, or you give in. Easy."

For a long time, there was silence between them. The fire crackled, sparks popping as the logs slowly began to collapse in on themselves. Heat radiated outward, making her cheeks flush, but inside she felt a deep, dreadful chill.

"Teddy never said anything."

Curling her legs up to her chest, Camille wrested her chin on her kneecaps and dared to look at him through the shimmering heat of the flames. "Well, it's a sensitive subject, particularly for him. Thaddeus was always a little crazy, but it was the pull that drove him over the edge." Fiddling with the cuff of her slim black pant leg, she quietly added, "Besides, after... well, I made him promise not to tell."

He shifted his weight in the sand, restless and tense. A muscle ticked in his smoothly shaved jaw. "Why?"

"Because you would have felt obligated to be with me if you knew." Disgust soured some of the warmth in her stomach, made it a sickly, feverish heat of unfulfilled longing. "Anything — anything at all — was preferable to *that.*"

Camille had spent her life balancing one obligation after another. From the moment she could walk, she stood between her mother and her brother. Supporting both, shielding them from one another, she carefully managed her mother's rages and Cameron's tender heart. She kept Marian in line and fulfilled her obligations to the main family. She took over as head of the family and then as her mother's caretaker when she declined.

The burdens were endless. The guilt was even worse. She had no desire to become a chore, an added weight, to someone else.

"Cam..." Viktor planted one hand in the sand in front of him and rose onto one knee, as if he wanted to launch himself across the fire but held himself back at the last second with rigid control. His expression was hard edged, desperate. The skin around his eyes was tight, his brows pinched in a ferocious frown. "Cam, you have to know that you would never have been an obligation to me. You certainly aren't one now."

She shook her head. The wind whistled through their little alcove, singing a haunting melody with the rushing waves. "Doesn't matter now. I—"

"No, this is important." Viktor's eyes flickered back and forth between cornflower blue and coyote gold. "I need you to know what you mean to me. You need to understand how afraid I was for you."

She tucked her arms around her middle. "Your father?"

He swallowed and slowly leaned backward, dropping out of his crouch to sink into the cool sand. "Yes. When you asked me to run away with you, I... Gods, I *wanted* to, but it was all wrong. I knew that I wasn't strong enough to take on my father yet, and if he came after us, he'd kill you first. And even if he didn't, I still would have been leaving my mom, the rest of the pack. I'd be asking you to leave everything you loved behind, too, and I wouldn't even be able to protect you, provide a pack for you to lean on... I couldn't do that."

Viktor breathed out slowly, the muscles of his neck and jaw working hard as he clearly wrestled with some great internal force. When he spoke again, his voice was low, tight. "You were this beautiful bright spot in my life, Cam. When I was with you, I felt like I was worth a damn. Like I wanted to make a future for myself, not just run headlong into the ground the moment I took out that sonuvabitch. But running away with you— it scared the shit out of me. I'd be putting you at risk, and even if I wasn't, I had no idea how to care for a mate, how to build a life with you outside of everything we'd ever known. I reacted on instinct." He blew out a noisy sigh.

Camille had the strangest sense of something unraveling inside of her — a knot of hurt buried so deep, it felt like it was being drawn from the pit of her soul. Almost to herself, she said, "We were sixteen, Vik."

And that was the long and short of it. They were sixteen and in the foolish sort of love that you never forgot, never let go of. It shaped who they were, but it was not all they *could* be.

"Yeah, well, I shouldn't have said what I said," he admitted. "I didn't know how— I didn't know what to say, how to tell you about my father, what I should have asked... Honestly, I fuckin' panicked, sweetheart."

A startled laugh bubbled out of her, surprising them both. Camille covered her mouth with the tips of her claws as some old and brittle ice began to thaw inside her.

It wasn't funny — especially not when she knew how cruel his father had been, how he'd terrorized his son and mate, his pack. Dominic hated elves, but Camille had always gotten the sense that he hated his pack and his obligations to them more. Perhaps if he had less of an ego, he could have given it all up and provided a little peace to everyone involved, but he was too possessive, too dominant to do that.

Not that Viktor had ever, ever let her meet him, of course.

Everything she knew of Dominic Hamilton was gleaned from context, rumor, and Viktor. The teenager she knew had been obsessive about her safety, always going out of his way to make sure his father had no knowledge of their relationship. The only reason he let her come so close to the pack's land at all was because his father, a childhood victim of a vicious school of mermaids, wouldn't go within a hundred yards of the beach.

Nothing about that was funny. What made her chuckle with disbelief was the idea that the alpha sitting across from her, always so self-assured, could possibly *panic* because of something she did.

When Viktor looked at her like he couldn't decide if he wanted to be offended or amused, she promised, "I'm not laughing at you. I'm just— I actually can't really picture you panicking about anything, let alone me."

A slow smile curved his lips up. "Sweetheart, I hate to break it to you, but you drive me crazy. I don't think I've *stopped* panicking since the day we met."

Pleasure suffused every inch of her, rushing like bubbles

through her veins to make her head feel light. Camille hugged herself tighter, as if she could lock in that feeling, hold it close for a little longer.

Viktor's smile widened even as his eyes got softer. They flickered back to blue and stayed there. "Now, I promised we'd get to know one another like two people who *don't* have a fucked up history."

She arched her brows. "And how do you propose we do that?"

"Wanna play twenty questions?"

Another bubble of laughter escaped her. A grin, irrepressible, cramped her cheeks. "Are we twelve?"

"Nah, I'm just in love with you." Viktor stared at her mouth with a faintly dazed look before muttering, half to himself, "Damn, that's the prettiest smile I've ever seen."

Nah, I'm just in love with you. He said it so casually, so unremarkably, like it was a fact of life and not a declaration that shook her to the core.

Camille held her breath. *Gods, I feel like I'm going to come apart at the seams.* Stripped of her anger, overflowing with treacherous hope, she had nothing to hide behind. With effortless ease, he had once more revealed the softness she tried so hard to conceal.

Flustered and needing a distraction, she said, "Okay, fine. Twenty questions. You go first."

He didn't need to think. Viktor volleyed questions at her like he'd been saving them up for years. *What time do you normally wake up in the morning? What's your favorite color? Have you ever seen Kaz having a bad hair day? What's it been like on the vineyard? Do you want to keep running it? Did you go to college? What did you study?*

The serious mingled with the silly and the blessedly mundane. Camille gave back as good as she got, though she did her best to steer around the landmines of their past. Instead, she asked about life in the pack, how he'd become so good at making investments in m-tech startups, what his favorite — disgusting — food was, and whether he could sleep sitting up.

It was *fun,* and it had been so very long since she had fun that Camille almost forgot what it felt like.

"How about you tell me exactly how this elvish courtship is supposed to go? Aren't we technically skipping ahead? I'd hate to get you in trouble with your big bad cousin for not following the rules."

Camille hid her smile behind her knees. She had always broken the rules for Viktor. The moment she laid eyes on him that day in the garden, she broke her *own* biggest rule: never love like her mother had.

And yet there was no stopping it now. As inexorable as the hope that blossomed in her chest, her feelings for Viktor had their own power, their own agency. They fought to survive even when she did everything in her power to kill them.

They were strong, and now that they had hope, they were *unstoppable.*

"Well, you could say this is the second meeting," she allowed, feeling the giddy, if cautious, urge to play with him. To tease. "We're supposed to have some sort of chaperone, though. And *no one* would have a second meeting so soon after the first. That implies favoritism."

Viktor didn't move, but she got the uncanny sense that he sank into a hunting crouch, as if he was prepared to spring at the slightest provocation. His smile turned just shy of wicked when he purred, "Does that make me your new favorite?"

Heat pulsed between her legs. Camille's breath shortened. Flushing, she lifted her head to primly inform him, "I never said that."

"So you're still trying to convince me you've got another favorite? Cute."

"I *do* have an elvish favorite," she shot back, though it sounded weak even to her own ears.

He tilted his head to one side, sending several blond curls

tumbling across his tanned forehead. The way he narrowed his eyes did not convince her that he actually believed her bluff.

"Hm, interesting. I wonder if he could make you come as hard as I did, or if he knows that you like it a little rough." A distinctly lupine smile turned his expression into something feral, hungry. "I wonder if he knows how badly you want *my* bite."

Camille opened her mouth before she thought about what might fly out of it. "Well, seeing as I've slept with him—"

A growl shook the air between them, cutting her off before she could say something even more stupid.

In one smooth motion, Viktor was on his hands and knees, his lethal body lowered in a deep, predatory crouch. Golden skin rippled over tense muscle as magic, wild and animalistic, permeated the air. His eyes were two furious circles of luminous gold.

She should have been afraid. Viktor looked about half a step away from shifting, and being an alpha of his strength meant he might actually be able to do some damage to her if he chose to.

And yet, she didn't feel any fear.

Her blood pumped faster, rushing in her ears, as adrenaline and lust came hard on the heels of her sense of danger. Uncurling her legs from her chest, Camille flexed her claws on her thighs. *Play,* instinct whispered, sending a shot of pure joy through her chest. *Finally, he wants to play!*

"You really want to test those claws on me, don't you?" he rumbled, lip curling over straight white teeth and rapidly elongating canines.

Strangely breathless, she answered, "Maybe. I'm not sure you can handle it, though."

Another hair raising growl made her squeeze her thighs together. Desire was a molten heat between her legs, only made worse with every beat of her pulse.

"Sweetheart, I don't care if you slept with every man on the West Coast." His voice dropped into a low, low purr. The light of the fire danced in his heavy-lidded eyes. He rose up onto his knees slowly, one hand resting on the elastic band of his athletic pants, above the tantalizing outline of his rigid cock. Every deep breath hollowed out the arch under his ribs.

He hooked his thumb under the waistband, taunting her, and murmured, "I wouldn't care if you fucked the entire UTA, sweetheart, as long as you admit I made you see fuckin' stars."

She swallowed a whimper of pure, unadulterated *want*. "And if I don't?"

His smile was a knife's slash, hard and sharp. "Then I guess I'll have to try harder next round. By the time I'm done with you, you won't even remember his name."

She barely remembered his name *now*. "Oh?"

He pushed his hand down, ever-so-slightly, baring more tantalizing skin and a sprinkle of crisp blond hair. The mouthwatering arches of his Adonis belt drew her eyes downward, until she was gazing hungrily at the hard outline of his cock.

His reply was a silken purr. "Yes, *oh.*"

Camille's heart raced. She wanted to lunge around the fire and tackle him into the sand. She wanted to lick every salty, delicious inch of him. She wanted to feel his fist in her hair and his mouth on hers. Gods, she wanted him more than she'd ever wanted anything in her life.

She felt that deep unraveling again, faster than before. If they made contact, that was it. No more choice. No more ice baths. No more union. Her life would be over.

Or it would finally begin, her heart whispered.

Her heartbeat thundered in her ears as she stared at him. He didn't move, though he nearly vibrated with tension. He didn't breathe. He waited, despite what she guessed was a crushing wave of instinct, for her to choose *him.*

Because she was his mate. Despite the obstacles and the years, he loved her still. He wanted her. More importantly, he wanted her to want him back.

Everything in her shifted.

Affection glowed, rich and vibrant, in her chest. *He's a good man — and better, he could be mine, if only I had the courage to give myself to him in return.*

"Vik, I—"

A low whine, barely audible over the whistle of wind, was their only warning before the bolt slammed into Viktor's shoulder.

CHAPTER TWENTY-TWO

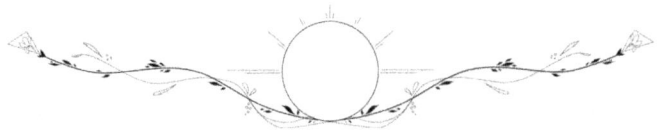

AT FIRST, HE ONLY REGISTERED THE IMPACT.

Viktor felt the slam of some great force into his shoulder, throwing him back into the sand. His teeth clacked together, clipping his tongue, and the coppery tang of blood filled his mouth. There was a dull roar in his ears as his mind fought to catch up with what had happened.

In the space between blinks, reality bled into his awareness. So did pain.

I've been fucking shot, he realized, trying to breathe through the agonizing burn. Pain threatened to blot out his vision. Black spots floated in front of his eyes, muddying the glow of the fire, the sight of Camille lunging around it to cover him with her own body as sand sprayed in a wide arc around her.

Dazed, it took him a second to figure out why that was bad and why on Earth she would do it in the first place.

Someone is still shooting at us.

Bolts of superheated plasma whizzed over their heads and into the sand around them, making it pop and crackle as it instantly turned to jagged glass.

Viktor's senses returned to him, vicious and wild. "Fuck!"

Ignoring the pain, he slung his good arm around Camille's

svelte waist and flipped them over. Using his wider frame, he guarded her from the onslaught as best he could, cursing himself for his lack of caution.

They were in perhaps the worst possible place to be caught by a damn sniper. The only cover the alcove offered was a sandstone boulder a few yards away from their fire, but it was in no way big enough to provide any real protection for long. Other than that, they were completely exposed.

Fear was a cold drip down his spine, numbing the sharpest edge of his pain. Camille was in danger. His *mate* was in danger.

Never, in all his life, had he felt such visceral, stomach churning terror.

Not when he thought Valen would kill him for breaking into the Solbourne apartments. Not when he watched his mother wither away under his father's cold cruelty. Not when he ripped the old bastard's throat out.

Nothing compared to the feeling that he might lose his mate moments after getting her back.

Viktor took advantage of a brief lull in bolt fire — about the time it took for a power cell to be changed out — to haul them both toward the boulder. The agony in the torn and cauterized wound that once was his shoulder and upper chest made movement seem impossible, but he gritted his teeth and did it anyway. Sweating profusely and using his one good arm, he managed to get them both at least somewhat covered by the sandstone seconds before the bolts started up again, this time aiming for the space around the rock.

Whoever it was behind the gun wasn't the best marksperson, but what they lacked in skill, they made up for in quantity.

"Vik." His name was a harsh breath against his cheek. Her voice was raw when she said, "Vik, you're hurt."

He turned his head, desperately trying to get a good look at her, but they were plastered so close together that he didn't see much beyond the side of her face. "Were you shot?"

She shook her head. He felt the prick of her claws somewhere around his waist and realized, with an awful jolt, what he'd done.

"Gods," he choked out, wishing he could push her away and yet entirely unable to do so. Guilt stole the air from what was left of his lungs. It was worse than the pain, worse than the fear. *I stole her choice.*

"Gods, Cam, I'm so sorry. You shouldn't be touching me—"

She drew back just enough to look him in the eye. Away from the fire and tucked into the shadows between the boulder and the sandstone wall of the cliff, her beautiful face was wrought in deep blues and violets. He had no trouble seeing her clearly in the dark, and didn't miss the way her pupils had expanded to nearly eclipse her irises, nor the deep flush that settled into her cheeks.

Camille might have looked dazed, even a little drunk, if she wasn't also wearing a wild-eyed scowl. "Shut *up!* We are being *shot at!* Do you think I care?" A bolt whistled overhead and slammed into the cliff wall, sending chunks of red hot sandstone raining down around them, but she didn't seem to notice. A snarl curled her plump upper lip over her fangs when she brought her face close to his. "After I rip the head off of the man who shot you, I'm going to bite every inch of you. Got that?"

Viktor blinked. The pain made thinking difficult, and although he was pretty sure he wasn't losing any blood, his mind felt sluggish, uncoordinated. A cold sweat drenched his skin as his body began to slide into shock. That had to be why he thought he heard her say she wanted to *bite* him. Certainly, if he'd been in his right mind, he would have heard her scathing condemnation for stealing her choice from her.

"Cam," he rasped, "what are you—"

A gloved hand curled around the back of his neck. Claws tickled the skin of his jugular as she yanked his head down for a kiss that turned his world upside down.

Camille tasted like wild honey — sweet, with a tart, earthy bite. It was a taste he remembered with perfect clarity from the single kiss they'd shared just moments before she asked him to run away with her.

The taste of that kiss had haunted him for twenty years.

Her lips were smooth and plush, her tongue sleek and hot as it slid hungrily against his own. Viktor sucked in a shuddering breath through his nose and took in the wildflower scent of her overlaid with the delicious warmth of her desire.

For a single, breathless moment, he felt no pain, heard no shots, knew no fear. There was only Camille and the howl of victory that rose up from his very soul.

My mate, his coyote howled. *My mate!*

Just as he was lifting his hand to bury it in her hair, determined to bring her closer, she pulled away with a low, terrifying growl. "Don't you fucking die on me while I'm gone," she hissed, pressing another hard, fast kiss to his lips.

Fear returned, bigger and colder than before. The coyote went perfectly still inside him before, with a yowl of outrage, he lunged against the cage of his mind. "Cam, *no!*"

It was too late. Camille was as sleek and graceful as a cat. His only chance of holding her in one place involved two arms and brute strength. Injured and taken by surprise, he didn't stand a chance of pinning her down.

He lurched forward, but his good arm only caught cold air and sand. In one graceful roll, she was out from behind the boulder and sprinting toward the opposite cliff wall — *toward* the shooter.

Camille didn't think. She didn't doubt. She was an elf, and that meant she *acted.*

In the moment between watching Viktor fly back into the sand, his shoulder and upper chest obliterated by a plasma bolt, and her next breath, Camille decided that there was no going back.

Presented with the possibility that Viktor may simply cease to exist in the world, every fiber of her being balked.

That was not right. That was not *possible.* He was hers. When he left Burden's Earth for the Underworld, it would be in lockstep with her. No other outcome was acceptable.

He was *her* consort. His life, his future, belonged to *her.*

And someone tried to take him from me.

Camille was familiar with anger. Elves tended to run hot, and she could nurse a grudge better than anyone she knew, but *this*—this was a fury she had never felt before. It was all-consuming. It was bigger than her, wilder and smarter than her.

It was so, so cold.

Alongside the flood of endorphins that came with touching Viktor, tasting him, a deadly, adrenaline-laced calm settled over her. Every sense sharpened, and every thought was clear, precise. Camille had never been a particularly violent person, but she was an *elf.*

And all elves were predators.

They were fast, graceful, and almost impossible to kill. Taught from childhood to manage their immense strength through intensive martial training, there was not a single elf who could not kill if necessary.

It's really fucking necessary now, she thought, darting across the narrow gap between one wall of the alcove to the other. The sandstone was craggy and uneven, jutting out around her in places to provide partial cover from the bolts that sporadically aimed her way.

That alone told her everything she needed to know.

The shooter was not even really aiming for her. Almost all of his focus, even when she made herself a clear target, was on her consort.

And that's why he has to die.

Ducking behind a small outcropping of stone, Camille took a second to fish her phone out of her pocket. With her free hand, she touched the *SOS* sigil carved into the back of the Solbourne pin stuck into the lapel of her coat. A small burst of magic made her skin tingle.

Vik's down. Bring Margot.

That done, she shoved her worry for Viktor's health into a tiny box and cast it aside. He would survive. He didn't have a choice.

With her worry compartmentalized, all that remained was fury and the laser focus of the hunt.

Lips curling over her teeth in a snarl, she bent her knees and leapt. Just before she began to fall back to the ground, she hooked her claws into the soft sandstone and began to haul herself up the cliff with dizzying speed.

Going by the direction of the bolts and knowing what any half-trained lout with a bolt gun would do, she used the pock-marked stone as hand and toe holds as she made her way up to the highest point. Above her, a cluster of vegetation-covered boulders loomed.

When a bolt went off, a tiny flash of light illuminated a juncture where two of the boulders leaned against one another.

That the fool hadn't bothered to use an m-dampener for his assassination was both insulting and a relief. He'd made her job easy.

Camille pulled herself up and over the ledge a few yards from the boulders with one graceful, soundless move. Crouching low, she sucked in a deep breath.

Cat shifter.

She didn't have time or the wherewithal to be surprised by that. All she needed was his scent in case he ran. Everything else was secondary.

Her steps were silent as she drifted toward the shooter. Each bolt that went off was another rake of her claws against his flesh, another bite she would take.

If one more bolt hits my consort, I will rip his spine out and show it to him.

Camille flexed her claws as the rush of the hunt settled into her bones. It only made her rage expand, its permeating chill radiating out from a solid core of possessiveness.

Circling wide around the rocks, she spied a figure crouched between them, dressed in black from head to toe. It was pure luck that she wore an all black outfit herself. While the figure focused on trying to aim a weapon he clearly barely knew how to use, she was a dark wraith drifting behind him, soundless and deadly.

He didn't notice her until it was too late to run.

The smell of a burning fuel cell and sharp, sweet ozone lingered around him. As did the bite of singed flesh when he scrambled to change out the cartridge again and burnt the tips of his fingers. Cursing under his breath, he sucked his thumb into his mouth even as he jostled his gun, shaking it like that might make the redhot fuel cell fall out on its own.

Amateur, she thought, stepping behind him with a cold sneer. *A dead amateur.*

Camille lunged.

While one hand snapped out to wrench the gun from his hands and throw it aside, the other tore into his throat — not enough to kill, not yet — but enough to make him bleed. The shifter froze for a heartbeat before he threw himself backward, attempting to break her hold by throwing her off balance.

He weighed more than she did, but Camille was quick and determined to see him hurt. Letting go would give him the chance to shift, and since he would be that much harder to subdue as a cat, she could not let that happen.

Somewhere far below them, a huge burst of magic rent the night air, but neither she nor the shifter noticed it. They grappled, shifter against elf, claw against claw. He caught her side with his shifted claws and, with a vicious bite, caught her gloved hand between his teeth. Bone snapped, though she barely felt it.

Tearing her hand out of his mouth, Camille let loose a beastly snarl and leapt up. Curling her knees into her chest, she dropped all her weight into the center of his back, sending them both crashing to the ground.

The air was ripe with the scent of crushed plants and blood as she tore at his back, her claws shredding cloth and skin with terrifying ease. The shifter yowled in agony. He bucked, attempting to dislodge her even as his muscles bunched and heated, trying to change even when she had her claws in them.

"You tried to kill my consort," she hissed in his ear, bloodlust a high, keening song in her mind. "Do you know what that means?"

Fear and anger were ragged notes in his voice when he gasped, "Fucking— I don't even know who you—"

"So you *were* only after him. You probably should have stayed quiet." She dug her claws in deeper, until they hit the solid mass of bone. Unlike hers, *his* bones were brittle with soft, spongy marrow that could easily be snapped between her jaws.

The shifter let out a hoarse scream and bucked again, but it was no use. Staring down at him like he was little more than a writhing bug, she asked, "Do you know what the punishment for hurting an elf's consort is, *cat?*"

Panting, he rasped, "No, you fucking crazy el—"

"Put before an elvish tribunal, I would be expected to break every limb before I sliced open your chest, cracked your sternum, and *ripped out your beating heart.*" Camille felt him jerk, like her words sent an electric current through his entire body. Leaning in close enough for him to feel the scrape of her fangs against the shell of his ear, she finished, "You are lucky I don't have time for that. My consort needs me, so I have to make this quick. Not painless, though. You haven't earned that."

He thrashed, his fear perfuming the air with an acrid, sour smell. "Wait, wait! I—"

Growling, Camille wrestled with him until she had both of his sturdy wrists pinned behind his back. Shifters were strong, but they couldn't match the sheer power of an elf — even one as deceptively willowy as herself.

Keeping his twitching hands pinned with only one of her

own, Camille dug her bloodied claws into his hair and wrenched upward, pulling his head back into an uncomfortably sharp angle.

Instinct was clear and sharp in her mind. Millennia old, it passed from one generation to another unbroken, unchanged.

Go for the fucking throat.

Rearing her head back, she bared her fangs and swooped down toward his pounding jugular just as Kaz's familiar baritone boomed, "Cammie, *stop!*"

CHAPTER TWENTY-THREE

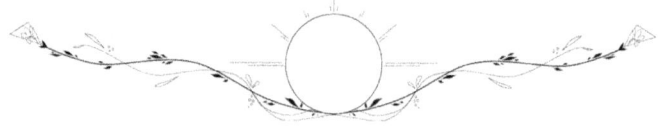

It took Kaz and three seasoned Sovereign's Guard to pry her off of the shifter. Even so, it was not their brute strength that finally uncurled her claws from torn flesh, but the relentless call of reason.

Stroking her hair back from her sweaty face, Kaz rumbled, "Hey, sweet. I know you're itching to make a pelt outta this cat, but you need to listen to me, okay?"

Camille could barely hear him over the rush of blood in her ears, over the pounding din of bloodlust. The need for retribution was a great, heaving wave inside her, rolling forward and back, crashing against the walls of her mind again and again and again.

Instinct recognized that neither he, nor the three hulking soldiers currently crouched, hovering over her prey, were threats. It was the only reason that bloodlust didn't extend to them. If it had been anyone else, she would have lashed out, fighting to keep her right to the kill she'd claimed.

But Kaz's touch was soft. His voice was familiar. The smell of buttery soft leather and woodsmoke filtered in through the haze of copper and ocean salt.

Kin.

Kaz was kin. She trusted him.

"That's a good girl," he crooned, using that famous, orcish baritone to praise her as she slowly, slowly unclenched her claws. Her face still hovered barely an inch from the shifter's pounding jugular, but as her cousin's words began to slip through the thicket of her rage, so too did a tiny amount of reason. "That's it, sweet. It's okay. We have him now. You don't want to let him die, do you? We won't be able to figure out who wants your consort dead if he doesn't have a head."

She blinked. *Someone wants Viktor to die.*

The thought was muddied, distorted. It rang with truth, but she had trouble coming to grips with what exactly it meant. The beast in her recognized only the immediate threat. It wanted her to finish what she'd started, to the Underworld with Kaz and his murmuring.

But the woman was stronger than the beast. It had to be, to survive as long as she had, denying what that miserable creature demanded was their due.

"Ah, good girl. Good, sweet girl. That's it. Everything will be okay, I promise." She didn't even realize she'd begun to lean backward until Kaz motioned for the soldiers to take over her position, pinning the writhing, babbling shifter to the sandy ground. As soon as they had a pair of m-enhanced stun cuffs snapped around his wrists, Kaz looped an arm around her middle and hauled her off of him completely.

Immediately, warmth enveloped her, chasing out a cold so deep, it left her trembling. Kaz crushed her to his chest, one big green hand sliding over her cheek and down, searching for wounds. It was only then that she noticed the pain in her side.

"Oh," she breathed, beginning to shake in earnest. "I didn't realize he got me."

She felt Kaz's breath hitch when his fingertips grazed the jagged slice in her coat. Now that the adrenaline was beginning to wear off, she could feel a strange coolness there — the cold night air stealing the warmth from the blood soaked into the thick wool.

Agony bloomed in her side, as well as up and down her arms, where the shifter had clawed to be free. During the fight she didn't notice even a hint of pain, but it rushed to the forefront of her mind now, alongside the crushing weight of worry.

"I'm going to pick you up," he warned, crouching to slide one muscled arm behind her knees. The sudden change in position cruelly jostled the wound in her side. Black spots floated in front of her eyes and she let out a strangled cry.

Somewhere down on the beach, a haunting roar of rage went up. *Viktor.*

Camille curled her claws into Kaz's leather covered shoulder. Cold sweat broke out across her chest and behind her knees. "Kaz — Viktor, is he—"

Her cousin was already walking, his long legs eating up the distance to what she knew was a narrow trail leading down the cliff with ease. "He's okay. We've got a squad down there, and we called his second. Teddy's there, too, and so is Margot."

She might have felt relief, except she couldn't quite believe it until she saw Viktor with her own two eyes. *My consort was almost stolen from me.*

Bile raced up the back of her throat with a violence that made her head swim. Camille pressed hard against Kaz's shoulder. "Put me down! Put me down!"

"Cammie, wh—"

Ignoring the pain in her side, she thrashed until he was forced to ease her down onto the ground. She fell to her hands and knees. Sand and grit stung the shredded skin of her palms as she emptied her stomach into the thick greenery.

Gods, I almost lost him just when I'd begun to find him again.

Was it not enough that she'd lost her mother? That she'd never known her father? Did the gods need to take her consort from her, too? It was enough to make her wonder just what spectacular sin she had committed in a past life; what incredible blasphemy she must have offered to those capricious deities to warrant a punishment such as this.

Muscles of her throat and shoulders cramping, she looked up through the sweaty fringe of her hair to see the three Guards hauling the shifter to his feet. He slumped between two of them, the look on his face dazed. One leg was clearly broken, and nearly every exposed patch of skin was torn by her claws — including one of his eyes, which was little more than a socket covered in shredded flesh and stringy viscera.

And in that instant, Camille understood her mother as never before.

Rage as she'd never felt coalesced with a grief so sharp, so poisonous, it threatened to slice through whatever remained of her sense of self.

She needed to kill that man. She needed to gut him with her own hands. She needed to find out who he worked for and then do it all over again. Nothing, not even her own wounds, would stop her.

Camille's body tensed, ready to pounce. *He almost took Viktor from me!*

"No, Cammie." A heavy hand landed on her back, drawing soothing circles. "Not yet."

Her voice was wrenched from her scalded throat, raw and agonized. "He tried to *kill* him!"

"Yes," Kaz answered, "and your mate needs you now. Do you really want to waste time cutting that shifter up when you could be with him?" She stiffened, suddenly torn, and Kaz was quick to drill down on that sign of weakness. "He's in pain, Cammie."

Damn, ruthless orc.

Wiping her mouth with the back of one trembling hand, Camille forced her eyes away from her prey and nodded.

Wasting no time, her cousin swept her back up into his arms and hustled down the winding trail. It was a much longer trip than the one she'd taken to get up there. Every step hurt her side and every minute dragged by, increasing her anxiousness to see Viktor, to know that he was well.

In her mind, the image of how satisfying the shifter would look with his head removed was replaced with that of Viktor's contorted expression, his ravaged shoulder.

All that beautiful golden skin burnt and blackened. The scent of blood and charred flesh. The sound of his labored breathing as he wrestled them back behind the boulder. Her empty stomach rolled again.

"Hurry, Kaz."

"We're almost there." Her cousin tightened his arms around her. When she looked up at him, she found his beautiful face stark, each feature hewn with the jagged edge of fury. He looked as fierce as she'd ever seen him — which was saying something, since Kaz was one of the most handsome and terrifying people she'd ever met.

They rounded a bend and she felt his gate change, shifting to accommodate his stride in the sand. Ten more steps and they turned another corner. The beach opened up before them, once deserted, now swarming with glamoured Guards, shifters, and the unmistakable form of Theodore himself.

The bulk of people were clustered around one spot near the opening of the alcove. The faint glow of the fire gilded a woman's back as she knelt beside a prone figure. Even in the dark, her red hair gleamed.

Margot. Relief swelled. *She's healing Viktor.*

That was a good thing, but as her eyes darted around the beach, taking in all the shadowy figures, tension pulled her muscles into rigid readiness. Camille wanted to struggle, to fight to be let down so she could run to her consort and put herself between him and so many unknown people, but her limbs had turned to jelly as the adrenaline finally evaporated from her system. All she could do was manage a weak, keening sound of distress as she watched people move around Viktor, only granting her the smallest glimpses of him.

She thought that Theodore would be the first to notice them, but as they neared, a tanned arm shot out from somewhere beside Margot, claws digging into the sand as Viktor fought to sit up. His agonized bellow echoed off of the sandstone cliffs. *"Cammie!"*

She sucked in a jagged breath, her sight blurring as tears of relief came.

"She's here!" Kaz called back, his arms tightening. His heart beat fast against her side.

Theodore took off like a shot. It didn't seem to matter that he was dressed in a suit and dress shoes. He loped over the sand with the ease of a deadly predator, every movement well-oiled and perfectly timed. He was by Kaz's side in seconds.

His expression was hard, his eyes dark with barely restrained rage when he looked down at her. "Is she hurt?"

"Yes." Kaz answered at the same time that Camille replied, "No."

Kaz and Theodore shared a look. "She *is*. I didn't get a good look at it, but the shifter got her side pretty bad, and I think she might have broken some bones in her hand."

That was news to her. Camille flexed both of her hands and was surprised by the sharp bite of pain that radiated from the delicate bones in the palm of her right hand. It took a moment to recall that the shifter had, at one point in their struggle, *bitten* her.

Huh, she thought, strangely impressed, *I didn't know shifters had the strength to break elvish bones.*

Theodore swore. Both men picked up their pace until they were nearly jogging through the sand, bringing Camille closer to where she needed to be. The pain in her side was growing, as was the new, terrible ache of crushed bones in her hand, but when they were near enough to Viktor, she clawed for a final reserve of strength and threw herself out of Kaz's grip.

Both he and Theodore reached for her as she stumbled in the stand. "Cammie, what are you *doing?* Stop!"

But she didn't stop. Panting through the pain, she lurched

forward, the toes of her shoes digging into the sand, until she was close enough to reach him. She dropped to her knees and *crawled.*

"*Cam,*" Viktor rasped, his coyote eyes locked on her as she crossed the remaining distance between them. Someone had laid him on the blanket he'd brought. It bunched under his palm as he struggled to sit up, the muscles of his arms and chest straining hard against his golden skin.

On his other side, Margot didn't even look up as she firmly pressed him back down. Her eyes were down, her expression one of honed focus, as she rested her hands on the skin around his wounded chest. Magic hummed in the air around her.

Camille didn't realize she was crying until she pressed her face into his cool neck. Viktor fell back, freeing up his uninjured arm to wrap around the back of her neck in a crushing, possessive hold. He buried his face in her hair as he sucked in great, gasping breaths.

"Can't believe you ran *toward* a shooter. Don't you ever, *ever* do that to me again," he grated against her ear. She felt his breath hitch, then wheeze with an awful, rattling finish. "Don't you leave me, Cam. Not again."

Camille shuddered. "I won't. I swear, I won't."

"Thank you," he gasped, arm slackening. "Thank you. I'm— Love you so much—"

His arm fell away to fall limply into the sand.

Camille raised herself up just enough to peer into his face. His eyes were closed, his lips parted. Her ears rang when she whispered, "Vik? *Vik.*"

She didn't hear any rustling of clothing, the soft sound of sand moving beneath shoes, nor conversation before strong hands grabbed her upper arms and pried her away from him. Panic stole the last of her strength. She strained against the hold, but couldn't break it as she demanded he wake back up, that he open his eyes and *look* at her.

She kept yelling even as Margot changed her position, moving to place her hands directly over his heart.

Some small part of her recognized that it was Theodore who held her up, that shifters were filling up the beach, that she was losing blood. The world outside of Viktor existed, moving around her in a sluggish current, but she could not acknowledge it.

All she saw was Viktor's chest as it rose and fell, rose and fell and... stopped.

Chapter Twenty-Four

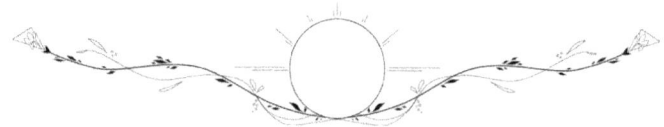

Viktor woke to the sound of birds outside his window and his mate in his bed.

For a moment, he drifted in a golden haze of sleepy contentment. His mind was fuzzy, his senses dulled by the drugging pleasure of Camille's nearness. He stared up at the familiar ceiling of his bedroom with a slow, drowsy smile.

Camille was a soft weight against his side. Her back was pressed against him, and she'd commandeered one of his arms to use as something of a body pillow. He felt the grip of her fingers, unyielding even in sleep, around his bicep. Her breaths were a gentle rhythm in the quiet of the early morning. Her feet, bare and cold, were pressed against his shin.

Careful not to wake her, he slowly turned on his side and curled his body around hers, drawing her into his chest. A deep, animalistic sound of contentment rattled out of his throat.

Sweet like honey, he thought, drawing in a deep breath of her scent as he buried his nose in her hair. She never smelled sweeter than she did in his bed, covered in his deeper, muskier scent. *A perfect fit.*

Viktor slid his hand down, over her hip and across her stomach. Her skin was bare and silky smooth, her muscles lithe and gracefully molded to her willowy frame. Desire was a steady heat in his gut as he traced the dip of her belly button with the pad of his thumb.

So soft.

Like hot silk, her skin tantalized the coyote in him, who loved soft things and warm, lush sensuality. He wanted nothing more than to learn every curve of his mate's body. He wanted to taste her, to discover what made her go soft and pliant for him. Drunk on the feel of her in his arms, Viktor lowered his head to kiss the gentle swell of her shoulder. He scraped his teeth against that delicate skin and felt his longing for her expand in a heady rush.

His jaw ached. Magic, the wild kind that overtook him in the glorious seconds it took to change into his other form, burned hot and fizzy under his skin. It begged for an outlet — for *her.*

Want to bite her, he thought, man and coyote melding into one seamless, hungry being. *Want to sink my teeth into her and make her mine forever.*

Why hadn't he done that already, anyway? She was in his den, in his arms. He'd felt her softening toward him, knew that he was on the way to winning her completely. The fact that she was in his bed was a triumph he couldn't have imagined only a month ago. His mate was *his.*

Viktor's breath quickened with raw excitement. His cock hardened against the sweet curve of her backside, aching for release, for all that luscious, slick heat he'd known so briefly. His jaw cramped, flexing hard with the desire to extend his fangs and—

His questing fingers met the edge of something strange on her side. It was filmy, almost rubbery, like one of those special m-bandages hospitals used to quickly stop blood loss. He ran his thumb over the edge again, his mind stalling. A budding sense of dread began to burn away the delicious arousal coursing through his veins.

Brows furrowing, he reluctantly lifted his head to peer down at Camille's body.

It *was* a bandage. A big one.

Awareness spread like ice through his mind, pricking him until it felt like his insides were nothing more than a frozen mass of thorns.

The beach. The way she looked at me. The firelight in her eyes. The gunshots.

Viktor began to shake. Terrified he'd wake her, he gently extracted his arm from her hold and sat up against the headboard. He lifted one trembling hand to his injured shoulder, but found it undamaged, the skin taut but otherwise unharmed.

Margot was there, he recalled, staring down at the slumbering form of his mate with wide eyes. *I was shot, and Cam...*

Camille ran after the shooter.

He felt his gorge rise as he remembered the sight of her slim back getting smaller, running away from him. He remembered watching from behind the boulder as bolts whistled by her head. He remembered the visceral terror of seeing her scale the cliff with her claws. He remembered the exact moment his excellent night vision failed him and he lost sight of his mate as she vaulted over the cliff's edge.

Sweat broke out over his bare chest as he raked his fingers through his tangled, salt-crusted hair. This was no leisurely wake-up after a sultry evening. This was the morning after what was very nearly the greatest tragedy of his life.

Gods, I almost lost her.

Not to another man. Not because he'd done something stupid. He almost lost her because she'd fought to *defend* him.

A lump grew in his throat until it felt like he couldn't breathe, let alone swallow, around it.

No one had ever defended him before. That was an alpha's job. He was the one who defended his pack, not the other way around. While they took his safety seriously — he was their leader, after all — no one had ever gone so far as Camille had. Not even when his father was at his worst, his most cruel to his vulnerable cub and mate, did someone risk their life to protect him. He was grateful that since his father's death, there had been little opportunity.

Viktor's eyes watered as he traced the edge of the bandage again. Remorse and pride and tenderness and horror waged a war in his chest. He was gutted, and yet he felt stretched too far; his strong, shifter's heart rendered brittle by the love he felt for her.

Camille shifted and rolled onto her back, one arm thrown up to rest on the pillow above her head. His blankets were tangled around her hips and long, lithe legs.

Gods.

Viktor held his breath as he took her in. His mate was so beautifully wrought it made him *hurt.*

Lavender skin stretched over trim muscle and elegant, sloping bone. Her waist was a neat dip above lean hips. Her ribs, moving slowly with every deep breath, were a divine arch. Her breasts were soft swells tipped with dark nipples. Her neck was long and bare, stretched in a way that tempted the coyote into a frenzy — triggering that deep, instinctive compulsion to lick and kiss and *bite.*

It was the most arresting sight he'd ever had the privilege of seeing, and it was utterly spoiled by the clear bandage carefully applied over the wound in her side.

It was a series of jagged lines, five in total, that split her beautiful skin to reveal the yellow fat and pale blue flesh beneath.

Claw marks.

He ground his teeth as he probed at his own healed shoulder. Why hadn't Margot tended to Camille? Why was he fully healed and his mate *wasn't?*

Camille was no fighter. She was born elvish-strong and trained like all of her kind were, but he was certain she hadn't been in a real fight before that moment on the beach.

For all that her mother was a spiteful, self-centered woman, she did her best to shield her twins from violence. Whisking them away to Napa did more than keep them out of the Solbourne family's reach. It also kept them away from potential squabbles and that oh-so-elvish need for dominance and territory.

Camille had been inadvertently cosseted by her mother and had likely run on nothing more than instinct and adrenaline when she fought the shooter. For all her spine, she was delicate, breakable.

And she still risked her life to protect me.

Viktor pressed his palm against his chest, as if that small gesture could contain a heart that had never belonged to him.

The sound of someone walking barefoot through his den snapped him out of his staggering realization. Too quick for the average eye to follow, he had the sheets pulled up over Camille's shoulders and his body between her and the door.

In a voice so low only a shifter's ears could pick it up, Benny called out through the door, "Vik, you awake in there?" He paused, waiting for an answer, before he continued, "I thought I heard you moving. If you're awake, come out soon. The pack's worried sick and I've got a pushy sovereign incoming."

Instinct prowled close to the surface of his mind. His coyote gnashed its jaws, too caught up in the fever to care that Benny was a dear friend, not a foe. It took several deep breaths for him to get that protective rage back under control.

Benny was in his den because he was guarding his alpha and his alpha's mate. He was doing the work of a good packmate, a loyal second.

Still, his coyote balked at the idea of someone being in their den when his mate — not even marked yet, gods help them — lay vulnerable and injured in their bed.

He can't come in here.

Viktor wasn't used to being out of control or quick tempered. He was as easy-going as a dominant alpha coyote could be, really. It was jarring to admit to himself that, should Benny step through that door, he couldn't say his friend would safely make it over the threshold.

Careful not to jostle Camille, Viktor slid out of bed and

planted his bare feet on the cool floor. He was in his boxers, he noticed, and though he was grimy from spending so much time laying in the sand, a quick check showed that he was no worse for being shot.

Margot really is something, he thought, trying to tamp down his agitation over the fact that *he* was healed while his mate wasn't. Standing up to quietly find a pair of pants, he rolled his shoulder experimentally. *Not even a twinge.*

He'd been to his fair share of healers with a myriad of gruesome injuries. Not once had he come away feeling *better* than he had the day before. Margot hadn't just patched him up: she made him *stronger.*

Shaking his head in disbelief, he pulled on a pair of sweatpants before he padded back to the bed. Camille had moved slightly; just enough to fall into the divot he'd left and bury her pert nose into his pillow.

His breath quickened again as he leaned down to press a featherlight kiss to her cheek. She stirred, her head turning towards him with sleepy yearning, but he didn't dare disturb her more than he already had. His mate needed her rest. As soon as she woke naturally, he'd take her to see Margot. With her skills, she was the only healer he trusted with his mate's health.

After he quietly left his bedroom and closed the door behind him, Viktor found Benny in the open living area. He was on the couch, which had been hastily made into a bed with a throw pillow and one of the spare blankets he kept in the ottoman by the feed screen.

Incredibly, Benny looked worse than Viktor felt.

"You look like shit," he announced.

Benny stood up from the couch and turned to scowl at him. The skin under his eyes was dark, his hair was a mess, and he hadn't changed clothes since Viktor saw him last. Worry grooved his rough features. "Damn," he breathed, circling the couch to haul Viktor into a hard embrace. *"Damn,* Vik. Fuck. I thought we were going to lose you."

Viktor clasped his hand around Benny's nape and drew him close, bringing him into the shelter of his alpha's embrace. He felt his second shudder, as if a great tension had finally begun to loosen inside him.

It didn't matter how old a packmate was, nor how strong they were — they needed the physical reassurance of their alpha's touch.

"It was just a shot to the shoulder," he gruffly replied. "Nothing to cry over."

Benny took a step back and shook his head. His expression was stark. "No, Vik, it wasn't. What do you remember about last night?"

"I coaxed Cam to meet me at the beach. We were there for a few hours before someone started shooting from the cliff. I got hit and Cam nearly took a shot before I pulled her behind that boulder." He shook his head, trying to dispel the goosebumps that broke out across his skin at the memory of how close his mate came to death. "Then she went after him. Things get kind of fuzzy after that, but I remember Teddy and Margot showing up, and then Cam being there. Past that it's all blank."

In the shadows of his mind, there was a vague sense of movement, of warm, foreign magic mending shattered bone and singed muscle, but when he dug for more, Viktor came up empty.

Benny's lips thinned. "Vik, you almost died last night."

That drew him up short. He made a face of disbelief. "What? No, I didn't. The shot hit my shoulder."

"It was a long range bolt gun set to maximum," Benny bit out. "It didn't just hit your shoulder. It shattered two of your ribs, took a chunk out of your lung, and sent you into shock. Healer Goode was working on you almost the entire night. She barely had enough left in her to heal your mate's pulverized hand and stop her bleeding before the sovereign forced her to stop."

"What happened to Cam's hand?"

"Did you not hear what I said?" Benny ran a shaking hand

through his hair, messing it up even more. "You almost *died*, Vik. Right there on the beach."

Viktor wasn't entirely certain what he was supposed to make of that. How exactly did one process a brush with Grim? All he could manage was a slow blink.

He'd never been one to obsess about the what-ifs, nor the fact that he would die one day. One did not challenge their father to a death match at eighteen and *not* understand one's own mortality.

Death was a fact of life. The animal knew it as well as the man.

What he *did* grasp, perhaps for the first time, was that his death would not simply belong to him.

Staring at Benny's stark face, the memory of Camille running away from him fresh in his mind, Viktor was rocked by the knowledge that his death would have devastated his entire pack.

It was one thing to know that and quite another to see it written plainly on his second's face, to feel the worry and the jagged fear in the bond he shared with every member of his pack. He hadn't thought twice about going out alone, without notice, but he now recognized that he'd put himself — and his pack's stability — at risk without a single fleeting worry.

This is why Teddy travels with the Guard, he thought, staggered by his own ignorance. *Not because he can't defend himself, but because there's no sense in putting his people at risk if he fails.*

"I'm sorry," he found himself saying, voice hoarse.

"Shit, man, just..." Benny scrubbed at his face for a moment before he cracked a small, tired smile. "Just don't scare us like that again, okay? I don't fuckin' wanna be alpha, got me?"

Viktor swallowed. He'd taken his father's place as alpha at eighteen and had to learn a lot of hard lessons along the way, but none of them felt quite so hard to stomach as this one. "Yeah, I got you."

Sniffing hard, Benny nodded toward Viktor's bedroom and changed the subject. "How's your mate?"

Viktor glanced over his shoulder and was pierced by an acute longing. He wanted nothing more than to slip back into his bedroom and hold her. It was a cruel twist of fate to finally have his mate in his bed, only to not be able to actually be *with* her. "Sleeping. Her side doesn't look great."

"Margot said it isn't as bad as it looks." Benny made a face that said everything about how serious *he* thought Camille's wound was. "She took a nasty swipe, but apparently he missed anything vital. Her hand was the worst. Margot used up the last of her energy piecing the bone back together and didn't have anything left for her side."

Viktor paced away from the couch and into the kitchen. He moved restlessly, bare feet whispering over the cool tile, and grappled with the animal that howled in rage at the thought of his mate being harmed. In a voice distorted by a low, coyote growl, he asked, "What happened to her hand, Benny?"

"Looked to us like the motherfucker *bit* her."

He stopped by the kitchen island, grasped the edge of the countertop, and bowed his head. *"Fuck."*

His mate shouldn't have been put in the position of defending him. The only bite she should have been concerned with was *his* — the one that would be gentle even in its ferocity; the one that would tie them together until Grim called them to the Underworld.

Struggling to hold the horror and the fury in, he grated, "Who was he?"

The click of the knob and the soft *whush* of the door opening came seconds before Camille's sleep-roughened voice answered, "Cougar shifter. That's what he smelled like, anyway."

Viktor's head snapped up. His muscles coiled, ready to spring. The cold knowledge that Andreas almost certainly had a hand in the mess of the previous night took a backseat to the awareness of his mate.

She stood in the doorway of his bedroom, dressed in her ruined clothing from the night before. Her tight black pants were streaked and her navy turtleneck was torn on her right side, revealing hints of the bandage. Her short black hair was mussed and her face looked drawn, but she stood with her shoulders back and her spine straight, as if she was about to walk into a ballroom, not the living room he'd designed with her in mind.

"Cam, you shouldn't be up," he exclaimed, pushing away from the island. He was in front of her a second later, one hand pressed against the small of her back to gently urge her into the bedroom. Unconsciously, he eased himself between her and Benny, blocking her from sight.

"I'm fine," she murmured. Violet eyes stared up at him like she was seeing him for the first time. They were so damn soft, he almost couldn't stand to meet them.

Palming his cheek, she leaned in to press her lips to his in a trembling kiss. "I thought I lost you last night," she whispered into his mouth.

Viktor cupped her neck with both hands. "Never. *Never,* Cam."

Her shaky exhale burst across his lips. "Damn right, *never.* You're not allowed to leave me just when I decide to keep you."

"Yeah? Sounds like a good deal to me." He smiled against her mouth. Not caring even a little bit that Benny was standing only a few feet away, he tilted her head back with his thumbs and deepened the kiss. It was the drugging kind of kiss that held no urgency, no pressure. It was a kiss *shared,* each person giving as much as they received.

Fuck, he thought, forcing himself to pull back. *I could kiss her like this for hours.*

Husky, he murmured, "Sweetheart, go lay back down."

"No," she replied, pressing her palms against his bare chest. Her fingers skated over the fresh skin there. "No, I need to talk to you about last night."

"Cam, your side..."

"Does not affect my ability to speak, does it?"

Viktor let out a low growl and attempted to steer her back toward the bed anyway.

Of course, she wasn't having it.

Camille sidestepped him and padded into the living room. Though he was annoyed, he was still relieved when she trailed her fingers — *ungloved* — over his forearm as she passed him. His eyes were glued to the sight of her claws.

Retracted, he thought, chest swelling with pride, *just like she said.*

"I'm *fine."* She peered at Benny, her dark brows lowered. "Why would a cougar shifter come after my consort, Benjamin?"

Benjamin? Viktor choked on his laugh even as he winced. He knew that look, that *tone.* She was advancing on his second with a keen, distinctly ruthless expression, as if she intended to get the information out of Benny with her claws if necessary. "Cam—"

"That's pack business," Benny answered, cutting him off. His second raised an eyebrow at Camille, his expression stony. "Sorry, Miss Solbourne, as much as I respect what you did out there, I'm not about to tell you all our secrets."

Viktor didn't like that. He didn't like that at *all.*

Frowning at his second, he slowly informed him, "Cam is *pack."*

"No, she's not. Not yet, anyway." His response was cool, quick. "How do I know that she's got your best interests at heart? How do I know that she wasn't the one who set you up? I don't." He pinned Camille with a hard look. "Look, I don't *think* you did anything wrong, and I *want* you to be good for my alpha, but until I know for sure, I'm not putting Vik or this pack at risk."

"Benny."

"I know, Vik," he said, a deep frown grooving lines around his mouth and eyes. "I know, but this is how it is. We almost lost you last night. I'm not risking that shit again. Period."

Viktor took a step forward, hackles raised. A deep, resonant growl rumbled in his chest. In an instant, he was more coyote than man, though he didn't look it. "She didn't have anything to do with what happened last night," he bit out. "You know that as well as I do. And if I decide to tell her our secrets, that's *my* call, not yours. Understood?"

He didn't often play *alpha* with his pack, since it was his father's favorite intimidation tactic, but in this he was immovable. His mate deserved respect — if not for the fact that she was his, than because *she saved his fucking life.*

Benny held his gaze for longer than anyone else in his pack would have, but it was only a handful of seconds before he had to tear his eyes away, his jaw clenched hard enough to make the muscles in his rugged jaw twitch.

"It's not about *her,*" his second argued, face flushing. "It's about—"

"I'm a stranger." Despite Viktor's insult on her behalf, Camille did not appear fazed.

Laying a cool hand on Viktor's arm, she said, "I understand. I wouldn't tell *you* all my family's secrets either, Benjamin." Eyeing him shrewdly, she continued, "However, I know for a fact that my cousin is going to demand answers. Not only was his friend put in danger, but an alpha was nearly assassinated on his watch." She arched a dark, winged brow. "And, of course, I'm his *cousin.* Whoever is behind this chose to die the moment he pointed that gun in my direction."

"Even if doing that might start a war?"

Camille didn't hesitate. "Yes. We're kin. There is no price we would not pay to protect one another." She paused, her expression darkening. "Or to get revenge on their behalf."

Viktor caught Benny's eye. They shared a look of grim understanding.

What had once been a private bid for a better life had just become something much, much more complicated.

CHAPTER TWENTY-FIVE

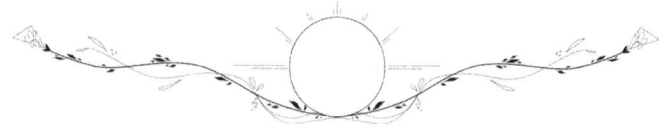

"I KNOW WE HAVEN'T BEEN CLOSE IN A LONG TIME, VIK, but you could have at least had the courtesy to tell me you were planning to *leave.*"

Viktor braced his elbows on his knees and looked up at Theodore from under his brows. Camille sat on his left, her back ramrod straight, and Margot perched on the armrest beside her, one hand on his mate's bare shoulder. Camille's shredded turtle neck lay neatly folded in her lap, leaving her in a silky black bra and that awful bandage.

Magic hummed in the air and made his teeth ache as Margot worked to close the wound on his mate's side.

He had to force himself not to peek at her, to try and gauge her reaction to the news. Anxiety was a tight band around his lungs, squeezing the air out of him. *Gods, we only just started to get things settled between us. Now this?*

Did she even want to live in the wilderness with his small pack? She was an elf. Elves usually lived in cities, where they lived comfortable lives surrounded by steel and glass and wealth. They had no time to discuss what they wanted for their future — they'd barely even *kissed* — and now he was being forced to lay everything out without preamble, without care, with an *audience.* He couldn't think of a worse way to get her feelings on the subject than that.

On the other side of the room, Theodore stood with his hands on his hips, his suit jacket spread out like purple silk-lined wings and his expression thunderous. Every few seconds his eyes darted to Margot and Camille. Every time they came back to Viktor's they were darker, angrier, than before.

"It wasn't your business," he argued, knowing that he had to stand his ground. Neither he nor his pack had done anything wrong when they initiated contact with the Alliance. They might live under the thumb of the elvish government, but they were not beholden to it. "If we want to move to a new territory, the only thing you're required to know is the day we move out."

Theodore made a sharp sound with his tongue and teeth. "Did you even think about what would happen to this territory when you left? What kind of chaos you could invite into the city if you just abandoned Merced with no warning?"

"Of course we thought of it." Viktor shifted a little, seeking the calming effect of contact with his mate. When their knees touched, his heart rate slowed a fraction, but it was not enough to completely douse the agitation burning in his chest.

"There was no point in opening our mouths until the negotiations went through, was there? Imagine we started looking for a pack to take our place and then the deal fell through, or they voted against letting us in. You want chaos? That might have opened up the door to my pack being attacked and the territory taken anyway."

Shifters didn't take well to broken promises, after all.

"So instead of telling me *privately,* you went behind my back and *then* put my cousin in danger." Theodore's expression was rigid, his eyes two black chips of fury.

"That's not fucking fair and you know it," Viktor shot back, temper rising. Gods, he was just trying to do what was right for his people. How was he supposed to know that the path would lead *here?*

"Isn't it? You entered a high stakes negotiation with some of the most dangerous shifters in the UTA and you didn't think to even have a detail with you? One fucking guard? Was my cousin supposed to be the one to—"

"Theodore." Margot's soft voice cut through the thickening aggression in the air. There was no reprimand there, but a firm command. *Stop.*

Theodore locked eyes with his wife for several heartbeats, communicating with her on a level that only they understood, before he drew his shoulders back and turned away. Pacing to the windows, he growled, "Just tell me who I need to behead."

"Well, that's going to be complicated," Viktor grimly replied, "because my money is on Alpha Andreas."

Theodore sent him a blisteringly exasperated look. "The same Alpha Andreas who keeps trying to fucking sabotage any proposed treaty between the EVP and the Alliance? *That* Alpha Andreas?"

Viktor rubbed his eyes. "Yes. I don't know what he has against elves personally, but he was one of my shithead father's best friends. He's had it out for me since I took over, and he's been loudly accusing me of essentially being an *elvish spy* since I petitioned the Alliance. In the last meeting he made it very clear that my connections to your family were tantamount to me working directly for you." He didn't mention the call, simply because he felt foolish for ignoring the very real threat the bully posed. Regret roughened his voice when he finished simply, "He wanted my bid thrown out."

"The assumption being that you would serve our interests in the Alliance."

"Yes."

Silence stretched. Outside, the faint sounds of Benny and Kaz having a low conversation drifted in through an open window. The vague shadows of Theodore's Guard flitted back and forth in front of that window — a whole unit, ready to lay down their lives for the sovereign and his mate at any moment.

He thought it was overkill before, but now... Now he understood. There would never be a moment's peace for him after this.

It was Camille herself who broke the tense quiet that had settled over them. In a low, detached voice, she said, "I'm a Solbourne. What will happen if they find out about... us? If they were against even an informal alliance, wouldn't they balk at me being your mate?"

Viktor felt every eye settle on him. Breathing out slowly, he turned his head to look at her.

Camille was sitting stiffly against the couch cushions, her violet eyes fixed on him. Her expression was reserved, impassive, giving nothing away.

His coyote hated that look. It was distant, too far from him. It wasn't the vibrant mate he knew, but someone cold, out of his reach. He wanted his soft, trusting Camille, not this beautiful, brittle creature who hid her thoughts from him.

It cut him to the quick to know he had that softness in his embrace so very briefly.

"It doesn't matter what they think," he answered, his voice a serrated edge of pure emotion. "You're my *mate*. They would have to accept it."

"But they wouldn't necessarily have to accept your *pack*, would they?" she pressed. Out of the corner of his eye, he watched Margot's pale hand tighten on Camille's shoulder in a supportive squeeze.

Sweat began to dew on the exposed skin of his chest. He didn't like where this was going at all. "If you wore my mark, they wouldn't—"

"They could still reject your pack." Camille blinked, and for just a moment he saw behind the shields she'd put up. The devastation he spied there nearly took his breath away. "Or they could try to kill you again, just to be rid of the problem altogether."

Desperation no longer tickled the edges of his mind. It sank into every fiber of his being. *"No,* Cam, that's not going to happen. If Andreas was desperate enough to actually send someone to kill me, then that must mean the Alliance is voting in my favor. They *want* us."

"But you don't know that for certain, do you? Who's to say that learning about me won't tip them over onto the other side?" With each word, her expression grew starker, the skin around her eyes and mouth tighter. "Your whole pack could lose the chance of a lifetime because of me."

"That's not going to happen," he pressed, heart beating hard and fast in his chest. Panic ran over his insides like tiny razors, skinning him of all the golden contentment he'd so briefly known. "Cam, if you took my mark, no one would be able to reject us on those grounds. You'd be *pack.*"

Viktor reached for her hand, but she jerked it out of his reach to settle it in her lap. He stared at it numbly.

He'd been shot only hours before, but Viktor was certain nothing had ever hurt him as much as that small rejection.

He watched, throat tightening painfully, as she turned her eyes on her cousin. Theodore met her gaze squarely. His expression was grave. The tiniest tilt of his head conveyed a wealth of sympathy, of understanding, as if he knew exactly what his cousin was about to say but wished he didn't.

Camille, sounding dazed, murmured, "Teddy, I think I'd like to go back to my apartment now. I need... I need to think."

"Okay, Cammie," he replied. "We'll take you home."

Viktor felt like the life was being squeezed out of him. "Cam, don't."

One beautiful lavender hand reached out to touch his arm. Her skin was cool and slightly clammy against his. "I'm not leaving you. I can't. You're mine, Vik," she whispered, breath hitching. "I just... I need to clear my head."

The coyote didn't see the difference, and the man struggled with the concept, too. Choked, he asked, "Can't you do that here? With me?"

Camille squeezed his arm. "No, Vik. I don't think I can."

"Are you sure you don't want me to stay?"

Camille turned to look at Margot hovering by her bedroom door. She was dressed in a crisp white blouse and dark green skirt, her red hair braided over one shoulder and her face clear of any strain, any sign at all that she had spent the better part of the night saving a man's life.

She looked bright and beautiful and full of life. In Camille's current state, that was utterly intolerable.

"Thank you, Margot," she rasped, striving for a tone that didn't bely how very close she was to stepping off of an emotional cliff. Camille wasn't in the habit of revealing her vulnerabilities to anyone besides her brother, but even he wouldn't be privy to her coming meltdown. "I just— I need to be alone for a while."

Margot's angular brows pinched together. Her lips pursed, and when she sucked in a deep breath, her narrow shoulders rose. Every line of her body spoke loudly, *I don't think that's a good idea.*

"I understand," she said at length, "but... I just want you to know that I get what you're feeling right now."

Camille couldn't stop the strained laugh that bubbled like acid up her throat. What did this dignified, sweet-faced little halfling know about having her world completely yanked out from under her again and again? "You do? How?"

"Yeah." Margot smiled, but it wasn't a happy expression. It was soft and sad and full of memory. "Like you want to keep fighting for a chance to have a little bit of happiness, but every choice presented to you is the wrong one. Like there is no good outcome, no path that doesn't lead to misery. Like you just... can't win."

Her throat convulsed around a jagged shard of glass, as if the tears she locked away had crystallized and shattered inside her. Speaking was almost impossible, and yet she managed to whisper, "How did you figure it all out?"

"I decided that, if my life was already over, then the last thing I wanted was to go out friendless and alone. I wanted to know what it was like to trust someone, just once." Margot stepped into the room. Her feet, bare except for the thin, shadowy tights she wore, whispered against the plush carpet as she came to stand in front of Camille.

Margot's eyes flickered from one spot on her face to another, as if she was reading some message only she could see.

"I know it isn't easy, but letting someone else take a little bit of the weight of that despair for a moment can change everything." She touched Camille's arm, gentle but firm enough to feel it through the layers of her ruined clothing. "Let me take a little of the weight for you, Cammie. Just for a minute."

Gods, I'm falling apart.

Camille could feel her walls crumbling, letting loose a torrent of pain and anxiety and guilt that threatened to break her bones, drown her, and sweep her body out into an endless, churning despair.

Her chin wobbled and she watched, horrified, as Margot's unusual eyes watered with sympathy. In a ragged voice, she asked, "Why would you do that? We don't even really know each other."

Margot was quiet for a moment. Finally, she answered, "Because sometimes it's easier to let a stranger into your darkest moment than someone you love."

The words hit her like an m-lev. Camille couldn't bear the idea of Theodore witnessing her meltdown, knowing he would only seek ways to fix it, and she knew she couldn't stay with Viktor and watch it torture him, either.

But if she was honest with herself, she would admit that she didn't really want to be alone, either.

She'd been alone for far longer than the months since her mother died. Making sure that her brother could live his life how he pleased meant putting herself between him and Marian — effectively isolating herself from both the rest of the family and the outside world. The unintended side effect of her mother's scheming was making their branch of the family pariahs. Until Camille grew into adulthood, very few wanted to risk their young by associating them with the woman who boldly declared her hatred for the Solbourne family.

Even Linnea, who grew up on the estate with her, had never been allowed to publicly appear alongside Camille until she was an adult.

For a handful of golden years, Viktor had been her only real connection, her only companion. She'd felt that connection again so briefly. It was like a soft rain on a parched and broken field.

And now that taste of cool, sweet water only left her wanting more. For just a moment she wasn't afraid of the future. She didn't think of politics or her promise to her mother. She thought only of her consort and the joy that rushed through her veins when he looked at her like he couldn't imagine a life without her.

Now... now I don't know what I'm going to do.

The shock of almost losing Viktor, of watching Margot hold his life in her capable hands on that beach, and then the horror of discovering that their relationship might put the future of his pack at risk, finally set in. Grief and guilt meshed with the acute terror, gathering like a twisting cyclone in her mind.

"I don't want to ruin this for him," she gasped. "But if I don't — if I can't— I'll end up just like *her*. And I won't— I won't have *him.*" Camille's breath hitched once, twice, before the dam broke.

"Oh, Cammie," Margot breathed, stepping forward to enfold Camille's crumbling form in her arms. "I know it hurts. I know."

Though Margot was much smaller than she was, her embrace managed to feel all-encompassing. She stroked Camille's dirty, briny hair back from her face and murmured soft assurances as she slowly guided her toward the bathroom.

"Let's get you comfortable, okay? I'll run you a bath and—"

Through her tears, Camille managed to gasp out, "N-no baths, please."

Margot didn't miss a step as they passed through the doorway and into the marble and chrome temple that was her master bathroom. "No baths. A nice hot shower, then, and after we'll get some food into you."

"No baths," she blubbered again. "I *hate* baths."

Margot smoothed her hand up and down Camille's spine. "Shh, it's okay. I'll start the shower now, Cammie."

She couldn't bear to take another bath, perhaps ever. Just the thought sent ripples of remembered pain across her skin.

Her stomach turned. *It's too late to go back now even if I wanted to.*

She'd touched him, breathed him in, kissed him, spent hours pressed up against him in bed. There was no way she could escape the pull now.

Did she want to?

Camille's thoughts were a tangle, each one overlapping and knotting with the next until she couldn't tell one apart from the other. While she cried, she couldn't rightly tell exactly what she cried for.

Was it for herself? For the fear and adrenaline drop that had only begun to hit her? Was it for the near loss of her consort? Did she cry for the guilt she felt for what may be her pivotal role in wrecking the future of his pack?

The more she tried to follow each thread, the more tangled they became and the more tears flowed. She was a sobbing mess by the time Margot gently helped her out of her ruined clothes and guided her into the glass walled shower.

While Margot used the wall panel to set the right temperature, Camille huddled under the spray, her arms clasped around her middle. Despite the fact that her side had been healed, she swore she could still feel the claw marks. That pain, at least, might fade.

She wasn't sure the confusion and guilt would be so easily banished.

CHAPTER TWENTY-SIX

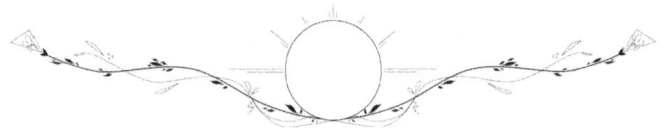

HOURS LATER, CAMILLE SAT ON HER LIVING ROOM couch alone. Theodore and Margot had reluctantly departed a short time before, claiming the need to visit a certain cougar shifter, though it took more than a few assurances on her part that she would be fine in their absence to get them to actually leave.

Theodore was dead-set on bringing her back to the Tower, but Camille refused. Even when she felt so very brittle, she knew that she would not be staying anywhere except in her coyote's den.

After her meltdown in the shower, where Margot had quietly let her bawl until the tears dried up, Camille felt marginally better. Not *good*, certainly, but settled. The tears had drained a deep well of guilt she had filled over the course of years, *decades,* in both drops and tidal waves. Now she felt... lighter.

You made your choice, she heard her mother say, her voice echoing from memory. *Now act on it.*

Whatever else Marian was, she never shied away from the consequences of her actions. There was a certain honor in that — even if those actions usually harmed those around her.

Camille did not want to be someone who regretted her choices. She did not want to be a woman who merely lamented fate and never faced it head-on.

She'd chosen to make a mess of her life, just as she'd chosen Viktor the instant before that bolt hit his shoulder.

Now she had to figure out how to go forward.

First, she packed an overnight bag. In went her clothing, her favorite heels, and her toiletries. The rest of her things could be brought to the den at a later date. Next, she called Viktor.

He sounded hoarse when he answered, "Cam?"

Her breath hitched. "I'm ready to come home. I'll take a car and be there in a couple hours, okay?"

"Oh, sweetheart." Viktor sounded like relief had knocked the wind out of him. "I'll come pick you up. I don't want you traveling across the city by yourself right now."

"But the pack—"

"Want their alpha's mate safe," he firmly insisted. "You wait there and pack your things. I'll be over in an hour."

Her chest ached. Gods, she couldn't wait to hold him. Once they figured out the mess she made, she planned on sinking her claws into him and never letting go.

"I'm going to make some calls before you get here," she explained, voice rough. "To... to cancel the negotiations."

There was a beat of silence before Viktor harshly replied, "Damn right, Cam. Damn *right.*"

Camille sucked in a shuddering breath. "See you soon."

"See you soon, sweetheart."

Some of the pressure in her chest eased. *Now comes the hard part.*

Dressed only in a long, baby blue silk robe, she curled her legs underneath her and stared at the tablet in her lap. Her skin still felt too sensitive to wear much else, though the pull had temporarily eased its grip on her. She had emails to write, calls to make. The first step in untangling her the disaster of her life was pulling out of all negotiations with the only excuse anyone would accept: she found her consort.

Under no other circumstance would it be deemed acceptable to end talks with the interested families so soon. Finding a consort was not favoritism. It was fate, *biology*. Now that she had locked herself in, there would be no going back, no choosing another. It was Viktor or it was no one. The families would understand that.

So she had to make the calls and write the emails, even if she desperately didn't want to.

Camille chewed her lip and considered asking Theodore to handle it for her. It wouldn't look that strange to have the head of her family take on the task, but it felt like the coward's way out. He *had* warned her, after all. She wasn't sure her pride could take a blow like stooping to ask him to clean up her mistakes.

It was bad enough that she would have to call Cyrus personally and tell him that the union that felt all but official was now little more than smoke.

No matter the discomfort, she owed it to him. He was a dear friend, and he'd brought her comfort in the worst years of her mother's illness with his steady support and gentle care. She adored his family and hoped he would find a bigger, better love than the pitiful thing she could have offered him.

Knowing he deserved to hear it first and not through a vicious grapevine, Camille set aside her tablet and picked up her phone. She sucked in a fortifying breath.

Cyrus picked up on the second ring. "Camille?" Warmth glowed in his deep voice, making the guilt so much worse.

"Hi, Cyrus," she croaked.

Of course, he immediately picked up that something was wrong. A trained monkey would have been able to hear it. His worry came through the line when he asked, "What's wrong? Is everything okay?"

Gods, she felt *awful*. Tears stung her already bloodshot eyes and her nose tickled in that infuriating way it did when she was about to really bawl. *Again.* "I'm okay," she weakly assured him. "I..."

She sucked in a shuddering breath and thought, *Just get it out there, Cam. Putting it off will only be worse.*

"I'm just... I'm sorry, Cyrus, but I have to call off negotiations."

There was a beat of stunned silence before he asked, voice hoarse, "I... Can I ask *why?*"

She sniffled and hugged her robe tightly around her chest. At any other moment, with almost anyone else, she would have been humiliated to be caught openly crying in front of another elf, but after the last two days... Well, she didn't think Cyrus would judge her for her lack of composure.

As long as he doesn't hate me after this.

"It's not you," she rushed out. "If I was going to join with anyone, it was always going to be you, Cyrus. I *adore* you." That was the truth. Even when she considered the other families, it had always been sweet, gentle Cyrus she had in mind. It was simply the fickleness of fate that made it impossible for her to love him.

Closing her stinging eyes, she continued, "I... found my consort, Cyrus."

"Oh." She could imagine the stunned expression on his face. "And you... you are going to bind yourself to him?"

"It's already started." Camille could feel Viktor in her pores even then, hours after she'd left him. He lived in her skin now. There would be no going back. *Ever.*

She heard Cyrus's long exhale before he asked, "Are you happy, at least? Do you like him?"

Her heart squeezed. He sounded so hopeful for her it hurt. "Yes," she answered, finally admitting it aloud. "I love him."

It didn't matter that twenty years had passed. It didn't matter that they'd grown into new versions of themselves, that there were so many parts of their lives they had yet to share. Camille fell in love with him the first time he snuck into the Tower to visit her as a grinning, rain-soaked coyote, and she fell in love with him again when he begged her not to leave him on that beach.

Even when his heart began to fail, he begged her.

Despite years of trying to bury it, that feeling had only grown with every bit of news, every glimpse of him she dared catch. Every victory made her proud, and every whispered rumor about him made her ache with envy.

She had never stopped loving him, no matter how hard she tried.

Cyrus made a soft sound of relief in the back of his throat. "Then it's okay, Camille. I'm... I'm sad for us, but I'm happy for *you*. I only want the best for you. Finding a consort is a dream, and I'm sure he'll be able to offer you more than I ever could have."

"Oh, Cyrus," she breathed, "you would have made me happy, too. It's just..."

"Different," he finished for her.

"Yes."

"It's all right. I'll be okay, Camille. As long as I know this is what you want, then I can handle it." He paused. "My mother will be relieved, at any rate."

A startled laugh burst from her lips. "Did she dislike the idea of me joining the family so much?"

He sounded scandalized when he answered, *"No,* no! She just never liked the idea of me in a union, that's all. She wanted me to find my consort. You know how much my mother likes you. She calls you her *sharp little gem."*

Camille swiped at her eyes, unspeakably relieved to hear some levity returning to Cyrus's baritone. "She is lovely. Your whole family is. I really looked forward to getting to know everyone better." Her chin wobbled. "I wanted to be a part of your family, Cyrus."

"You still can," he promised her. "We love you. You will still be my friend, Camille. Nothing has changed there. Whenever you want to stay with us, you can."

"I'd love that. Maybe after..." Camille blanched, trying to think of some distant point in the future when she might be able to visit her dear friend. When could she do that? She struggled to imagine what *tomorrow* would look like, let alone months, years from that point.

"After things are settled," she finally finished, stumbling over the words.

"I understand," he replied, soft and gentle, like he didn't want to spook her. "This is a vulnerable time for you and your consort. Take as much time as you need."

"Gods, Cyrus, you are such a good man."

He laughed, but there was a note of self-deprecation in it that rankled her. "Not very elvish though, am I? I suppose I should be snarling or ready to fight right now. That's what a real elf would do, right?"

What he meant was a *dominant* elf.

Cyrus was elvish down to his bones, but he wasn't aggressive, didn't have the territorial streak that so many elves were born with. He was a kind soul, and she hoped that one day he would find a consort who would protect that softness in him, not demand something he couldn't give.

"You are *perfect,*" she told him, a low growl in her voice. "Anyone who tells you otherwise can come see me."

"Yeah?" There was a smile in that single word, as big and beautiful and soft as he was.

Relief made her dizzy. *He doesn't hate me. Thank the gods.* "Yeah," she answered, "and I'll send what's left of them to your mother."

Cyrus's laugh boomed through the speaker. "They'd never find the pieces!"

She mustered a smile, answering, "Good."

"Well, I don't know about *good,* but..."

"Certainly efficient, I thi—" Camille was interrupted by a knock on her door; two quick, hard beats that made her jump. The proximity alarm chimed.

Sliding her legs out from under her, she rushed out, "I'm sorry, Cyrus, someone is at my door. I'll call you back, all right?"

"Sure. Take care of yourself, okay?"

Fondness for Cyrus made her chest tight when she answered, "Of course. You do the same."

The line went dead. Dropping her phone onto the couch, Camille cinched the silk tie at her waist. She padded out of the living room and down the hall toward the front door. Some deep instinct told her it wasn't Viktor at the door, so she assumed it was either Margot or another relative sent to make sure she wasn't a sobbing mess on the floor.

It was for that reason that she didn't run to throw on something more appropriate, or at least put on a shawl to cover her neck, which was scandalously bared — an open invitation to bite or to slash, depending on one's mood. Kaz wouldn't care, and a guard sent to check on her would never say a word even if she'd answered the door stark naked.

Exhausted by the events of the day, she didn't think to check the intercom to ask who stood on the other side of the door. She merely unlocked it, disengaged the ward that acted as an extra seal, and pulled it open.

For a second, all she could do was stare at the man who stood on the other side.

Taller than her, with wide shoulders and long, muscled legs, he was dressed in a dark houndstooth coat and smart mahogany monk shoes polished to a high shine. One hand, gloved in supple brown leather with matte white claw-caps, loosely clutched a long velvet box by his muscled thigh.

His skin was a luminous teal and his features were aquiline, sharpened by age and framed by lashes, brows, and a neatly trimmed beard of deep green. His hair was swept back from his face in one sleek wave. He was strikingly handsome, but that wasn't what took her breath away.

It was the air of pure, unfiltered menace that radiated like a chill around him. She had never met him before — had never even spoken to him — but she *knew* this man.

Camille froze, one hand on the door knob, and found herself

numbly greeting him. "Epifanio, I... didn't expect to see you here."

She felt his gaze dip down her body, taking in her thin silk robe and her bare throat with a single, cool glance. His voice was a silky, emotionless purr when he replied, "Clearly."

Camille felt her cheeks heat. She knew she looked like a mess with her unkempt hair and her bloodshot eyes. Never in a million years would she have willingly shown a predator like *Epifanio Luz* such a vulnerable image of herself.

Feeling wrongfooted and with no other polite option, she took a step back and gestured for him to come in. *Well, I was going to email him anyway,* she thought, watching him cross the threshold.

She thought that Margot's brother Olivier was intimidating, but he at least had *some* warmth to him. This man, however, looked like he could snap her neck without a thought. Standing in her entryway, he seemed to suck up all the air.

Wishing she could scurry away but knowing that would only make her look weak, Camille led him into the living room and, summoning her most aloof voice, said, "This is highly unusual. I was expecting an invitation to a meeting from your father, not a man on my doorstep."

Epifanio didn't look even a little fazed by the barely concealed reproach. Pulling one hand out of his pocket, he unbuttoned his coat at the same time that he tossed the velvet box onto the gold-edged marble coffee table.

"I don't like to waste time. My father wants this union and I don't like leaving things undone." His eyes, a clear bottle green, pinned her in place. "We're finishing negotiations today. Next week, we will fly out to my chalet in Switzerland. While there, you will sign the paperwork and this will be done. We will hopefully conceive offspring in that time. What you do after that is your business."

Camille gripped the back of the couch, unable to mask her surprise. "Excuse me?"

One dark green brow lifted. "What about that did you not understand?"

Indignation flared. Fighting the urge to bare her fangs, she answered, "The part where you assumed I've decided to join with you."

"Of course you have." He tipped his head toward the coffee table, where the velvet box lay. "That is your union necklace. I expect you to wear it whenever you are in public."

It was her turn to raise her eyebrows. Stepping around the couch, she reached for the box with morbid curiosity. Popping the lid with the tip of her claw, she peered inside to find a necklace that would cover her neck from chin to clavicle. It was absolutely *bursting* with diamonds and vivid green emeralds.

Revulsion crawled over her skin like thousands of tiny, many-legged bugs. *He expects me to wear this?*

She loved fashion and jewels more than she probably should, but there was something about wearing such an ostentatious display of wealth — *his* wealth, *his* claim — that made her feel ill. There was not a chance she would ever wear a sign of Epifanio's ownership on her person.

Camille stared at the glittering necklace and realized, with a deep inner stillness, that the only necklace she wanted was her consort's bite.

Slowly, she looked over the lid of the box to find her guest watching her, his expression inscrutable. While she digested her own revelation, she asked, "Might I ask why? Union necklaces are awfully old fashioned."

Somehow, Epifanio's expression became chillier, the lines of his face starker, more deadly. "Las Vegas is not like San Francisco, Miss Solbourne. It is considerably more dangerous. Once you're mine, your protection will be my responsibility. That necklace will let everyone know who you belong to — and who they'll be dealing with if you are harmed."

"Right." Camille closed the box with a snap. "Well, I'm afraid that isn't going to be necessary."

Epifanio tilted his head to one side. It was a purely predatory action, the same way a lion might move a second before it pounces on the gazelle. "Oh? And why is that?"

Reaching over the couch to offer him the box, she answered, "Because I will not be joining with you."

He made no move to take the box, but leaned forward until both of his hands were braced on the back of the couch, his shoulders rounded in a hunting crouch. The tips of his matte white claws pricked at the velvet cushions. "That's not how this works, Miss Solbourne."

"I'm afraid it is." Camille swallowed her instinctive reaction to the sight of an elf much more dominant than her leaning closer, challenging her. The instinctive knowledge that Epifanio could maul her with one swipe of his claws was oppressive. The air he carried around him *demanded* submission.

But she was more than instinct, more than the beast that howled in the heart of all elves. She was a woman, too, and more than that, she was a *Solbourne*, a Dia, the last of her mother's line, and no shrinking violet. If Epifanio wanted to intimidate someone into submission, he picked the wrong fucking woman.

Delicately placing the box on the cushion in front of him, she continued, "I will not be entering into a union with *anyone.* I've called off negotiations."

"Why?"

She raised her chin. "Because I've found my consort."

Astonishingly, Epifanio didn't hesitate before he crisply replied, "Why should that matter?"

"I— what do you mean, *why should that matter?*" Camille made an expansive gesture to the room at large, and then at herself. "I'm taken."

"So?" Totally unbothered, he rose up from his crouched position to button his coat. Not once did his eyes rest on the velvet box — to him, millions of dollars in jewels seemed to matter about as much as a piece of litter. "I don't care if you have a consort as long as you remain publicly loyal to me. Have as many bastards as you want. I don't care."

The end of his sentence caught her ear in a strange way. *To me,* he said. Not to his family. *To him.* Goosebumps broke out across her skin as intuition whispered, *Watch out. There's trouble there.*

"You would be fine with me loving another man?" Camille peered at him suspiciously. It wasn't uncommon, of course, but with an elf like Epifanio, she struggled to imagine he would handle sharing *anything* well.

"I don't need you to love me. I don't even need us to be sexually compatible," he replied. His smile was sharp and close-lipped, as if he had already decided that was the case. With only a look, he'd deemed her somehow *incompatible.* She had absolutely no desire to find out why. "I just need your name."

"Well, you won't be getting it." Camille had no desire to provoke him, nor to make an enemy out of the Luz family, but she also knew that dominant elves didn't respond to anything except force. To them, everything and everyone was a nail. If they simply hit it hard enough, it would do what they wanted it to. The only way to be heard was to hit back.

Bracing her hands on her hips, Camille pretended like she was not alone in her apartment with a greater predator, nor that she was in nothing but a silk robe, with not even a stitch of clothing underneath.

"I will not be joining with you, Mr. Luz," she told him firmly. "Even if I had not found my consort, I don't believe we are compatible in any way and likely would have chosen another. I appreciate your offer and am sorry for any inconvenience this may have caused you, but our negotiation is finished. You may go."

A tense silence settled between them. Camille worked hard to maintain eye contact with him, to keep her body language loose and unaffected, though she wanted to shrink back, to tense in preparation for an attack.

She hadn't heard any rumors that he was particularly violent — no moreso than any other elf was, really — but she was no fool.

Denying a man like Epifanio, with no understanding of his temper, was a risk. Attacking her would be a damn foolish thing to do, but when an elvish temper lit, reason was the first thing to go.

So she made herself look as at ease as possible. She did not step back, fearing that it might trigger an instinct to chase, and she did not break eye contact. Camille held herself perfectly still and waited.

At length, Epifanio flexed his jaw hard enough to make his fangs squeak. He reached down to pick up the box. Curling his long, gloved fingers around its velvet surface, he said, "I am not a man most people feel comfortable saying no to, Miss Solbourne. My father even less so. He won't be pleased."

Your father can kiss my purple ass. Camille held the thought in with a swift bite of her tongue. Flesh stinging, she said instead, "That is unfortunate. However, I'm sure you can convince him that there are better alternatives out there."

Tucking the box into the deep pocket of his houndstooth coat, he replied, "Doubtful. Once my father gets the hunger for something, he is relentless."

"That is your problem, not mine."

Epifanio's eyes met hers. They were a beautiful, almost shocking green — the green of new leaves, or perhaps of some vicious poison. "For now," he purred, lips quirking in a dark smile. "I can't promise you he'll take this insult lying down."

Camille's brows snapped down. "What are you—"

The hair on the back of her neck rose. Her lungs seized, for just a moment, as an animal awareness settled over her. *Viktor's here.*

She didn't have time to panic before her proximity alarm chimed. He didn't even bother knocking, but simply called out, "Sweetheart, it's me."

Before she could react, Epifanio turned on his heel and strode toward the door. "Ah, this must be the consort," he drawled, ignoring Camille's choked protest. "I think I'd like to meet the man who stole you from under my nose, Miss Solbourne."

She scrambled around the couch, dashing toward his retreating figure. "Epifanio, do *not*—"

"*Cam, who's in there with you?*" Viktor's voice was guttural, nearly unintelligible beneath the deep, coyote growl.

Shit!

She sprinted, but Epifanio had a head start and longer legs than her. Reaching the door first, he twisted the knob and jerked it open to reveal Viktor's still form on the other side. Camille caught sight of him from around Epifanio's arm and gasped.

His brows were drawn down, his lip lifted in a feral snarl, and his eyes were a glowing coyote gold. His features were stretched oddly, caught somewhere between coyote and man, and an air of promised violence hung thick around him.

Her heart skipped a beat. Even half-shifted, he was *beautiful.*

The beast in her nearly wilted with relief at the sight of him. At last, her consort had come.

If only he had better timing!

"Who the fuck are you?" Viktor barked.

Epifanio casually tucked one hand into his pocket, as if he wasn't standing only a foot away from a shifter very near a mating-induced freak out. "I'm Epifanio Luz." He stepped six inches to the left and nodded, revealing Camille, who stood stock still behind him. "I am here to finalize our union."

Oh, you rat bastard. Camille snapped out of her shocked daze with a burst of fury. Rounding on her unwanted guest, she bit out, "I was *rejecting* your offer, Mr. Luz!"

He lifted one shoulder in an elegant shrug. "I'll be honest, I didn't expect a shifter." He *tsked.* "You still want to turn down my suit, Miss Solbourne? I wouldn't mind if you kept him as a pet. After all, we would only need to have sex once or twice a week until we produced a—"

Viktor crossed the space between them in a blink of an eye.

Nearly nose to nose with the elf, he murmured, "Finish that sentence and you're a dead man, *Epifanio.*"

Amusement colored his low voice when he replied, "Oh?"

"Yeah, *oh.*" Viktor smiled, but it was not one of the grins she was used to. It carried nothing but the promise of violence. "The only one Camille will be with is *me.* The only one she'll have cubs with is *me.* Now get the fuck out of my mate's apartment."

"Viktor!" Camille exclaimed, worry making her voice higher than usual. Cold sweat broke out over her chest.

Gods, she could *not* watch him get in a fight with Epifanio. She just couldn't. Watching helplessly as Margot struggled to save his life the night before was enough trauma for a lifetime. She didn't need to see him test his mettle on Epifanio, too.

Epifanio lifted a hand over his shoulder in a lazy, placating gesture. "Don't worry, Miss Solbourne, I don't have any plans to turn your mutt into mince meat today." Smoothly stepping forward until Viktor was forced to move aside, allowing him out of the apartment, he added, "Viktor *Hamilton,* I presume?"

Viktor swiftly took his place in the doorway, his hands shooting out to grasp both sides of the door jamb to completely block Epifanio's view inside. Camille rushed over to him. Hands spreading across the expanse of his back, she felt the trembling tension in the bunched muscles.

"Yes," he grated, leaning slightly backward, into her touch.

"Fascinating," he drawled. "Well, it was a delight, Miss Solbourne. I wish you all the best." She heard the hard heels of his shoes striking the floor with each measured step as he began to walk away from her apartment. The beat paused. "Oh, one more thing."

Viktor let loose a rattling snarl. *"What?"*

"I heard something interesting through the grapevine the other day," he answered, coolly amused. "I like to make it my business to know when someone offers a lot of money for murder. You might want to know that there's a bounty on your head,

Alpha Hamilton. I do believe someone is trying to have you killed."

Without missing a beat, Viktor snapped, "Old news. Now get the fuck out."

With one quick step back, he grasped the door and swung it back into place with *bang!*

Epifanio's laughter carried down the hall as he walked away.

CHAPTER TWENTY-SEVEN

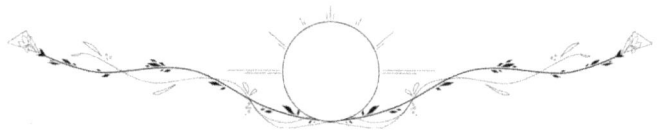

"Vik, I—"

He swung around to face his mate, breathing hard and fast. Grabbing her by the shoulders, he bent his neck to bury his face in the soft, fragrant skin of her bare throat. "Give me a minute," he rasped, struggling for calm, for some part of the man who would not go hunting for the elf who thought he could enter *his* mate's den.

The coyote bit and snarled inside him, worked into a frenzy by the fever that raked every nerve, every instinct. It couldn't fathom the sight he was treated to when Camille's door swung open. It was bad enough to know she'd left *their* den, but to find her with an unfamiliar, obviously dangerous man in her apartment, when she was dressed in nothing but a long silk robe, made every instinct scream in enraged protest.

The fever was relentless. It didn't understand reason, nor listen to caution. It was a tidal wave built by generation after generation of intense, bloody competition. Securing a partner had never been easy, after all. It took cunning, tenacity, and single-minded focus to win a prized mate, to build that sacred bond that rose above all other loyalty.

His coyote, separate from him and yet the same being, howled from a primordial place, one where competition had to be cut down with tooth and claw: *Not bitten, not safe, not mine!*

Viktor felt like he was losing his damn mind.

Trying desperately to calm himself down, lest the fever push him to do something stupid, Viktor walked them back until Camille's back hit the wall. He smoothed his hands down her arms, calluses catching on the soft fabric of her robe, until he reached the tips of her fingers.

No claws, he thought, for the second time that day. Pride swelled as protective rage began to bleed away, replaced by the pounding need to assert his claim. Wrapping his hands around her waist, he dragged his parted lips over the column of her throat, tracing the tendons and muscle that made such an elegant arch.

"Vik," she sighed, pressing her hands against his stomach. Muscle rippled under her firm touch. "I'm sorry. I had no idea he would—"

"Shh." He dared to nip her throat, teeth grazing a part of her he knew she rarely exposed to anyone besides close family, and felt her spine arch. He had only seen her throat once, so many years ago, when he convinced her to sneak into one of the many elvish training facilities late one night to swim in a pool.

Viktor groaned at the memory of what the sight of her in only her black panties and bra had done to him. He was too afraid to touch her then — gods, she was so out of his league it wasn't even funny — but he could touch her *now.*

Breathing hotly against her skin, he rasped, "We're not talking about *him* now, sweetheart."

He felt her breathy sigh ruffle his hair. "Then what are we going to talk about?"

"Nothing," he answered, fingers moving to the silken sash tied around her waist. He traced the topography of its bunches and twists before he found the knot. It unraveled with one sharp tug. "I don't want words right now. I just want my mate."

Her fingers curled into the shirt covering his stomach. There was no prick of claws, and for a moment he was stunned by the vulnerability she must have felt every time she came near him. Clawless, with her choices dictated by biology firmly out of her control, unsure of his affection — no wonder she had accused him of torturing her. With him, his fierce elf was helpless.

The trust it took to let him near, after everything, stunned him, humbled him, and aroused him beyond his ability to articulate.

"You have me," she whispered, so soft his coyote hearing barely picked it up.

Chest aching, Viktor pushed aside the tearing need to claim for just a moment. He lifted his head to peer into her face, needing to see the truth in her eyes when he asked, "Do I?"

She swallowed thickly, but didn't look away. "Yes," she answered, stronger. "Yes, Vik. I don't know how we'll figure everything out but I know— I *know* that I'm yours. That you're mine. You have me, body and soul."

He let the sash fall from his fingertips. Reaching up to cup her cheeks, he forced her to look him directly in the eye. There could be no second thoughts about this. No redos or cancellations — not simply because it would break him to let her go a second time, but because there was more than just their hearts on the line.

"I need you to be sure," he ground out, "not just about you and me, but about everything. If we do this, you become alpha of my pack, sweetheart. You won't just belong to me anymore. You'll belong to all of us. Are you okay with that?"

This was about more than lust, more than the fever. There was no way they could have sex and he *wouldn't* bite her. It was as deeply ingrained in him as the need to shift was. The need would override everything else.

And once she took his bite, everything would change. They would be mates in the eyes of the law and under the power of the gods. They would be leaders of their pack. It was vital that she understand those things before they went any further.

Camille's violet eyes searched his face, but he didn't see doubt there. "Would your pack accept me? Benjamin didn't seem to think so."

"Considering you saved my life? Yeah, I think they will." In fact, he *knew* they would, since he'd spent the better part of the day going from den to den, speaking with every family. He was relieved when every single one of them asked about his mate.

They were wary of outsiders, certainly, but Camille had scaled a cliff and took down a shooter on her own for their alpha. That sort of thing went a long way to earning trust. The problem was that now he *really* had to share her.

Viktor smoothed his thumbs over her cheekbones, saying, "Don't mind Benny. He's just doing his job." He sucked in a deep, calming breath through his teeth. "If you take my bite, he'll accept you."

He felt the cool touch of her fingertips sliding under the hem of his shirt like a tickling trail of water droplets. He shuddered when she asked, "And what about the Alliance?"

"One of their alphas tried to kill a prospective member," he replied, voice flat. "They don't have anything to stand on. Unless they want to come off looking like they sanction what Andreas tried to do, then they'll let us in."

Palms met the skin of his stomach next, making the muscles of his abdomen clench reflexively. His cock ached and his instincts were in a whirling rage, but Viktor pushed it all aside to focus on his mate, on the thoughts he could see churning behind her eyes.

"What happens next, then?"

A heavy weight settled on his shoulders the moment he heard his attacker was a cougar shifter, and it had only gotten heavier as the hours passed and the reality of what Alpha Andreas did set in. Viktor knew that only two options lay before them now. Neither of them were free of bloodshed.

"In the unlikeliest scenario, the Alliance will back Andreas and escalate things with the EVP. Teddy will have to bring it to the Congress floor." Unspoken between them was the specter of the Great War, which impacted so much of their lives, despite the fact that both of them were born decades after its end. "If they choose that route, then it may come to war."

A representative of the Alliance had attempted to assassinate a political leader — small and relatively unimportant though he was — on EVP soil. That could not go unaddressed.

That was the worst case scenario, but the best case wasn't much better. Firming his jaw, Viktor broke the news to her in a grim voice. "Far more likely is they won't back Andreas. If that happens, it will be one on one."

In the shifter way, the transgression would be met claw for claw, fang for fang: Viktor versus Andreas.

If he won, then Andreas would die and the future of his pack would be left in Viktor's hands. He could choose to expel them from the Alliance, though he didn't foresee doing so.

If he lost, then he would die before he ever even got the chance to enjoy matehood, to see his pack flourish.

Viktor tried not to flinch when he watched the blood drain from Camille's face. Her normally luminous lavender skin paled to an ashen gray when she whispered hoarsely, "You... you would fight him?"

"Yes."

For a moment, she simply stared at him, uncomprehending, before the slow creep of horror stole across her expression. Her voice broke when she said, "That's how my father died, Vik."

Gods, he wished he could take the fear out of her — just pluck it out with his fingers and crush it in his palm. "I know, sweetheart," he breathed, closing the distance between them to press his lips against her forehead in a hard kiss. "I know."

Everyone knew what happened to Theron Solbourne. It was in the history books, after all.

Theron Solbourne was Thaddeus's twin and at the height of his brother's tyrannical rule, he challenged him for the sovereignty. The citizens of the EVP were terrorized by the shadow Patrol, Thaddeus's secret arm of the military, and the Five Families who ruled the biggest cities were in open rebellion. At any moment, it looked as though the EVP would explode in a hail of bloodshed.

Though they were identical twins, and despite the fact that Theron was fighting for his mate and his unborn children, he was no match for the sheer, coldhearted ferocity of Thaddeus II. Where Theron still had a measure of love left for the sovereign, his brother had none.

He showed no mercy, no recognition that it was his brother under his claws. Theron died a brutal, bloody death, and left behind a pregnant mate traumatized by his loss.

Viktor couldn't imagine how it would feel to Camille to know that *her* mate might find himself in a similar position, though in vastly different circumstances.

"Whatever happens, I will not die, Cam," he promised her. "This is just a fact of life. Andreas is getting old and he's let anger make him irrational. If it comes down to a fight between us, I'll win it."

Camille's fingers spasmed on his stomach. Her blunt claws scraped his skin when she whispered, "I can't lose you, Vik."

"You won't." That he knew with absolute certainty. He had not waited twenty years and come this far to lose her now.

She leaned forward until her lips grazed his cheek. "Then I can handle everything else. I'll learn what it means to become part of a pack. I'll follow you anywhere you go. I'll even stop wearing heels if we move somewhere *really* rural. I don't care." Her breath hitched. "I just can't watch you die, Vik."

He wrapped his arms around her and crushed her to his chest. His heart slammed against his ribs as the enormity of the moment hit him all at once. *My mate wants me.*

She wasn't just signing up to be with him, but to be part of his pack, to stand by his side as they charted a new course into the future. Relief made his head spin.

"I would *never* ask you to stop wearing heels," he said, voice thick with emotion. "Not in a million years, Cam. I like watching you walk in them too much. Though I do think you'd look pretty fucking hot in a pair of hiking boots."

He felt her smile against his jaw. "Yeah?"

Sliding his arms down, Viktor dared to slip his hands past the lapels of her silk robe. He smoothed his palms over her ribs and down, until he could dig his fingertips into the soft flesh of her lithe hips. "Gods save me," he muttered, drawing her closer. "Are you not wearing any panties?"

She scraped her fangs against the corner of his jaw. "No."

Viktor swore he felt all the blood rush past his waistband in one huge rush. Thumbing the bows of her hip bones, he growled, "Wait, you weren't wearing anything underneath this when that elf was here?"

What was once a gentle scrape became a not-so-gentle nip. "Didn't know he was coming over, remember?"

Didn't matter. The possessive beast that lived in his heart only understood that a rival had been very, very close to his vulnerable, alluring mate, and that couldn't be borne.

So long as her neck remained bare, she could be stolen from him, and that was utterly unacceptable to every part of him.

Viktor skimmed one of his hands up, feeling the smooth expanse of skin and finely made bone of her side. Margot had done a magnificent job of healing the rest of Camille's injuries, it seemed, so he didn't have to worry about hurting her. *Good,* he thought, moving his hand back down to her hip.

Without warning, he hoisted her up, guiding her to wrap her sleek thighs around his hips. Camille squeaked and clung to his neck as he began to walk them back to where he knew the master bedroom must be.

"What are you doing?" she gasped, clutching at the back of his shirt. "I'm heavier than you!"

He gave her thighs an appreciative squeeze. "Yeah, and I'm *stronger* than you."

It didn't matter that she had those elvish bones — dense like heavy metal — he'd carry his mate if it pleased him. And it *did*

please him. The sway and bump of her body against his, the tantalizing view of all that naked skin under her open robe, the knowledge that he was only minutes from finally, *finally* claiming his
mate was almost *too* pleasing.

As they passed through the double doors that led to the
master bedroom, Camille dug her fingers into his hair and nuzzled
his ear. "Are you? Are you *really* stronger than me?" she purred.

Fuck me.

Viktor nearly stumbled. Her scent permeated the lavish
bedroom. Fresh desire perfumed the air. Her blunted claws
scratched at his scalp as she traced the shape of his ear with her
lips. It was all enough to make anyone weak-kneed. "I…"

"I guess we'll have to find out."

Without warning, Camille grasped two fistfuls of his hair and
pulled, forcing his head back. Lips hovering a hairsbreadth from
his, she challenged, "If you think you're stronger than me, *mate,*
then you'll have to prove it."

Heat exploded in his veins — popping and hissing like magic,
like the ecstasy of a shift. Lust was all-consuming, as was the need
to meet the challenge she lay before him like the sweetest offering.
If his mate wanted him to prove his worth, then he was more than
happy to—

Fangs sank into his lower lip in a swift, playful bite, and
Viktor saw *stars.*

Chapter Twenty-Eight

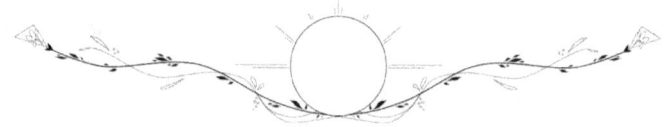

THE PULL WAS A MONSTER. IT CONSUMED EVERYTHING in her, made Viktor her only focus, her only craving — and yet, in that moment, Camille understood that it could also be *joyous.*

When she wasn't busy fighting it, the pull could be a sweet drug, a steadily unspooling warmth that tied her to her consort. It made her giddy. It made her combative. It made her want to pin him down and lick him all over. It made her *hunger.*

So when he playfully asserted his strength surpassed hers, Camille did not fight the spark of challenge that made her blood heat. Instead, she bowed to it.

Finally, her beast sighed, *we can play.*

She sank her fangs into his lip and everything in her howled with victory. When Viktor jolted, rough hands sliding down her thighs to grip her backside in a deliciously bruising hold, she felt a rush of power so heady, it made her head spin.

Viktor stumbled toward the bed, his hips grinding hard against hers. She felt the hard ridge of his cock through the rough denim of his jeans. Her skin was hyper-sensitive, her core already wet and aching for him. The rough scrape of fabric combined with the insistent rolling of his hips sent a sharp bolt of pleasure through her.

Camille gasped, back arching, as Viktor dropped her on the bed. He remained standing. Towering over her, he smoothed his hands down her legs to lock them around her knees, keeping her spread and pressed against him.

"Fucking beautiful," he rasped, staring down at where her cunt pressed against his fly. His eyes, coyote gold, roved over her, taking in her splayed arms and spread robe with an unmistakably feral look. "My mate is gorgeous and ready for me, isn't she?"

Flushed with desire and yet unwilling to give in so easily, Camille lifted her lip in a snarl. She twisted her hips, attempting to dislodge his grip and wriggle away. "Maybe I'm not," she challenged. "Do you think you don't have to work for me? For *this?*"

Instinct was a cacophony in her mind, egging her on, demanding she prick and prod until he wrestled her down and earned the privilege of her submission. Could he make her bend without hurting her? Alternatively, could he yield to her own dominance? Could he *play?*

Coyote eyes gleamed down at her. A dribble of bright red blood slid down from the tiny puncture wound decorating his bottom lip. It looked particularly wicked when he grinned.

"Sweetheart," he purred, "I'm a shifter — we *always* put in the work in bed."

Viktor swooped down, pinning her lower body to the edge of the bed, and closed his lips over one pert nipple.

"Ah!" Camille dug her fingers into the soft duvet cover, her back arching helplessly as he bit down on her sensitive flesh. It wasn't gentle. She could feel his fangs extending a mere breath before the sharp sting of another bite made her whole body jerk. She choked on a cry as her hips rolled into his, seeking friction that his weight refused to grant her.

Tongue soothing the sting, Viktor made a low humming noise of satisfaction. He switched to the other breast, clearly determined to give it the same treatment, but even blinding pleasure couldn't smother the need for challenge. Before he could bite her again, Camille dug her hands into his blond hair and wrenched his head back.

The move took him by surprise, giving her the opportunity to wrest herself from his grip. She was nearly out from under him before Viktor managed to pin her down again, this time with her thighs pinned to the bed, opening her obscenely wide for his perusal.

Rearing backward, he roughly tore his hair out of her hands and stared down at her with a wild-eyed gaze. "I am *not* letting you go," he snarled, punctuating each word with a hard thrust of his hips against her core. "You are *mine*. This cunt is *mine*. Do you understand me?"

Camille looked up at him boldly, defiantly, even as her heart sang a fierce, possessive song. "Prove it then, *alpha.*"

Viktor swore. Pressing one hand down against her stomach, pinning her, he reached down to swiftly undo the brass button of his jeans and then the zipper. Shoving his pants and briefs down as much as he cared to, he once more wrenched her legs as wide as they could go. His cock sprang free between them, flushed and perfect, the tip gleaming wetly with pearly pre-come.

The sight made her so hungry, so full of empty, aching *need*, that Camille began to squirm in earnest. Not to get away, but to get closer. When she made a halfhearted effort to pull her legs back together, seeking leverage, he gave the tender skin of her inner thighs a threatening squeeze and barked, *"Still!"*

Instinct responded at once. Camille froze. Even her chest stopped its quick movement as she held her breath, watching and waiting to see what he would do next.

Viktor was breathing hard. A look of dark satisfaction crossed his face when he slowly lifted his hands from her legs and she didn't move so much as an inch. "There's my good mate," he rasped, eyes locked on her slick skin even when he reached backward to tear off his faded t-shirt. He tossed it over his shoulder carelessly. That done, he swept his hands back down her thighs to frame her sex. "Look how pretty your cunt is, sweetheart, all wet and ready for your mate."

Camille's lungs started to burn. Sucking in a huge lungful of air saturated with the combined scents of their desire, she let out a soft, plaintive sound. It was a whimper that would have shamed her in any other moment except this one.

Here, now, she did not feel powerless in the face of her overwhelming need for him — she felt stronger than she ever had before.

"Shh. Let me look." Viktor used his thumbs to spread her even more. He hissed an oath under his breath as he traced every inch of her wet, swollen flesh with his eyes. She clawed at the duvet under her, aroused by the greedy expression he wore, the feeling of his hands on her starved skin.

"Touch me," she begged, momentarily giving up the dominance game. "Touch me, *please.*"

Viktor's eyes darted up to meet hers. He didn't say anything for several torturous heartbeats. At last, he breathed, "That is the sweetest sound I've ever heard."

Biting his lip, he fisted his cock and, keeping her spread with one hand, pressed the flushed head against her channel, coating it in her arousal, before he slid it up against the swollen bud of her clitoris.

Camille cried out as pleasure seared her. His skin was so hot compared to hers, the contact so potent, so lush with much needed pheromones, that it immediately overloaded her senses. A hard, fast orgasm held itself just out of reach as he began to rock himself against her, using his hand to keep himself pressed tightly against every sensitive nerve. With each pass, she felt the silken slide of the head of his cock, then every velvety inch of him, contrasted with the scrape of denim against her inner thighs.

Unable to do much else, Camille reached down to hook her fingers in his dangling belt loops. "Please, please, please," she begged, raw and desperate. "Please, Vik, I need—"

"I've got you, sweetheart," he growled. "I know what you

need."

He began to move faster, harder, increasing the pressure and the friction until, with a tearing cry, Camille's orgasm rippled through her. Ears buzzing, she followed Viktor with her gaze as he pulled back from her, curled his fingers around his cock, and gave himself several hard pumps before he came — directly on her cunt.

It was perhaps the most erotic sight she'd ever witnessed: the look on his face as he came; the ropes of pearly white release that stood out so starkly against her lavender flesh; the sight of his free hand moving to smear it into her skin in an entirely animalistic claim.

Camille panted, both sated and unfulfilled. Her skin prickled with the need for more. More contact. More of him. Always, always more of him.

When he reached down to untangle her fingers from his jeans, she let out a keening noise of protest, the fear that he was leaving her jumping to the forefront of her mind. "Vik, please, don't—"

Humming a reassuring note, he slowly lowered himself to his knees. She sat up on her elbows to watch him as he slung her legs over his shoulders and took a deep breath. A look of pure hunger tightened the lines of his features when he said, "Fuck. Nothing smells as good as you and me, sweetheart."

Before she could even start to think of a reply — almost certainly an enthusiastic agreement — Viktor buried his head between her thighs. His tongue, flat and hot and smoother than hers, swept over her from core to clitoris. In one long stroke, he gathered up the taste of them both and groaned long and low.

"Taste so fucking good together." He wrapped his hands around her upper thighs and jerked her toward the edge of the bed, plastering her to his hungry mouth. Suddenly boneless, Camille slid her fingers into his hair and held on for dear life as he tasted every part of her.

Instead of staring at the gently swaying chandelier over their heads, she closed her eyes and savored every stroke of his tongue, every noise of deep satisfaction he made. Nothing in her life could have prepared her for the tactile pleasure of his touch, nor the rush of power she felt when he knelt for her, lavishing her with his lips, teeth, and tongue.

As was expected, Cyrus had done this for her too, but it was nothing like when Viktor kissed her, licked her, *bit* her. When he went down on her, it was like he'd been starving, like he couldn't get enough no matter how much he ate. Her other experiences had been decent enough — reverent, even — but not like *this*. Never like this.

Camille felt the slow rise of another, deeper orgasm as he circled her clitoris with his tongue, wringing almost too much pleasure out of her. The fingers in his hair flexed as she began to rock her hips. Words spilled out of her, though she couldn't be sure what she said.

When he closed his lips around that hyper-sensitive bundle of nerves and began to suck in a swift, pulsing rhythm, Camille shattered.

Her muscles tensed as she tossed her head back and opened her mouth on a silent cry. Viktor murmured against her, something fierce and urgent, as he slid his fingers in and out, feeling the way her cunt rippled with each rolling wave.

It took longer to come down from her second orgasm than the first, mainly because Viktor refused to let it die. He kept coaxing her, working her from inside and out, demanding everything she had to give.

"That's my mate," he kept saying, voice a guttural rumble. "That's it. Give me more. I want all of you. I want you to feel me fucking *everywhere,* Cam."

"I do. I *do,*" she babbled. Gods, she was so sensitive the pleasure had begun to edge into pain. "Vik, please!"

He didn't stop. Instead, he began to thrust his fingers faster, harder, as if to make a point. "Tell me who your mate is. *Tell me who you belong to.*"

Camille twisted her hips, caught between needing more and

desperation to take a break, to get away. Instinct tangled with those warring desires. Speech was impossible, especially when he dropped his head to give her a punishing bite.

Her whole body jerked as a scream tore from her throat. "Gods!"

"Tell me!"

"You!" she finally managed. "You! I'm yours!"

"Fucking *finally.*" With that, Viktor suddenly released her. She lay there, dazed and out of breath, as he took a step back and hastily divested himself of the rest of his clothing.

He has such beautiful skin, she thought, watching in awe as he revealed all that lean perfection. A lifetime in the sun had burnished him a rich gold. Every line of his body, every small scar and crisp, blond hair, made him seem more vital, more *alive* than any other being she'd met. Viktor looked exactly like his namesake — a gilded victor, burnished in triumphant sunlight.

When he prowled back to her, he did not look even remotely human. The animal was alive in his gaze and etched into his posture. His fangs were extended and his normally blunt nails had shifted into razor sharp claws. He looked like he wanted to *eat* her.

A thrill burned through the haze of her orgasms, tensing her languid muscles once more. The predator in her recognized the predator in him. *Play,* it whispered, giddy. *Make him play.*

Viktor's voice was a whip when he commanded, "Turn over."

Her pulse jumped. A large part of her wanted to obey without question, yielding to the safety and comfort his dominance offered, but a bigger part understood that this dance between them was vital. Things would not be settled until they saw it to the end.

So instead of bowing to the very *alpha* command, Camille halted his approach with one slim foot planted in the center of his golden chest. Meeting his hungry gaze, she lifted her chin and breathlessly replied, "Make me."

Viktor smiled. "Wrong answer, sweetheart."

Chapter Twenty-Nine

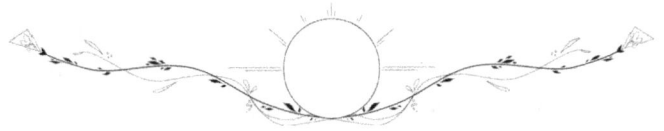

Viktor wrapped his fingers around her slim ankle. It felt perfectly weighted in his palm — all smooth skin and strong elvish bone, wrought in a shape so fine it felt divinely made in his unworthy hand.

For the span of a heartbeat, all he could do was stare at the creature spread out before him like an offering. Defiance made her violet eyes glow, but everything else about her was well-loved and marked by him. Her lavender skin shone with a thin layer of sweet, clean sweat, and her dark nipples were puckered. A single droplet of blue blood slid down the gentle curve of her breast.

Her chest rose and fell with short, excited pants, and her hair was a riot of short black waves on the pale gray duvet. When he squeezed her ankle, he felt the lithe muscle under his hand tremble.

Viktor took in all of this between one breath and the next. He wasted no more time than that.

Releasing her ankle, he tossed her leg to one side and grasped her waist, turning her over and moving her up the bed in one smooth move. A gusty exhale left her when her chest hit the mattress, palms flattening to catch her fall too late.

By the time she thought to push herself up, he was already

behind her. One hand ripped the robe off of her arms, revealing the smooth lines of her back and ass, while the other fisted her hair and pulled her head to one side. Pressing her cheek down into the pillows, he leaned in close to hiss, "Make you, sweetheart? I don't need to *make* you do anything. I think you'd bend over with a smile if I asked you nice enough."

He couldn't resist running his tongue along the line of her angular jaw, tasting the salt and sweetness there. "But you don't want me to ask nicely, do you? You want me to *take.*"

Camille made a low sound in the back of her throat — part growl, part purr. Her shoulders tensed, but before she could reach back to take a swipe at him, Viktor pinned her hands down with one of his own. Her clawless fingers dug into the downy pillows. Bucking her hips under him, she tried to crane her neck to snap her teeth at his throat.

A snarl pulled his upper lip over his aching fangs. The animal pressed close to the forefront of his mind, howling for her submission at the same time that it reveled in her fight.

Except that it wasn't really a fight. Somewhere in the back of his mind, he still understood that if Camille wanted to, she could have thrown him off at any moment. Elves were like quicksilver — hard to hold and faster than lightning. She fought him, but she wasn't *fighting* him.

The animal in him recognized that this was a dance, and it was one she led.

That didn't make it any less potent, any less *real,* though. Viktor knew she wanted him to win just as he knew he *had* to win.

Using his knees, he nudged her legs apart. His cock, aching still despite his earlier release, rested against the sweet curve of her backside when he leaned down, pressing his chest against her back. He could feel the roaring heat of her cunt against his skin, the sweet wetness that glided between them. He licked her clean, but with the way her body reacted to him, it didn't make a difference.

Still, she snapped at him. Elvish fangs, razor sharp and numbering four to his measly two, came within a hairsbreadth of his throat before he jerked his head back.

"If you keep trying to take a chunk out of me, I'm never going to be able to free one of my hands up," he coolly informed her. Thrusting his hips against her backside in a teasing rhythm, he asked, "Is that what you want? To keep my hands occupied so I can never be inside you, sweetheart? Did you want me to leave you aching? Because I can. I can get off this way no problem."

A very feminine growl rattled out of her chest and straight into his. "You wouldn't dare."

"Oh, I would." To punctuate his point, Viktor picked up his pace, sliding himself back and forth against her. Underneath him, her spine locked, trembling with tension.

She canted her hips back, trying to change the angle, but with his body weight holding her in place, there was very little room for her to move. Viktor watched her expression contort with frustration as her fingertips clawed the pillow above her.

Peering up at him through slitted eyelids, she bit out, "I guess you'll just have to find some other way to hold me, because the second you release me, I'm *really* going to bite you."

Fuck.

Faced with the intensely erotic image of Camille biting *him,* Viktor's cock jerked. The fever rose, hot and unstoppable, until a film of deep red covered his vision. *"You want a bite?"* he grated, each word a rumbling, inhuman snarl. *"Then you'll have a bite."*

Pulling her head up and to one side, Viktor closed his jaws over the juncture of her neck and shoulder and *bit.*

Camille made the softest, sweetest *buh* sound as his fangs sank into her skin. Every muscle in her body went suddenly lax. Magic roared between them, hot and wild, scalding them both.

And suddenly, Viktor *felt* her there, in that tender place where he carried every soul in his pack. She twined her threads into the tapestry, braiding herself around and through him, until they were one inseparable force.

Mine, his coyote howled. *Finally mine!*

Frenzied, Viktor released her wrists to position himself and then, with a deep grunt, sheathed himself inside of her.

Camille arched her back, pushing herself against him, taking everything he had to give her. She was hot and slick and so fucking perfect it punched the air right out of his lungs. *Like we were built for this,* he thought, marveling at the perfect fit and the hot glide.

With his jaws still clamped around her throat, he felt it the moment a purr began to hum its way out of her chest. It was a sound of such perfect contentment that he was momentarily too stunned to move.

This is what she wanted.

The thought was clear, absolutely certain. His mate had been angling for his bite the entire time, and now the dance was done.

He'd won her.

Viktor sucked in a shaky breath through his nose and slowly began to move. Magic pulsed in time with every thrust, tying them together in a way that could never be undone. His bite would leave a scar for all to see, and his magic would live inside of her until the day they passed into the Underworld. In exchange, she now lived in the heart of him — without her, he could not live.

Camille had always been his heart, but now she was his breath, his bread, his water, and his air. She was *everything.*

When he'd given her everything he had, Viktor slowly pulled his mouth away from her neck. The taste of her blood — so very different from every other race — lingered on his tongue as he rearranged her under him.

On her back now, with her legs wrapped snugly around his hips, he caged her in with his arms and kissed her hard.

Camille twined her arms around his neck and lifted her hips to match his pace. Her tongue slid sensuously against his in a languid caress. The kiss was deep, their rhythm slow and intense.

This moment was about more than sex, more than pleasure, more than the claim they now had over one another.

It was a joining in the truest, most primal sense.

In that perfect moment, he felt their future open up before him, welcoming them with open arms. He felt the joy of waking up beside her every day for the rest of his life. He felt her wildness, freed from the cage of elvish propriety and embraced by his pack. He felt the contentment of a family he did not yet know.

It was an avalanche of emotion, bright and multifaceted, that came and went in a moment.

When the euphoria of the bite finally began to fade, Viktor pulled back from the kiss to press his face into her hair. "I love you," he rasped, hips moving faster. "I've always loved you. I love you so much it hurts, Cam."

His mate hugged him close, plastering them together until he could feel the beat of her heart against his own. Her breath hitched when she replied, "I love you, Vik. Always have. Always will."

Tears blurred his vision. He squeezed his eyes shut as pressure began to build, tightening the base of his spine. Determined to wring one more orgasm out of her, he forced himself to slow his pace and reached between them, stroking her as he plunged deep, with enough force to rattle the bed.

When she came, Camille closed her fangs over his shoulder, biting hard, and instantly sent him flying over the edge.

Viktor cupped the top of her head as wave after wave of pleasure rolled through him, emptying him completely. Only when he couldn't take it anymore did he slow the roll of his hips.

Finally, *finally* spent, he stroked her hair until she released her bite.

Pride and satisfaction warmed every dark corner of his mind when he rolled them onto their sides. His healed shoulder ached something fierce and he felt like he'd been hit by a truck, but even so, he'd never felt better than he did at that exact moment.

Camille cuddled close, her eyes closed and her expression

blissed out. "You're mine now," she whispered. His blood smeared her lips like wine, or perhaps the lipstick of a woman well-kissed.

"I'm yours," he breathed. His chest felt too tight, too small to contain everything he felt for her. Choked by it all, he hoarsely added, "I am so damn proud to be yours, Cam."

She rubbed the tip of her nose over the swell of his shoulder, tracing a path to the bloody bite. Kissing the center, she whispered, "Of course you are. I'm a *Solbourne.*"

Laughter, like all that perfect contentment, bubbled out of him in a rush. "Yeah, you are."

~

They had an escort back to Lake Merced. Two of his senior packmates, both guards, and an armed contingent of Patrol led them back to his — *their* — territory. No one was taking any chances with their safety now, and Viktor was grateful to have a pack that cared enough to make it a priority.

Although it smarted his pride a little, he was grateful for Theodore's intervention, too. There was not a chance anyone would get through the battalion of Patrol soldiers he assigned to his cousin. While the coyote might have balked at the implication that he could not care for his mate with his own claws, Viktor knew better.

The coyote could fight tooth and claw, but it could not do anything against a sniper, or a bomb, or nasty spellwork. So even though it didn't sit well with his pride as an alpha and a mate, he was grateful for the extra protection afforded his elf.

The sun was beginning to set by the time they left the Patrol soldiers at the border. After parking their cars in a discreetly obscured spot behind a wall of trees, Viktor slung her overnight bag over his shoulder and took her hand.

As they wound their way through the trees, following a path worn down by countless paws and feet, they passed packmates moving around the territory, going from one den to another, or just returning home from work in the city. Cubs peeked out from behind legs to peer up at their alpha's mate, and older members stopped to introduce themselves.

Camille seemed shocked that they would bring their young out to meet her. When a toddler had been hastily deposited in her arms by way of greeting, she went white as a sheet.

Viktor frowned, concerned. "Are you not comfortable holding babies?"

"No, I..." Camille swallowed thickly, eyes darting around to take in the bemused expressions of the parents and her mate. "No, I love spending time in the nursery. I've just never been allowed to hold an Other child before." Her voice dropped to a whisper. "I'm worried I'll scare him."

The toddler didn't seem to notice her hesitancy, as he was busy tugging at one of her ears. Coyote inquisitiveness meant her heavy diamond studs were, at least briefly, the center of his universe.

Kate, the toddler's mother, let out a bark of laughter and dared to nudge Camille's shoulder. "Please. That's a coyote cub. You could dangle him off a roof by the toe and he'd just laugh."

Camille looked scandalized. "I'd *never* do that."

The parents laughed and, with an encouraging pat on her back, said, "Don't worry, you'll get used to it. You see enough feral cubs running around and eventually it'll feel normal."

"If you say so," his mate replied, looking entirely unconvinced.

There was a certain stiffness to the interactions at first, but after the third introduction and obligatory embrace, Camille's spine lost its starch. "I'm sorry if I'm awkward," she muttered as Mia brought her in for a tight hug. "Elves don't— we're not big huggers."

Again, his mate received that same good natured advice: "Oh, you'll get used to it!"

By the time they finally made it to their den, nearly the entire pack had come out to introduce themselves to Camille and not so subtly assess their new alpha. Viktor's chest swelled with pride every time their eyes met his, glowing with humor and approval.

While Camille was a little awkward, she was sincere. Every introduction was met with a solemnity and steady eye contact that made each packmate feel special, important. While he wasn't in a mood to share his mate with the whole world yet, he knew better than to interrupt or hustle her away. This moment was as important to his mate as it was to his pack.

This was her family now.

Still, he was relieved when they finally walked up the hidden path to his den. Only Benny stood outside, his brawny arms crossed over his chest and his expression unreadable.

Viktor tensed, the coyote immediately recalling how he rejected Camille only hours before. He held himself back from following instinct. Benny was one of his best friends. He was no threat to Camille. More than that, like the rest of the pack, he had to sense that the bond was made, that she was his alpha now.

He was owed the chance to reintroduce himself to Camille on those terms — but if he rejected her again, Viktor knew he would have to step in and handle it. Best friend or not, second or not, *no one* was allowed to make his mate feel as though she did not belong with her pack.

But that tension and readiness to act did not prove necessary.

As they strode up to the hidden door, Benny came to meet them. As one, they paused. For several long seconds, his mate and his second simply stared at one another.

In that stony silence, Camille drew herself up to her impressive height and, with a small tilt of her head, opened her arms.

It was perhaps not the most natural offering of a hug he'd ever seen, but it was genuine. Warmth rushed through his veins when he saw Benny's lips twitch upward in a crooked, bemused smile. Without hesitation, his second swooped in to wrap his arms around her middle and hoist her off the ground.

"Sorry I was hard on you," he gruffly apologized. "Didn't mean to make you think I didn't like you."

Camille caught Viktor's eyes over Benny's shoulder. She looked shyly pleased. "It's okay. I understand. In your place, I would have ripped out throats first, asked questions later."

Benny's laugh boomed off of the trees. Dropping her back onto her feet, he gave her shoulder a proud pat. "Pretty sure you did do that, grape."

"Grape?" Camille wrinkled her nose. "...Because I grew up on a vineyard?"

Viktor coughed into his fist, covering up his laughter when his second answered, "Because you're *purple!*"

Camille sputtered. "And you're *furry!*"

"Only sometimes."

Making a disgusted sound in the back of her throat, she gave his shoulder a solid punch with one deceptively dainty fist.

Benny stumbled backward, taken by surprise by the sheer wallop even a delicate-looking elf's hit could pack. "Damn!" He craned his neck to peer at Viktor. Rubbing his shoulder, he exclaimed, "She's strong as fuck!"

Viktor stepped close to his mate and slung his arm around her waist to guide her into the den. Speaking over his shoulder, he said, "I know! Isn't it great?"

Unlocking the door with the thumb scanner, he made a mental note to add Camille's ID code and biometric data to all the pack's systems in the morning. Now that she was pack, she had access to everything that was his *and* theirs.

The den was dark and cool when they stepped inside. He closed the door behind them, muffling the sound of Benny complaining about his "pitching arm".

Viktor felt a pang of regret when he watched Camille walk in ahead of him. "I'm sorry," he said, sighing. "I had this grand plan to show you the den for the first time, but all that's ruined now."

She turned to give him a curious look over her shoulder. "Ruined? How?"

"Well, you've seen it all already."

"Not to make it seem like I don't care, but honestly, Vik, I wasn't paying all that much attention last night." She paused, canting her head to one side. "Or this morning, for that matter. I was a little distracted."

Viktor set her bag down by the door and, feeling uncharacteristically shy, asked, "That's— well that works, then." Swallowing hard, he straightened his shoulders. "Mate, would you like a tour of the den?"

Camille's smile was absolutely heartstopping. "I *would*, my consort. Very much."

CHAPTER THIRTY

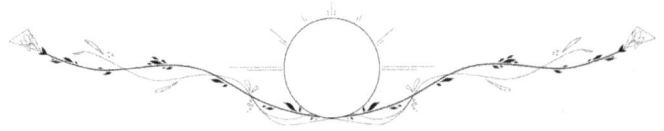

"So what happens when the pack moves to the new territory?"

"What do you mean?" Viktor rubbed her knee with one hand, his other busy stirring... something in a pan on the cooker. It smelled salty and tangy, which tantalized her, but one glance at the sodden vegetables in the pan made her firmly rethink trying a bite.

Camille was perched on the countertop beside the cooker, her long legs crossed at the ankles and her feet bare. After the tour, in which he'd proudly showed off every tiny detail of his beautiful, if strangely open den, he insisted on dinner. She had opened her mouth to politely inform him that he was unlikely to have anything she could eat in his kitchen, but he was already miles ahead of her.

Her eyes watered when he presented her with a refrigerator full of elvish food — raw meat marinated in spices or cured with smoke. There were even large filets of fish in the freezer, ready to be unthawed and enjoyed with a drizzle of citrus or soy sauce.

Gifts from our packmates, he told her. *To welcome you, you know?*

Like the den, everything was prepared for her, as if she had always been part of his home.

Camille watched her shirtless consort as he cooked, her eyes tracing the familiar musculature of his form with a possessive hunger. Swallowing her nibble of peppered salami, she elaborated, "I mean the den. You've put so much time and thought into it. Are you going to be okay just leaving it here and starting over wherever the Alliance puts you?"

Viktor smoothed his palm up and over her thigh. Giving her a gentle squeeze, he answered, "Nah. Our homes are modular. We build them knowing that at any moment the pack might need to leave, so everything here can be transported easily to the new territory."

Relief washed through her. "Oh, good."

He turned his head to give her a warm smile. "You like the den?"

Camille leaned over to give his bloodied shoulder a lingering kiss. "Yes. Very much."

It *was* an exquisite home. The lines were clean and modern, the wood was light, and the windows tall. It looked like a home built to highlight the nature around it, not the other way around.

She especially liked all the touches of purple. There were tiny violet glass tiles in the bathroom. There were deep plum pillows on the low couch. There were lavender curtains, so pale they were almost white, in the bedroom. When he opened a cupboard to pull out a plate, she even spied a handful of mismatched purple cups and bowls, some of them chipped and clearly well loved.

Each little pop of color stood out against the grays and greens he seemed to prefer, and every single one told the same story: *He never once stopped thinking of me.*

"I'm happy to hear it," he replied, grin widening as he scooped some of his dinner onto a baby blue plate. "But I'm happy to change anything you want. This is your den too. It should feel like it."

Her heart skipped a beat. "Maybe someday, but for right now I think it's perfect."

Holding his plate in one hand, Viktor turned to rub the pad of his thumb along her jaw. His gaze was intent on her face when he said, "We'll get your things moved in this week, okay? Not just from the apartment. I want you to get everything you need from Napa."

Because this is forever, a voice in the back of her mind whispered. The wound on the juncture of her neck and shoulder pulsed, further cementing the feeling of permanence.

She would leave her mother's estate for good. It was no great loss, really. Although she felt a deep kinship with the land she had helped cultivate for most of her life, Camille felt no real connection to the home itself. Not anymore.

Now it was a shell of what it once was, when she and her brother used to run through the halls together, evading their mother and their beloved houserunner. Even those moments of joy had been snuffed out over time, buried under the strain of her mother's clashes with Cameron and then her decline.

If she were being honest with herself, Camille would admit that staying in San Francisco for her mourning period and negotiations wasn't necessary. The real reason was because she found no comfort in the mansion that only reminded her of the years she spent taking care of her mother in secret. The food she ate at their table tasted of ash, and the air smelled of medical grade cleaning solution. Always.

"Cameron comes home with his consort next week," she told him. "I'll have him pack everything up and bring it with him when he comes to visit."

Viktor's lips twitched. "How is he gonna feel about you mating a shifter?"

"He'll probably be relieved."

"Yeah? Why's that?"

Camille smoothed her palms over the planes of his chest, soothing herself. "Cameron has always hated elvish society. It was half the reason he and our mother fought so much. She wanted revenge, but he just wanted her to let it go and move on. She accused him of being a traitor to our father's memory."

"Was he?"

"No, of course not." Camille shook her head. "He just couldn't live under the cloud of her grief like I could. Whereas I tried to redirect our mother, he just got angry and shut himself off. After that, they fought about everything. It was all I could do to keep the peace between them."

Viktor took her hand and tugged gently, urging her off of the counter. When she stood in front of him, he wrapped his arm around her shoulders and walked them back into the living room. "I remember you telling me how bad their fights could get, but I didn't know it was like that. That sounds like a heavy burden, Cam."

She shrugged. "It was what it was. I love— loved them both."

Guiding her to sit beside him on the couch, Viktor set his plate on his thigh and shook his head. "Loyal to the core."

Camille shifted uncomfortably. She wished that people would stop saying that. "I just did what I had to do. And, honestly, I don't feel very loyal right now."

She felt his sharp gaze on her face. "What? Why?"

Staring at the driftwood coffee table, scored with jagged claw marks, she answered, "I promised my mother on her deathbed that I would join with another family and get out of Solbourne reach. Instead I'm here." She swallowed the acidic taste of guilt. "I swore I'd do it, but today I..."

"You fulfilled your promise."

Camille's eyes swung upward, confusion tightening her features. "What? No, I didn't."

Viktor cupped her cheek. "Sweetheart, you *did*. All your mom wanted was for you to get out, right? Well, you did it." His hand slid down to cup her throat. The skin of his palm radiated with the same heat that came from his bite. "I got myself on the list, too, so she wouldn't even be able to complain about it not being a legit union. If you want, I'll even sign whatever bullshit paperwork Teddy can cook up. I don't care. It all means the same thing."

Camille's throat tightened to the point where speaking became impossible. Was he right? She didn't think her mother would have ever forgiven Viktor for rejecting her all those years ago — grudges were, after all, her specialty — but he was correct that Camille had fulfilled her mother's request.

She had negotiated a union with someone outside of the Solbourne sphere, who was actively looking for a territory beyond their reach, and would never again be in danger of losing her mind due to the pull.

Holy shit. I did it.

Seeing the astonished look on her face, Viktor let out a bark of warm laughter. "Sweetheart, whether or not your mom would have approved of me, you did exactly what she asked. I don't want to see that guilty look on your face ever again, okay?"

"Right," she answered, dazed.

Later, when they were curled up in bed, Viktor's arms tight around her middle, Camille stared into the darkness and listened to the sound of coyotes yipping in the distance. She knew from research that they had an incredibly complex system of communication, and that not all of those barks and yowls were shifters. Some of them were regular, wild coyotes — friends of the pack who helped patrol the territory and play with the cubs.

She listened hard, trying to learn the cadence, and felt a heavy warmth spread over her. *Pack*, the magic now coursing through her veins said. *Pack is home. Pack is safety. Pack is my responsibility.*

"Vik," she whispered, knowing he was still awake.

"Hm?"

"What's going to happen to the pack? What are we going to do about the territory?"

Worry pressed close. This was her family now. Every tiny cub, every elder, every smiling adult who welcomed her with open arms *belonged* to her. Had her mating to Viktor irreparably damaged their chances at a better future?

Viktor's palm flattened against her bare stomach and drew her closer still. He nuzzled the back of her head when he answered, "We're calling the Alliance tomorrow morning. We can't do anything until we know where they stand. And as far as the territory goes, there is no use in worrying about it until we have the all-clear to move." His fingers flexed, digging into the soft skin of her belly. "I meant what I said, Cam. Making plans with another pack prematurely can be deadly. I won't make a move until everything is secure."

She threaded her fingers through his and closed her eyes. Leaning into the warmth she could feel resonating through their primal bond, she tried to let go of the insistent terror that clung to her like a second skin. "Let's say it all works out. Do you have a pack in mind to take over Merced?"

She could feel his smile. "They'd have to be able to buy us out, and the land needs to go to good people who will take care of it, who need it — but yeah, as a matter of fact, I do."

Camille gave his hand a squeeze. "Are you going to share?"

Chuckle rumbling out of his chest, he replied, "Have you ever met Angelique Batacan?"

CHAPTER THIRTY-ONE

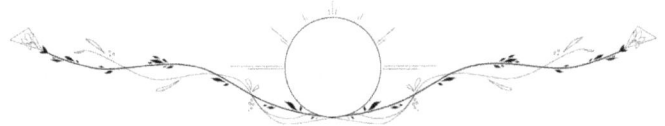

IDEALLY, VIKTOR WOULD HAVE PREFERRED TO HAVE this meeting alone. Unfortunately, Andreas didn't give him that choice.

They were gathered in Theodore's office. It was a large room walled with bookshelves and floor-to-ceiling windows overlooking the Bay, but it still felt crowded. Theodore was there, of course, as was Valen, Kaz, and Laurence, Captain of the Sovereign's Guard. Margot was perched on the edge of the live edge desk, her expression somber. Benny and another senior packmate, a lean wolf shifter named Diana, had accompanied him to the Tower as well.

And of course, Camille was with him.

Somewhere far below them all, in the bowels of the Tower, the cougar shifter had just confessed to trying to kill Viktor on his alpha's orders.

They were all silent as the feed screen played his taped confession. Torture hadn't been necessary — or even prudent, really. The cougar shifter looked like he was hanging on by a thread as he laid out his assignment to the Patrol officer sitting across from him.

"...and said that it was necessary. I don't know. I don't— he just kept saying that if we didn't, they'd come in and take our territory.

I fought in the war, man. I know what elves can do." His words tripped out over bruised lips, almost too fast to be understood. *"I got cubs now. What was I supposed to do? My alpha said he was a threat and told me to take care of it. What would you do? Do you have cubs? I couldn't let him— my alpha would have—"*

The Patrol officer held up a gloved hand, stalling the desperate, almost incoherent confession. Pushing a paper cup of water across the stainless steel table with one finger, he asked, *"Did your alpha threaten your cubs, Mr. Carter?"*

The cougar shifter took the cup in one trembling, bloodied hand. Water sloshed. *"I— Not outright, no. No. He just— You don't know him. He'd toss us out in a heartbeat. I've seen it before. And after Juan—"* He sucked in a ragged breath and, apparently realizing that he was trending toward disloyalty, rushed to add, *"He said elves were going to take our territory. I wasn't sure, but then I saw him with that— with that elf on the beach and I knew he was right. I had to defend the pack. Don't you get that? I had to—"*

Theodore stopped the video. The image paused just as the shifter was leaning forward over the table, as if he could beseech the cool officer to understand why he tried to murder another alpha on foreign territory.

Viktor swung his grim gaze over to his friend. He felt Camille's fingers tighten around his hand, offering wordless support. "Send it to Lee."

"Already done."

"We should get custody of the cougar," Diana piped up, her sweet voice pitched low. Her grandmother was a harpy, and though the physical signs were subtle, anyone with a tuned ear could pick up the almost unnaturally lyrical notes in her voice. That natural beauty didn't do anything to make her sound less lethal when she added, "He attacked our alphas. We should be the ones who handle his punishment."

Valen leaned forward in his seat and propped his elbows on his knees. He was aging, but Viktor felt it was the good kind of aging — the mark left by years of happiness after so much strife, rather than the ragged, worn expression he'd seen on others. His mother had aged like that until, one day two years after his father's defeat, she'd simply *gone*.

The man who had been more of a father to him than Dominic Hamilton ever was, did not have that ragged edge to him. He simply looked like he had lived a full life, and that he had put on a few more miles chasing after the young men he helped raise. It was good to see.

He still looked scary as fuck, though, when he answered, "I'd normally agree, but he was technically in our territory when he attacked Vik. That complicates things."

Diana's dark eyes, a deep, warm brown that was echoed in the rich tone of her skin and waterfall of silky brown hair, flashed with a pale, wolfish blue. She crossed her svelte arms over her chest and demanded, *"How?"*

"For one thing, the Merced territory is not technically independent. It is semi-autonomous, as dictated in the Allied Charter, not its own sovereign country," Theodore interrupted.

He stood beside his wife, one hand pressed flat against the desk by her hip, caging her in against his much larger body. Margot was small enough that, turned sideways, she could be completely blocked from view by her husband's body. "The EVP, however, is. Andreas sits on the council of the Alliance, making him a leader of a foreign government. That makes what he did technically an act of war. And *that* means, until we know how the Alliance wants to handle this, the cougar stays in elvish custody."

Diana opened her mouth to argue, but Viktor cut her off with a look. "He's right. Us getting ahold of Andreas's packmate could be viewed as the EVP ceding the right to retaliation, which would weaken our position. Believe me, I want to see that man pay for what he did, but if we don't play this smart, Andreas could just end up with a slap on the wrist."

A low growl circled the room.

Viktor agreed with the sentiment, though he wasn't particularly enthused by the idea of delivering just punishment himself.

It was an alpha's job and the shifter way, but he wasn't a naturally violent person. He didn't relish the idea of taking a father from innocent cubs. Taking his own father's life had been enough for one lifetime.

But justice was justice, and in the UTA, it had to be swift and unforgiving. The consequences of a failure to act could be too dire for anything else.

If Andreas was reckless enough to craft a plot as foolish as *this*, then the gods only knew what else he was capable of.

Besides, Viktor might have been able to forgive an attack on himself, but Damon Carter, father of two and mate to an arrant woman in data science, had gone after *his mate*. He owed the man no mercy.

Benny cleared his throat. "What about the bounty?"

They had shared the news from Epifanio with everyone before the confession came through. Theodore took the fact that the elf had shown up on Camille's doorstep without warning about as well as Viktor had — which is to say, *extremely poorly*.

However, it was Kaz who answered in his smooth baritone. "Handled."

Viktor arched his brow. "Yeah? How'd you manage that?"

The orc's smile was close-lipped and terrifying. "Trade secret, but let's just say that going after one of ours is widely considered a poor health choice. No one is going to take that bounty. Trust me."

He liked to think that he could be pretty scary when he wanted to be, but very few beings could claim the sheer menace of Kazimier Rione.

Camille laid her free hand on his thigh. He felt her anger and her concern throbbing through the bond they now shared. "We do, Kaz. If you say it's handled, then it's handled. Doesn't mean I'm not going to worry, though." Slanting a look at her cousin, she asked, "When do you think Alpha Seymour will—"

An urgent chime rang through the speakers on either side of the feed screen. Theodore looked down at the razor thin screen on his desk, checking the incoming alert, before he hovered his fingers over the projected keyboard below it. "That would be him. You ready, Vik?"

He lifted Camille's hand to give her knuckles a lingering kiss. "Yes."

When she nodded, lips pressed into a tight, bloodless line, he stood up and joined Theodore behind his desk. When he passed Margot, she hopped off the edge and gave his arm a gentle, supportive stroke. "You've got this."

He shot her a crooked smile. "Thanks, sunshine."

She moved to join Camille on the leather loveseat he abandoned. Margot reached for his mate's hand and twined their fingers together. They wore identical expressions of grim encouragement.

Viktor held Camille's eye for a heartbeat longer, but when Theodore answered the call, he was forced to turn his gaze toward the feed screen once more. The camera was angled at the desk, giving the impression that it was just Theodore and Viktor, side by side, confronting the de facto leader of the Alliance.

Lee Seymour's face appeared on the screen. He was in what looked like a sleek, modern office and dressed in a crisp white dress shirt that stood out against his dark skin. His normally inscrutable expression was gone, replaced by one of dark anger.

His pale blue eyes shifted, taking in Theodore and Viktor standing side by side, before he said, "This is not how I wanted my morning to go."

Viktor stuffed his hands in his pockets and arched a brow. "Yeah, well, join the club. You weren't the one shot yesterday."

"You're looking pretty good for a man who claims to have taken a bolt."

Theodore smiled, slow and sharp. "He has a *very* good healer."

Lee shook his head. "I really don't want to hear the story behind that confession, do I?"

"No," Viktor answered, "but you have to."

And he did, though Lee's expression only got darker, stonier, as the details came out. When Viktor finished, Lee was silent for several long moments. His jaw ticked. "Well, fuck. I knew he had piss for brains, but I didn't think he was *that* far gone."

"He trespassed on my territory," Theodore added, tone as icy as Viktor had ever heard it. "And he shot at *my* cousin."

Lee's brow furrowed. "Your cousin? Who..."

Viktor pushed his shoulders back and stared hard at the feed screen, daring Lee to react when he answered, "My mate, Camille Dia Solbourne."

He was so attuned to his mate that he heard her suck in a breath from across the room. Viktor couldn't look at her, though. He didn't want to see the dread on her face, the worry that she would be the reason their pack lost this chance. If they were rejected after all of this, it would be on him, not her — though he was smart enough to know that guilt did not follow lines of logic or responsibility.

Lee was experienced enough not to show any outward sign of surprise. "I see. When did this happen?"

"Recently." Viktor did not feel the need to elaborate on just *how* recent their mating was. That was none of his business.

"And it's official?"

In answer, Viktor simply tilted his head to one side and pulled down the collar of his t-shirt with a crooked finger. His expression was fiercely proud when he showed off his mate's bite.

Icy blue eyes locked on the juncture of his shoulder for several heartbeats before Lee let out a breath and cut his gaze away. One large hand came up to scrub at his jaw. "So Ruben not only tried to have you shot on Solbourne land, but he also went after your mate, the sovereign's *cousin?*"

He wasn't sure what Lee found more upsetting: that a mate had been targeted, or that one of his fellow alphas had brought the Alliance to the brink of war.

It was a cardinal sin to go after a shifter's mate unprovoked. Losing a mate was the end. A done thing.

Once they were gone, a shifter had nothing left to lose. It didn't matter that Andreas couldn't have known who Camille was, nor that she would be with him when his would-be assassin tracked him down. That didn't matter. Incidental or not, the man had aimed his gun at his mate. That was the end of it.

"Yes," Viktor answered, releasing his shirt. The worn cotton settled over the mostly healed wound in a mildly irritating way. He would have preferred to strip and walk around in his skin, letting it continue to heal unbothered. He loved showing his bite off to everyone who looked, but only his fellow shifters would have been comfortable with something like that, so he politely refrained.

"Shit." Lee pursed his lips and, just out of sight of the camera, appeared to prop his hands on his hips. His white shirt stretched over his barrel chest, emphasized by the two undone buttons at the top. "Well, what are we gonna do about this, then?"

"That's entirely up to you," Theodore replied. He dropped his balled fists on the desk and leaned forward to look at the screen from under the shadow of his brows. "This can go one of two ways, Alpha Seymour: either you condemn the attack on my land or I take this to the Congress floor."

Lee scowled. "You want me to take this public? That'll cause chaos."

"It'll be even worse if I lodge a complaint in United Washington, I promise you."

"I'm not saying we're taking Ruben's side," he pressed, arching a dark brow. "I'm saying we don't need to take this to the public. If we do that, faith in the Alliance would take a hit and it could turn into a bloodbath out here — especially if upstart alphas get it into their heads that they can make a name for themselves during the commotion."

Theodore narrowed his eyes. "That's not my problem. He shot at *my* fucking cousin in *my* territory, where she should have been safest in the world." His jaw clenched hard enough that Viktor could make out the sound of his fangs squeaking against one another. "And he very nearly killed my best friend. If you think I'm going to allow you to bury this and let him off the hook, you have no idea what kind of *chaos* I'm capable of."

Viktor, though touched by Theodore's furious defense, dropped his hand onto his friend's shoulder. "There's a middle ground here," he insisted. "You don't want to announce it to the public while we want justice. We *can* have both of those things."

Lee eyed him skeptically. "Do tell."

"Easy. You tell Ruben that it's me and him, one on one, at Alliance Landing. I'll take our justice, and you can say that it was an internal dispute settled in the circle."

"It won't look good." Lee shook his head. "Either way it's shit, but I mean it won't look good for *you*."

"Why?"

"Because we were going to call you and tell you that you'd been voted in today," he grimly informed him. "Andreas was the only dissenting vote, which will be made public when we make the announcement. If you kill him in a fight, it'll look like reprisal."

Elation was immediately tempered by cold reality. Lee was right. That was a bad look for anyone, but most especially a fresh alpha just accepted into the Alliance.

Viktor sighed and dropped his hand from Theodore's shoulder. There was never going to be an easy way out of this mess. So long as he could live to build a future with his mate, he'd just have to deal with the mess. "If it's my reputation versus inter-territory bloodshed, then I'm going to throw my reputation under the bus, Lee. It is what it is."

"As long as you understand how it could look, Vik. You want to do this, then I'll support you." The older alpha nodded, the skin around his eyes tight with anger, and shifted his gaze to Theodore. "And what about you, Sovereign? Would you be willing to accept the outcome of a fight and let the transgression go?"

"Sure, but I want a meeting with the Alliance in exchange."

Theodore straightened to his full height. His eyes, dark enough to obscure his catlike pupils, gleamed with challenge. "I want to discuss a formal alliance with your territory — *really* discuss it."

"There's a good section of the Alliance that doesn't want anything to do with the EVP. I can't promise that they'll be any more open to hearing you out than they were yesterday, formal meeting or no."

"All I ask is that they meet with me." Theodore waved a hand in a deceptively casual gesture. It would have looked harmless if anyone else had done it, but with the light streaming through the windows at his back and his hands ungloved, his claws looked particularly menacing. "What they decide after that is up to them."

"Fine. Consider it done." His eyes, a shockingly pale blue that looked almost white in the early morning sunlight, moved back to Viktor. "When do you want to do this?"

"As soon as possible." There was no way he wanted this hanging over them all.

"It'll take a few days to get the other alphas on board and force his hand," Lee cautioned. "He's a damn coward. He'll do everything he can to get out of stepping into the circle."

Viktor nodded. "As long as you get him there, that's fine. I have arrangements to make, anyway."

Now that they were formally accepted into the Alliance, he had people to talk to, logistics to coordinate. Viktor did not dwell on the other plans he had to hastily put together — like what would need to happen if Andreas won. He was determined to focus on the future, and that did not involve his untimely death in the desert.

Hopefully.

Chapter Thirty-Two

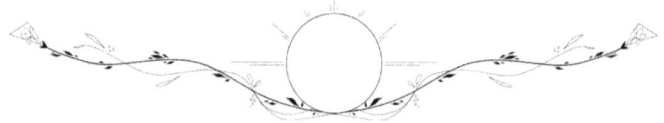

"I HATE THIS."

Camille had been quiet ever since they left the Tower. They were alone in Viktor's car, though they were escorted by Benny and Diana, as well as two Patrol cars that drove a discreet distance behind them.

"I know," he answered, finding her hand on her thigh. He gave it a small squeeze, knowing it would do little to soothe the fear that made her look like a ghost. "I know, Cam. If I could do this any other way, I would. There just... isn't."

She blinked furiously. Her eyes were glossy with tears when she finally turned her head to look at him. Her expression was almost *angry,* though he didn't feel that it was directed at him. "Did you ever wish that you'd said yes?"

He didn't have to ask what she was referring to. "Yes," he answered, exhaling a long, painful breath. "I wished I'd run away with you all the damn time, sweetheart. I don't think a night has gone by where I didn't wonder what kind of life we would have been living if I wasn't so damn scared."

"I know it's selfish," she whispered. "I know that it would mean your pack lost out on you, but I wish we could run away now."

Viktor couldn't resist bringing their twined hands up to kiss her fingers. She wasn't wearing gloves, perhaps because she'd picked up on how the sight of her retracted claws made him puff up with pride.

"They aren't just *my* pack," he steadily reminded her. "They're yours now, too. If we ran then or we run now, they would miss out on us *both*."

She let out a watery scoff. "They don't even know me. It's not me they'd miss."

"Maybe not today, but you don't know about tomorrow, or the day after that. You think that just because they don't know you *now*, that you won't matter to them as much as I do in the future? Families aren't built in a day, Cam."

He felt the tremor that ran through her. "I... I want to be part of it, Vik. I want it so much it hurts. I'm just scared."

Her fear was his. He felt it deep in the heart of the coyote, who whimpered, helpless and confused. All it wanted was to soothe its mate, but there was no loving this problem away. They had to face this terrible moment together if they wanted the future they dreamed of. It was just exceptionally bad timing.

Just like every other part of their relationship, really.

If only she'd had a little more time to adjust to the pack, she wouldn't feel this hopeless, he thought, gripping the steering wheel with his free hand until his knuckles were bleached white. *She'd feel anchored, supported.*

As it stood, there was no remedy for the rush. Trust could not be developed in a day, though she'd come damn close by saving his life. All he could do was promise her everything would be all right.

"What can I do?" Viktor cut a look at her, desperate for some clue to easing her fear.

Camille met his gaze and asked, "When we get back to the den, can I see him?"

Viktor's heart jolted. His throat felt dry when he hoarsely replied, "It's been a long time, but I'm sure I can make the arrangements."

They held hands the rest of the way home, and when they slipped into their den, Viktor drew her in for a series of deep, drugging kisses. "Everything will be all right," he whispered against her lips. "I promise, sweetheart."

"I trust you." The words skated across his lips. Even though they were shaky, he knew they were sincere.

"Good."

Taking a step back into the living room, he began to shuck his clothing. His shoes came first, then his t-shirt. His jeans, briefs, and socks were discarded just as quickly, leaving him in nothing but his skin. Camille's eyes roved over him hungrily. His blood heated at the sight of her pupils expanding, but he forced the lust aside. Temporarily.

"After," he promised her with a wink.

And then the magic in his blood erupted.

Bone shattered and reformed. Skin moved. Fur burst out to cover a sleek new form, bigger than a normal coyote but thinner, more agile than a wolf. The shift only took a handful of seconds, but when it was done, Viktor gave himself over to the animal. He had waited long enough to spend time with their mate, impatient though he was. He had earned the right to take the lead for a while.

The coyote tilted his head back to look up at their mate, golden eyes fixing unerringly on her familiar face. The smell of wildflowers and honey and salt filled his lungs — the smell of home, of den, of pack.

His claws clicked on the tile floor when he padded closer, moving slowly, instinctively wary of scaring her off.

This wasn't the first time they'd met. For a very long time Camille had been more comfortable with the coyote than the boy. That first time he snuck into the Tower to see her, he'd chosen to come as the animal based on instinct and the burning desire to see his mate through the coyote's eyes. Twenty years later, he was still surprised he had been welcomed into her den even when he was rainsoaked and barely more than a cub himself.

Perhaps it was because the coyote never asked anything of her — nothing more than her presence, her touch, and her attention.

But it had been a very, very long time since they'd come face to face, and the coyote was wary of sending their mate running again. Though she wore their bite, he did not yet feel entirely secure in its claim on her. How could he, when he had been restrained from contact with her for so long?

Stopping barely a foot away from her, he slowly sat down. Careful to keep his posture nonthreatening, he let out a low, crooning sound and gazed up at her longingly. *Do you remember me?*

Camille sucked in a deep breath. He watched, ears twitching with concern, as her lower lip trembled.

"Hello, my love," she whispered, slowly raising her hand. "It's been a long time."

The coyote whimpered as a deep ache resonated through his soul. He did not understand why they had been apart for so long, nor why she had continued to reject them. All he knew was yearning and loneliness, the pain of their separation a serrated blade in his heart.

Even so, the animal was not the man. To him, the past was done, the wounds of time already fading into distant memory. They would never be entirely forgotten, but he did not know hate, nor hold grudges.

My mate is here now, he thought, tilting his head into her tentative hand. *All is well again.*

And things got even better when she sank to her knees in front of him. This way, they were the same height. When he closed the distance between them, just as he used to, Camille shuddered and curled her arms around his neck. She buried her face in the ruff of fur there and inhaled deeply.

The coyote rested his chin on the back of her neck and rumbled a soft note for her. It pleased him endlessly to hear her purr back. Even though the fur she clutched was getting wet with tears, he didn't care. He loved the sound of his mate's unique purr almost as much as he loved the scent of her, the taste of her skin when he ran his tongue over her cheekbone.

They stayed in that position for some time, but eventually they ended up on the couch. Camille curled up with him under a blanket, one hand fisted in his blond-tipped fur, and whispered to him as she used to.

Once, the coyote had been her first friend. The boy had come second, though in their heart they were truly one being. But his mate needed the wild, unflinching acceptance of the coyote first, so it was what she got. Before she ever let the boy see her vulnerable, she told her secrets to the coyote, and let him wrap his furred body around hers in secret.

The longer he stayed with her, cold nose buried in her fragrant hair, the less he felt the ache of such a long separation.

His mate was safe now. He had given her a den that pleased her, and he would defend her from every threat. He won her. Someday they would have cubs, and their pack would grow, and everything would be as it should be.

Underneath the wild heart of the coyote, Viktor felt something taut and painful in his heart finally relax. For the first time in twenty years, he did not feel as though he was at odds with his other half. He did not need to fight the clawing loneliness and the heartbroken confusion. All he needed was right there, curled up against him.

The future loomed dark and uncertain, but it did not take away the contentment of the moment. And later, when the coyote gave way to the man, it did not stop him from finding pleasure in his mate again.

Man and coyote both relished the softness of her skin. They basked in the sight of her fresh bite, ringed with deep green bruises that looked like a coiled string of emeralds. They relished the taste of her when they sipped at her lips, stroked her with their tongue. They both felt the claim on her sink into the very fiber of their souls when she clutched them close, welcoming them into the slick heat of her with a pleased sigh.

When he sat back on his knees and hitched her lithe thigh over his hip, Viktor picked up a slow, deep rhythm. Both sides of his nature basked in the pleasure that tightened her expression. They watched, transfixed, as her pretty lavender breasts moved, the way her stomach flexed with every thrust, the gorgeous sight of their cock disappearing into her perfect cunt again and again — gold disappearing into amethyst with the sweetest glide.

The fever was a low burning fire in their soul, a deep well of heat that made every touch, every glance, every bite a lick of flame.

They had never felt closer to another being than when they breathed the same air as their mate. They had never felt pleasure like they felt when they thrust harder, faster, and slid a hand between them to stroke her until she came with a hoarse cry.

And when she was languid under him, they gave into impulse and sat up, dragging her into their lap to admire her as he lifted her and brought her down again. Was there ever a sight so arresting as their mate throwing her head back as she rode out the last ripples of her orgasm on top of them? Was ever there a pleasure greater than the feeling of her clenching hard as he thrust upward once, twice, a third time, until they came with a ragged gasp?

No, they thought, an orgasm stealing their breath, their sight. There was nothing better than knowing his mate was *his*, as man and animal were *hers*.

Nothing, not even an uncertain future, could tear her out of their claws now.

CHAPTER THIRTY-THREE

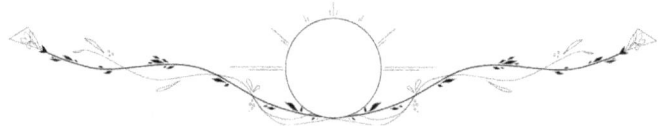

PACK LIFE TOOK SOME GETTING USED TO.

Camille didn't think about the way her life would change when she moved into the den. All that concerned her was being near her consort, being in his life in the way that every part of her craved. It was a joy to leave her lonely apartment behind, and she felt giddy with pleasure when she unpacked her things in the empty closet Viktor saved for her.

Together, they did their best to pretend like every phone call, every message, did not make them tense. They willfully ignored the sword hanging over all their necks. The brittle peace was grasped with the ferocity of two people desperate to pretend that their world did not stand on the brink of cataclysm.

She loved discovering that he slept on the right side of the bed. It delighted her to find his much-loved surfboard leaning up against the back of the house. She even found humor in the fact that he liked to leave dirty towels on the bathroom floor.

The intimacies of the mundane were a balm to her bruised soul. Living with him was effortless.

Living with the *pack*, however, did not prove quite so seamless.

For someone that had only a handful of close relationships, it was immediately overwhelming to suddenly be embraced by so many people. Each new packmate came with a new social expectation, a new path to blindly navigate as she attempted to make a good impression.

That was the problem, though. She knew what a good impression was for an *elf,* but for a shifter? She only had her experience with Viktor to go on.

Touch was important. That much she learned from her first introductions, and she thought that she was getting better at offering it to people who were packmates but strangers still. It was a struggle. Once they reached adolescence, elves became very choosy about who they let into their personal space. It went against the grain to open up her arms to every elder and every senior packmate she met.

Of course, not everyone expected it, and not every packmate was a shifter. There were a handful of arrants, a witch or two, and even a lovely vampire. Meeting them helped Camille feel less like an interloper. Certainly, if a *vampire* could find a place in the pack, she could too.

It was awkward for the first few days, but Camille firmed her chin and pushed through it. Had she not been trained by a lifetime of awkward smalltalk about her mother? She could deal with nosy shifters asking blunt questions about whether she ate people, and she could absolutely traverse the assessment she underwent every time a new packmate sized her up.

Truly, the main stumbling block came the day she woke up to the sound of someone letting themselves into their den.

Viktor was sprawled on his back, one arm thrown over his eyes and the other limp next to her, his fingers half-curled like he had begun to reach for her in sleep but couldn't quite make it. He didn't stir when the front door *whushed* open, but Camille did.

She was jolted out of her light doze by a deep sense of unease. *Intruders,* her instincts roared. *Threats!*

Her ears twitched at the sound of feet moving over the bamboo floor of their entry way. Adrenaline rushing and still waking up, Camille felt the sickly terror of the night on the beach return with a vengeance.

Had Andreas sent someone to kill Viktor in his sleep? Another packmate? Or was it some fool after the bounty?

The driving need to protect her consort was a loud drumbeat in her mind, drowning out everything else. Gliding silently out from between their sheets, Camille snatched up the robe hooked on the bedpost and shoved her arms through. Cinching it tightly around her waist, she prowled toward their bedroom door on bare feet.

She picked up hushed voices from somewhere in the living room as she silently eased the door open and slid through the gap.

Movement caught her eye. Without waiting for someone to pull out a bolt gun or shift, Camille darted down the short hallway and burst into the living room, a vicious snarl tearing its way out of her throat.

For a taut moment, the two toddlers and one very surprised teenager that were making themselves at home on her couch only stared at her. Then, as if the fear took a second to properly register, both little ones gasped and immediately broke out into huge, wracking sobs. They scrambled away from her to cling to the teenager, who had gone starkly pale.

"I'm sorry, Camille!" He croaked, hauling the wailing children into his thin arms as he quickly backed away. "I didn't mean to intrude! Vik usually watches Fiona and Thomas while Aunt Cherry checks on the elders. I was just dropping them off. I— I didn't think—"

Camille was mortified. She recognized the teenager as one of Mia's children, as well as the two toddlers, who were both about three years old, dressed in smart outfits and tiny sandals, and bawling uncontrollably. Now that she had some sense knocked into her, she realized how ridiculous it was to assume that they were intruders.

They had tight security on their home, with biometric scanning as well as warding. Only packmates would have the ability to enter, and even if someone *did* get past all that, they certainly wouldn't do so at eight in the morning.

Holding up her hands, Camille tried to make herself look as non-threatening as possible. "No, no! I'm so sorry, Johnnie! I didn't know it was you." She took a quick step toward the children, but stopped when they took one look at her and cried harder. Camille paled. "Oh, babies, I'm— Oh no, please, please don't cry. I didn't mean it."

"Whoa, whoa. What is goin' on?" Viktor's sleep-roughened voice came from behind her. "Johnnie? Why are the cubs upset?"

Camille turned a panic look on her consort and gestured helplessly to the shaken teenager and wailing toddlers. "I thought— I didn't know who they were and I... scared them."

Gods, she felt like a monster, too.

She'd gone out of her way to make sure she didn't appear threatening to the children she met, and then she went and undid all of that by scaring the daylights out of the trio in her living room.

"Ah, shit. I forgot that it was Cherry's day with the elders. I should have warned you they'd be coming over." Viktor was shirtless and tousled, but his eyes were keen when he strode across the room to swing both toddlers into his arms. "Shh. You're okay. I know you were surprised, but Cam didn't mean anything by it."

"No, I didn't. I—"

The toddlers, who had begun to calm down some, wailed again. Johnnie looked abashed and Viktor wore a pinched, resigned expression as he attempted to soothe the children clinging to his bare shoulders.

Camille shrank back into the hallway. Speaking low and fast, she said, "I'll just— I'll just go into the bedroom. Sorry."

Viktor made a soft sound in the back of his throat. "Cam, it's okay, just—"

She didn't listen. Camille hurried back down the hall and dashed into the bedroom. Standing in the center of the room, she clenched her hands into fists and fought the wobbling of her chin.

I scared them so much they can't even look at me, she thought, agonized by guilt. She wanted to fit in *so badly.* It cut her to the quick to know she blundered so terribly. What would the pack think of her now? Would Johnnie run off to tell his mother that she bared her fangs at the children? Would they accuse her of threatening their young?

Feeling sick, Camille looked for something to do to calm herself down. There was no way she was stepping outside of the bedroom until after the children left. She'd rather sequester herself all day than have them look at her like she planned to eat them one more time.

She decided on a shower. There was little else to do, and it only made her feel worse to stand there and hear the muted sounds of Viktor attempting to soothe the children across the house.

Grabbing her clothing, she fled into the bathroom and locked the door. Maybe after she got ready, she could sneak out the bedroom window? It wasn't dignified, but leaving the house while Viktor took care of the children sounded like a better plan than waiting around. Eventually he would try to coax her out. Best that she removed herself from the situation entirely.

Camille showered and dressed quickly. When she ducked her head out of the bathroom, she was relieved to hear that the muffled crying had stopped. It sounded like they were on the other side of the house — probably the kitchen.

Good, she thought, insides twisting with guilt. Viktor was probably making them breakfast. She would have loved to be a part of that, but she knew that her presence would only upset them more. *Best that I retreat for now.*

Maybe it was running away, but she couldn't feel too bad about it. There was a unique kind of hurt that came with the knowledge that a child thought you meant them harm. It grated against something foundational in her to think that she'd terrified them so badly.

Would they always look at her like that? Would she slip up again with others? Gods, she hoped not.

Feeling hopelessly out of place, Camille grabbed her shoes with one hand and padded over to the large window that over-looked their wild backyard. It wouldn't be hard to pop out the screen and slip out. She could text Viktor as soon as she left the territory and ask him to let her know when the children had gone.

In the meantime, she could take the m-lev downtown and maybe meet Linnea for lunch. Perhaps she'd have some tips on how to reverse the damage she'd done to the poor babies.

Camille paused, reconsidering that plan. The last time she visited her friend and came back to the pack's territory, Benny wouldn't stop asking where she got "that great new perfume". Seeing as Camille was relatively certain he was picking up on her friend's natural vanilla and spice scent, she stalwartly refused to tell him. There was no way she was sending someone like Benny sniffing around her sweet, naive friend.

But he was a shifter, so of course he pressed. They did love a game, after all. Too bad she was more stubborn than he was. He annoyed her so much that she ended up pushing him off the tiny dock by their house and into the lake. That ended the conversation well enough.

Maybe I'll see if Margot has time for lunch instead.

She was prying open the window when the sound of the bedroom door opening made her jump.

"What are you doing?"

Camille snapped her head towards the door, her eyes wide. "Ah..."

Viktor stood in the doorway. His arms were crossed, his feet spread, and his eyes narrowed on her frozen form. "Do *not* tell me you were trying to sneak out of our den, Cam."

She glanced at the shoes dangling from her hand. "...Okay, I won't."

He followed her gaze. A look of intense exasperation crossed his expressive face when he exclaimed, "For fuck's sake, sweetheart, *everyone* startles cubs sometimes. They're *fine.*"

Camille fidgeted with her shoes and refused to meet his gaze. "You didn't see the way they looked at me when I..." She swallowed hard. "They think I'm a monster, Vik."

His footsteps were little more than whispers over the bamboo floor. Warm hands skated down her upper arms. "They don't think you're a monster, Cam, I promise. Come have breakfast with us. I promise that if you give them ten minutes, they'll be crawling all over you like a jungle gym."

She shot a look at the window. "Or I could leave for the morning and—"

"Nope. You're helping us make pancakes." Viktor plucked her heels out of her hands and tossed them onto the floor. Ignoring her squawk of outrage, he grabbed her by the shoulders, spun her around, and began marching her toward the kitchen.

Speaking under her breath, she protested, "I don't even eat pancakes! And if they're uncomfortable, they won't either! Hey! Do *not* push me, mutt!"

"You can have your own breakfast, but you *will* help me make pancakes," he commanded, steering her down the hall and into the open living area. "Pack doesn't run when they make a mistake. Pack stays to fix it, Cam. That's how we build trust."

"Easy for you to say! You grew up in a pack, remember? They trust you automatically. They looked like they were afraid I'd suck the marrow out of their bones."

"And you're a part of this pack now. You have to learn how to handle these things. I'm not going to let this shake your confidence." He paused to chuckle. "That's a good threat, though. Maybe we should use it when they misbehave?"

Camille seethed. "Don't you *dare.*"

Laughing, he gave her shoulders a squeeze and steered her out of the hallway. The kitchen was to their right. Camille dug in her bare heels, but Viktor kept pushing her until they stood by the corner of the kitchen island.

The children were sitting on the floor by the kitchen table, two synthetic bowls of apple slices and sippy cups of what looked like water within reaching distance. At some point since she saw them last, Thomas had shifted and Fiona had lost her jaunty headband and her sandals. Johnnie was nowhere to be seen, so she assumed he had run off to school.

The toddlers were talking merrily, as if they hadn't just suffered a terror-induced meltdown. They were exchanging mostly coherent words and unintelligible coyote yips until the adults stepped into their line of sight.

Instantly, both children froze. Fiona stared up at Camille with wide eyes, one bruised apple slice in each fist, and Thomas halted his attempts to leap onto the kitchen table. His ears flattened and his tail lowered as he glanced between his alpha and the elvish interloper.

Was there anything more awful than children being afraid of you? She had never frightened an elvish child in her life. They understood instinctively that she would never harm them. It made her feel sick to her stomach to see the uncertainty in their eyes, the way Fiona's lower lip began to wobble at just the sight of her.

Camille wilted and tried to shrink backward.

"No, no." Viktor stopped her with a firm hand on the back of her neck. "I know you know how to win cubs over, Cam. Don't be a chicken."

"I am not a chicken," she tartly denied.

Fiona squeezed one of her apple slices and, in a thoughtful voice, informed her alpha, "Chickens not purple."

"You're right, Fi, only pretty elves are purple." Viktor gave Camille a gentle shove toward the table. "Are you okay with Cam helping us make breakfast?"

Fiona and Thomas shared a wide-eyed look. "No growling?"

Camille hovered by the table, afraid to come closer. "No growling," she promised, hands open. "I'm sorry I growled earlier.

I didn't know it was you, or I wouldn't have. You just... scared me."

Fiona took a thoughtful bite of her crushed apple slice, while Thomas slunk under the chair he had attempted to climb. He peered out from under the seat and let out a low, inquisitive whine.

"S'okay," Fiona finally replied. "Everybody growls *somedays.* "

Viktor beamed. "That's right. Even I growl sometimes, don't I?"

Both children gave their alpha identical looks of baffled amusement before Fiona argued, "Nuh. Alpha doesn't *ever.*"

Bending down, Viktor scooped up Fiona and held her up to his face. Growling playfully, he pretended to nip at her snubbed nose several times until she burst into a fit of giggles and dropped her mauled apple slices onto the floor.

The tight ball of anxiety unwound in Camille's chest. Everything was fine. The children were fine. It was all *fine.*

Feeling almost too relieved to stand, she sank into the nearest chair — which happened to be the one Thomas hid under.

Soft fur brushed her bare foot. Camille jumped.

Bending at the waist, she peered under her seat to find Thomas crouched, his backside in the air and his tail wagging. Smiling tentatively, she asked, "Little one, what are you—"

The attack came with sharp baby teeth, a sloppy tongue, and dull claws. Camille yelped, more surprised than anything, as Thomas wrestled with her bare foot. His tail thumped wildly when she attempted to lift it away, only for him to go after the ankle of her pants with a wild, playful growl.

"Seems *real* worried you're gonna eat him, doesn't he?" Viktor teased.

Camille glanced up to find him by the cabinets, Fiona on his hip and a purple mixing bowl in one hand. She flushed dark purple. "Shush!"

Leveling a stern look at the cub currently attempting to maul her toes, he said, "Don't you go hurting my mate, Thomas. She might just climb out a window and never come back."

Outraged, Camille stooped down, swiped an apple slice from one of the bowls on the floor, and sent it sailing across the kitchen to smack him in the head. Fiona squealed with laughter, while Thomas released her foot long enough to dance in a circle, yipping like it was the best thing he'd ever seen.

"Hey! No throwing food! That's a bad example for the cu—" She got him again, this time on his nose. He went momentarily cross-eyed. "Guh! Stop that!"

The cubs dissolved into hysterics as Viktor sputtered with mock offense, and Camille felt fear loosen its grip on her heart just a little.

Everything is okay. For now.

CHAPTER THIRTY-FOUR

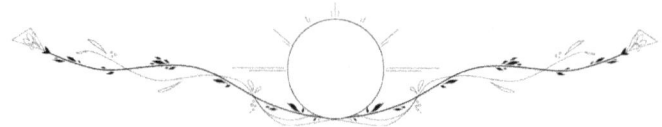

CAMILLE GOT SIX DAYS WITH THE PACK BEFORE THE fragile peace was shattered.

She knew it was coming. Sickly fear had churned in her gut all morning — her unnaturally keen intuition warning her that their time was up.

She was on her phone with her brother when the message came through. Cameron was desperate to hear the whole, sordid story and rightfully horrified when she got to the part about the shooter, but as soon as Viktor looked up from his phone with that hard expression, she knew it was time.

"I'm sorry, I have to go." Her brother protested, but she didn't hear him. Camille hit the *end call* button and lowered her phone to stare at her consort.

He stood in the doorway of their bedroom, his brows drawn down over his cornflower blue eyes and his shoulders stiff.

Her throat was dry when she croaked, "When?"

"Tomorrow."

Camille closed her eyes and forced herself to breathe, to remember that her consort was strong, in his prime, and had too much to live for to die under the claws of *Ruben Andreas*.

But didn't her father have all those things, too? Having everything to live for, being strong and determined to fight for what was right, didn't save *him*.

Warm hands cupped her face. Her lashes fluttered against her cheeks as she fought the sudden, terrible urge to cry. "It's going to be okay, Cam," he promised for the hundredth time.

She sniffed hard. "I know, but I can still worry, can't I?" The words came out tart, though she wasn't truly upset with him. How could she be, when he might leave her so soon?

"Yeah, you can." Viktor sat down next to her on the bed and drew her into his lap. His heartbeat was a steady rhythm against her side. Holding her tightly, he said, "When this is all over and we're settled in the new territory, what's the first thing you want to do?"

When this is all over... He said it so casually, as if it was a given that things would work out. She knew better than anybody that nothing was a given, nothing was ever truly promised. Her parents should have had forever. A love match, two consorts who were utterly devoted to one another, and they'd only gotten a measly thirty years together before they were torn apart.

Would she be even less lucky? Would she only get a few golden *days* with her consort and her new pack before the gods yanked him out of her life once more?

Camille dug her blunted claws into his shoulders and clung as tightly as she was able. "I don't know. I can't picture a time after — after everything right now."

Viktor skimmed his lips over her forehead. "I can. I can see us in our den, in our new territory. I can see us with the pack, having picnics and playing with the cubs in the lake. I can see us arguing about the best place to put the sofa and trying to hide what we got each other for our birthdays. And I can see us going camping, too. Just the two of us, when we need an escape from the pack for a little while."

She let out an incredulous laugh. "Camping? Elves don't go camping."

"My elf can," he playfully asserted. "I want to take you deep into the woods and have my wicked way with you."

"*Outside?*" She balked. Sex was for their sturdy bed, the couch, the shower, and sometimes the kitchen counters. Not *outside*. "Why in the world would we do that?"

She liked nature more than any other elf she knew, certainly, but Camille still had a brain in her head. There was nothing sexy about dirt, bugs, and having to pee behind bushes.

Viktor tangled his fingers in her hair and slowly tilted her head back. Looking down at her with dark eyes, he rasped, "Because I want to see my mate wild and free in the world. I want to know what it's like to hear her scream my name and hear it echo off of a fucking mountain." He dipped his head to skim his lips against hers. "I want to know how it feels to lay you down in the leaves and fuck you raw; to see the sun shine on your body as I lick your cunt."

Camille's breath hitched. Bugs aside, that didn't sound too bad at all.

"Vik..." She trailed her hand down his bare chest to rest her fingertips on the waistband of his sweatpants. He rarely wore more than that when they were home. Her coyote preferred to walk around in his skin.

It was jarring at first to see so many of his packmates wandering around in so little, if anything at all, but in the brief time she lived among them, she'd begun to acclimate. It made sense, after all. Shifting at will meant clothing had to be optional.

Besides, she liked being treated to the sight of her bite on his neck. The silvery scar told everyone that he belonged to her, just as the much larger bite on her shoulder proclaimed to all the world exactly who *she* belonged to.

Viktor used his free hand to cup her between her thighs. Her breath quickened as the heel of his palm slowly ground down against her. "Yes, sweetheart? Does that sound like a good plan to you?"

She made a soft sound in the back of her throat. Her eyes fluttered closed as she spread her thighs for him, demanding more.

He let out a husky laugh. "Yeah, I thought so. I think you'll like being fucked outside, sweetheart. I think you'll *really* like it."

Camille bit her lip and wiggled her fingers past his waistband. Her searching met hard, hot flesh that beat with his quick pulse. "Anywhere," she breathed, freeing him from his clothing. "Don't care where. I'll always like it."

Viktor hissed when she gave the head of his cock a small, proprietary squeeze. "As long as you bring *this,* I'm game."

He smiled against her cheek. "Well, I can't exactly leave it at home, can I?"

Her laugh was watery, but when he kissed her, she let him sweep away her fear in a wave of desire.

Viktor broke their kiss to peel off her shirt. When they were home, she generally forwent a bra, so his seeking mouth met the soft skin of her breast as soon as it hit the floor. Bending her slightly over his forearm, he trailed his lips over her shoulder to kiss her bite before moving them back down, over the rise of her clavicle, to gently bite the swell of her breast.

Camille's fingers flexed on his cock as a streak of pleasure ran through every nerve. Gods, she loved it when he bit her.

With his free hand, Viktor continued his torturous pressure against her aching center. The steady grind of his palm stood in stark contrast to his sharp nips to her breasts. His tongue chased away the sting, but not for long. Soon, her breasts were peppered with dark purple marks, her nipples hard and aching, while she was a wet, panting mess in his arms.

Squeezing him impatiently, half-retribution for the exquisite torture and half-desperation, she gasped, "Vik, you're driving me insane."

"Mm, that's the point, sweetheart," he breathed. "I want you crazy for me. I want you wild when you ride me."

He closed his teeth around her nipple and carefully rolled the sensitive flesh between his teeth. When the pressure bordered on pain, he sealed his lips over it instead, alternating between sucking and biting until she couldn't tell up from down any longer.

Camille made a strangled sound. The ache between her legs was becoming more and more painful by the moment, and his slowly rubbing palm was only making it worse.

Releasing his flushed cock, she placed her palm in the center of his chest and *pushed.*

Her dark nipple popped free from his lips as he fell back onto the mattress. Gold eyes stared up at her with a keen, hungry look. His cock, hard and wet at the flushed tip, pressed against his stomach under the tension of his elastic waistband.

Reaching for her with semi-shifted claws, he snatched her by the hips and dragged her over him. Those claws made quick work of her thin, comfortable leggings. "I love it when you get bossy with me. Makes me want to bite you even more," he breathed. "I love it almost as much as I love watching you ride me."

Camille shimmied his sweatpants down his hips with jerky, impatient movements, freeing him completely. Bracing one hand on his tense lower abdomen, she quickly positioned him against her and lowered herself down.

They both let out a hiss as he slid home. There was always a slight stretch, a tantalizing burn, and then the sense of fullness that never, ever got old. They were a perfect fit, and Camille loved it when he was inside her, filling her with everything he had.

She flexed her fingers on his stomach and leaned back, savoring the feeling. Her muscles fluttered around him. Pleasure bubbled in her veins. Liquid heat and deep, delicious pressure made her want to stay there, locked together, until the whole world faded into nothing.

Viktor's warm palms smoothed over her thighs and up over her hips. Digging his fingers into the soft flesh there, he commanded, "Start moving, sweetheart. I want to watch."

Oh, she wanted to *bite* him when he told her what to do. Not because she hated it, but because she *loved* it.

Camille flattened her palms against his stomach and tilted her head forward to watch him as she began to move. Friction sent shocks of pleasure through her, quickening her breath, but the feeling was greatly enhanced by the look on his face.

The muscles of Viktors neck and shoulders bunched as he strained underneath her rolling hips. His cheeks flushed and his lips, swollen and shiny, parted. His eyes were coyote gold and locked on where their bodies came together.

"So fucking pretty," he muttered, half to himself, as he used his grip to urge her to move faster, to take him deeper. When he canted his hips up at a steep angle, Camille dug her blunted claws into his stomach and cried out, *"Vik,* gods, that's too much!"

"Take it," he demanded, doing it again. "Be good for me, Cam. I want to see you make yourself come while you ride me. I want it to *wreck* you."

At this rate, she didn't think there was any other option.

Camille increased her pace, chasing the bright, hot orgasm that built and built and built. Beneath her, Viktor panted hard and snapped his hips up to meet her. The pleasure bordered on agony when he snatched up one of her hands and pressed it to where they were joined and grated, "Touch yourself."

Her fingers slid against her slick skin, pressing hard against her clitoris as she tried to keep the pace he set, the one they both needed. It was brutal, almost desperate, as they fought to hold off the world for a little longer.

It was too much. Camille lost the rhythm and fell forward on one hand, her other still stroking, circling. Their faces inches apart, Viktor lifted his head enough to snarl against her mouth as he took over completely. His hips jackknifed off of the bed with a bruising beat. Each stroke knocked the wind out of her, threatened to break her apart, until at last she came with a ragged whimper.

Viktor sealed his mouth over hers in a deep, possessive kiss as he brought her down sharply, burying himself to the hilt. His spine arched as he came, bowing that gorgeous, shifter's body beneath her own.

Gradually, the kiss softened. Viktor clasped the back of her neck with one hand and smoothed a path up her spine with the other as he lavished her with reverent nips and licks. He was not a man who gave pecks, or who would ever be content with the vanilla kind of kissing.

When Viktor kissed her, it was like he wanted to take as much of her in as possible. She *loved* it.

Eventually, as their hearts began to slow and the sweat began to cool on their flushed bodies, they turned to lie on their sides. Viktor softened inside her, but they didn't separate. Instead, he hooked her leg over his hip and held her closer, until it felt like they might blend into one seamless being.

Burying her face against his sweat-slicked throat, she whispered, "You're not allowed to leave me, Viktor Hamilton. Do you understand? You're *mine*."

His arm tightened around her back. "I lost you once, Cam. Never again."

She pressed her nose against his pounding jugular, willing tears away. "Promise."

"I promise, sweetheart. I'm yours, from now until the day we're too old for this world. Even then, I'll belong to you."

Incapable of speech, she clung to him, desperate to hold him close, as if her grip alone could stop the creep of sour dread in her gut.

CHAPTER THIRTY-FIVE

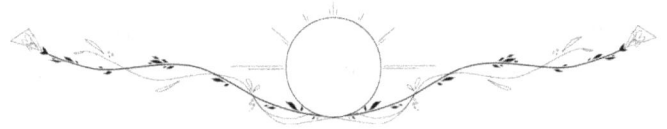

VIKTOR DIDN'T LET HIMSELF WORRY. HE HAD TOO much to live for to bother with it.

But he wasn't a fool. He was young, and perhaps he hadn't taken his mortality very seriously before his near-assassination, but he was not reckless.

He wouldn't leave his pack vulnerable if something happened to him. In between reveling in his mate and setting their move into motion, he'd made sure every member of his pack was prepared for what could happen and understood what they would need to do if he didn't make it back to them.

I will, though.

It didn't matter that Andreas was a damn big cat and he was a lean coyote. Muscle did not count for everything.

It certainly didn't make a difference when he fought his father.

As they boarded the m-jet that would take their party of shifters and elves to St. George, Viktor's mind lingered on memories he'd long ago left behind. He didn't enjoy violence, and he didn't relish his father's death, no matter how big of a bastard he was. Like the fight with Andreas, it was simply something that had to be done.

It was a fact of shifter life that sometimes death was the only option. If an animal was not smart enough to back down when cornered, it died. Full stop.

In many ways, the moment felt almost identical to when he finally challenged his father. Again, the future of his pack rested on his shoulders. Again, he was forced to fight someone he had no wish to. Again, he wondered if he would live to see his loved ones.

But as he pulled his mate into his lap and tucked her head into the crook of his neck, Viktor acknowledged that things were also entirely different. He looked around the cabin of the m-jet with clear eyes, taking in the sight of his second sitting beside Kaz and the strange tableaux that was his other senior packmates mixing with jewel-toned elves. It was a visually baffling party, but when he looked at the entourage that had come to support him, he felt... strong. Stronger than he ever had.

Theodore couldn't come, as it would be seen as direct interference by another territory, but Valen had come in his place. His second was with him. His packmates were there. Even the elves he hadn't spoken to in decades had quietly volunteered to act as Valen's security detail.

And I have my mate.

Camille clutched him close. The tip of her nose was cool when it skimmed the warm skin of his throat, and a soft, heart-breaking sound hummed from her chest. It was the softest purr he'd ever heard.

Never had he been more supported than he was at that moment. The Solbournes couldn't be there for him when he challenged his father, though they had endorsed his claim after the fact. Even his pack, wary of retribution should he lose and traumatized by their alpha, hadn't fully stepped up to support him before Dominic took his last breath.

Now, though, he had more trust, more support than he could have ever dreamed of.

The trick would be making sure he didn't lose it.

Though the air was thick with tension and Camille damn

near vibrated with worry, Viktor didn't let doubt steal his calm. He had not come this far only to lose his life to an old, bitter alpha in the rocky desert of Alliance Landing.

Time passed too quickly as he held his mate, praying that he would not let her down. It was early afternoon when they stepped off of the m-jet to meet the Alliance entourage.

As they approached the small group of shifters waiting by the tram that would take them to Alliance Landing, he and Camille stiffened. They glanced at one another before he cleared his throat and called out, "Where's Lee?"

Alphas Taisia and Asbury stood with a small group of Alliance security, all dressed in the signature Alliance white with an orange insignia on their biceps. It was Taisia, a deceptively soft-looking bear shifter, who answered, "He had to take an emergency call just before we got on the tram. He'll meet us at the Landing." She eyed Valen and Kaz with a hard, suspicious look. "We weren't told that there would be elves with you. This is shifter business."

"My mate's an elf," Viktor coolly reminded her.

Taisia waved a hand dismissively. "She's got a bite. It's different."

Viktor felt Camille start with surprise. He smoothed his hand up her back to settle it between her shoulder blades and let out an almost imperceptible sigh of relief. He had hoped that they would react that way, and he had even explained how important the bite was, but he couldn't be *sure* they would accept her until that moment.

It was a different story with Valen, though.

Adjusting the fit of his suit jacket over his trim waist, the old elf said, "Considering one of *yours* attacked our sovereign's own cousin, we have a vested interest in seeing the outcome of the fight, Alpha Taisia."

Damn, but the man could manage cold contempt like no one else. Viktor rolled his shoulders, shaking off the instinct to wither under that familiar censure. *I really don't miss being on the receiving end of that look.*

Taisia and Asbury shared a telling glance. He could see them weighing the benefits of pushing the issue, but Viktor knew they would not fight it and risk adding an offense to what was already a grave situation.

Asbury, a dark-skinned wolf shifter with an intense, reserved mien, was the one to sigh and gesture to the tram over his shoulder. "Fine. Just know that if you try to interfere with anything, the entire Alliance will have a problem with it."

Valen stepped toward the tram's open doors, but paused briefly to stand beside the wolf shifter. With a cutting smile, he said, "Boy, I'm older and meaner than your *Alliance.* You want a fight, I'll be happy to give it to you."

Clapping one heavy, jewel-toned hand on the alpha's shoulder, he strolled into the tram.

Asbury scowled after him, but didn't say anything before he turned and followed the old general in. The Alliance guards and, after a moment of clear reluctance, Taisia followed.

Viktor shared a look with his packmates before he jerked his chin toward the tram. They filed in, leaving him and his mate alone in the hangar.

He turned to look at her and found Camille already staring up at him, her face ashen and her lips pressed into a thin, determined line. Fear stole the fire from her eyes. Viktor's chest ached.

Cupping her jaw with both hands, he nuzzled the soft, fragrant hair just above her forehead and whispered, "Everything will be okay, sweetheart. I promise."

"Why isn't there a way out of this? I have a terrible feeling about this. My gut says it's going to go bad, Vik. Why does it have to be you *again?*" Her breath hitched. Clutching his t-shirt with trembling fists, she rasped, "Why can't it be someone else? I know that I should— I should support you and be proud of your courage, but I don't give a fuck about pride. I can't—"

He pressed his lips against hers, silencing her protests with the intimate contact they both craved. "I know, sweetheart," he whispered against her mouth. "I know, but there's no other way. If I didn't have to fight him, I wouldn't. I wouldn't risk our future for anything."

He felt a hot tear land on his thumb. "But why does it have to be *you?*"

"Because I'm the alpha, Cam. It's my job."

She was quiet for several heartbeats. Eventually, Camille sucked in a deep breath and shuddered, as if to shake off some terrible feeling. "Okay," she announced, leaning back to look him in the eye. She still looked queasy, but managed to say what he needed to hear anyway. "Okay, Vik. I support you. You'll do this and then we'll go home. Everything is going to be okay. It... it has to be. It just does."

It sounded like she was trying to convince herself more than him, but he took her words at face value anyway. If he dove any deeper, the thin veneer of her confidence would shatter, and he couldn't do that to her.

"My brave, beautiful mate, thank you." Viktor pressed one last fierce kiss to her lips before he wrapped his arm around her waist and began to walk them toward the tram.

Chin lifted, eyes shining with unshed tears, and dressed to the nines in an elaborate, high-collared emerald green leather coat and stilettos, his mate looked ready to take on the world for him.

Gods willing, she wouldn't have to.

As soon as they took their seats in the tram, the doors closed with a cheerful chime and the hiss of smooth hydraulics. Camille chose their seats. Nestled between Valen and their packmates, they were completely surrounded by allies as the tram lifted smoothly out of the hangar and took off toward Alliance Landing.

Viktor pushed up the arm rest between them to wrap his arm around her back, while Valen quietly reached across the aisle to hold Camille's hand. They shared a glance over her head.

There was not a hint of doubt or uncertainty in Valen's expression.

Gratitude for Valen, for all that he'd done for him, swelled in Viktor's chest. Without Valen, he might have abandoned his pack as an angry, lost teenager. He never would have learned to fight for himself, to defend others. He never would have become an alpha. He never would have become friends with Theodore.

He never would have met Camille.

Viktor owed the old general *everything*.

For all of that, it was the least he could do to win this fight, to see it through to the end, and give Camille the love she deserved.

They touched down at Alliance Landing and found a crowd waiting for them.

The air was already hot to the point of discomfort when they stepped out onto the platform. Heat shimmered off of the white, extremely durable material used to make the entire Landing compound, giving the air a shimmering, ethereal look. The sky was a huge, cloudless dome of vivid blue over their heads, and the arms of Alliance Canyon stretched out around them in two ridges of buttery orange and red-flecked brown. A plaque stood proudly beside the landing pad, reminding all who stepped off the tram what the Alliance stood for.

Communication. Cooperation. Courage.

Viktor gazed out at the small crowd assembled on the platform, seeking Andreas.

He stood by where the fight would take place: a faintly etched circle in the center of the platform — several feet away from the perilously unguarded edges, left open for the landing and takeoff of winged shifters, but not anywhere near the tram's docking zone or the entrance to the building, which sat on the opposite side of the platform.

Andreas stood with his arms crossed over his chest, his eyes bright with the shift and the lines of his body fairly *vibrating* with rage. Viktor could only imagine what it was the Alliance used to pressure a man like that into the circle.

Viktor expected to feel fury when he looked at the man who nearly killed his mate, but he didn't feel anything at all. Andreas simply wasn't worth it. When this was all over, Viktor was certain he wouldn't spare the bastard a single thought.

Two of Andreas's packmates stood beside him, their faces grim and lined with the sort of belligerent anger one typically associated with men who made themselves feel big by making others small. Everything in their body language spoke of a threat, but Viktor wasn't worried about them or particularly surprised by their growling. Only men with death wishes would dare interfere with an alpha-alpha fight.

What *did* surprise him was the sight of Lee walking out of the shining glass doors of the building with a svelte woman dressed in slim-fitting black athletic gear. Her long black curls were secured in a loose braid down her back and her golden brown skin glowed in the sunlight. Her full lips were pressed into a bloodless line.

Camille shifted closer to his side and whispered under her breath, "Who's that?"

Benny answered for him. "Lana Andreas." He shared a bemused look with his alpha. "Her father threw her out of her pack last year for insubordination. What the fuck is she doing here?"

Viktor's gut tightened with unease. It was never good when unexpected shit came up with these things. They were bad enough without being *unpredictable.*

Ignoring Andreas for now, he pressed a fleeting kiss to Camille's temple before he walked over to meet Lee and Lana.

"What's going on?"

Lee, looking troubled, braced his big hands on his hips and tilted his head toward his companion. "We've got a complication."

Viktor raised his eyebrows. "I see that."

Lana fixed him with a fathomless look. Her eyes were hazel bordering on a peculiar natural gold, and when she looked at him, he felt like she was trying to peer *inside* him.

A natural born alpha, she had a presence that immediately raised his hackles. "Alpha Hamilton, I'm here to ask you if you would be willing to cede your place in the circle to me today."

Viktor stared at her. "You... want to fight your father in my stead?"

"Yes." It was an unflinching affirmative.

His eyes bounced between the two somber faces, looking for answers. "What is happening here? You do know that this is a death match, right?" Protective rage, summoned by the awful memory of that night on the beach, strained the muscles of his neck when he added, "He tried to have my mate *shot.*"

Lana was perfectly calm when she answered, "I understand. That is exactly why I'm here."

It took a second for it to click, but when it did, Viktor could only rub his palm across his face. "Gods, you're challenging him for the pack, aren't you? That's what this is."

"Yes." She cut a look at her father. There was not even a hint of warmth in her gaze when she looked at Andreas, and it appeared he felt similarly. A snarl lifted his lip when they locked eyes. There was no love lost between father and cub. "That man is going to get my pack expelled or killed or *worse*. It's time. It's well *past* time."

Viktor shook his head. "Lana, I'm not going to request your pack's expulsion as recompense. You don't have to do this."

"I do. It's about our honor, Alpha Hamilton. If it was your pack, *your* father, what would you have done? Would you let him send one of yours out on a fool's errand like he did to Damon? Would you let an alpha like that represent your pack?"

It was well known amongst shifters that Viktor had challenged his father when he was eighteen, the youngest age a person could claim the legal status of an alpha. He couldn't very well deny that he did exactly what Lana was trying to do — killed his father before he could drive his pack into the ground.

"*Shit.*" Viktor scuffed the toe of his shoe against the platform. Glancing over his shoulder, he soothed himself with a brief look at his mate's grim, expectant face before he asked, "Did you give him the choice?"

"To step down? Or his choice between fighting you or me?"

"Both."

Lana gestured to Lee with one long-fingered hand. "Lee gave him the choice and he picked me. And yes, the pack's seniors gave him the chance to step aside. He refused."

Gods. Viktor struggled to imagine what kind of monster voluntarily *chose* to fight his own daughter. He didn't care what kind of bad blood might exist between himself and his offspring — he would never willingly raise a hand or a claw against them. He'd die first.

"It's up to you, Viktor." Lee's voice was a dark rumble. Nothing about the situation pleased him, and that came across loud and clear in the harsh lines of his normally reserved expression. "If you let Lana do this, it's over."

Unspoken was the knowledge that if she *failed,* he would have also forfeited the right to his justice. Their laws were the wild kind, but that didn't make them any less firm than that of the EVP: Once a challenge was issued and accepted, it could not be done so again without severe censure to the challenger.

Shit.

"Let me talk to Lana alone for a second, Lee." When he stepped away with a solemn nod, Viktor said, "Listen, Lana... I know that you feel like you have to do this to save your pack's reputation, but you shouldn't *have* to. If they're already behind you, then you'll become alpha anyway. Why risk it?"

Why do this to yourself?

"Because I have to." Her expression grew stark. Tension stretched her skin taut over high, blade-like cheekbones and around her hooded eyes. In an inflectionless voice, she explained, "The bastard killed my brother."

He stared at her blankly for a moment. Over their heads, a hawk let out a piercing cry that tore through the silence.

"I... *what?* I thought Juan died in a boat accident."

"That's what he had the pack say, yeah." Fury made her hazel eyes look like two hard chips of green-gold stone. "Who could tell the difference between a cougar's bite and a gator's after a few days in a swamp, right?"

A deep chill spread through his veins. It was one thing for Andreas to be a lying, manipulative bastard. It was quite another to know he was a cub killer. "Why?"

Lana shrugged. She wasn't particularly muscled, but every movement was catlike, almost *silky* in its gracefulness. "Because Juan disagreed with him? Because he didn't like the shirt he wore that day? Because he argued against my exile? It doesn't matter. He did it, and now I'm here to kill him for it."

"Gods." Viktor rubbed at the back of his neck. "I can't fault you for wanting to. Fuck me, *I* want to kill him even more than I did ten minutes ago, which I really didn't think was possible. But Lana, you have to know that this isn't— it's not just about me. It's about my pack, and it's about what this could do to you. If you lose, I legally can't pursue the matter any further. If you win, it'll change you. I promise you, it will."

Lana clenched her jaw. Speaking slowly, she replied, "I know, and I understand that I'm not sure what I would choose in your place. But I *have* to do this. Let me."

Viktor's stomach turned. He glanced over his shoulder again and caught Camille's eye. Her expression was stiff with worry, her complexion ashen. Her eyes were locked unerringly on his back. She stood tall next to Valen and Benny, but he could see past the cool elvish exterior to the broken heart underneath.

If something happened to him, she would not recover.

This is her worst nightmare, and Lana is giving me an out.

His pride demanded he not take it. Andreas had sent someone

after *him* and *his* mate. Honor demanded that he be the one to take his head off of his shoulders, to feel the slide of viscera between his claws. Righteous bloodlust was a raw howl in his blood.

But he was not an angry boy any longer. He was a man, an alpha, a mate. Someday he dreamed of being a father, a grandfather, an elder. *That* man could not think with the mind of the animal.

It was a risk to let Lana take his place, knowing that she might lose, that he might have to watch Andreas murder his own daughter in the circle, but it was one he had to take.

For his future. For *their* future. For Lana herself.

Reaching out to clasp her shoulder, he rasped, "Okay, Lana. If you're sure, then I concede my place to you."

Relief was a flash across her features — there and gone in a moment. "Thank you, Viktor."

"Don't thank me yet," he warned. "You can do that after you come out of the circle alive."

He turned to walk back to his mate and second, but a fleeting touch to his arm forced him back around. Lana's expression was still hard, but her eyes had softened with concern when she asked, "What are your plans for Damon?"

Viktor's lips thinned. "He shot at and mauled my mate, Lana."

She didn't flinch, but he caught the bob of her throat when she swallowed. "I know. I just— it's important to me that you know he wasn't always a bad man. Fear made him stupid, but he wasn't the one who gave the order. My father is manipulative, cruel. You know what that kind of alpha can do to someone weak-willed, Viktor."

"What do you want me to do with him?" Viktor gestured sharply toward Camille and Valen, whose stares he could feel burning a twin pair of holes in his back. "I can't let that shit slide, Lana. And even if I could, my mate is the sovereign's *cousin*. If I don't take his head off, Teddy will. With relish, I might add."

Neither man loved violence for its own sake. Fighting together in the ring, learning side by side what it meant to be a man and a leader, they both understood that it was a tool honed for protection and used only when absolutely necessary. The only true difference between them was that Theodore viewed threats to his loved ones as a golden opportunity for an example.

You hurt one of mine, your life is over. No second chances. No negotiation.

The only exception to that rule, of course, was when the threat came from one of his own.

"He's a father, Viktor. A good one." Lana squared her shoulders. "I'm not saying let him go without consequence. I'm just asking you to remember how easy it can be to be led astray by a bad alpha — and that maybe he doesn't have to die."

The coyote heartily disagreed. A threat to his mate was a threat that had to be extinguished. Permanently.

Still, Viktor nodded once, sharply. He respected Lana's bravery, her sense of honor, and wouldn't disrespect her by dismissing her request off-hand. "I'll think about it."

"That's all I ask."

Waving a grim-faced Lee back over, Viktor told him, "Lana's taking my place."

"You sure?"

He felt the thrum of magic in his veins, the connection that tied him to his mate and to his pack, and answered, "Yes, I'm sure."

Lee sucked in a deep breath. Looking tired but resolute, he turned to Lana. "Then it's time. Good luck, kid."

Lana inclined her head once before she turned on her heel to walk across the platform, toward that faintly etched circle where her father waited. The wind, hot and dry, whistled through the canyon to scour the compound. It carried the scents of the high desert — sand and stubborn greenery and that indefinable quality that was Glory's light.

Soon, it would also carry the coppery tang of blood.

Viktor and Lee watched her walk away, both lost in a moment of bloody remembrance. For Viktor, the sight brought back vivid memories of his own challenge; the worst and best day of his life.

For Lee, who knew? The man had seen and done everything. Only the gods knew what horrors lurked in the mind of a man who helped carve a better world out of the bloody soil left by war.

"You think this is a good idea?" Lee's voice was so low, not even keen shifter ears would hear it over the wind. Viktor, standing less than a foot away, barely caught it.

"I don't know." Viktor eyed the circle and its silent, seething occupants with dread. "It's better than how it used to be, but..."

Lee inclined his head. "There was something cleaner about the old ways."

"Cleaner, but not necessarily more fair."

"We've never been good about that, have we?"

Viktor ran a hand through his hair, pushing back the golden strands kicked up by the wind. "No, we haven't."

The old ways would have seen them fight with no witnesses, no holds barred. There would have been no rules of the circle, no consequences for intervention or discussion of terms. They would have been little more than two animals trying to rip each other's throats out.

Simpler, certainly, but the people who embraced those ways could never have functioned in an Alliance. Getting shifters to cooperate would never be *easy*, but having rules that made bloodshed the last resort at least gave them all something to hold onto. Rules gave them a singular sense of identity.

Trust. It was about *trust*.

If the Alliance was going to work, they had to trust one another to follow the rules, to understand that there would be consequences should they be broken, and that violence would not be nondiscriminatory. They would never be rid of the animal entirely — and wouldn't want to be even if they could — but they could learn to trust one another and build a better future for everyone in the process.

Lee clapped a heavy hand down on Viktor's shoulder and rumbled, "I'm really not sure if you did her a kindness or not, Vik."

"I'm not sure either." Shaking his head, he stepped back. The need to be with his mate drummed at the back of his mind. Her fear was his own, and now that his life was no longer on the line, he needed to see it gone. "I should be with my mate."

Lee's eyes, icy blue, darted toward where Camille stood rigidly with her packmates. He let out a low whistle. "An elf, huh?" He glanced down to where Viktor knew Camille's bitemark peeked out from under the collar of his shirt. Lee's full lips kicked up in a smile. "Damn, that's a deep bite. She must really like you."

Viktor pressed a hand against the silvery scar and grinned. "Yeah, I'm a lucky sonuvabitch."

"You are." Lee nodded toward where she waited. "Get back to her, then, before she marches over here and turns her claws on *me.*"

Turning on his heel, Viktor threw over his shoulder, "If you think I can stop my mate from doing *anything,* you're delusional."

Lee arched a brow. "Is that an elf thing or a Solbourne thing?"

"Both."

CHAPTER THIRTY-SIX

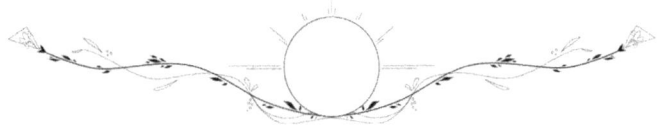

As soon as Viktor was within arm's reach, Camille curled her fingers around his forearm and pulled him closer. "What's going on?" Bile crawled up the back of her throat. "What's wrong, Vik?"

Viktor wrapped his free arm around her waist and ran the tip of his nose along her hairline. A low, soothing rumble built in his chest. "Everything is okay." Pressing his cheek against the side of her head, he met the eyes of his packmates and assembled EVP representatives. "Lana Andreas requested that she take my place in the circle. I accepted."

If she hadn't been holding onto him so tightly, Camille was fairly certain her knees would have buckled. Her breath left her on a wheeze as all the sick anxiety and fear bled out in a dizzying rush.

He's not going to fight. Thank the gods, he's not going to fight.

Fuck honor. Fuck pride. Fuck justice. Camille didn't care about any of it. All she needed, all she *wanted* was her consort to live.

Curling her arms around his middle, she dropped her head onto his shoulder and shuddered. "Thank you," she whispered, ragged. *"Thank you."*

Viktor cupped the back of her head with one warm hand in a

wordless gesture of understanding. She did not need to hear the words to know he'd given up the chance to exact shifter justice for her sake. She *knew* it, just as she knew that her cloying fear over the past week was not simply the past catching up to her — it was *instinct.*

The Solbournes didn't advertise the fact that they routinely bore Seers, but Foresight ran in their family like a wide, turbulent river. Unlike Delilah, Camille couldn't boast any real skill with the ability, she knew the difference between knowing and *knowing.*

She *knew* that something was going to go terribly wrong if Viktor fought Andreas like she knew that Elio was a threat and that her mother's end had loomed closer every day.

Relief was a lead weight in her stomach. It threatened to drag her down to her knees, but Viktor wouldn't let that happen. With his arms wrapped tightly around her, he told Benny, "Lana's got the support of her pack. It didn't feel right to fight her on it if she really wanted to handle her father herself."

"It's the honorable thing, sure, but what if she loses?" Camille didn't have to lift her head to know Benny had a deep, dark frown etched into his expression.

Kaz answered for Viktor. "If she can't do it, then we'll handle him. Quietly."

"That's against UTA law, my dude," Benny dryly fired back.

"Only if you get caught," Kaz answered, equally dry. Camille felt rather than heard Viktor's quiet snort.

"We can talk about that later. If we're lucky, it may not even be a conversation we have to have." Viktor's fingers stroked through the short strands of her hair, soothing the anxious beast that paced inside of her. It railed against the threat that stood so close, to so many strangers in his proximity. All it wanted to do was hide him away from the world and rub her skin against his until they were drunk on one another.

But that wasn't possible. At that moment, she could only be thankful that she would not have to watch her consort step into that circle.

Camille pressed a lingering, reverent kiss to the base of his throat before she lifted her head and took half a step back. Viktor didn't let her go, but loosened his arms around her enough to allow her to shift to his side. "Okay," she said, looking around at all the hard, angry faces of her family and her new packmates. "What happens now?"

~

She had never witnessed a challenge, but she had lived under their shadows for all her life.

Elves had once been famed for their death matches. In the first few months after Delilah's abdication, Theodore was challenged six times for the sovereignty — and won every match without killing his opponent. They couldn't afford to lose even a single elf, so what had once been fights to the death rarely went quite so far in the modern day.

Shifters, though, were just as vicious as they had always been.

She never thought she would need to see a challenge herself and had certainly never desired to change that. Why would she, when her family had been so very scarred by one?

Though she was relieved that Viktor would not be the one fighting today, she still felt a deep unease as they gathered at the circle's edge. They were flanked by their entourage, with Benny, Diana, Kaz, and Valen just behind them, watching their backs. Across the circle, the assembled alphas and the Alliance guards watched with somber faces. Between the two groups, Andreas's second and his brother stood with arms loose at their sides, their eyes bright with aggression.

In the middle of the circle, with their backs to one another, Lana and her father stood. They were naked, their skin glowing gold in the relentless sunlight, with several feet of empty space stood between them. While Andreas faced his packmates, Lana stared out over the jagged expanse of the canyon and its dome of baby blue sky, her expression clear of everything except a serene determination.

Camille wondered what kind of person it took, what kind of pressure was necessary, to drive the young cougar shifter into the circle. It would have been easier to simply let Viktor take the risk. If he won, her understanding was that Lana would become alpha by default.

Was it courage that drove her? Revenge? Pride?

She tried to imagine herself standing there, facing off with her mother. Camille could picture herself turning around and seeing Marian there, her skin glowing with the deep amethyst that had been Theron's Solbourne's favorite feature. Could she have looked in her mother's eyes and still decided to kill her?

Certainly, there were many moments in their relationship that Camille was certain she *hated* her mother.

Marian's rage and grief was directionless and more often than not found purchase with her children. When Camille guarded her brother from it, she opened herself up to take more. Marian would often berate her for hours at a time, relentlessly pulling at every little thread in her daughter's self-esteem until she simply shut down, waiting quietly for the rage to flow back the way it came.

When the tide washed out, Marian was left more grief-stricken than before. She often felt deep regret for what she'd said and done, but never asked for forgiveness. Instead, she leaned on the daughter she had just railed against for comfort, to be cosseted and coddled until the pain went away.

Camille loved and hated and pitied and understood her mother in those moments.

But Marian was not simply volatile. She was proud, and she loved her children even when she couldn't bear to look at them. She lived in fear of what elvish society would do to them. She nursed them and played with them and watched indulgently as the twins splashed in the river behind the estate.

Marian held Camille as she sobbed that night twenty years

ago. She stroked her hair and did not ask questions, didn't berate her for entertaining a secret relationship with a nobody shifter. She simply held her daughter as she cried. The next morning, she handled the situation with brusque efficiency, and Camille had never, ever been more grateful to have her as a mother than she was then.

So no, Camille thought, she could not have turned around and unsheathed her claws on her mother's fine skin. She could not have looked in her violet eyes and still chosen to end her life.

Love existed between them even when old grief threatened to swallow her mother whole. She couldn't see even a spark of that between Lana and her father.

When the shifters turned to face one another, they locked eyes. While Andreas nearly vibrated with unconcealed rage and contempt, Lana appeared coolly aloof, her hazel eyes clear of regret or fear or pain.

From his place by the edge of the circle, Lee cleared his throat. "Last chance, both of you. If you want to back out, say it."

"Not a chance. It's about damn time we did this." Andreas shifted his stance and lifted his upper lip over rapidly elongating fangs. Magic was a deep, disconcerting shimmer over his skin as the cougar hovered just below the surface. "Come on, Lana-bean. If you think you've got the fucking stones to take on your father, then *do it.*"

Two jagged, rumbling growls spilled from Andreas's pack-mates. When Camille glanced at them, all she saw was furious agreement. Edging closer to Viktor, she breathed in his ear, "They hate her, don't they? Look at their faces."

He nodded once, but never took his eyes off of the two shifters in the circle. In a voice that was not at all subdued, he answered, "Yeah, they do hate her. They're loyal to the alpha that lets them have power. You take that away and they're nothing. No one wants to be nothing, but *especially* two pieces of shit like that."

"Watch your fucking mouth, *dog,*" Andreas's brother, a

younger, leaner version of the man who wanted her consort dead, snarled from across the circle.

Viktor smiled. "That's my mate's job, actually, and I'm pretty sure she doesn't have a problem with it."

"Enough," Lee barked. Focusing back on the pair in the circle, he inclined his head toward Lana and asked, "You still want to do this?"

She didn't hesitate. "Yes."

Lee sucked in a deep breath and propped his hands on his hips. A beat of tense silence passed before he announced, "This is a fair challenge. You both know the rules. Only one of you leaves. No interference from the outside. Anyone who tries will be executed. Understood?"

They answered in unison, "Yes."

"All right." Lee inclined his head. "Go."

Magic was a liquid ripple around both of their forms. She'd seen Viktor shift a hundred times, but it never felt normal, or commonplace. The universe seemed to tear itself apart and reform around them as bones snapped, ligaments tore, and fur burst from what was once sun-warmed skin. The entire transformation took less than a handful of seconds, but one of them was ever-so-slightly quicker.

The moment her paws touched the ground, Lana launched herself forward. Her body was a sleek, sun dappled blonde with vivid black markings around her face, tail, and heavy paws. A terrible yowl tore from her throat as she descended on her father mid-shift.

The shifters collided with a flurry of claws and snapping teeth, their great cougar bodies locked in a life or death struggle as each tried to get the upper hand. Lana was slightly smaller than her father, but that wasn't necessarily a bad thing. No matter how he tried, he couldn't seem to get a firm hold on her. She darted out from under him and leapt on his back. Her claws came down on his flank just before he shook her off and dove for her throat.

Next to Camille, Viktor shifted his stance, subtly putting

himself between her and the battling cougars in the circle. Every single person gathered around the edge looked ready for anything as the fight got worse.

Heavy cougar jaws snapped and tore at beautiful, tan fur. Razor sharp claws sank into thick muscle. Growls and deep, pained yowling echoed all around them, bouncing off of the canyon walls to fill the valley below with the song of violence.

It was hard to tell who was winning. They both looked so similar, and when they were in constant motion, grappling with one another, they were simply two tan and black blurs. Red blood splattered the white platform. It smeared under scrabbling paws, creating a macabre painting baked by the sun.

Camille watched with the eyes of a predator and a deep internal stillness. It was horrible and yet astonishing to watch. Two shifters, so alike, clashed in a remarkable display of strength and skill. The beast in her was impressed by their speed, their viciousness. The woman could only find deep, aching relief that she was not watching her own consort out there.

It was not his blood smeared across the platform. They were not his howls of pain and rage that filled the air.

He stood beside her — strong, grim-faced, with one arm wrapped firmly around her waist. His scent was a heady perfume in the air, guarding her against the metallic stink of blood and magic, and his nearness was a balm to her pressing fear.

Somewhere in the tangle of limbs, there was a deep, bone-chilling *snap*.

Camille started, her eyes widening as one of the cougars — gods, she wished she could tell which *one* — managed to pin the other down. Blood smeared their muzzle and eyes of wild gold were locked on their opponent as they bore down on its neck.

One of the pinned cougar's legs collapsed at an odd angle, destroying their balance and sending both to the ground. Camille could only guess by the wet sheen and glint of white bone that the snapping sound was the cougar's right foreleg.

Digging her fingers into Viktor's side, she breathlessly whispered, "Who—"

"Lana's on top," he answered, voice raw. "She's got him."

She swung her eyes back to the pair just in time to see Lana close her jaws around the back of Andreas's neck. He thrashed hard, trying to shake her off, but she would not be budged. Pride for the woman Camille didn't know and horror for what she had to do swelled in her chest. *I cannot imagine the strength it takes to do this for your people.*

For her mate, she would rip out any throat, put herself at any risk, but for her *people?* Camille was not sure she could have killed her own mother, no matter the circumstance.

Viktor did.

She risked looking away from the bloody spectacle to check on her consort. He stood stock still beside her, his beloved face carved from stone. Did he suffer when he watched Lana do what he'd done? Did he have regrets? Did he feel guilt and yet know that it was the right choice — the *only* choice?

Camille's throat thickened as she peered at him from under her lashes. In that moment, she got the acute sense that they had both suffered a great deal in the twenty years that lay between them. Perhaps that suffering had made them strangers, but it also made them akin.

There was so much she didn't know and she—

Movement outside the circle caught her eye. Over her shoulder, she watched as magic rippled around Andreas's packmates just as their alpha let out a horrendous roar.

All eyes were fixed on the death match, so she was the only one who caught the split second it took for them to turn from man to cougars.

"Stop!" Her bellow came too late. Two sets of heavy paws slammed down inside the circle. Both cougars were already bounding forward, ready to leap onto Lana's back and tear her from victory before anyone else in the circle could turn their heads.

In an instant, everything changed.

Magic burst like bubbles around them as one shifter after another burst into their other forms. Viktor howled in outrage and shoved her back into Kaz's waiting arms. Her cousin snatched her to his chest and hauled them both backward, toward the cover of the tram, as Valen and the rest of their entourage waded into the melee.

Everyone arrowed toward the brawling cougars. Coyotes mingled with lynx, wolves, and swooping eagles. Elves moved to guard the tram, matte black claws at the ready, and Lee, unshifted, barked orders for everyone to stop from somewhere near the center.

Camille tried to follow the figures, her eyes moving, searching for her familiar coyote, and found him guarding Lana's back as she struggled to snap her father's neck and defend herself at the same time.

The cougars were thoroughly outnumbered, but they were close enough to Lana and her father to make separating them a difficult and dangerous task. All the shifters were bigger than their natural animal counterparts, but cougars in particular had a muscle advantage over nearly everyone except the wolves and, notably, Taisia the bear shifter.

"Gods, would you look at that," Kaz muttered. Together, they watched as Taisia's huge body launched into the fray, clearing a path toward Viktor and Lana. Viktor was outmuscled by his opponent, but he was quick enough to keep them busy until Taisia took one heavy paw to their side and simply swept them off the platform.

There was a blood curdling yowl as the cougar tumbled over the edge and down into the canyon below.

There was a split second of stunned silence, followed by the soft *whump* of a body making contact with the ground and, from the center of the fray, the meaty crunch of a neck being broken.

For a frozen moment, no one moved, nor breathed, nor dared

to make a sound as Lana opened her jaws and let her father's corpse fall to the platform.

She lifted her head and, opening her blood-streaked muzzle, let loose a roar of triumph that shook the canyon walls.

Viktor and the other cougar were the first to recover. Two things happened at once: the last of Andreas's loyal packmates lunged for Lana's throat, and Viktor leapt at him from the side. Her coyote knocked the surprised cougar to one side and, in the coyote way, was immediately joined by his packmates.

Letting out a musical, yipping howl, they worked together to pin the larger shifter down. Jaws clamped on legs, digging into heavy muscle to wrench him onto his back, and coyote claws shredded a soft underbelly.

Viktor, snarling muzzle smeared with blood, dropped all his weight onto the cougar's prone chest. In one smooth move, Camille's consort lowered his head, ripped out the cougar's throat, and tossed it over the side of the platform to join the corpse below.

In the calm that settled over them, Lee sighed, "Well, that's one way to do it."

CHAPTER THIRTY-SEVEN

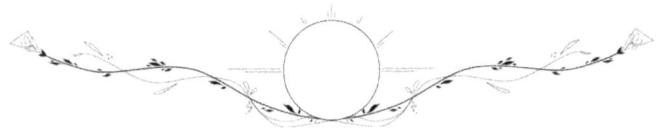

THE TRIP BACK TO THE EVP WASN'T EXACTLY celebratory, but it wasn't somber, either. The tension of knowing what lay ahead had vanished, leaving a tram full of predators to mingle and discuss the mess that was the challenge.

Impressed by the shifter ferocity they witnessed, the elvish guards that accompanied them broke their usual stony silence to talk to the bloodied and rowdy coyotes. Kaz sprawled in his seat and stared out the window, his expression darkly satisfied, and Valen had broken the usual code of conduct and gotten his phone out to call Theodore as soon as the tram lifted off the platform.

Benny was in a heated discussion about the best way for a coyote pack to overcome a larger threat — say, a dragon — and Diana sat in the back, calmly polishing a wicked looking harpy knife with a tiny rag pulled from the pocket of her jeans.

Camille sat in Viktor's lap. Her legs were slung over the arm of their chair, and her head rested beside his on the seat. They were set away from the rest of the group, and with all the talking, it was easy to feel like they were in their own little world.

"Were you scared?" he asked, skimming his palms up and down her back.

She stared at a fleck of dried blood on his cheek. He missed it when he'd washed in the compound's bathroom, probably because it was hidden in his usual scruff.

Lifting her hand, she used her thumb to ever-so-gently scrape it away from his skin.

"No," she answered. "Not after I knew you weren't fighting. I *knew* something was going to go wrong if you did. Once Lana took your place, I was okay — even when shit hit the fan."

She shuddered to think of what might have happened if things had gone according to plan. Would she have been too focused on the fight to catch the two cougars mid-shift? Would Viktor have been slaughtered before they even felt the need to break the rules? Camille couldn't possibly know and didn't want to.

My consort is safe in my arms. Nothing else matters.

"It didn't bother you seeing me fight?"

She shook her head. "No. I knew you would be okay."

"You trusted me." Viktor turned his head to brush the tip of his nose against her cheek. His voice was soft, husky with feeling. "You knew I'd keep my promise to come back to you."

Camille swallowed the lump in her throat. "Of course I did. I'm your mate."

"You are. Gods, I don't know how I got so lucky, but you are." He curled his arms around her middle and hugged her close. Burying his nose in her hair, he whispered, "Thank you for being here with me, Cam. I know how hard this was for you."

"I don't care. You don't do anything without me anymore. We're a team."

"No," he said, pulling back just enough to give her a wide, coyote grin, "we're *pack.*"

"Right." Camille stroked blond waves back from his cheeks, her expression tender. "We're pack. You and me and Benny and Diana and all the babies and everyone else. Right?"

"Right."

Trailing her fingers down across his brow, she asked, "Are you okay? Did this bring up..."

She couldn't quite figure out how to finish that sentence, so instead she left it hanging. There was no good way to ask if seeing Lana execute her father had brought up trauma from his own death match, after all.

And of course, Viktor understood what she couldn't say. Gaze darkening, he answered, "It'll never be a good memory, Cam. There will always be a part of me that hated doing it, that hates myself for doing it — that will always hate him for *making* me do it. But I don't regret it and I don't think Lana will, either."

Viktor pressed the softest of kisses to her lips, seeking and taking comfort, before he continued, "My father terrorized his pack. He stole money and nearly bankrupted the pack. He didn't even like *cubs*. I don't think he was always like that, but by the time I came around, I think he'd grown to hate being an alpha — maybe even having a pack at all. I don't think I would have begrudged him that if he just did the right thing and walked away, but he couldn't seem to give it up."

"Some people become trapped in their own power," she said, thinking of her uncle Thaddeus and his half-orc son sitting at the far end of the tram. "Even when they want to leave it behind, they can't seem to fathom ever doing so. It's somehow better to destroy everyone else's life than give up control."

Viktor touched their foreheads together and closed his eyes. "You're right. And because they're miserable, selfish fucks, they make their pain everyone else's problem. So to answer your question, yeah, today hurt. It brought up shit I wish I could bury, but it also reminded me that what I did was right, just as what Lana did was right."

They were quiet for a while, half-listening to the buzz of conversation and their own steady breathing, until Camille dipped her head to give him a long, thorough kiss.

When she pulled back, Viktor looked up at her from under eyes gone half-mast and asked, "What was *that* for?"

"I'm proud of you," she answered, blinking back the sting of tears. "You're a good alpha, Viktor. I am... I am so proud to be your mate."

Instead of speaking, he let out a huff of air and bent to bury his face in her shoulder. Strong arms locked around her back. His muffled "I love you" barely made it over the hum of the tram and the current of conversation ebbing and flowing around them.

But she heard it.

Nearly the entire pack met them on their return. Their elvish entourage waited on the city side of the green corridor, their vehicles idling quietly in the final splash of sunlight before sunset. The Merced pack had set up tables and barbecues while they waited for their alpha's return. Cubs tumbled together in the grass, shifted and un-shifted, while the adults mingled with beers in their hands.

A cheer of relief went up when Viktor climbed out of their car. Unwilling to make them wait a moment longer than necessary, Benny had called the waiting pack seniors with the news well before they touched down in San Francisco. Still, they rushed toward the cars to pull their alpha into a series of bone crushing hugs.

Little ones swarmed around, eager to get in on the action, and exuberant yips mingled with the childlike howls of delight when cubs were hoisted up onto shoulders and swung playfully in the air.

While Viktor was busy, Camille slowly climbed out of the car and hung back on the border, where the sidewalk met the line of lush green grass. Other doors opened, too, and soon an uneasy group of stern-faced elves joined her.

Kaz slung a heavy arm over her shoulders and pulled her into his side. His rich scent of wood smoke and leather was a familiar comfort. When he spoke, his voice was dark with the protectiveness that made him exactly who he was. "You okay, sweet?"

"Yeah," she answered, leaning into him. "It's good to see Viktor with his pack, is all."

He nudged her back. "Aren't they your pack now, too?"

She glanced down at where the tips of her stilettos touched the grass. "Yes. It'll take a while to get used to, though."

Elves didn't share well. That was part of the reason they could never manage the close-knit pack system that the shifters had. Instinct made her want nothing more than to hide her consort away from the world. She wanted to dig her claws into him and keep him to herself.

While they had their own version of alphas, they didn't have... *this.*

Camille stared longingly at the crowd of semi-familiar faces. She tracked the progress of two wobbly-legged toddlers chasing a ball under a picnic table and then the serene-faced elder who wandered indulgently after them. She looked for her mate in the throng. He was speaking animatedly with Mia, two howling teenagers held under his arms in playful headlocks.

It was a sprawling family. It was *Viktor's* family.

She needed to be a part of it like she needed to breathe, and being shy would get her nowhere. The coyotes would not tiptoe around her. They would not indulge an alpha who couldn't insinuate herself amongst them. Camille had to forge her own path through the thicket of their pack.

Turning her head, she peered up at Kaz's beautiful, jewel-green face. He gave her a bittersweet smile. "It's okay, sweet. I know you've got to go be with your pack now. But you'll always be ours, too, all right?"

Because she wasn't sure that she had ever said it to him before, Camille breathed deeply and told him, "I love you, Kaz. You know that, right?"

One green knuckle brushed the curve of her cheek. His expression, normally closed off, briefly cracked. For just a moment, she spied the depths of something great and tender in her stoic cousin. "I love you too, Cammie."

He pressed a hard kiss to the top of her head. "Go on," he muttered gruffly, nudging her over onto the grass. "Go be with your flea-bitten coyote already."

"I do *not* have fleas."

Camille turned her head to find Viktor waiting for her. At some point, he'd managed to lose his shoes and socks, but had acquired a gray-furred cub that couldn't have been more than a few months old. The cub looked right at home tucked into his elbow. Reaching for Camille with his free hand, he looped his arm around her waist and drew her under his arm.

"You don't think I have fleas, do you?" he teased.

Camille wrinkled her nose. "I share a bed with you, so I certainly hope not."

"We do not have fleas in this pack!" Adjusting his one-armed hold on the sleepy cub, he demanded, "You look Bea in the eye and tell her she has fleas."

Bea stared up at them all with eyes of the sweetest whiskey brown and, as if on cue, unrolled her tiny pink tongue in a canine yawn.

Camille made a soft sound of delight and, after glancing at Viktor to make sure it was okay, gently stroked the cub between her tiny triangle ears. "I would *never* say something like that to Bea," she promised. "Would you, Kaz?"

Sneaking a look at her cousin, she found him staring at the cub with the same unease she felt when Viktor introduced her to the pack. His dark eyes shifted over their shoulder, towards all the milling shifters, and back to the cub with open discomfort.

Before she could say something, Viktor asked, "You good, Kaz?"

Kaz gestured to the stiff guards standing a few feet away. Valen had left them at the m-jet hangar to go home and be with his consort, but Camille was confident he would have been included in Kaz's gesture, too, if he stayed.

"Should we go?"

Viktor peered at the orc's tense expression before slowly asking, "Why would we ask you to leave?"

Camille shot him a look. She knew for a fact that he understood why the elves and her cousin might be uneasy, but he clearly wanted Kaz to *say* it.

Frowning, he answered, "Because you've got young here. We wouldn't want to make anyone uncomfortable."

Viktor didn't say anything for a moment. Apparently making some decision, his expression was thoughtful when he met Camille's eyes. She knew what he was going to do approximately half a second before her consort stepped away from her and — *gently* — shoved the cub into Kaz's bulky arms.

Panicked, he said, "What the fu—"

"Don't swear in front of the cubs," Viktor admonished him. Clapping Kaz on the shoulder, he gave him a nudge toward the party. "You get cub duty until she wants to be let down. Then just put her on the grass. She'll find her way back to her parents."

Ignoring the way Kaz was actively attempting to hand the now much more awake cub back to her alpha, Viktor made a swirling gesture with his hand, motioning toward all the assembled guards. "Join the party, folks. It's about time we started trusting each other, don't you think? I mean, my guess is your sovereign has already invited himself and is..." Viktor checked an imaginary watch. "...about five minutes away. If *he* thinks he can be around our cubs, then I think you can, too."

The guards looked at one another, then at Kaz, who was busy being gnawed on by tiny puppy teeth and looking positively terrified. When he was no help, they looked to Camille for direction.

Straightening her spine, she turned to walk fearlessly into the fray. Camille waved over her shoulder and proudly called out, "Come on! We can't have the shifters thinking we're *cowards,* can we?"

CHAPTER THIRTY-EIGHT

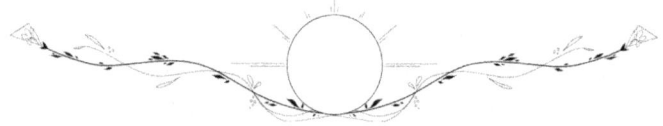

"SEEMS A LITTLE OSTENTATIOUS, IS ALL," VIKTOR muttered, pulling at the stiff collar of his barely buttoned dress shirt.

They were sitting by a massive wall of windows that overlooked Union Square and its soaring column topped with a triumphant, winged harpy cast in bronze. The day was beautiful and blue. Viktor wished he was outside, running along the jagged edges of the lake or the sunbaked beach, enjoying the weather as only a shifter could.

"Even an animal can sit at a linen-covered table for a minute," Theodore teased from his side of the table. He had removed his suit jacket and rolled up his shirtsleeves to reveal powerfully corded blue forearms. One was draped casually over the back of his wife's chair. Claws blunted, he slowly dragged his fingertips through the loose strands of her hair.

Camille, seated beside Viktor, leaned across the table to flick his other hand, which was resting by a glass of whiskey. "Don't call my consort an animal, you oaf."

Theodore flashed his fangs at his cousin, but there was only humor in his eyes when he replied, "I'm the sovereign and head of this family. You can't call me an oaf!"

"And *I'm* an alpha," she shot back, saccharine sweet. "So I can do whatever I want."

Viktor grinned and squeezed his mate's thigh beneath the table. "She's got you there, Teddy."

Theodore opened his mouth to retort, but Margot smoothed her palm down his chest and dryly interjected, "Isn't today supposed to be serious? *Monumental,* even? Why are you poking at your cousin, baby?"

Viktor coughed into his fist, covering up a bark of laughter.

He didn't care how many times he heard it: listening to the tiny, red-haired healer call the terrifying sovereign of the Elvish Protectorate *baby* would never, ever get old.

"I can be serious *and* annoy my cousin," Theodore smartly replied. Catching his wife's hand, he brought it up for a brief kiss to her palm. "I can *multitask,* as you so love to say."

"Besides," Viktor added, smiling, "they're not here yet."

Theodore nodded. "See?"

"Angelique will be here with her mate any minute." Margot dared to tap the tip of the sovereign's blue nose. "Be *nice,* okay? No growling."

"Hey, I'm only here for mediation. This one isn't on me." Theodore arched his brows at Viktor. "My wife is right, though. This is some monumental stuff you're trying to pull off. You ready for the big time, Vik?"

"It's time," he answered, sharing a look with his mate. "I've been thinking about this for years. They deserve this chance, Teddy."

Not that the weres couldn't manage it well enough on their own, but Viktor knew what it was like to feel like the world was against you. If he could help out a pack that had never been offered even a *chance,* he was going to do it. No one should have to fight for every scrap they got.

Margot reached across the table to touch his knuckles with the tips of her warm fingers. Immediately, magic hummed from the contact like a low-grade electrical current. "You're doing the right thing, both of you," she said, eyes suspiciously shiny. "They're good people. Very, very good people."

The sound of a door opening echoed across the cavernous room that was The Rotunda. If he peered over the railing of the balcony, he would see shoppers moving about their business, unaware of the world-shaking deal that was about to take place just over their heads.

Camille turned in her seat to peer over the open area that separated them from the far end of the restaurant. "They're here."

The strange, opulent restaurant had been cleared out for their use. Only a skeleton crew of waitstaff remained, giving them much-needed privacy. Conversation and soft music floated up from the floors below. It was the only sound in the restaurant as the maitre'd escorted the diminutive form of Angelique Batacan and her mate, Anders Batacan, around the circular room toward the only occupied table.

Angelique was a small, soft-looking woman in her mid-200's. Her skin was a soft brown and her hair was a long, straight curtain down her back. Laugh lines and crow's feet had just begun to kiss her skin, but her most striking feature was her two different colored eyes — the mark of a were.

Her mate, a lanky Dutchman with straw blond hair, one pale blue eye and one dark brown, walked beside her, his expression cheerful. Angelique, on the other hand, could only be described as suspicious. Her dark brows were drawn in a deep frown and her body language read, *Look at my mate wrong and I'll claw your eyes out.*

He respected that.

As they neared the table, everyone stood up to greet the new arrivals. Viktor took the lead.

Sticking out his hand like he'd never met the woman before, he said, "It's good to see you, Angelique. You too, Anders."

Angelique gave his hand one firm shake. "Well, it's nice to see *some* of you." She gave a pointed nod in Margot's direction. "You doing well, Healer Goode?"

"She's just as well as she was the *last* time you asked her if she needed rescuing, Alpha Batacan," Theodore deadpanned.

Margot elbowed her husband in the stomach, but Viktor was certain the blow bounced off with little to no impact. "I'm doing *great,* thank you."

"It's always worth checking," Angelique sniffed.

Hoping to defuse some of the tension, he gently pulled Camille up beside him and proudly announced, "Angelique, Anders, this is my mate, Camille Dia Solbourne. Cam, this is Angelique and Anders, the alphas of the San Francisco were pack."

Camille inclined her head and offered them a small, close-lipped smile. "It's nice to meet you both. Margot's told me some very... interesting stories about your teens."

Anders slung his arm around his mate's shoulders and let out a hearty laugh. To Viktor, it sounded a bit like an accordion dropped down a staircase. "Ah, you know how it is! Teenagers are always getting into trouble, and were-teens are even worse. Absolutely *no* impulse control. We're just glad that Healer Goode hasn't become too busy to make house calls."

Margot smoothed a lock of hair back behind one dainty ear. Her cheeks were flushed when she answered, "Any time, Anders. I like to help."

"How's Frankie?" Theodore's voice took on a somber note, drawing attention back to him.

Viktor had only heard bits and pieces of Margot and Teddy's encounter with the weres, but he knew that at some point Theodore had reflexively threatened a young man's life. Knowing how seriously his friend took that sort of thing, Viktor wasn't surprised by his remorse.

Theodore's normally affable expression was a little more rigid when he pressed, "Is he in school?"

There was the most minute softening in Angelique's tough exterior when she answered, "Yes. He's doing great. Thank you for writing his recommendation letter. I don't think they would have let him into the university otherwise."

The air lost the last of its levity. Unspoken was the truth that, even nearly two hundred years on from their creation, weres continued to be rejected by many.

Theodore nodded. A little bit of the tension left his expression. "I'm glad to hear it worked out. You know you can contact me if he needs help with anything else."

Angelique neatly bypassed that statement when she asked, "And how is Roger? Still rotting in your dungeon?"

There was no love lost there, apparently. Not that it surprised Viktor overly much. Angelique was the alpha of a volatile pack. That meant she had to be a strict enforcer of rules to keep order.

When Roger, a member of her pack, went rogue and accepted Delilah's offer to bomb Margot's Healing House in return for some cash, he directly defied his alpha's order to treat her as one of their pack.

As far as Viktor knew, the only thing that spared him from a quick and dirty death at his alpha's hands was Margot's intervention.

That, and Viktor privately speculated that the only reason he was still alive was because he didn't actually know who the elvish woman who hired him was. If word got out that Delilah Solbourne had bombed a Healing House, it would have been very, *very* bad.

The healer in question shared a look with her husband before she answered vaguely, "No. He's... working for us now, actually."

"Doing what?" Angelique asked, eyebrow arching.

Theodore smiled a small, cold smile. "Don't worry about it."

The were shook her head. "Probably best I don't know. As long as he's out of sight and out of trouble, I'm content. We don't need a dipshit like him making our reputation *worse.*"

Which is why this is important, Viktor reminded himself. *This matters.*

Clearing his throat, he gestured to the empty seats. "Please sit. They should bring our lunch out soon, but I'd like to get business out of the way first."

When everyone was in their respective chairs, Angelique eyed him from across the table. "So, Vik, what's all this about?"

Viktor found Camille's hand beneath the table and intertwined their fingers. Smiling slightly, he said, "So, you might have heard that we're moving."

"Yes." Angelique looked begrudgingly interested. "I heard you got into the Alliance and received a cushy bit of territory in Minnesota for your trouble."

"It's in a place called Prairie," Camille explained, as proud of their new home as an acquisitive elf could be. "Not too far from Minneapolis and with a gorgeous lake for the cubs to play in."

"Sounds like a dream." Anders nudged his mate's shoulder with his own. "Our sons love to swim, but it's hard to get them to a pool in the city regularly."

Viktor held Angelique's gaze when he asked, "What if you didn't have to find a pool for your boys to play in?"

He watched her eyes narrow. "What are you talking about?"

"I'm talking about selling your pack the Merced territory."

There was a moment of stunned silence, followed by Angelique slowly easing herself backward. She swallowed before deadpanning, "You aren't serious."

"We're *very* serious." Viktor braced his elbow on the edge of the table and leaned forward. "I've looked at your public investments and the estimated profits from your restaurants. I know that you can afford it, and I also know that you've been looking for a piece of land."

"If you were looking, why haven't you left the city?" Margot asked, gentle but firm in the way only a healer could manage.

Anders's voice was hushed, his joviality subdued by shock when he answered, "The virus spreads most in the cities and it's where new weres go to look for help. If we went too far, more weres would fall through the cracks. We don't want that to happen. We want to be where we're most needed."

"That's why I'm offering you Merced," Viktor continued. "You wouldn't have to leave the city, but you could finally have your own territory, your privacy. You could really build something for all those weres who need your help."

Angelique's voice was thready when she asked, "Why would you do that?"

Viktor sat back in his chair and pulled Camille's hand up. Pressing their twined fingers to his heart, he looked around the table at Theodore and Margot, at Angelique and Anders, until his gaze came back to the violet eyes that held his heart and soul.

"Because," he answered, "we are all trying to build a better future. We all want something more than rivalry and suspicion. We want our cubs to grow up in a better world than the one we were born into." Looking back at Angelique, he said, "You want to help people, Angelique. It's all you've been doing since you came to this city. I think it's about damn time someone made that a little easier for you."

No, the weres weren't perfect. He knew for a fact that they had their fingers in plenty of smuggling operations and black-market trading in the Underground. But the elves had their spies and the shifters had their death matches.

No one was perfect.

Angelique blinked hard and clenched her jaw. For a moment, there was no sound but the murmurs from below the balcony and the faint squeaking of ice cubes melting in glasses of water.

The were cut her eyes to Theodore, who watched the scene play out with a reserved expression. "And what about you? You're okay with this?"

Theodore shrugged. "Don't see why I wouldn't be."

"If we buy that land, we'd become a legally recognized pack," she shot back.

"The *first*, as I understand it."

"You are just... *fine* with a new faction being born right in the heart of your capital?" Angelique scoffed. "What's the catch? If we sign off, you'll revoke the semi-autonomous status of the land?"

"There isn't a catch," he calmly answered. "The land stays the same, and the pack that occupies it gets the benefits afforded to it by the treaty my grandfather signed. That's it."

Viktor jumped in to add, *"You* would become the Merced pack, Angelique."

"If you do this," Camille murmured, "you will set a precedent for all were packs. Someday you might even have your own representatives in the UTA Congress. Don't you want that?"

Anders stared at the table, his expression awestruck, and said, half to himself, "Imagine how much easier it would be to look after the orphans, Angel. We could— we could build a school. We could let everyone build homes." His voice cracked. "They could make families. Bring their mates home. Angel—"

Angelique grasped her mate's hand and gave it a squeeze. The fight had drained out of her expression when she said, "I know, Andy. I know. I... I just don't know what to say."

"Say yes," Viktor playfully demanded. "Say yes, or I'll have to take the offer to the wolves."

Half the table wrinkled their noses at the suggestion. "No," Theodore replied. "I don't get a veto but I'm vetoing that. Wolf shifters are insufferable."

Angelique tilted her head toward the sovereign and grimaced. "Agreed."

"Then take it. Save us all some trouble," Camile encouraged.

Angelique shared a long look with her mate, communicating silently as only a mated pair could. Something profound passed between them before Angelique turned back to Viktor and rasped, "We'll do it."

Theodore brought his hands together with a resounding clap. *"Fan*-tastic! Now let's get some meat in us. I'm godsdamned *starving."*

Margot leaned over her husband's arm to excitedly suggest, "Let's get the cookies, too. This is a celebration now!"

"And wine," Anders piped up, jubilant. "Lots and *lots* of wine!"

Chapter Thirty-Nine

"What made you think of the weres?"

"Hm?" Viktor stood at his glass-topped desk and peered down at the tablet in his hand. They had made a pit-stop at the pack's business office in the Castro District to make sure all of their physical copies of important documents had been properly packed out and ready to go, but he couldn't resist glancing at the never-ending cascade of emails while he was there.

The door to his office clicked shut. It was followed by the dull thud of the old fashioned bolt sliding into place, and then the click of his mate's metal-studded heels as she walked across the wood floor.

Bare lavender arms slid around his waist from behind. "What made you think of the weres when you first started planning this move?"

He looked down. Her skin was such a beautiful color, and when the sunlight filtered in through the slatted blinds, pulled nearly closed, it gilded her in hues of green and gold and pink. He would never get sick of admiring just how fucking gorgeous his mate was.

Viktor leaned back into her embrace. Covering one of her hands with his own, he set the tablet down on his desk, his focus drawn inexorably to the center of his universe. "You know, I'm not really sure. I never really considered them before last year."

She nuzzled her nose against the back of his neck, tickling the sensitive skin there. "What changed?"

Viktor laughed. "You know, I think it was the teenagers."

"The teenagers? Weres or ours?"

His chest swelled with pride when she so casually referred to their young packmates as *ours*.

"Both. They started running into each other a lot when they visited Margot's Healing House, and because I escorted so many of our kids there, I got to know them." He shrugged. "I don't know. I think one day I just had this realization that they and their caretakers were so similar to my pack that it made me sort of... ache for them, I guess. I empathize with them. After that, it just seemed like a natural fit."

"Do you think they'll be able to make it all work?"

"I do, yeah." He turned around in her arms. Cupping her cheeks, he continued, "I think they were well on their way before now, but a little helping hand never hurts."

Camille tilted her head into his palm. A smile pulled at her plush mouth, soft and full of tenderness. He loved it when she took bites out of him, but Viktor almost couldn't stand it when she was so sweet. Every moment felt like a gift he hadn't earned; every smile a kiss of sunlight on a cold soul.

"I'm excited for them," she said, "and I think they'll take good care of the land."

He smoothed his thumbs over the swells of her cheekbones. "I'm excited for us, too."

Camille was quiet for a moment. Her eyes roved around the room, perhaps taking in the hushed atmosphere, the semi-darkness provided by the shades, and the nearly barren landscape of what was once a cramped office.

Outside, tourists and locals alike strutted up and down the springy, magic-heavy sidewalks. The sounds of cars and conversation was a dull white noise through the thick walls of the old building.

"You know, this reminds me of someplace," she said, slanting a look at him through her thick black lashes.

Viktor leaned forward to brush the corner of her mouth with his. "Hm? Does it?"

"Yeah."

"Where, sweetheart?"

Her arms slid down from his waist. Fingers danced along the top of his leather belt until they rested on the buckle. "The meeting room."

Viktor's spine locked. A rush of instant arousal made his blood heat. Voice dropping, he rumbled against her skin, "Does it, now?"

That day in the meeting room felt like a lifetime ago, but he knew it would be forever seared into his memory. It was the first time in twenty years that he got to hold her, taste her, be *with her* as the man he had become, not the scared, angry boy he was.

Slipping his hand under her silky dress, thrusting his fingers into the cunt he'd fantasized about for so very long, was a moment of such profound eroticism he *still* shuddered when he thought of it.

Camille's nimble fingers made quick work of his belt buckle. The sound of metal jangling and the quiet scrape of leather were loud in the quiet of the office.

"I think we should get a redo on that day," she whispered. There was a husky note to her voice that he'd come to associate with her desire. Just hearing it was enough to make his cock ache.

Her lips trailed over his jaw to nip at his ear while her hands undid the button and zipper of his slacks. He turned his head, trying to catch her lips in a kiss, *needing* the taste of her on his tongue, but Camille only let out a husky laugh and moved in the opposite direction.

"Cam..." He groaned when she shimmied his slacks and briefs down his hips, freeing his cock. Viktor let out a low growl of frustration when she turned her head again, evading his kiss. "Cam, you not letting me kiss you is *not* my favorite memory of that day."

"Oh, I couldn't tell," she sweetly replied. Palming his cock in her gloriously bare hand, she purred, "And what *was* your favorite memory of that day, Alpha Hamilton?"

Viktor collared her throat, pushing upward until her jaw was framed by the junction of his thumb and fingers. It forced her to hold still as he slid his tongue along her lower lip.

Fuck, he thought, *she put on some berry lip gloss or something.*

There was nothing — absolutely *nothing* — hotter than licking a woman's lipstick off. When it tasted like spun sugar and berries and his *mate,* it was utterly incomparable.

Wrapping his free hand around the one she had on his cock, he forced her to give it a hard, almost painful squeeze. "Sweetheart, you have no idea what it felt like to touch your cunt for the first time. Never felt much for the gods before, but *that* — it was like I had my fingers in something *holy.*"

He watched, rapt, as her slitted pupils expanded in a rush. Hardly anything remained of her violet irises, giving her eyes the illusion of limitless depth — like she wanted to swallow him whole.

Her breaths puffed against his mouth as he gently bit down on her plump lower lip. The feeling of her thumb skating over the flared head of his cock, spreading a bead of pre-come across his flushed skin, made him bite her just a little harder, just how he knew she liked it.

Camille let out the loveliest little growl and lifted her chin. Viktor let her lip go with a snap. "You thought that was holy?" she taunted, dark eyes glinting in the half-light. "You haven't even tried my mouth yet, *alpha.*"

His hips flexed involuntarily, seeking relief from the ache that was now bordering on full discomfort. "You want to suck my cock, sweetheart? Go ahead."

Her lips, flushed and swollen from his bite, formed a taunting moue. "Hm, I don't think I will."

Viktor grinned a large, coyote grin. Using his grip on her throat, he dragged her face back to his to grate against her mouth, "You want me to make you, sweetheart? I can do that. I know how wet it makes you when I tell you what to do."

Challenge glittered at him from eyes gone half-mast. "Oh?"

"Yeah, *oh.*" Releasing her throat, Viktor fisted his fingers into the short strands of her hair and nudged her down. "On those pretty knees for me, sweetheart. I want to see you suck my cock. And when that's done, you're going to show me the come on your tongue. Got it?"

Camille sank onto her knees. It was one of the headiest things he'd ever experienced, watching his proud, gorgeous mate lower herself before him with no resistance at all. Her short black skirt rode up her supple thighs, stretching across them and showing off just a glimpse of her lacy black thong. The red soles of her heels flashed behind her.

Viktor had no idea which god he'd pleased enough to earn *this,* so he shot out a quick, silent prayer to the whole lot of them.

A smile twitched the corners of his mate's mouth. Locking eyes with him, she deliberately turned her head, half-heartedly attempting to remove his grip on her hair. Viktor *tsked* and dragged her closer, forcing her to brace her palms on his thighs. Using his free hand, he squeezed her cheeks until her lips parted.

"Be a good girl for me," he growled, "and maybe afterward I'll lick you until you scream."

Camille blew out a hot breath against his hand. "Promise?"

"Promise." He released her cheeks, but just before she dipped her head, he added, "And watch those fangs, sweetheart. I'd hate to have to start withholding orgasms from you, but biting my cock will get you there."

His mate, gorgeous, contrary thing that she was, flashed said fangs in a saucy snarl. "Afraid of me now, alpha?"

Palming his cock, Viktor guided it toward her mouth until the flushed head rested on her lower lip. He arched a brow. "Do I look particularly afraid to you?"

A small, dark green tongue snaked out to lick a bead of pre-come from the slit. Viktor's fingers flexed in her hair as a ripple of pleasure ran up his spine.

Slowly, like she wanted to both tease him and savor the moment at once, Camille slid her tongue along the sensitive underside of his cock. When his skin was slick, she parted her lips and waited. An open invitation.

Breathing hard, he guided himself into the hot well of her mouth.

"*Fuck.*"

Her tongue was ever-so-slightly textured — though he'd be damned if he could pinpoint exactly what the texture was — and it felt like heaven as it pressed against him. Viktor could only watch, slack-jawed, as his cock slid past her plump lips. His skin was flushed a livid red that stood out against her darkened lips.

He wondered if she knew how many times he had imagined this moment when they were teenagers. It used to drive him crazy. They'd only ever shared the one kiss, but it was a constant, torturous fantasy of his teens.

Shit, even when he was a full-grown man, he used to fantasize about what it would be like to watch her swallow him down, to hold her gaze as he came in her mouth.

Since she wasn't moving, Viktor let loose a rumbling growl and changed his grip on her hair, forcing her to move back and forth as he slowly matched her rhythm. Pressure built as he watched her take him more and more, her lips stretching taut around him with each shallow thrust.

"Open for me," he bit out.

Camille tilted her head back *just so* and slackened her jaw, as well as the muscles of her neck and shoulders. She was utterly pliant, completely at his mercy, and *his.*

"Good girl," he crooned, going deeper. "All that talk is just that, isn't it? You love it when I make you do things, just as much as I love *making* you. Look how well you suck my cock, sweetheart. Open a bit more for me— *there.* Fuck, you are perfect."

His cock slid past the feeble resistance of her throat as she relaxed completely. Viktor cupped her head with both hands and thrust faster, moving them together so she could take breaths between each stroke. Her fingertips dug into the muscles of his thighs, holding on tight as he chased the rising swell of his orgasm.

His words burst out on a gasp. "Remember what I said, sweetheart. You're going to show me my come on your tongue. Don't you fucking swallow until I tell you to. Do you hear me?"

She couldn't speak, but when her fingers flexed and relaxed on his legs in quick succession, he knew that she understood.

Groaning long and low, he pulled back to pump shallowly into her mouth. Quickly guiding one of her hands to his shaft, he used her grip to pump the rest of him as the pressure built and built and built, drawing his balls up tight before he came with a ragged gasp.

Gently extracting himself from her mouth, Viktor grasped her cheeks with one hand, pinching until she opened her mouth to show him the pearly release that coated her pretty green tongue. "That's my good girl," he rasped, tugging her up.

Camille unfolded herself gracefully from her kneeling position. Cupping the nape of her neck, Viktor dragged her mouth to his. Their tongues tangled in a wet glide — tasting of him, of her, of *them.*

My favorite taste in the entire godsdamned world.

Without breaking the kiss, he turned them around to face the desk. He bent her backwards until she lay on the glass surface, her legs sprawled around his hips and her soft, needy moans melting with the muffled sounds of the city. Every sound passed from between swollen, flushed lips, reminding him of how damn pretty she was when she sucked his cock.

Lifting his head, he dragged his hands down to her bunched skirt and commanded, *"Now* you can swallow."

Camille's elegant throat worked with her deliberate swallow.

A look of hazy-eyed bliss crossed her face, but it didn't stop her from teasing, "Is it *my* turn now, bossy alpha?"

"Fuck yes it is," he answered, yanking her thong out of the way with a deep disregard for its continued usefulness. "You made me thirsty, sweetheart. It's *my* turn to drink."

CHAPTER FORTY

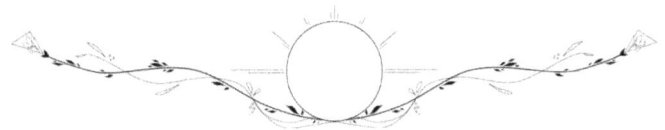

THE PACK WAS ALL ACTIVITY FOR TWO WEEKS following their lunch with the Batacans. Organizing everything was a logistical nightmare — and exactly the sort of thing Camille was best at. Years of co-managing a huge vineyard and all its operations, from staffing to production to shipping and sales, gave her the perfect toolkit to take on the task.

Viktor, for all that he was a wonderful alpha who knew how to keep his people centered and safe, was absolutely *terrible* at detailed work.

"I'm good with numbers and coyotes, not organizing shit," he complained after one particularly difficult afternoon spent attempting to arrange for all the modular homes to be shipped to Prairie. Getting anything shipped across territory lines was difficult, but a whole pack's worth of homes and possessions was a Herculean task.

"That's why you have me," she assured him, tapping her claws against the kitchen table as she stared at the phone resting by her elbow. She had been on hold for over an hour, but she wasn't worried. They wouldn't scare her away. Once she had someone with authority on the line, she would get things in order.

Very, very few people would dare say no to a Solbourne, and

she intended to leverage the entirety of her family's name against the infuriating bureaucracy that made moving so very difficult.

In the end, it took nearly a full week to make every plan — and contingency plan, for all worst case scenarios — and required she make trips to every home to make sure everyone knew what was going on and where they needed to be. By the time the big moving day came, Camille was intimately familiar with every packmate's needs, their belongings, and their concerns.

She relished the challenge of getting all the pieces of the puzzle in the right order, and there was something deeply satisfying about being immediately useful to the pack. They were grateful for her deft handling of such a complicated series of arrangements. Even those few packmates who were wary of her quickly came around. When they thanked her, she assured them all that even if she disliked the work, Camille would have done it without question.

Finding her place within the pack was what mattered. If she had to work her ass off for two weeks to make that happen, then she would do so without a complaint.

Even so, she was helped enormously by her brother, who returned from his trip through France's countryside just in time to assist in the operation. Like her, he'd spent most of his life running the vineyard. He knew the ins and outs of getting things across territory lines even better than she did, and his consort, Rufus, was a skilled urban planner who helped them parcel the land with expert attention to every family's needs.

Between the three of them and the rest of the pack, who came with more than their fair share of skills, the move managed to go relatively smoothly. In what felt like a blink, they were ready to leave Lake Merced behind.

Benny escorted half the pack, including most of the younger families and elders who would require more time to settle in, while Viktor and Camille planned to escort the rest. While their homes had been packed up and shipped off to Prairie, they all stayed in the Solbourne apartment building downtown, graciously provided for their use by the sovereign himself.

The night before their flight out, Camille caught Viktor standing by the window overlooking the street. His upper body was bare and limned with the neon lights below. Her bite was a beautiful white scar on the thickest part of his shoulder.

She normally loved the sight of it, of *him*, but in that moment, her normally sunny consort wore an air of grief that cut her to the quick.

He'd been like that off and on ever since they got off the phone with Lana. They had finished negotiating the terms of her packmate's punishment just that morning. The discovery of Juan Andreas's murder had shed more light on the cruelty and manipulation Damon must have lived under. While neither would *ever* forgive him, Camille and Viktor were in agreement that executing him wasn't the right choice.

There had been plenty of death, and too many cubs had been robbed of their parents. They didn't need to perpetuate the cycle of violence and loss.

Besides, he'd already lost an eye, three fingers, and suffered severe nerve damage in one leg that would take years of regular healer visits to fix. That and the Aucilla pack's hefty tribute payment for the damage done seemed like enough punishment.

He would be shipped back to his pack, worse for wear but *alive,* for them to deal with as they saw fit. It was more than he deserved, perhaps, but they stood by their choice even when Theodore snarled about it. They were building a better future. What better place to start than their own lives?

What better tenet to stand by than *mercy?*

But it wasn't the thought of Damon that troubled her consort. The melancholy settled over him after he checked in with Lana about how she was handling her father's death. Camille had quietly left him to it, knowing that it was a private thing between the two of them, and returned half an hour later to find Viktor quiet.

Sidling up behind him, she pressed her cheek to his bite and asked, "My love, why do you look so sad? This is the night before your big triumph. Shouldn't we be celebrating?"

Viktor pulled her around to tuck her into his side. His skin was hot, several degrees warmer than her own, and littered with the tiny scars of a life lived to the fullest. She had only just begun to memorize their constellations. Camille couldn't wait for the day when she could close her eyes and map them unerringly with her fingertips.

Viktor tilted his head to press a kiss to her temple. "I am happy. I'm just— I'm also sad to say goodbye to this place. More than I thought I'd be."

"We'll be back."

Viktor's smile was bittersweet. "I know, but it won't be the same. This is saying goodbye to the place that helped raise me."

Camille stared at his profile. He was so beautiful it made her want to cup him in her palms and keep him close forever. Every time she looked at him, she saw that moment he nearly slipped from her grasp and only wished she could hold on tighter, more fiercely, until even the memory of terror faded into nothing.

"I didn't really say goodbye to the estate," she told him. "I loved the land, but..."

Looking away from the window, he murmured, "You said goodbye to your mom, though. That was enough."

And she didn't care enough about the house, tainted by memories as it was, to feel what Viktor did. There would always be a pang of nostalgia when she thought of the dusty, sandy soil of the vineyard and the verdant hills that sprawled around it, dappled with twisted oak trees, but she didn't cry when she left.

Camille could *feel* how wrenching it was for him to leave his home behind.

"All my memories are here," he continued, husky with feeling. "I was born here. My mom died here. I became an alpha here." Viktor looked at her with eyes of liquid gold — coyote and man grieving for the past. "I found a family with the Solbournes and my pack here. I met *you* here. This is where every good and terrible memory lives."

Gently, she reminded him, "We'll make new memories in our new home, Vik."

His smile was painfully sad. "I know and I'm excited for that. But it doesn't mean I can't grieve for what we're leaving behind."

"No, it doesn't."

Viktor sucked in a deep breath and pulled her closer. His eyes wandered back to the window as she pressed a soft kiss to his cheek. In a choked voice, he confessed, "I don't think I'll be able to sleep tonight, sweetheart. Thinking of the land empty right now— it hurts too much."

Cupping his jaw, Camille gently turned his head until he was looking at her. "Let's go, then."

"What?"

"Let's go spend the night there."

Viktor looked startled, then torn, when he said, "We leave tomorrow morning, Cam, and the weres plan to start moving in at dawn."

"We'll be gone before then." Stepping back, she trailed her fingers down his arm until she found his hand. With a tug toward the apartment door, she cajoled, "Come on, Alpha Hamilton, let's go for a run around the lake. Remember how you used to promise me we'd do that someday? Now's our last chance."

His throat worked around a hard swallow. "You're sure? I know you're tired from all the planning—"

Shoving her feet into her black running shoes, left by the door when they came home, she cast him a look over her shoulder. "I want what you promised, thank you very much. I'm your mate. Aren't I supposed to be treated to nice things?"

Viktor's voice was full of tenderness when he muttered, "Brat."

Camille passed him his shoes with a wink. *"Your* brat."

～

Walking into the dark woods surrounding Lake Merced on the cool summer night was not quite eerie, but it was... heavy — as if the trees and the water and the tracks worn down by paws and feet over a generation knew they were leaving.

In the light of day it hadn't felt so real.

In the dark, it was impossible to escape the profound sense of emptiness that echoed across the territory. There was no background hum of magic from the individual wards around the dens. No thrum of life from the packmates who called the land home. The air was still and quiet without the howls and yips of coyotes stalking one another in the night.

Even the breeze felt somehow melancholic when it slid through her hair.

They stood in the clearing that had once been their pack's meeting place. The huge firepit that sat at its center had been disassembled; its stones carefully packed and shipped to their new home with Benny. Where there were once well-loved picnic tables, there were simply impressions in the grass. At the far end of the clearing, a small building that had housed their nursery school and a community center stood silent and watchful, waiting for its new occupants. The pack had voted unanimously to leave it for the incoming pack.

Camille watched Viktor walk up to the filled in circle where the fire pit once sat. He crouched, the muscles of his bare back flexing, and pressed his palm against the freshly turned earth.

The moon was new and the sky was clear. No fog obscured the stars, nor bounced back the light of the city to illuminate her consort's form. But she was an elf, and she did not need it to see him — to feel the bittersweet ache of separation that raked his soul.

A fine sheen of sweat cooled her skin as the breeze blew in off of the water. The faint hint of salt touched her tongue, conjuring memories of their trips to the ocean, of the taste of his skin.

Their run took them around the entirety of the tiny territory and back through the hidden arteries of the trails. They wound around thick, gnarled tree trunks and through spiky reeds. They brushed the treeline where the sandy cliffs gave way to the glittering beach, and they wandered back, circling the impressions each den left in the soil as a final goodbye.

The meeting area was their final stop, and where she knew Viktor would bury a piece of his heart.

Camille joined him at the fire pit. Disregarding how the silty, ash-strewn dirt would ruin her expensive athletic leggings, she dropped onto the ground beside him and brushed her fingertips over the edge of the circle.

A silent thank you to the place where her consort was born, forged, and found home.

"I'm not sorry for any of the terrible stuff that happened here," he murmured. "Not to me, at least. I wouldn't change any of it."

Camille leaned her side against his, sharing her warmth and her strength with him. "I understand. I wouldn't change my life either, awful as so much of it was."

She used to dream of things being different, but now she couldn't imagine a single change. Any wrong step, any missed chance, and she could have missed out on *this*.

Viktor sifted his fingers through the ashen dirt before letting it fall back into the pit. "I hate that bullshit saying that everything happens for a reason — that the gods have a plan and suffering is necessary. Used to piss me off when people would see what my father did and say it was making me tougher. Like his cruelty would make me *better*."

He smoothed out the small impression he made in the dirt, as if to comfort the soil they were leaving behind. "Suffering isn't necessary. It doesn't make you tougher. It just hurts. That's why I pushed so hard for this, why I believe the weres should have the territory. The future can be kinder. It *should* be kinder." Viktor turned his eyes, glowing green with a predator's night sight, on her. "I shouldn't have had to suffer. You, too. Still... if it risked being with you now, then I would do it all over again."

She breathed deep. The scents of the trees, the water, and her mate blended into the sweetest notes of home. "I love you, Vik. The kid you were and the man you are now. If I loved you any more, I wouldn't be able to contain it all."

"I love you, too, Cam. Always." A crooked smile lifted up one corner of his mouth. "Even though you called me a furry dunce last night."

"You tried to out-bench press *Kaz*—" Camille stopped. Her ears twitched, picking up sounds that would have been far below human hearing. Moving on instinct, she swiveled to one side. Her eyes locked on the treeline opposite the clearing, nearest to the lake. The hair on the back of her neck rose as a low, threatening growl rattled in her throat.

"Shh, it's okay." Viktor closed his hand around the nape of her neck. "It's some friends."

She opened her mouth to ask who it could possibly be, but the words died on her tongue when several pairs of green, glowing eyes slowly faded into view. They were lower to the ground than a shifter's might be, but she recognized the shapes of their ears, the lean builds and long legs.

Coyotes.

Her heart skipped a beat. Things had been too busy for her to make time to meet the *other* coyotes who called the territory home, and with all the activity around the dens, they had made themselves scarce.

It was thrilling to finally see so many together, their lithe forms melting out of the shadows to cautiously approach the center of the clearing. Their ears were low, their bushy tails still, but their heads weren't cast down with fear or aggression. They wandered closer with clear intention. Viktor held their focus unerringly, drawing them in.

Camille gently touched his thigh. "Should I back off so you can have some time with them?"

"No, you should be here, too. Just let them approach you on their own and slowly lift your arm. They'll smell me on you."

She slanted a curious look at him. Keeping her voice low, she asked, "How well do you know them?"

Viktor held out his hand. The coyote that appeared to be the leader of the group moved a little faster, his tail lifting, until he could press his nose against Viktor's palm. "Well," her consort answered, "considering this one chewed up my shoes when he was a cub, I'd say I know them pretty well."

As soon as Viktor reached up to scratch the coyote behind his ears, the rest of the small pack — a tiny number of the coyotes that actually made their home in the shadowed corners of the city — closed in around them. Their breaths made quiet rasping sounds, and their slender paws dug impressions in the loose dirt.

Camile did her best not to tense. It wasn't like they stood a chance of hurting her, of course, but still, she didn't enjoy the idea of fending off six or seven furious canines if they turned against her.

"Relax, sweetheart." Viktor ran his fingers down her arm to find her hand. Lifting it slowly toward the coyote, he crooned, "There now, see? She's with me. You know she's my mate, don't you?"

She held perfectly still, not even daring to twitch her fingers, as the coyote's nose skimmed her knuckles. It was cold and wet. Almost as soon as it happened, though, the coyote hopped back a step. His gray ruff rose and his head lowered with clear unease. Around them, the other coyotes tensed.

Viktor huffed. "Don't be like that. I *know* you smell me on her."

"It's okay." Camille tugged her arm. She swallowed a bitter pang of disappointment. Of course, she didn't *need* to be accepted by the coyotes, but it would have been nice. "Most animals aren't huge fans of elves. I can't expect them to be any different."

"Hold on."

Viktor stood up and kicked off his shoes. When he hooked his thumbs in the waistband of his pants, she looked up at him quizzically and asked, "What are you *doing?*"

"I think they'll understand better if I shift, and I didn't bring a spare change of pants." In a handful of seconds, her consort stood in the clearing stark naked. He was entirely confident, without even a hint of unease or self-consciousness as he cast her a grin.

Damn, he's gorgeous.

It didn't matter how many times she saw it. Camille *loved* ogling her mate's beautifully sculpted ass.

Magic rippled like heat over dry earth before it bubbled out in a searing wave. One moment her consort stood there in all his glory and the next, her coyote settled down on his haunches beside her.

Opening his mouth in a huge, coyote grin, he leaned his weight into her side and proceeded to cover her cheek, neck, and ear with playful licks.

"Ugh!" Camille laughed, swatting playfully at him. Golden eyes gleaming with mischief, Viktor paced around her in a circle, his tail wagging and his upper body lowered in a playful crouch. His fur brushed her sides and covered her in his natural, musky scent, before he padded forward to dance around the wild coyote.

There was a moment of hesitation as the coyote gave him a good sniff, wondering, perhaps, why the shifter smelled like an apex predator that could eat him, but it only lasted a handful of seconds. Camille watched the transformation with wide eyes. In an instant, all the coyotes sprang into motion — tails wagging, jaws opening to let tongues loll, and elegant legs moving in a spirited dance around one another.

The wild coyotes yipped with joy when Viktor pretended to snap at them, herding them closer to where she sat.

Suddenly she was overwhelmed with gray and brown and white fur as canines bobbed and weaved around her. Cold noses explored the back of her neck and her hair. Dirty paws tested the texture of her leggings. Jaws gently clamped on the fabric of her sweaty t-shirt and tugged.

A delighted laugh bubbled out of her. Camille raised her arms, not entirely sure what she was supposed to do with them, and let the coyotes rub themselves against her sides. When one got particularly bold and tried to bump her over onto her side, Viktor was there to give her a sharp nip on her haunch and a low warning growl.

Cowed, they were more gentle after that. Kisses to her neck and chin followed, though Camille doubted they were for her benefit. They were certainly more for Viktor, who watched them all with a look of intense pride.

Camille didn't mind. They were damn cute. They could use her to ingratiate themselves with the alpha all they wanted.

While they frolicked around, trying to tempt Viktor into a game of chase, she indulged in petting the canines who decided to lounge beside her. She watched Viktor fall, tackled by a well-coordinated cluster, as she stroked velvety ears.

He's giving up so much, she thought, pride and sorrow welling up with every delighted bark.

She knew that the pack needed to grow and that this was for the best, but watching him romp with the wild coyotes, she came to a new level of appreciation for what he was leaving behind.

A while later, as dawn crept closer and their time in the territory dwindled, Camille felt her consort settle his big, furred body beside her. Several more coyotes had joined them. Most were piled on top of one another around her legs and behind her back. Viktor had to muscle a sleepy canine out of the way to take his spot next to her.

With one last gentle lick to her cheek, he shifted back into his other form. His brows were drawn tight, but there was a soft smile on his lips when he reached for her.

Resting against his chest, she listened to the steady beat of his heart. "Better?"

"Yeah," he answered, husky, "much better."

Looking up at him through her lashes, she asked, "The weres will take care of them, right?"

Viktor caressed her cheek with a knuckle. "They better. I put it in the contract. No culling, no traps, no poison."

Camille kissed the skin above his heart. "Good. Though I kind of wish we could take them with us."

"I don't think the wolves would appreciate that too much," he replied. "There's a shitload of them up that way, and I'd really rather not deal with a bunch of pissed off wolf packs — shifters or wild."

"And they're better off here, where they're comfortable." She sighed, thinking of soft fur and cool noses. "It would be nice, though."

Viktor's arms tightened around her. "Trust me, sweetheart, you'll have plenty of coyotes around. As soon as the pack gets comfortable, I expect at least four or five new families *and* a lot of new cubs." He winked. "If there's anything coyotes know how to do, it's make babies."

Camille snorted with laughter. "Well, that'll be nice at least. I do love the cubs."

"You say that now, but wait until they get a hold of your heel collection."

She waved a hand, totally unconcerned. "You'll just have to buy me new ones, Alpha Hamilton."

"Or you could make baby teeth holes the new chic," he suggested.

"Or that." They shared a soft smile. "It'll be good, no matter what."

Viktor bent his neck to skim his lips over her forehead. "Yeah, it really will be, sweetheart."

≈

In the end, they stayed long enough to watch the vehicles begin to arrive at the green corridor. Sitting beneath the boughs of a leafy maple tree on the university's side of the street, they silently tracked the progress of the weres as they officially took control of their new territory.

It was time to go.

When dawn broke through the gray, pre-sunrise haze, they quietly climbed in their car and headed to the Financial District, where their pack was only beginning to rise.

They had an m-jet to catch and a home to make.

EPILOGUE

"I REALLY DON'T UNDERSTAND THE APPEAL," CAMILLE grumbled. She was perched on a mossy boulder to the left of their small, state of the art tent, and deeply disgruntled. "We *live* in the woods. Isn't that camping? Why would I willingly go without hot showers, a toilet, *and* my tablet when I could do the same thing by just sitting in our yard for twenty minutes?"

"Because, sweetheart, it's about freedom. Nature! Besides, we *need* the vacation. If we didn't go soon, half the pack would have mutinied and forced us onto an m-jet to Cabo or something."

And as much as he appreciated the pack's concern for their mental health and their appreciation for all the work their alphas did in getting their new territory up and running, he knew that neither of them would be able to relax so far away from their people.

That didn't mean they were wrong, though. Viktor knew he and his mate needed a break. Six months of non-stop work hadn't left much time for relaxation, nor alone time. They had families to settle, dens to help reassemble. They needed to begin work on the neglected, war-damaged ghost town of Prairie. Schools had to be built, relationships with the locals made, and bonds with the land to create.

The work was constant and the emergencies never-ending. Viktor and Camille had thrown themselves into settling their pack into their new territory, but it was time for a break.

And it was about damn time he delivered on that promise he made.

Viktor finished setting up a small metal folding table by the fire pit. Striding back to his bulging backpack resting against a pine tree, he began to pull out their utensils and various necessary things like a portable water purifier, his mate's carefully packed meals, and the peanut butter cup he had stashed in the side pocket — his favorite camping treat.

"I like nature plenty. More than most elves, even," Camille argued, eyeing him from her place across the campsite. "I just like it better when I have regular access to a bathroom."

Shoving the peanut butter cup into his mouth, he mumbled, "Trust me, Cam, you'll learn to like it."

He carefully arranged everything they needed on the table before he made one more trip for the bundle of firewood he collected on their hike in. He knelt to assemble the wood in the pit, but only got about halfway before Camille tartly demanded, "Please remind me why you thought I would enjoy this? Is it the *atmosphere* or something else that I'm missing?"

Viktor dusted his hands. The taste of chocolate and peanuts lingered on his tongue. "All right."

"All right *what?*"

"All right, I'll remind you." Standing up, Viktor prowled across the campsite to where his mate sat on the boulder, her long legs crossed.

She looked damn delicious in her fancy, previously unused hiking boots and shorts. Mosquitoes and ticks didn't bother trying to bite her tough lavender skin, so she could breeze through

the woods in little more than a tank top and tight shorts that
showed off every inch of her pretty legs.

He *loved* it. Even the pout she currently wore, which he was
fairly certain was just for show. Camille knew how much he liked
it when she growled at him. It only made him love her more.

It *also* made him want to lick every inch of her.

"No, no," she protested. Planting the soles of her boots on the
loamy earth, she placed her palms primly on her knees and
warned, "I know that look and I'm not having it, Vik. There are
bugs out here."

"Uh-huh." He dropped his hand to his belt and watched her
eyes follow the movement. Biting back a smile at the sight of her
pupils expanding to eat up all of that pretty violet, he used his
own boot to kick her legs apart, making room for him to stand
between them.

"I promised I'd show you why fucking outside is the best —
and now we're far enough away from the pack that no one will
hear you or see you. It's about time."

Her breath quickened, but still she protested, "I don't want to
get dirt in my hair. I *won't* get dirt in my hair."

Sliding his fingers into the silky strands by her pointed ear, he
arched a brow. "Sweetheart, just yesterday I caught you making
mud cakes with Ivy, Thomas, and Alejandro. You had way more
than dirt in your hair."

"That was different!"

"How, exactly?"

"Well," she huffed, "they're cubs. It just is."

Viktor considered her flushed cheeks and tart little pout for a
moment before he shrugged. "Fine."

"Fine? Really?" She blinked up at him, clearly taken aback by
his easy acceptance. Was that disappointment in her narrowed
eyes? Viktor bit the inside of his cheek, stifling a smile.

"Sure. You don't want to get dirty, then you won't get dirty."

He *knew* he didn't imagine the flash of disappointment in her
eyes that time. "Oh, that's—"

Of course, he didn't let her finish. Stooping, he swiftly tucked his shoulder into her stomach and hoisted her up with a cheerful grunt. Camille squealed with surprise and clawed at his back as he marched them through the underbrush, toward the cool lake just beyond their campsite.

"What are you *doing?!* Put me down! The campsite is back that way, Vik!"

Giving her pert ass a proprietary squeeze, he glibly replied, "I know, sweetheart. We're not going that way."

"*Why?*"

"Because you said you didn't want to get dirty. I do so aim to please my sweet mate, so we're gonna fuck where it's clean."

Jabbing him between his ribs with one irate finger, she growled, "And where could that *possibly* be? Unless it's the tent, you're a damn liar."

They broke through the treeline and out onto the rocky shore of Lake Adley — from which their pack got their new name. It didn't have much of a beach to speak of, but neither did Lake Merced. Instead of their old territory's scrubby, swampy drop into brackish water, Adley was all stones and cattails.

All in all, he actually enjoyed Lake Adley more, since it wasn't occasionally fed into by the frigid, salty waters of the Pacific. The water was cool and crisp and clean. Exactly what his mate needed after a hot day of hiking.

She didn't seem to agree. At the sight of the rocky shore, she squawked, "Don't you fucking *dare,* mutt!"

He only hummed and gave her pert ass a possessive squeeze. "What my mate wants, she gets."

Camille squirmed over his shoulder, protesting at the top of her lungs. When he walked straight into the water, heedless of his boots or the fact that he was still fully clothed, she squeaked, "Do *not!* Do not do this, Viktor! I will smother you in your sleep, so help me go—"

Grinning wide enough to make his cheeks hurt, he tossed her into the water.

She came up sputtering, soaked to the bone, and mad as hell. Her lip lifted in a snarl even as she watched him strip off his shirt and toss it ashore with a familiar, greedy gaze.

Though the urgency had dimmed over the months since she took his bite, Viktor knew the fever would never completely leave him. He would always hunger for her. He would always feel that lick of flame up his spine, that instant, mind-wiping arousal for his mate.

Looking at her, hissing mad and soaked, made that ever-present lust a roar in his blood. The coyote loved to play with her, and the man thought it was the hottest fucking thing in the world when she used her claws on him.

He was working on the zipper of his cargo pants when she sat up on her knees to swipe her soaked hair out of her eyes. "I am going to *bite* you, Viktor."

"Aw, sweetheart, we both know I'll bite you back." Palming his cock and giving it a teasing stroke, he told her, "Now it's your choice: standing up or on your knees in the water."

Camille licked her lips. Despite the cool kiss of water, her cheeks were still flushed a dark purple. She rose slowly from the water and, with an expression that was an erotic mix of annoyance and arousal, she peeled off her soaked tank top and threw it right at his face.

"Standing," she tartly informed him, "and *then* on my knees. If you're going to make me do this, you're going to put in the *work,* Alpha Hamilton."

Gods, he thought, tossing her shirt onto the shore to join his. *I fucking love this woman.*

He couldn't wait to lick all the clean, living water from her pretty purple skin. Biting her would be damn good, too.

Viktor wrapped his fingers around the back of her neck and dragged her in for a drugging kiss. Breathing into her mouth, he commanded, "Shorts off, sweetheart."

"Bossy alpha," she muttered.

He trailed his lips down her throat to deliver a series of firm bites as she slipped her thumbs under the waistband of her shorts and pushed them down.

She could complain all she wanted, but Viktor felt the way she melted when his teeth clamped on her throat. Even over the smell of trees and water, he could scent the sweetness between her thighs. His mate was as insatiable for him as he was for her.

When he felt her free her boots from her shorts, Viktor changed his hold on her neck to grasp her throat. Spinning her around, he dropped one hand to pinch a dark, straining nipple and then lower, skimming her damp stomach.

When she arched under him, he gently kicked her legs apart and speared his fingers between her thighs.

"Ah!"

Viktor rumbled against her back. Nipping her pointed ear, he purred, "So wet for me, sweetheart."

Her breath came fast and hard as she turned her head to glare at him. "You *threw me in the lake.*"

Giving her clitoris a possessive little tap, he replied, "And now I get to look at you, all soaked and ready for me in the sunshine."

Viktor let go of her throat just long enough to gather both her wrists in one hand. Pressing them against the small of her back, he pushed her over until she was bent in half, the wet strands of her hair dangling against her cheeks.

They stood knee deep in the water. Above them, the sky was a perfect azure, the clouds a pristine white and fluffy. The sun bounced off of her lavender skin in shades of electric green and hot pink, making the water droplets that beaded on the dip of her spine look like diamonds.

Back arched, ass out, ripe and ready for him, she made a glorious picture.

"You belong out here, Cam," he told her, stroking his fingers around and around. Her hips rocked as she keened a low note. "Look how gorgeous you are. Your skin is so fucking beautiful in the sun, and with the way the water glitters around you, it's like a damn dream."

She strained, making her back arch at an even sharper angle. He watched her rippling reflection in the calm water and felt his cock twitch. *"Vik."*

"When we get home, I'm buying us a big fucking mirror for our bedroom," he told her. Reluctantly moving his hand from her slick skin, he grasped his cock and slowly began to push himself into the tight heat of her cunt. His eyes bounced between the beautiful bow of her back and their shifting reflection. "I could get used to watching myself fuck you, sweetheart. What do you think?"

Her voice was breathy when she asked, "What... what if someone sees us out here?"

Viktor smoothed his free hand down her spine. His fingertips met cool water on hot skin. He felt the bubbling of magic in his veins when his eyes shifted to coyote gold. "No one will, but if they did, then they'd see me fucking my gorgeous mate and think, *Damn, I wish that was me.*"

Camille could only moan. She rolled her hips back, giving him more of her weight until he could use his grip on her wrists to swing her back and forth, matching his slow, deep thrusts.

Viktor took his time. The pleasure was intense, her submission heady, but he wanted to make this experience last. He wanted to *relish* the sight of his mate in the wild, giving herself to him in the most primal sense.

Tossing his head back, he stared up at the open sky and said a prayer to anyone listening.

Thank you, he thought, picking up his pace. *Thank you.*

Water lapped around their legs. Camille rocked backward, throwing her weight behind each swing, and gradually his control slipped. Slow thrusts became quicker, his movements more brutal, and his mate threw her head back in response. Going deeper, knowing she needed that hot, hard strike of flesh, he growled her name.

Forcing her to still so he could go faster, he slid one hand around her front to roughly circle her clitoris, forcing a hard orgasm that made her knees buckle and her muscles contract around him like a vice.

Viktor lost his rhythm. His fingers, shifted to claws, dug into the softness of her lean hips as he thrust once, twice, and then buried himself as deep as he could go. *Gods, I fucking love camping,* he thought, an orgasm rippling hot and fast down his spine. *It's the* best.

Later, when they'd made love on their knees in the lapping water, as Camille requested, *and* against a tree, Viktor held his mate against his naked chest and soaked up the heat of their fire. The sky above them was an open wound in the flesh of the universe, overflowing with the light of galaxies too far away to properly comprehend.

Insects buzzed in the bushes, and somewhere in the distance, an owl called its curious notes into the night.

Camille was drowsy as he delicately selected another slice of cured bison for her. Her lips parted, accepting the morsel without hesitation. Everything he was, man and coyote, alpha and lover, felt a ripe, golden contentment in the fire's light.

When his mate began to purr, he buried his face in her half-dried hair and sing-songed, "Tell me I'm right."

"No."

He scraped his teeth against the shell of her sensitive ear. "Why not?"

Tilting her head back to peek at him with sleepy eyes, she answered, "Because you love it when we play."

Viktor gathered her close. Smiling against her cheek, he agreed, "I do, sweetheart. I really, really do."

THE END

ABOUT THE AUTHOR

 Abigail Kelly is a writer and illustrator of alternate histories, love stories, and women with drive. Her work is heavily influenced by both her modest family roots and her passion for history. She is also a bookseller at an independent bookshop where she gets to badly influence impressionable young minds and put her favorite books in eager hands, as well as the host of the Kingdom of Thirst podcast, a show all about romance novels and why they matter.

Her favorite authors are Shirley Jackson, V. E. Schwab, Ursula K. Le Guin, Kresley Cole, Nalini Singh, and just about anyone who writes about the weird and wonderful. She lives in San Francisco with her dog, Babs, who remains stubbornly illiterate.

Glossary

A full character directory and map can be found at Abigailkkelly.com

Places

United Territories and Allies: What we would consider the continental USA. A loose federation of sovereign states established after the Great War. The UTA capital is United Washington, in the Neutral Zone.

The Elvish Protectorate: Also known as the EVP. Stretches from Oregon to New Mexico. Capital city is San Francisco. Led by the elvish sovereign Theodore Thaddeus Solbourne.

The Coven Collective: Also known as the Collective. Encompasses Washington state. Capital city is Seattle. Led by a large coalition of witch covens, with Sophie Goode acting as their leader.

The Orclind: Encompasses much of the Midwest. Led by the Iron Chain, a close-knit government made up of orcish clans and family groups. Capital city is Boulder.

Shifter Alliance: Takes up a section of the midwest and all of the south. (Unfortunately includes Florida.) Run by a very, very loose alliance of shifter packs from three capital cities — Minneapolis, Oklahoma City, and Atlanta.

The Draakonriik: Also known as the 'Riik. The second smallest territory, it takes up all of the Great Lakes region and stretches to New York. Led by Taevas Aždaja, the *Isand* (ee-zand) of the dragon clans. Pronounced: *dra-kon-reek*

The Neutral Zone: Also known as the New Zone. Technically it is held by a coalition government consisting of representatives from the UTA, but in reality it is run by a syndicate of feuding vampire families. It is a small strip of land squeezed between the Draakonriik and the Shifter Alliance.

GODS

Light & Darkness: The primordial gods who created all the others. Also known as The Lovers and First Union. Both are generally represented as female.

Loft: God of the sky and creator of flying beings. Twin sibling to Tempest. They know no gender. Also known as the Boundless One.

Tempest: God of the ocean and creator of all water beings. Also known as the Hungry God and the god of love.

Burden: God of the Earth, creator of all beings who live within it — most notably the orcs. Husband of Glory.

Glory: Goddess of sunlight, magic, and creator of elves. Worshipped by witches for giving the gift of magic to humanity.

Blight: God of forested places and disease. He works in partnership with his daughter Grim and shares her dominion over demons and all reviled creatures.

Grim: Goddess of death. Known as the Merciful One and the Brilliant Lady. She is widely beloved.

Craft: God of change, newness, and messengers. Creator of humanity and viewed warily by non-worshippers as the Chaos Maker. They change their gender frequently, but generally is referred to using he/him pronouns.

TERMS

Alpha: a broad term used by many communities generally associated with a leader — either of a small family group, a pack, or even a territory.

Anchor: a vampire's mate. Anchors are carefully chosen and usually longterm-to-permanent arrangements, as they take considerable energy to make/become. A vampire must inject their venom into a host many times before their blood chemistry adjusts such that they become unsuitable for consumption by another vampire and their sleep cycle switches to a nocturnal pattern. At this point, they can can also produce/carry to term a vampiric child. Temporary anchors do exist, although they are relatively rare due to the intense withdrawal symptoms associated with ending the regular venom intake.

Arrant: someone born without m-paths, or the ability to channel and use magic.

Change: an elvish term for a sudden shift into adulthood. This is marked by 5-14 days of "madness", usually triggered by some stressful event around the age of 16-18. The elvish body is flushed with hormones to the point where sudden growth, overwhelming hunger, and aggression take over. Viewed as an incredibly vulnerable time, only immediate kin are charged with the care of their loved ones — which includes isolating them, preventing harm to themselves/others, and feeding them. The change marks the second phase of an elf's life, when they are no longer coddled children but young adults who can accept challenges and family responsibilities. Formal adulthood is attained at 30.

Changeling: a term first used to refer to fey children fostered out to non-fey homes, now more widely used to mean any person raised by people who are not the same beings. *Ex:* A dragon couple raising a human child.

Chosen: the formal term for a dragon's mate. The act of finding a mate is called *Choosing,* and is considered sacred.

Consort: an elvish mate. A term used exclusively by elves to refer to someone they are biologically compelled to pair up with. This usually involves intense sexual attraction, but can vary from person to person.

Dragon: a person with a dual form. In their bipedal form, they have claw-tipped wings, horns, and a tail. In their quadrupedal form, they are roughly the size of a standard SUV and can fly at extremely high altitudes for weeks at a time. They come in a variety of extremely saturated colors that shift with the time of day (light to dark). They breathe cold blue fire and can see the Earth's magnetic field. Identifying mating feature is marked change in behavior, including the overwhelming urge to nest.

Elemental: a being created by a spontaneous magical eruption. They often take on the attributes of whatever weather they happen to be born into, *i.e.* a lightning storm might produce a lightning elemental, or a blizzard might make a snow elemental.

Elf: someone born with jewel-toned skin, claws, pointed ears, and four fangs. Very secretive and considered apex predators who require a strict hierarchy to function. Average height of 6-7ft. Identifying mating feature is the retraction of claws.

Fever: shifter mating imperative triggered by the "animal's" choosing of a mate. Marked by a perpetual near-shift — elevated body temperature, increased aggression, build-up of magic, and the compulsion to mark. A shifter displays their readiness to find a mate by creating a den.

Fey: a person with nearly vestigial, insect-like wings, small fangs, and claws. Usually live in large groups. Identifying mating feature is bioluminescence.

Foresight: the ability to see multiple possible futures. The average number is between 2-4, with the likelihood mental instability increasing with each subsequent possible future.

Halfling: the elvish term for an elf with mixed heritage.

Healer: a person who possesses the ability to see into and heal bodies through touch.

Isand: the title of the leader of the Draakonriik. Pronounced *ee-zah-nd*

M- : M- is frequently used as shorthand to denote when something is infused or otherwise combined with a magical element.

Marriage Sigil: a custom symbol branded into the foreheads of spouses (pairs or multiples). Each one is unique and infused with a small amount of magic as a reminder of the power love holds. They are typically sought out by worshippers of Glory — mainly witches and arrants. Elves, though worshippers, don't usually take a marriage sigil when they find their consort or form a union with another elf.

Mate: a catchall term for a significant other. Used by many cultures, it has varying degrees of weight. To shifters, orcs, and demons, the word mate is synonymous with family, monogamy, and dependence. It is much more loosely used within arrant society, as well as amongst elves, who generally prefer the term *consort*.

Met: acronym for *magically enhanced tech*. A branded home assistant that can do everything your Alexa can, as well as small, low-level magic to help around the house.

Metallurgic Inoculation: a vaccine given to all elves within hours of birth to make them immune to iron poisoning.

M-siphon: a containment device used to imprison a magical being and siphon off their magic. Highly illegal.

R-siphon: also known as *reverse siphon*. New technology that redistributes magic away from the siphon instead of into it.

M-lev: a play on *maglev,* meaning a high speed train that levitates using magnets. In this case, magnets *and* magic.

M-weather: magic weather. Very common, but can result in "clusters" or storms that wreak havoc if not properly contained. In rare circumstances, it can also produce a sapient being known as an *elemental*.

Orc: a person with green, gray, russet, or blue skin, two fangs, and claws. Widely renowned for their strength and beautiful voices. Identifying mating feature is "the kohl", or altered, dark pigmentation of the hands and feet developed after meeting their mate.

Pixie: a small, winged creature with compound eyes with about the same level of intelligence as a rat. In the wild they live in trees and in burrows, but have adapted to living in walls, pipes, mailboxes, etc.

Pull: elvish mating imperative. A sudden hormonal shift caused by exposure to a compatible partner's pheromones, marked by the retraction of claws and volatile mood shifts. The pull is only "satisfied" when hormone binding occurs — the term for long term exposure to a mate, resulting in permanent biological dependence on their pheromones. This process increases fertility and often results in the conception of multiples. Lack of exposure to a mate can cause severe physical reactions (lack of appetite, muscle pain, headaches, insomnia) as well as the deterioration of mental stability.

Shifter: a person who can shift into an animal form. They can partially shift (changing only parts of their bodies at will) and often take on characteristics of their other half. Famous for their strength and tenacity, as well as their dual-voiced "shifter purr" which many people find deeply attractive. Usually found in packs.

Sigil: a symbol used to channel magic. Western countries use the alchemical alphabet formally codified in the 1800's, though many, many variations are used all over the world.

Sovereign: the title of the ruler of the Elvish Protectorate. It is capitalized when used in place of a name.

Turbo Virgin (c): Theodore Thaddeus Solbourne, Sovereign of the Elvish Protectorate and Head of the Solbourne Family.

Union: an elvish marriage. Usually done for financial, political, or procreational benefit. The parties involved are not fated or biologically compelled to be with one another, and might have many lovers or even a consort outside of their union.

Vampire: a person who drinks blood to survive and cannot go out in sunlight. Vampirism can only be "caught" with the exchange of fresh blood, and as of 2045 is much more widely spread through procreation. Vampires can only breed with their *anchors.* Identifying mating feature is marked change in behavior, including overwhelming desire and need for total isolation.

Ward: a magical barrier with varying levels of protection. A ward can be something as simple as a proximity alert — "someone walked into my garden" — or as complex as full on defense — "someone crossed the threshold and have now burst into flames". The severity of the ward depends on the complexity of the sigils used to create them, and wards can have many layers, each one with a unique purpose. Personal wards can also be used, such as in clothing or embedded into jewelry, though they tend to be expensive and difficult to foolproof.

Were: a person infected with the were virus, a much mutated strain of the vampirism virus, resulting in altered physiology and magical ability. They can be identified by their heterochromia, or different colored eyes. They are the newest magical race and viewed warily by the general public for a variety of earned and unearned reasons. Identifying mating feature is marked change in behavior, including highly increased territorial instinct and the urge to nest. Pronounced *ware.*

PRONUNCIATION GUIDE FOR NAMES OF IMPORTANT CHARACTERS IN THIS BOOK

Camille Dia Solbourne: kam-eel dee-ah soul-born

Viktor Hamilton: vick-tor ham-uhl-ton

Margot Goode: mar-goh good

Theodore Solbourne: thee-oh-door soul-born

Valen Yadav: vah-len yah-dahv

Andy Yadav-Coran: an-dee yah-dahv cohr-an

Kazimier Rione: kaz-eh-meer ree-own

Benny Reeve: ben-ee ree-vuh

Ruben Andreas: Roo-ben ahn-dray-ahs

Linnea Stafford: Lin-ee-ah staf-ord

Also by Abigail Kelly

Find all new releases, bonus chapters, and exclusive content on the Works by Abigail Patreon!

Strike: The New Protectorate Stories Volume Three

Passion is electric.

After a millennia of longing, Hele has finally gotten her chance to live. A lightning elemental with a voracious hunger for knowledge and experience, she takes to her new life with a gusto that surprises everyone she meets. After two years of learning how to navigate the world she's been thrust into, Hele is only missing one thing: love. She wants one particular dragon, but when he turns her away, she decides that life is too short to wait.

Vael has been a loyal soldier of the Draakonriik for nearly one hundred years. He's never wanted anything more than to serve his clan and his leader... until the day he snatches a beguiling elemental from the sky. For two torturous years, he's resisted the call of his Chosen, trying to give her a chance to fly before he claims her and hides her away in his nest.

But when Hele decides to set out on a quest to find a mate, that resolution goes up in smoke. His lovely elemental is about to learn a very valuable lesson: a dragon will do *anything* to win his Chosen.

Available in Kindle Unlimited, ebook, and paperback in May!

Burden's Bonds: The New Protectorate Book Three

He's chosen to be alone.

Kazimier Rione, half-orc spymaster of the Elvish Protectorate, doesn't want a mate. He's got too many rough edges and too much baggage for any woman. That's why he's done everything in his power to stay away from a certain lush little witch that makes every instinct bristle. A glimpse was all it took to seed a dark obsession, but it's one he knows he can never act on.

She was burned by fate.

Atria Le Roy learned her lesson a long time ago: the blessing of a mate is not for her. A witch groomed for a secretive priestesshood from birth, she's spent years throwing herself into her potentially world-changing research and running from her complicated past. Now that research is about to come to fruition — if only she and her research partner can survive being hunted by the factions desperate to get their hands on it.

Keeping their distance is impossible.

When his witch is threatened, Kaz knows that rescuing her will mean giving in to the pull of fate, but doing nothing is not an option. He'll do anything to protect her, even if that means kidnapping her and going on the run himself. With every mile they cover and danger they face, the fire between them burns hotter. She wants to escape her past, the bounties on her head, and the overbearing, beautiful orc holding her captive. He wants to possess everything she is — to be the breath in her lungs and the magic in her soul — and be utterly possessed in return.

Surviving will mean giving in, leaving the past behind, and letting the fire burn...

Available in Kindle Unlimited, ebook, and paperback in December!

CONSORT'S GLORY: THE NEW PROTECTORATE BOOK ONE

Margot Goode, healer extraordinaire, knows that being noticed is the fastest way to getting herself murdered — or worse. But even with a secret like hers, she can't stay cloistered forever. On her own in San Francisco, she's on the hunt for the one person who can stop her magic from turning against her in a catastrophic meltdown.

Margot doesn't expect things will be easy, but even *she* is surprised when someone plants a bomb in her Healing House, nearly killing her and wiping out her anonymity in one fell swoop. Attacking a healer is an egregious breach of the laws that keep the races from war. Attacking Margot Goode, granddaughter of the terrifying Goode Matriarch and leader of the most influential coven in the country, is not just blasphemous — it demands retribution.

Theodore Solbourne, newest sovereign ruler of the largest Elvish territory in the West, has waited his entire life for the woman he will one day claim as his consort. With the power to keep her finally in his grasp, he's planned their meeting down to every last detail... only to have all the carefully crafted steps in their courtship blown away when she's nearly killed before he can even say *hello*.

With her life and his kingdom on the line, there's no time for subtlety. Earning the trust of the woman he's been mad about his entire life just became much harder: the speculation of war is sweeping through the city, a goddess's acolytes call for justice, and a traitor's shadow looms over his household. But nothing, not even Margot's single-minded determination to keep him out, will stop him from winning her heart.

Available in Kindle Unlimited, ebook, and paperback!

EMPIRE: THE NEW PROTECTORATE STORIES
VOLUME TWO

Love blooms in the dark.

After a lifetime of service to the Amauri vampire family, retired assassin Harlan Bounds lives his life exactly as it pleases him – on his private estate, surrounded by beauty, and unbothered by the bloody politics of the criminal underworld he left behind. He doesn't need or want for anything... except, perhaps, the tantalizing witch hired to look after the acclaimed rose garden on his grounds.

Zia North has nursed a crush on the mysterious vampire that is her boss for nearly a year. They've never spoken, and she knows the rules by heart: never stay on Empire Estate's grounds after sundown and never, *ever* bother Mr. Bounds. There's no chance for her to fulfill her sensual fantasies, so what's the harm in indulging a crush that will never see the light of day – or the kiss of darkness?

It's all daydreams until she makes a mistake that finally brings her face to face with the intimidating vampire. Harlan's dark intensity draws her in, and Zia's light sparks a craving that can't be denied. Fantasy clashes with reality when his dangerous past threatens to bite them both, but not even the violent conflicts of the vampire syndicate can sever a bond forged in blood.

Available in Kindle Unlimited, ebook, and paperback!

CONTENT WARNINGS

Content warnings: Past parental abuse, past child neglect, past parental healthcare, past parental mental health issues, parental death, patricide, discussions of fertility, violence, blood, biting, light d/s themes, and explicit sexual situations.

www.ingramcontent.com/pod-product-compliance
Lightning Source LLC
Chambersburg PA
CBHW072337020726
47506CB00004B/908